ALL BETTER NOW

ALSO BY NEAL SHUSTERMAN

Novels
Bruiser
Challenger Deep
Chasing Forgiveness
The Dark Side of Nowhere
Dissidents
Downsiders
The Eyes of Kid Midas
Full Tilt
Game Changer
The Shadow Club
The Shadow Club Rising
Speeding Bullet

(with Jarrod Shusterman)
Dry
Roxy

(with Debra Young and
Michelle Knowlden)
Break to You

Arc of a Scythe Series
Scythe
Thunderhead
The Toll
Gleanings

The Accelerati Trilogy
(with Eric Elfman)
Tesla's Attic
Edison's Alley
Hawking's Hallway

The N.O.A.H. Files
(with Eric Elfman)
I Am the Walrus
Shock the Monkey

The Antsy Bonano Series
The Schwa Was Here
Antsy Does Time
Ship Out of Luck

The Unwind Dystology
Unwind
UnWholly
UnSouled
UnDivided
UnBound

The Skinjacker Trilogy
Everlost
Everwild
Everfound

The Star Shards Chronicles
Scorpion Shards
Thief of Souls
Shattered Sky

The Dark Fusion Series
Dread Locks
Red Rider's Hood
Duckling Ugly

Story Collections
Darkness Creeping
MindQuakes
MindStorms
MindTwisters
MindBenders

Graphic Novels
*Courage to Dream: Tales of Hope
in the Holocaust*

ALL BETTER NOW

NEAL SHUSTERMAN

SIMON & SCHUSTER BFYR

NEW YORK AMSTERDAM/ANTWERP LONDON TORONTO SYDNEY NEW DELHI

SIMON & SCHUSTER BFYR

An imprint of Simon & Schuster Children's Publishing Division
1230 Avenue of the Americas, New York, New York 10020

Text © 2025 by Neal Shusterman
Jacket illustration © 2025 by Matt Roeser
Jacket design by Chloë Foglia
Jacket stock image by Brankospejs/iStock

SIMON & SCHUSTER BOOKS FOR YOUNG READERS
and related marks are trademarks of Simon & Schuster, LLC.
For information about special discounts for bulk purchases, please contact Simon & Schuster Special Sales at 1-866-506-1949 or business@simonandschuster.com.
The Simon & Schuster Speakers Bureau can bring authors to your live event. For more information or to book an event, contact the Simon & Schuster Speakers Bureau at 1-866-248-3049 or visit our website at www.simonspeakers.com.
Interior design by Hilary Zarycky
The text for this book was set in Adobe Caslon.
Manufactured in the United States of America
First Edition
2 4 6 8 10 9 7 5 3 1
CIP data for this book is available from the Library of Congress.
ISBN 9781534432758
ISBN 9781534432772 (ebook)

For the Kirton, Ingham, and Lewis families
and all the other relatives I never knew I had!
It's wonderful getting to know you!

PART ONE
CROWN ROYALE

1
Mariel Rides Space Mountain

It was the wrong time to be living on the streets.

Not that there was ever a right time, but this new disease—it was picking up steam, threatening to be another pandem—No. No, Mariel didn't even want to invoke the *P* word. As if just thinking it would make it so.

"It's not so bad, baby," her mother told her. "It's not like we gotta be near people. Even out here we can find ways to isolate. We don't gotta be near anyone if we don't want to be."

Mariel's mother lived in denial. Truly lived there. If denial were a solid piece of real estate, Gena Mudroch would have a mansion on it. Or at least a garage so they'd finally have a safe and legal place to park their beat-up Fiesta.

Right now it was parked, all right. Behind a fence at the impound. Which was why Mariel and Gena were standing on a dark street in the seediest industrial part of town, in the middle of the night, waiting on someone who was, in theory, going to help them break their car out.

Unlike her mother, Mariel did not live in a constant state of denial. She was practical. A realist. She had to be; practicality was more than a survival skill—it was her superpower. Because without it, her mom would probably be dead, and Mariel would have been swallowed whole by the foster care system years ago.

"Maybe . . . ," began Mariel. "Maybe we *should* be with people."

"What, and catch this thing? No way!"

"But maybe we should get it over with quick. You know—before the hospitals get full, while there are still services for us."

Her mom brushed her straggly hair out of her eyes. "I know what you're thinking," she said, giving Mariel her suspicious look—the one she usually reserved for anyone and everyone else. "You can't really believe what the nuts out there are saying?"

"I know it sounds . . . *out there* . . . but there's always a chance it could be true."

"Since when do you listen to rumors, huh? You, who's gotta have scientific proof of everything under the sun!"

Her mother was right—rumor was the currency of ignorance. But anecdotal evidence had to count for something. "I've seen interviews with people who've had it," Mariel told her mom. "They seem . . . I don't know . . . different."

"How can you know they're different when you didn't know 'em to begin with?"

Mariel shrugged. "There's something in their eyes, Momma. Something . . . wise."

Her mother guffawed at that. "Trust me, no one gets smart from getting sick."

"I didn't say 'smart.' I said 'wise.'"

But "wise" wasn't really the word for it either. "Centered" was more like it. Being at home. Even if you don't have one.

"You're dreaming," her mother said. "That's okay, you're allowed."

As practical as Mariel needed to be to survive life with her mother, she wasn't immune to the occasional flight of fancy. Especially when it gave her hope. She told herself that hanging on to hope was nothing like her mother's perpetual state of denial, but deep down, she knew hope and denial were reluctant neighbors. They glared at each other from across the same silty river of circumstance.

Across the lonely street, a man walked with a purposeful gait, which also seemed a bit loose, like his joints were made of rubber. Although he was mostly in shadow, Mariel could tell he glanced over at them. Was this the guy? Or was this just someone who was gonna bring them trouble? Turned out he was neither; he just continued on his merry way toward whatever place a rubbery man goes at two in the morning.

"That's not true, you know," she said to her mom, who had already forgotten the conversation and needed to be reminded. "People do grow from being sick. What about Grandpa—he changed. He had a whole new perspective after he beat cancer."

Her mother gave a rueful chuckle. "I wouldn't want to go through *that* just to get some perspective. And besides, a heart attack got him not a year later, so what good did that perspective do?"

Mariel had no answer for that one. Now it was her mom sounding like the realist.

"We'll be fine, baby," she said. "We'll find a place where we can park safe and legal, and then we'll hunker down and wait it out, once we get the Grinch out of impound." The Grinch was their green Fiesta. Mom had a thing about naming inanimate objects.

The guy who was coming to help them was late. Her mother had said "*two-ish*," but that was from the guy who knew the guy that knew her mom. Three degrees of separation from a nameless man who already had their money.

Realism told Mariel he wasn't coming. Hope told her that maybe something better was.

Mariel always did her best to align her need for hope with her practical nature. In this case, both told her that maybe it was best to lean into this pandemic—and yes, she used the *P* word, because clearly that's what it was becoming. But a different one. A *very* different one.

The previous one, of course, was devastating. Millions dead worldwide. People fighting science, grasping at absurd conspiracy theories, hearsay, and random social media posts, even as they lay dying. While people who *did* follow the science and the rules wished death upon those who didn't. *That* pandemic exposed the very worst of human nature on all sides.

Her mom, of course, was one of the deniers, and went out partying during the worst of it. She caught it early, and although Mariel never did, it seemed her mom had it bad enough for both of them. Bad enough to land her in the hospital. They still had insurance back then, but it didn't matter, because there were no ventilators to be had. Her mom made it through—but it took forever. She had the long syndrome—not technically sick anymore, but not actually better. She couldn't work for months, and once she could, her job was gone. The restaurant she had worked at, like so many restaurants in San Francisco, went permanently out of business.

After that, it was Space Mountain.

That's what Mariel called her mother's tumultuous downward spirals—which her mom always rode with her eyes firmly closed and in the dark. And although her mom managed to get occasional work here and there when the world opened up, the damage had been done. Damage on too many levels to count.

So now they were here. On a deserted street, where nobody in their right mind should be, at an hour nobody in their right mind should be there, waiting for a guy who probably wasn't coming.

"Wouldn't it have been better to just use the money to pay the ticket and the impound fee, instead of paying some guy you don't even know?"

To that, her mother just grunted.

That money, which had been demanded in advance, was basically all the money they had left. The last bit given to them by Mariel's uncle, who said it was the last time. Which was what he always said.

"This asshole ain't showing," her mom finally proclaimed. Then she sighed. "Sucks to be us." That was her favorite expression. Right up there with *It is what it is.*

Well, Mariel refused to accept it being what it was. And she refused to accept a sucks-to-be-me attitude. Feeling sorry for herself wouldn't help anyone, least of all her.

But that latest interview she had seen . . . If what she suspected was true, it could help everything. *Change* everything. Maybe.

It was just a few days ago. They had been sitting in a bar and grill that called itself a gastropub so they could charge more, and eating a meal that her mom would pay only about a third of before bailing. Mariel respected that about her mother: she wouldn't just dine-and-ditch; she would always leave something.

"I won't stiff the servers," she told Mariel. "They deserve

better than what we can give." It was her hope that the server would pocket that money as a tip, and let the restaurant write off the meal.

The gastropub had three TVs, and although two of them were showing sports, the third showed the news. A man who had been hospitalized for "Crown Royale"—which was what they were calling this new coronaform virus—was being interviewed. For a man who had just been at death's door, he looked pretty happy—and it wasn't just relief at being alive.

"How do you feel now?" the reporter asked. A dumb but obligatory question.

The man smiled a genuine smile and seemed to focus on the reporter as if seeing something wonderful in her eyes.

"I feel better than ever!" he said. "Really—better than *ever!*" And then he laughed. He actually laughed. As if all his cares and worries had lifted with his fever, never to return.

Mariel could definitely use some of that.

"Hi, I'm Rón, with a pretentious accent above the O. You must be the Hogan family."

Although the door was open, the four members of the Hogan family seemed afraid to step inside. Like everyone else who booked a stay here, they were guarded—convinced that it must be some mistake, or maybe even a practical joke. Like maybe they were on hidden camera.

Rón didn't have patience for it today. "Or we could ride the elevator again if you like. It's the fastest express elevator in the city!" Rón said. That motivated them to step in the front door.

"Don't forget to put on masks," Rón reminded. "They're mandatory during the walk-through."

The family, as befuddled as they were, were even more so now. "Oh," said the woman. "But we don't have any. We didn't think—"

"On the table, in the bowl." Rón said, pointing to a Waterford Crystal bowl just inside the entryway.

They grabbed a few, still cautious; still worried that the elaborate nature of this place was an elaborate trick.

"Mom," said one of the kids—a boy, maybe about ten, "these are those digital masks! I read about them."

The masks were a filament fiber screen that projected an approximate image of your face, making it look like you weren't wearing a second-generation N95 mask at all. Of course, it didn't get your facial expressions quite right, so at best it was a little creepy.

"Aren't these expensive?" Mrs. Hogan asked.

"They're included in the rental fee," Rón told her with a smile that never completely left his own masked face—because he had tweaked the output on his own mask to be a little more cheerful than he actually felt.

Finally, Mr. Hogan voiced what they all must have been thinking. "I'm . . . I'm afraid there must be some mistake. I don't think we're supposed to be here. . . ."

"Trust me, you are. C'mon, I'll show you around." Rón swung his arm, beckoning them to follow him into the expansive penthouse. "We're on the sixty-first floor, facing west. From the living room you can see the Golden Gate Bridge. And there's a bedroom and bath to the left, but since there's just four of you, you won't need it. The main bedrooms are upstairs.

"There's an *upstairs*?" breathed out the girl, who seemed the same age as the boy. Maybe twins.

"It's this way. Follow me."

Upstairs were three more bedrooms, including a primary suite that was as large as most people's homes. "The bathroom floors are all heated," Rón told them. "Blinds are controlled by your phone—just connect by Bluetooth. And if you're worried at all about earthquakes, don't be; the building's on rollers, like the ones in Japan."

The family was breathless. Speechless. The two kids were oohing and aahing, pulling out their phones to play with the blinds, and already posturing for their bedrooms of choice.

The father, who didn't seem like a timid man, was pretty

timid right now. "But . . . but we're only paying one hundred dollars a night."

"Yeah, I know. For four nights."

Still, they just stood there, looking around like they had popped into an alternate dimension and were about to explode. Rón sighed and took it upon himself to explain. "My father believes everyone should have a chance to experience this level of luxury. So he rents this penthouse out on Airbnb way below market price."

"Who is your father?" Mrs. Hogan asked.

Rón chose not to answer. They'd figure it out. And if they didn't, it didn't really matter, did it? "Enjoy your stay. This is the west penthouse—but I'm just across the hall, in the east penthouse—so if there's anything you need, you can call me anytime." Then he left them to their own devices—of which there were many.

When your father is the third-richest man in the world, it's hard not to be defined by him. Hard not to define *yourself* by him. No matter how hard you try. Especially when he sees you as an extension of himself.

"You are overwhelmed by my notoriety, I know. The only remedy is to climb your way out of it and establish a stronghold of your own above it."

His father loved to give advice, but his advice often felt more like cheerleading than anything useful. Although Rón had to reluctantly admit that being forced to be the host of his father's jackpot-surprise Airbnb was good for him. His illustrious father insisted that Rón be more sociable and interact with strangers on a regular basis. Vetted strangers, perhaps, but strangers nonetheless.

"In this world you must learn how to conduct yourself with all types of people from all types of backgrounds, and in the most awkward of situations. Developing social skills is like learning to drive. With enough practice it becomes second nature."

Yeah, well, maybe until there's a crash and burn—and there's no insurance for a social fail.

To be a top-notch host in an international city like San Francisco, Rón was required to memorize his Airbnb spiel in seven languages, which was even more of a chore than he thought it would be.

Leona, the kindest and least superficial of his siblings, had the most useful take on it all.

"Think of being his son as a part-time job. You get to live your life, but for a few hours a week, you have to be what he needs you to be."

"So why don't you do it?" Rón had asked.

Leona had shrugged like it was nothing, even though Rón knew it must have hurt her in a way he could never understand. "I would, but he didn't choose me." Then she had flown off to Paris.

He never imagined that greeting starry-eyed strangers would become a highlight of his day. The thing he liked most was the look of wonder on their faces as they stepped into the penthouse. It was nice to live vicariously through their amazement. It had been a very long time since he had experienced that kind of wonder, and it reminded him that his life was anything but mundane, even when it felt that way. Besides, renting the penthouse out on Airbnb violated the building association rules in a major way and pissed off the other owners, a fact that Rón liked as much as his father did.

"Don't go anywhere," said Kavita, his father's current girlfriend, calling to him from the living room as soon as he stepped inside. "He wants to talk to you."

Where would I go? Rón wanted to say, but instead just said, "I'll be here."

He went up to his room, peeling the smile off his face—literally—and threw himself on his bed.

Rón's father invented the digital N95 mask. Rón's father invented a lot of things—or, more accurately, came up with the concepts and paid other people to invent them. Blas Escobedo was past the age of invention—he was an idea man now, because he could afford to be.

"Intelligence can only get you so far. True genius isn't in merely being smart; it's knowing how to wield your own intelligence, and that of others."

His father was prone to pontification on any subject he was an expert on. Which was everything. He was even writing an inspirational book filled with aphorisms and uplifting advice. Or rather, he was paying someone else to listen to him talk, and write the book. Even before publication, it had already presold nearly a million copies. Because everyone wanted a piece of Blas Escobedo. Either a torn chunk of his flesh, a slice of his fortune, or just his attention—which is what Rón's dad loved more than anything. Negative attention, positive, it didn't matter as long as a sizeable number of the world's spotlights were turned toward him.

And the brighter the light on his father, the darker the shadow for Rón to hide in. Or, more accurately, get lost in—because even in the rare moments he didn't feel like hiding, he was stuck in his father's shadow anyway; a territory as vast as the dark side of the moon.

There were times that Rón had tried to escape it. Forever. Only once seriously, though.

Rón was not short for Ronald, or Ronaldo, or anything remotely typical. His full name was Tiburón Tigre Escobedo—Tiger Shark—because that was his father's favorite apex ocean predator. All his siblings were named for apex predators. It was his father's little joke that they all had to live with. (Of course, it turned on him ironically—as Rón's brothers and sisters were increasingly predatory against their father.)

While his father had called him TeTe ever since he was small, it was far too diminutive for a sixteen-year-old who was already taller than him. He preferred Rón. It was simple and straightforward—but he kept the accent mark, which was entirely unnecessary in a single-syllable name; however, he wanted to give a nod to his actual name. While also being iron-ically pretentious.

Rón was the youngest of six siblings and half siblings, and the only one living with their father. For some reason, above all his other siblings, Blas Escobedo chose Rón as his mini-me, keeping him close at hand. While all the others spent their time and money partying in the Maldives and Ibiza, Rón stayed home in San Francisco to learn how to be rich and famous in a world that would rather he wasn't.

"There are many people who don't want to see someone with a name like Escobedo be the third-richest man in the world. And many more who think someone with a name like Escobedo must have gotten there through illegal means, instead of through educa-tion, inspiration, and hard work. Let them eat their sour grapes as we prove them all wrong."

It was another quote from his father's book. By "we," he

meant himself and Tiburón. He often included Rón in state-ments about himself, and always did his best to never let Rón feel left out, although he invariably did, because the world wasn't interested in the young man in Blas Escobedo's shadow. Not when his siblings were so much more flamboyant, photo-genic, and badly behaved. Which was the reason why his father wasn't grooming any of them to take over his various busi-nesses. He'd made it clear that Rón was to be his successor in the world of high-stakes tech.

"It used to be that inheritance went to the eldest. The old ways are fine and good when they make sense. In this case they do not. Your brothers and sisters would squander, and bicker, and tear each other apart. Better to just give them a stipend enough to satisfy their appetites and send them on their way."

That particular morsel wasn't going into the book, but he had spoken it to Rón as if it was. Any potential inheritance, of course, was too far off the horizon to see. His father was still relatively young, and besides, he had a good portion of Silicon Valley working on ways to live forever.

"The way I see it, there's big money in longevity. Because human greed for money is only surpassed by human greed for time. Someone has already come up with a pill that can add several years to a per-son's life. I think we can do better."

His father wasn't a terrible person. Far from it. But the world loved to paint the filthy rich as filthy in every way. As for the money, Rón knew the truth. What people don't understand is that money doesn't change you. Instead, it constrains you. It limits who you are allowed to be in the eyes of the world, in the eyes of your friends, and even in the eyes of your family. When you have as much money as the Escobedos, it becomes a

Victorian corset. Wear your wealth long enough and it cuts off your circulation, until you can barely breathe.

And so sometimes you don't even want to breathe anymore.

Because although Blas Escobedo could buy his youngest son anything under the sun, he couldn't by him the one thing he wanted. A reason to be here.

They called Rón's first two attempts cries for help. Perhaps they were. But he got help. All sorts of help. His mother came back to live with him for a while—because divorce suddenly seems insignificant when your child's life is at stake. His father put his entire tech empire on hold to be there for Rón.

Medication, therapy, support. And it all helped for a time. But the black hole always came back.

Rón's third attempt was the serious one. He lost more blood than a person should and still be alive. But like his father, he was a fighter. A survivor, even if survival hadn't been his goal. And the fact that he lived through it made him think that maybe his body knew better than he did. That leaving was not the answer.

His father sat by his bedside the whole time he was in the hospital, praying over Rosaries Rón didn't know he had, and then in Hebrew, which Rón didn't even know he knew. Old Testament God, New Testament God. Yahweh, Jesus, Allah, Vishnu—it didn't matter as long as one of them answered.

Tiburón had never seen his father so humbled. So human. He remembered many of the things his father said to him when he was too weak to respond. He didn't orate or pontificate; he spoke in whispers from the heart. And sometimes he still did.

"You don't know this—only your grandparents do. But when I was your age, TeTe, I had similar thoughts of leaving this life. And like you, I tried, but luckily it was one of many things I wasn't very good at."

"Neither was I," Rón had croaked, which had made his father smile.

"*Was*," repeated his father. "I hope that means you're starting to see it as something in the past."

His father had taken his hand then. Gently, so as not to disturb the bandages. "I found my passion in technology and invention. It answered the *why* of my life. You know . . . destruction and creation are two sides of the same coin. And self-destruction? It can become an act of self-creation given time and perspective. You will see. I promise you will see."

Everyone at the hospital was paid handsomely to keep his attempted exit quiet, so Tiburón Tigre Escobedo did not become a banner headline, and the subject of media attention. Surprisingly, they all kept their silence. Not even a single tabloid exposé. It was the one time Rón was truly grateful for being invisible.

That was more than a year ago. And although the black hole was still there, he had become better at skating around its event horizon. But that didn't mean there weren't bad days.

"TeTe, are you home yet? Come downstairs and let's talk a bit."

Rón hauled himself up and went down to his father's home office. It was a corner of the penthouse where the glass walls came together, kind of like a fish tank. His desk was turned at forty-five degrees. A lot of their furniture was cornered like that; damn the feng shui, Rón's father loved angles.

"All good?" his father asked. It was a catch-all question— like the set of five red-to-green emoji buttons they have outside restrooms to let management know your general impression of their hygiene. Today Rón gave him the second green button. Good but not great. Which was a respectable place to be.

"New family's in. They want to know who to worship."

His father chuckled. "Whoever they want, as long as it isn't me." A call came through on his phone, and he dismissed it. One thing about his father: he never let work interfere when he was having a conversation with Rón.

Through the fishbowl corner of the room, Rón could see across the mouth of the bay to the picturesque communities of Sausalito and Tiburon. When he was very little and thought the world revolved around him, he used to think Tiburon was named for him. Then, when he got older and realized that the world revolved around his father, he accepted there was no connection between himself and the place across the bay.

"Some sad news, TeTe. Bennett, the evening doorman."

"Oh no. . . ." Rón knew what was coming before his father said it.

"He died of Crown Royale this morning."

Rón had spoken to Bennett, couldn't have been two weeks ago. Talked about the Giants, and their prospects for the season. Now he'd never see another game. "Is there anything we can do?"

"I've offered to help his family . . . but when someone goes like that, nothing you do will ever be enough. But there's something I'd like *you* to do, TeTe. It's too late to help Bennett, but maybe it will help others. He cleared his throat, and hesitated. That's how Rón knew it was the kind of ask that would hurl Rón way out of his comfort zone. "I'd like you to record a speech to help galvanize young people to fight Crown Royale."

"A speech . . ."

His father waved his hand. "Speeches are easy. If you don't want to write them, they can be written for you. The important thing is to mobilize people early. Prevention matters when facing a contagion this serious. You could make a difference and save lives."

Maybe . . . but would a speech given by Blas Escobedo's shadow matter to anyone? And if people did care, Rón didn't know how he'd fare as the center of attention. He had seen how some of his older siblings had suffered when the spotlight flicked from their father to them. Pitón's drug problem, Jag's anger issues, Pantera's nude photo shoot. While his father was both loved and hated, Rón's siblings were universally reviled by the press, even when they weren't doing anything particularly obnoxious. The world simply hated the offspring of the rich and famous. Which was why Rón's father had tried so hard to shelter him from that world. Until now.

"Leona should do it. People will listen to her more than they'll listen to me. I'm fine just hosting the west penthouse."

"I'm winding that down," his father told him. "Crown Royale is getting worse—we shouldn't be renting anymore. The CDC now says there's a four percent mortality rate—one in twenty-five people who catch it will die. And there's reason to believe you might be at greater risk, Tiburón. It is best to limit your close interactions. Perhaps isolate entirely."

Rón suppressed a sigh. His "greater risk" was still only hearsay, but when it came to Rón, his father approached things with an abundance of caution.

"I'm not worried," Rón said. "Your masks work."

"Yes, but they're not one hundred percent. Nothing is. And

besides, we'll soon be leaving the city, because you know how the city gets during these things."

"But what about school?"

"So you'll be remote when the school year starts."

"And my friends . . ."

"If they're true friends, they'll stay in touch. And if not, best to know now, so you can make others."

Rón took a moment to gauge his father. There was something in his eyes Rón didn't like. A certain rare kind of fear. Like the kind when he was by Rón's bedside in the hospital last year. Over his career, Blas Escobedo had watched his rockets explode. He'd seen his stock take nosedives. He'd even had an attempt on his life. But those things hadn't rattled him. Rockets get rebuilt. Stocks rebound. Attackers get put away. This look was different. And Rón thought he knew why.

"Is it true what they're saying about Jarrick Javins?" Rón asked.

His father shifted in his seat. Rón could practically feel the man's blood pressure go up. "The news will report it tomorrow. The moment Javins recovered from Crown Royale, he gave all his money to charity, resigned from all of his companies, and vanished."

How does the richest person in the world vanish? Rón wondered.

"No one's seen him for days. Rumor has it he's walking the world with nothing but the clothes on his back."

Rón didn't know what to say, except, "I guess that makes you the second-richest man in the world now."

His father pursed his lips. "That's not how I wanted to get there." Then that look again. That look of secret terror. "This disease . . . if it doesn't kill you, it steals your agency. Your ambition. It turns you into someone you're not and ruins you."

Rón tried to shrug it off. "You've always been charitable."

"If I give my money to charity, it's because I *choose* to—not because I've lost my mind. That's what's happening, TeTe—people are losing their minds." He tapped his fingers on his desk for a moment. "Have you ever heard of Howard Hughes, TeTe?"

Rón nodded. "Airplane guy, right? Richest in the world, like, what, fifty years ago?"

"On top of the world, then he disappeared. He lost it up here," his father said, tapping his temple. "I'm not going to become that."

"If you get Crown Royale, you'll deal," Rón said. It was weird being the one to talk his father in from the ledge like this. "You always deal."

"If I go the way of Javins, there'll be nothing left for you. You know that, don't you?"

"Who says I care all that much?"

"You'd care if it happened. It's easy to imagine yourself happy without money, TeTe, but the reality is very different. It's true that money can't make you happy—but lack of it can't make you happy either."

They both let it sit for a while, allowing all the simmering fears to stew. Then something occurred to Rón.

"Didn't Howard Hughes go into hiding because he was afraid of germs, too?"

His father grunted and tried to wave that off, but it still hung heavy in the air.

Looking back, Tiburón Tigre Escobedo would mark this as the moment he realized he was stronger than his father.

3
Morgan Suits Up

It was a full-blown space suit. Not a mask, or a rebreather, or even a hazmat suit, but the thing that astronauts wore.

"Really? Do I really have to wear this?"

"I'm afraid so, miss. It's nonnegotiable. Dame Havilland requires it. Come; there are four of us to help you put it on."

Morgan had come a long way for this interview, but now it was feeling like a really bad idea. What was up with this weird internship? This place—this grand estate in the lush English countryside—was already overwhelming. But on the other hand, it suggested she wasn't going to be merely shuffling papers in some cubicle. The internship would pay well if she got it; she knew that much. And thankfully, while her luck was running both hot and cold today, it had gotten her here on time.

Well, not exactly luck. The only luck that Morgan Willmon-Wu believed in was the kind you made yourself.

But right now, Morgan was eying that space suit with serious concern. "What if it doesn't fit?" She really did not want to get into the thing. What—were they sending her off to Mars or something?

"Oh, it will fit," said the butler, or footman, or whatever a stodgy person in his position was called. "It was made precisely to your measurements."

There were so many red flags that statement sent up,

Morgan felt herself tangling in them. What the hell had she gotten herself into?

Morgan's day had begun early, and with an intensity bordering on panic, taking her through a chain of events that was maddening.

It started with her trip to the airport. Knowing it was hard to get an Uber at the crack of dawn, she had scheduled two in advance, willing to accept the cancellation fee for the one that showed up second. But both of them canceled at the last minute—and of course none of the ride-share apps could pull down another driver. In the end, she had to call in a favor from one of her dormmates and have her drive, bleary eyed, to Zürich Airport from the university at five a.m. so Morgan could make her flight.

The queue at security was a Kafkaesque nightmare, and the tension hung heavier than usual, thanks to Crown Royale. People who had masked up glared daggers at those who hadn't, but since masks were not yet mandatory, they glared right back. Morgan had to slip between disgruntled travelers who were more than happy to be solid obstacles before her—until she had the bright idea of coughing in their direction as she pushed. Suddenly people, masked or not, were more than happy to part just to get her out of their airspace. Every errant cough, sneeze, or sniffle was another reminder to people that Crown Royale's bass was about to drop.

Her gambit got her halfway through the line, but then she encountered a security guard, who took his job way too seriously.

"*Nein!*" he said. "*Sie müssen wie alle anderen in der Schlange stehen.*"

Ha! "Wait in line like everyone else." As if that was even an option today.

The security officer, Morgan noted, spoke German with an Austrian accent—and so she responded by putting on her own fake, but convincing, Austrian accent, while turning on tears so suddenly it was as if she had burst some internal water main.

"Bitte, bitte, bitte!" she cried. "Please, please, please! I can't miss this flight. You don't understand! My father! You don't know what he'll do to me!" Then she suddenly, spasmodically, began tugging her hair as if in a fight with herself. "Please, please, please!"

The combination of it all—the tears, the disturbing hair pulls, and the fact that this girl, who was clearly Eurasian, was speaking like someone from his hometown—was just enough to do the trick. He not only let her pass; he escorted her to the front of the line.

Then, just past passport control, as if to reward her performance at security, a man, who was also racing to his gate, dropped a fifty-Euro note.

Morgan stepped on it before anyone else saw it. She had two choices here. She could be the Good Samaritan, catch up with him, and give it back . . . or she could keep it for herself.

It really wasn't much of a dilemma.

With the bill in her pocket, she picked up her pace to her gate—but then fortune turned against her once more.

"I'm sorry, Fräulein," said the gate agent. "You were late to arrive, and we've already given your seat to someone flying standby. There's another flight this afternoon."

Again, not an option. She considered the waterworks again, but a quick assessment of the woman made it clear that she had seen it all, and would not be moved. In fact, this woman's picture was probably in the German dictionary right next to the word "schadenfreude." The more miserable Morgan looked, the more pleasure the gate agent would derive from it. This called for a different approach.

Morgan looked over the counter to see a boarding pass the agent had just printed out for the individual about to take her place on the flight. Morgan noted the name.

"Who's Jern van Vleck?" Morgan asked.

The woman's eyes flicked to an elderly gentleman sitting nearby, looking forlorn and morose.

Morgan pulled out her passport. "I understand that you have no choice but to rebook me on the next flight," she said, sounding resigned. "But I'd be forever grateful if you'd reconsider."

Then she slipped the fifty Euros into her passport, and slid it across the counter toward the gate agent.

Jern van Vleck did not fly to London that morning.

The flight was less than two hours, and gave Morgan some time to consider how she might best present herself. She had applied to this particular internship on a whim. She never thought her bullshit essay would be considered. After all, she was probably younger than most applicants. She had started university at fifteen, barreled her way through to two degrees, and was still only nineteen.

She was surprised when an invitation for an interview arrived at her dorm just a month before graduation. The invitation didn't come by email—it came by post—and it wasn't for a virtual interview, as all the others had been. They wanted her in person. In England. A flight that they were paying for. They. The Havilland Consortium.

Their website was minimal and vague. A bunch of philanthropic pursuits. With degrees in linguistics and international marketing, Morgan couldn't imagine what they wanted with her, but she liked their style. The fancy gold invitation. The free plane ticket. And the chocolate bar that inexplicably came with it. It had melted, of course, in the student mail center, but its presence had intrigued her nonetheless.

Problem was, the interview was on the same day as her graduation. It would have to be one or the other. The way Morgan saw it, commencement was for parents and egos. Well, in spite of her pleas to the security guard about an abusive father, her father was actually dead, her mother was not likely to attend, and her ego was plenty healthy without a cap and gown to bolster it. The decision had been easy.

A space suit was not easy to walk in. Aside from looking, and feeling, like an idiot, Morgan found it hard to balance, hard to even shift her feet forward. And what made it worse was that the grand salon she was led to was full of fragile things. Bone china; glass figurines; furniture with spindly legs that looked like it belonged behind the velvet ropes of a museum.

And in the midst of it all was a woman who seemed as fragile as her belongings.

She sat in a wheelchair, with a plastic tube snaking from an oxygen tank clipped to her nostrils by two tiny nubbins.

"Sit, sit," said Dame Glynis Havilland, for whom the Havilland Consortium was named. "I trust your journey here was uneventful," she said, her lips slightly screwed into an unsettling smirk. She spoke the sort of English that the most upper echelons of society spoke, although there was the faintest hint of Eastern European to it. Morgan considered matching her way of speaking, but instead took on a "Home Counties" accent, which made her sound like a standard middle-class Londoner.

"Are you sure the furniture is sturdy enough? This suit makes me all the more heavy."

"We'll find out soon enough, won't we?" the old woman said—then raised her cane, pushing it against Morgan's chest. The suit was so top heavy, it shifted Morgan off balance enough to plop down in the antique chair behind her.

The chair creaked with sorrowful complaint, but in the end held.

"So glad you could make it!" Dame Havilland said. "Originally you were to wear that suit for *my* protection. But as it turns out, it's now for your protection instead."

The woman let that hang in the air for a few moments, then explained.

"In spite of extreme precautions, I have recently been exposed to Crown Royale by a careless, and possibly spiteful, member of my staff, who has since been fired. As you probably know, the incubation period is three to six days, and I am on my fourth day, which means filling this internship position is an extremely high priority—and it is critical that I don't infect the applicants."

"I'm sorry to hear that," Morgan said. "But I still don't know what the job is."

"And you won't until I'm ready to tell you."

Then the woman coughed several times. It was a dry cough.

Could have been just the musty room. Could have been something more. Morgan had once heard that most household dust was dead human skin cells, and a palatial estate like this one must have had several centuries of the stuff haunting the halls like Shakespearean ghosts.

"Did you like the chocolate, by the way?" Dame Havilland asked. "It's the best in the world by my reckoning. Puccini Bomboni. Sounds Italian but it's Dutch."

Morgan didn't tell her it had melted. "A strange thing to send to a girl from Switzerland, the chocolate capital of the world."

"It was for my own amusement," the woman said. "An homage to Roald Dahl, after whose most infamous work I modeled my internship program."

"Then should I expect little people to hop out of the woodwork and burst into song?"

The old woman chuckled. "Had there been more time, perhaps I could have arranged it. Truth be told, Mr. Dahl was quite a miserable human being—but if we judge the work by the sins and temperament of the creators, the world would be virtually void of art, literature, and music." Then she raised a crystalline glass full of some spirit Morgan could not share in, or even smell, due to the space suit. "Here's to tortured souls! They vomit forth the most interesting Rorschachs."

And as Morgan looked around, she could see sculptures and paintings featuring the most tortured of souls. Works brooding and evocative. The types of things you wouldn't want to be alone with at night.

"I narrowed the field of applicants down to five finalists," Dame Havilland said as she put down her glass, "and then set out to test each of them to see who had the mettle to meet my exacting requirements. All were given approximately the same test. The first four failed."

"So I'm here to be tested?"

"You already have been. Your test was this morning, dear." Then Dame Havilland gave that twisted, smug smirk again. "I was the one who canceled your rides this morning, forcing you to be resourceful in getting to the airport in time for your flight."

"Okay . . ."

"Upon arrival at the airport, my representative—you may call him Slugworth—witnessed your stellar charade that got you through security. He is also the one who dropped the fifty-Euro note, which you wisely chose to keep rather than return. Had you returned it, you would never have gotten on that flight—because the gate agent was instructed to allow you on only if you bribed her with that particular marked bill."

"I suppose the sad old man was in on it too."

"No, he was just a sad old man. Probably still waiting there in the airport for all I know." And then Dame Havilland laughed long and loud.

"You're a very odd woman," Morgan dared to say.

Dame Havilland was not offended. "I enjoy games. Especially ones of my own design. You could say my whole life is a long game, as I've spent much of it in strategic maneuvers, reinventing myself when necessity warranted."

Morgan was still trying to process the woman's byzantine manipulation at the airport. Was there method in this madness?

"I was Hungarian by birth," Dame Havilland continued,

"then a British aristocrat by marriage. Although I was well and truly hated by others in that putrid social class. But I endured."

"And your husband?" Morgan asked.

"Dead. I had nothing to do with that; I was honestly widowed by a heart attack. I loved him, he died, and I mourned. But I knew all the while that broken hearts mend. And in time, I was able to use my modest fortune to turn the tables on those pompous stuffed shirts who so despised me. Because it is not good enough to merely succeed; one must also push those you despise into the tar, and watch them slowly sink like the dinosaurs they are."

The vitriol in the woman's voice made Morgan smile. And it also made her think back to one of her classes. A math class with an old-school professor who graded on a strict curve. Morgan's greatest joy in that class was acing the test, and throwing off the curve, ensuring that several kids toward the bottom flunked out. Kids who might have been fine had she not been there to shift the curve against them. It felt good to have that kind of power.

"But enough about me," said Dame Havilland, rolling forward. "Let's talk about you. Morgan Willmon-Wu. Fluent in Cantonese, German, French, Spanish, and English. Born in Hong Kong to an Anglo mother and Chinese father. Identified early on as exceptionally gifted." Then she wagged a finger. "There's one bit of your vitae that's misinformation, though, my dear. Your father wasn't really your father."

"Excuse me?"

"My research team is thorough, and you'd be amazed at the things you can dig out of the dark web. In this instance, they found an ancestry test that your father had done for you when you were very young. Apparently, your mother had an affair with one of his coworkers. We're not certain which one."

Morgan suddenly found herself wanting to fling the woman through the stained-glass window, but controlled her anger. Perhaps this was also a test. But she doubted it was a lie.

"Why are you telling me this?"

"Because you deserve to know why your late father became so distant before he died, and why your mother moved to Zürich with you all those years ago."

"I've heard enough." Morgan tried to stand, but found the chair threatening to buckle beneath her if she moved another inch.

Dame Havilland laughed. "My dear, you can't effectively storm out in a space suit. Your righteous rage loses all credibility when you need my domestic staff to peel you out of that thing. Now let's get down to the crux of the matter. I am most likely going to come down with Crown Royale over the next few days. At my age, and in my poor state of health, it will probably kill me. But if I survive, it will be much, much worse."

Quite honestly, Morgan was heartened by the thought of the old woman dying, but held her tongue, and listened.

"I'm sure you've heard rumors about the effect of the disease on its recovered victims. The rumors are apparently true. Which means, should I survive, I would likely give my property, and everything I own, to my staff, or to my bogus charity, or, God forbid, to my no-account nephew. My eyes shall miraculously be opened to the simple things in life, the joy of giving, Tiny Tim will walk again, and God bless us, every one." But the scowl on her face made it clear she was not that kind of Scrooge. "Let me make this perfectly clear. I do not wish my legacy to be one of graciousness to my fellow human beings. No one in this world is worthy of my grace. But to bring about the legacy I have in mind, it will take someone with more life in them than I currently have. . . .

"Therefore, I needed to seek out a youth. A jaded, self-interested, shrewd, and savvy youth. With whom I could trust with all that I hold dear. Someone to take up the mantle after I am either gone, or transformed into a person I do not wish to be."

Suddenly Morgan's hatred of the woman seemed a small and insignificant thing. "Are you saying what I think you're saying?"

Then Dame Glynis Havilland stood up from her wheelchair on legs that were not quite as weak as they appeared. "Morgan Willmon-Wu, I wish to turn over to you all that I have. Because I trust you'll know what to do with it. And because time is too short to find someone better."

Morgan found herself lightheaded and wondered if she was getting enough oxygen within the suit.

"Do you accept my offer?"

"If I accept," said Morgan, "what is it that you want me to do?"

Dame Havilland hobbled close, locking eyes on Morgan through the curved glass of the helmet.

"I wish to have one legacy and one legacy alone," Dame Havilland said. "I want to eradicate Crown Royale from the face of the Earth."

4
Victimless Staycation

"It was there on the bench—what was I supposed to do? Let someone steal it?"

Today, after a miserable night of not getting their car back, Mariel's mother decided the world owed her something, and had taken a businessman's wallet.

"I only just borrowed it," she told Mariel. "I gave it back, didn't take a penny—he didn't even know it was gone!"

What Gena did take, however, was a credit card number, expiration date, and CVC code.

"Mom, you can't do things like that! You worry about being at the shelter—this kind of thing will land you in jail!"

Her mother had done this once before—or at least once that Mariel knew of. That first time it was from someone they knew. A friend and neighbor. The woman had a daughter Mariel's age, although they only tolerated each other. Nothing in common except that their mothers were friends. Then, when Mariel and Gena's world came crashing down, that "friend" dished out a shallow casserole of sympathy and wiped her hands of them. They all met for lunch sometime later, when Mariel and her mother were living at a run-down motel. You could tell that they were afraid that nouveau poverty would rub off on them.

The woman insisted on paying for the meal of course—made a big show of it. Then Gena went to the bathroom. Only instead of going to the bathroom, she caught the waiter and gave him her credit card instead—because they still had a functional one at that time—and paid for the whole meal. "Because we don't need her holier-than-thou charity."

Turned out when she switched cards, she also got the woman's credit card number, which Gena then used to order them Grubhub for weeks. One meal in exchange for more than a dozen.

Mariel should have stopped her, or at least tried. But she resented that woman and her perfect prissy daughter, too. Knowing that they were paying for Wingstop and Wendy's made the food taste better. After all, it was a victimless crime, right? Because when the card statement showed up with all these charges, the woman would complain, and the bank would cover it.

So rather than stopping it, Mariel became an accomplice, picking up the orders herself, since delivery would have given the bank a beeline to their motel room door. "Fraud's not fraud when it's simple payback," her mother had said.

But revenge on a fair-weather friend wasn't the same as taking an Amex number from a total stranger.

"You have to throw that number away," Mariel insisted.

Her mother tapped her temple. "Can't. It's right up here."

Exasperating. Her mother was good with numbers. Too bad she couldn't find a way to put that skill to use. Or at least legitimate use.

"Just because you remember it, doesn't mean you need to use it!"

"Already did when we were back at the library. But I swear, crisscross applesauce, I'm only gonna use it once."

They often spent time in libraries—where you could stay

all day without being asked to leave. She had seen her mother on one of the library computers. Mariel assumed she was posting her usual opinions on social media. But this time she was up to something else.

She put her hand to Mariel's face, cradling it. "I did it because we deserve one nice thing in the middle of all this, don't we? *You* deserve one nice thing."

Mariel sighed. What was done was done. "So what did you buy?"

"I bought us one night where we don't have to worry about the Grinch, or the rain, or assholes who take our money and don't show." Then she smiled. "Tonight we're staying at an Airbnb."

The guests showed up early, but the doorman was instructed to keep any prepunctual guests in the lobby until four o'clock.

Tiburón was waiting for them when they were finally sent up in the express elevator. These were unexpected guests, in that they had made a one-night booking before Rón could suspend the account as per his father's orders. All future bookings were canceled, but this one slipped in under the radar. Rón was glad for it; with his whole life about to be put on indefinite hold, he was determined to savor this last in-person interaction, before it all became faces on a screen.

From the moment they arrived, Rón could tell that this woman and her daughter were not like the usual tourists that booked the place. They were pungent. A more judgmental person would say that they reeked. And on top of it, there was a weariness about them that was palpable. Like they were both caught in the undertow of a relentless ocean.

Both the girl and her mother were blond but clearly had not, or had not been able to, attend to their grooming. The mother's hair was beginning to go gray before its time.

Rón spent much of his life trying not to be defined by the privilege of wealth the way so many were defined by the privilege of their birth. He knew what it meant to be rich, but he also knew what it meant to be Brown—and, as his father pointed out—there were many people who couldn't accept those two things going together. So Rón fought to never look down on anyone in any circumstance. But it was hard to keep himself from forming an opinion of these two. Whatever their situation, this night was to remind themselves of their humanity, which the world was stripping from them, layer by layer. Even so, he could sense a spark to the girl, which he found interesting. He was never intrusive into the guests' lives, but this time he definitely wanted to know more.

Then, before he could welcome them and give them his standard spiel, the girl gasped. Not at the penthouse, but at the sight of him.

"No way! You're Tiburón Escobedo!" she said.

That threw him for a loop—because nobody ever recognized him. Even when people figured out who owned the penthouse, they never figured out who *he* was, or at least not by name.

His first thought was the realization that he had forgotten to put on his mask—although since the mask projected a reasonable approximation of one's face, he wondered if the girl would have guessed who he was anyway.

He grabbed one of the digital masks from the bowl on the credenza and quickly slipped it on. "Masks, please," he said, and handed them each one.

"Holy crap!" said the mother, looking around. "This is an Airbnb?"

But the girl wasn't taking in the penthouse; she kept scrutinizing Rón. "So . . . your father rents out a penthouse to make himself feel less guilty for being the third-richest guy in the world?"

No one ever nailed it so quickly. "Pretty much so, yeah. But now he's the second richest."

"Baby, look at this view! Jesus, we won the fucking lottery!"

"Language, Mom." Then she smirked. "He might think we're too common and kick us back to the curb."

Rón found he couldn't hold her gaze when she smirked like that, so he glanced at his tablet. "It says the reservation is under the name Vincent Cornell. . . ."

"Yeah, that's me," said the woman a little too quickly. "My parents wanted a boy, so whatcha gonna do?" Then she moved toward one of the sofas.

"Momma, don't sit down till we've showered," said the girl, then turned a little sheepishly to Rón. "We've been traveling all day. Got a little ripe."

Well, if that was her story, Rón was okay with her sticking with it. He didn't comment on the fact that they had no luggage.

"C'mon, I'll give you the grand tour . . . Miss Cornell."

"You can call me Mariel," the girl said.

"And you can call me Rón."

"Right. With a pretentious accent."

That made Rón smile—which was much broader on his tweaked mask. "It's *ironically* pretentious."

She shrugged, and grinned right back. "Which makes it even *more* pretentious."

Mariel and her mother probably didn't want the grand tour—he imagined they just wanted to be left alone, and explore the place by themselves. But Rón had his script to go through, and besides, he wasn't in a hurry to leave. His curiosity was piqued by them in multiple ways. When he finally wrapped up the tour, he said, "I'll be back with wine and cheese at five thirty. It's included."

"Cool," said the mother from across the room. "Hope it's fancy-schmancy cheese."

"Only the best," Rón said.

"Great," said Mariel. "See you soon."

Then Rón crossed the short hallway to his own penthouse. Of course, he had made up the whole wine-and-cheese thing on the spur of the moment, but he was sure he could put something fancy-schmancy together by five thirty.

Espresso-rubbed fontina, and black truffle Camembert. Fancy enough cheeses—although Rón had to cut them into neat wedges, because he had already gouged chunks out the day before. For wine, he brought a robust Malbec. He knew absolutely nothing about wine; he just heard his father call it robust.

"Even if your palate isn't educated, your wine knowledge will send the right signals in any pompous circles you wish to advance in," his father once told him. *"Rich fools don't need to be drunk to be under the influence of wine."*

By the time Rón returned, Mariel and her mother—who still claimed to be named Vincent—had both bathed, and Mariel had on fresh clothes that must have been in her backpack—the only item she had arrived with. The clothes were worn out and a little torn—but not in a fashionable way.

And yet it still looked fashionable on Mariel. Her mother was wearing the bathrobe that the Escobedos provided all their guests, and didn't seem at all shy about being so indisposed. The antithesis of his father's girlfriend, Kavita, who had to get dressed in order to get dressed.

"Very nice," said the mother, looking at the writing on the wine bottle. "French?"

"That's not French, Momma," Mariel said.

"It's an Argentinian wine," Rón told them. "My father is partial to South American vineyards."

"Well," said the mother as they sat down, "the cheese looks French."

And since the wrappers were long gone, Rón could only agree.

While Mariel had fully blown out her hair, her mother's was still damp in places, as if she didn't have the patience to dry it completely. From the few interchanges he had heard, Rón knew their dynamic without having to be told. Mariel was more the parent here. Not by choice but by necessity. While her mother seemed a force of nature, Mariel could wrangle it—and someone with the power to control the weather was far more intriguing than the storm itself. Rón didn't comment on any of it, though. His father had raised him to be acutely observant, but he also knew that sometimes it was best to keep the things he observed to himself.

Mariel was also observant, but for an entirely different reason. For her, it was a matter of survival. If you couldn't read between peoples' lines, you could get taken advantage of, or worse. Her mother was bad at reading people, and it had left them in trouble more than once. But reading their host was hard. Having not been in the company of someone as rich as Rón Escobedo before, she wasn't sure what to make of him. She didn't know whether this was a game of chess or a game of chance. With him, she was up for either.

While her mother chowed down on cheese and crackers, drinking her wine in gulps, Mariel ate more deliberately. Took only the smallest sips of her wine, slipping her mask down, then back up.

"So is your company part of the package?" Mariel asked.

"My company?"

"You said wine and cheese was part of the deal, but you didn't say anything about you sitting there watching us eat." She had said it to prod him just a little. To test the timbre of his intentions. But he suddenly became awkward, and even though his mask still showed him smiling, his eyes were not.

"Do you want me to go?"

Then her mother chimed in. "Absolutely not!" she declared. Then she refilled her wine and got up. "I'll leave you two to get acquainted." Her parting shot to Mariel was a conspicuous wink that could probably be seen from street level. Then she and her bathrobe swished away, taking half of Mariel's self-respect with her.

Mariel sighed. "Clearly my mother thinks you're a catch."

"Like every mother in the world."

He might have meant that to be quippy, but it rubbed Mariel the wrong way. "Well, it must be such a burden to be Prince Charming."

"You do realize that if you go there, that makes you Cinderella."

She gave a halfhearted guffaw that puffed up her mask. "Right. So if I leave my ratty old sneaker here when we go, will you try to find me?"

He shrugged. "Honestly? The cleaning service would throw it away before I even saw it."

She took another sip of wine. He just kept on smiling, and she had to ask.

"Why do you keep smiling like that?"

"It's not me, it's the mask. I . . . uh . . . programmed it that way."

"So if *you* programmed it, it *is* you."

He hesitated for a moment, then reached up and took off the digital mask. He was still smiling, just not nearly as much. "I know the pandemic is still in its early stages, but I need to be careful. I'm colorblind."

Mariel was going to take her mask off, too, but stopped herself. There were several factors affecting the prognosis of anyone who contracted Crown Royale. The aged, the sickly, the diabetic, and, oddly, the colorblind were most at risk. As if God threw a dart at a wall of random biological traits, and color-blindness took the hit.

Tiburón Escobedo was high risk. So what was he even doing here?

"Oh," she said, trying to find the least awkward thing to say. She failed. "I guess that makes it hard to see traffic lights and stuff."

"That's a myth. And anyway, that's red-green colorblind-ness. I can see red and green just fine. I have tritanopia. Blue-cone deficiency."

"You can't see blue?"

"So I've been told. Yellow's pretty iffy too."

Mariel looked at the wine bottle between them, then picked it up. "What do you see when you look at this label?"

"Greenish gray," he responded.

"Maybe because it's greenish gray," she said.

His grin took on a slant. "Trick question. No fair."

Mariel took a moment to reassess. Maybe this wasn't chess at all. Maybe they were partners in a hand of bridge.

"Anyway," he said, "I just need to be more careful than most." But he didn't put his mask back on. Stupid, considering he didn't know them or where they'd been.

Then, noticing he hadn't touched the cheese, or poured himself a glass of wine, she asked, "Aren't you going to have any?"

"I brought it for the two of you," he said. "So you'd . . . have something."

And there it was. Pity. That was a game she definitely didn't want to play.

"Thanks, but we don't need your charity."

"It's not charity. It's hospitality."

She responded by pushing the cheese plate back toward him. "Whatever you think you know about us, you don't."

He looked at the plate for a few moments, then back at her.

"You couldn't afford the hundred dollars you paid for this place. You haven't been eating regular meals. You may not live on the street, but you don't have a home address. And you'd *never* leave your sneaker, because you know you'd have to replace it."

And since he was right about all of it, there was only one thing she could say.

"You're an asshole."

Then, to her surprise, he folded. No—he *imploded*. Like a

shell that couldn't withstand the pressure of whatever place his billion-dollar head was at.

"I'm sorry," he said, and stood, turning toward the door. "I should go. Enjoy the place."

Mariel jumped to her feet. "That's it?" Mariel said. "You get called an asshole once, and you bail? Are rich people really that fragile?"

He turned back to her, palms open and neutral. "Listen, I just wanted to help."

"With wine and cheese . . ."

"What do you want? A house?" he blurted. "A Lambo? A hundred grand?"

"All of the above would be nice."

And he stood there, like he was actually considering it. She let out a bitter laugh. She could play him. The way her mom played people. She could, if she was that person.

"So you want charity instead of hospitality after all," he said.

Mariel found her self-respect flagging. She wished her mother would come out and shamelessly conduct the orchestra of his pity, but she had already been distracted by some other shiny object in the massive penthouse.

"Maybe you could let us stay here a few more nights," Mariel suggested. "Until we can . . . figure out our situation."

Rón pursed his lips. "I can't. You're our last guests—the place is being mothballed. A whole team is coming in tomorrow to cover the furniture and prepare for lockdown. My father's orders. I'm sorry."

Mariel nodded. She should have known that any doors that open in a place like this would have security chains.

"So . . . are you at least gonna bring us breakfast in the morning?"

He perked up. "Do you want me to?"

There was something sad about what an eager puppy he was. Sad and maybe a little endearing. "Turning a billionaire's son into my bitch is very tempting," she said.

She meant it as a playful barb, but it didn't land well. He frowned, clearly feeling laughed *at*, rather than laughed *with*. Then he slipped his mask back on. "The fridge is fully stocked. Eggs, juice, whatever you want."

She secretly wished he *would* be back for breakfast, but she had killed any hope of that.

"I'm sorry," she said, "I didn't mean to—" But she realized anything she said would just make it worse. Crash and burn. Move on; nothing to see here.

"You have my number if there's anything else you need," he said, slipping back into his hosting script. "Enjoy your stay."

"Thank you for the wine and cheese," Mariel said. "It was nice of you."

He nodded instead of saying "*you're welcome*." Only after he had left did she realize he had done that on purpose. To make sure she had the last word.

That night, with the lights of the bay twinkling outside the floor-to-ceiling windows of their luxurious suite in the sky, Mariel and Gena watched comfort TV. Cheesy episodes of some show that aired years before Mariel was even born. Mariel leaned into her mother, who gently stroked her hair, while two smooth Miami detectives, dressed in pastels, chased criminals that they always caught.

"This is like the old days, baby," Gena said.

"We never had a TV this big, or a couch this comfortable," Mariel pointed out.

"I know . . . but still."

And she was right. There were plenty of good times before the dark spirals of Space Mountain became a regular occurrence in their lives.

"Y'know . . . that boy likes you," Gena commented.

Mariel shifted her shoulders. Not uncomfortably, but settling in. Maybe her mother was right about Rón. And maybe the feeling was mutual. But what did it matter?

"He's on a different planet, Momma."

"You mean in a Mars/Venus kind of way? Men and women are all from the same planet, baby. Earth. We each gotta face that sooner or later."

"No," said Mariel. "I mean, he lives in penthouses, and limos, and private jets."

"And five'll get you ten he's tired of his own kind of people."

Mariel shifted again and sighed, not willing to entertain her mother's pie-in-the-billionaire-sky kind of thinking. They'd shared too much disappointment lately to add one more thing to the list.

There was a quiet moment between the car chases and the nightclubs of mythic Miami, and Gena surfed to other channels, landing for a moment on a news report. A descending graph and some loudmouth saying that commodity futures were plunging.

"What does that even mean?" Gena griped.

"It means people aren't buying stuff," Mariel told her. "Or at least they don't *think* people will be buying stuff tomorrow, or next month, or whenever."

Gena razzed, either in disgust, or dismissal of the notion. "People are people. They don't stop buying; they just get it cheaper somewhere else."

"They don't buy what they don't want anymore, Momma."

Gena threw her a suspicious look. "Are you talking about Crown Royale people again?"

Mariel grinned. "Maybe."

"Yeah, well, maybe let's just watch stuff blow up in Miami." Then she flipped the channel back, and within seconds guns were blasting and things were comfortably exploding again.

5
Theater of Concern

The hammer came down.

Dame Havilland knew it would. She thought she was prepared; that all the hatches of her worn and weathered soul were battened down for this final storm. And final it would be. She would go down with this ship. Because what choice did she have? She was old; she was frail; but more importantly, she was ready. This mortal coil, as Shakespeare had called it, had become too constricting. Too chafing. She despised things that lingered when they ought to be gone. She supposed that now included herself.

She took pride in how worthy an opponent she had been to death all these years—for he had tried to take her more than once, but failed. Scarlet fever in her youth. Malaria on her honeymoon. Ovarian cancer in her middle years. And then, finally, a car accident that had killed her driver, and left her Bentley an unrecognizable hunk of crumpled steel a hundred yards from the road. Yet she endured. Not only endured, but thrived, thumbing her nose at that dark specter.

But death was patient, and ever present. Always breathing behind her, making the small hairs on the back of her neck rise.

"Someday I will have you, whether you're ready or not," it seemed to say. *"But it's oh, so much easier if you're ready."*

And now she was.

Crown Royale was upon her, growing and replicating in her blood, ripping into her cells and replacing her RNA with its own.

She knew the basic symptoms, and marked them as they arrived. It began as a tickle in the back of her throat. Then her fingertips and toes began to tingle, and her lips to burn. There were bruises in unpredictable places. And a smell. A cross between burning lavender and yeasty bread right out of the oven. Everyone claimed to smell something, although for everyone it was something different.

Before the fever came on, she called Rooks, her butler, in. She was already isolated—hermetically sealed within her bedroom suite. Only Rooks and her lady's maid, Anna, were allowed entrance, in their own sealed suits. Simple white hazmat suits, for there was no need for the same overwhelming caution she had demanded for Ms. Willmon-Wu.

The maid, however, had become far too nervous once she donned the suit, making interactions unsettling. Besides, she was a sweet but dim-witted girl. Dame Havilland did not want her last human interactions to be empty calories.

"Sit with me, Rooks," she said as he entered. "I have a rare desire for conversation; be so kind as to indulge me."

"Of course, Dame Havilland."

She pursed her lips into a grin. "In all your years in my service, it's always been 'madame,' or 'Dame Havilland.' Never once have you called me 'Glynis.'"

Although she couldn't see clearly through the protective faceplate of his suit, she liked to imagine he reddened a bit.

"Had I done so," Rooks responded, "I have no doubt you would have discharged me instantly for such inappropriate familiarity."

Dame Havilland guffawed at that. It hurt her chest to do so, but sometimes things struck a person so that a burst of laughter could not be avoided. "You're right! I would have—and without so much as a letter of recommendation for your troubles." She thought about it a moment more. "Then a day or two later I would have hired you back out of the 'kindness of my heart.'"

Rooks remained stoic about it. Still, he asked the most curious question. "And would I have been grateful, madame?"

"Oh, you would have pretended to be. But really you would have just been relieved." She shifted positions in her wheelchair. She could get around without it, but she had fallen once. Hurt her hip. Bruised, not broken, but even so, that helplessness was unbearable. The very idea of being sprawled on the ground without the leverage to pick herself up. She had needed both Rooks and two others to get her to her bed. After that humiliation, a dependence on the wheelchair felt like the lesser evil. The problem was the more she used it, the harder it was to get around without it. Well, she wouldn't be needing it for much longer. She was already feeling the onslaught of the illness. The telltale aches, the hint of chills. It was beginning. But she wasn't ready to let Rooks leave her alone with it just yet. . . .

The silence between them was only broken by the sound of her breathing, which was labored even on the best of days. To keep the moment from becoming too unsettling, Rooks took it upon himself to engage in small talk.

"I've heard the crowds are still strong at Cornwall Castle."

"My charitable efforts at work!"

"Yes, people are still coming in droves, in spite of . . ." Then he faltered. Glynis found his hesitance irritating.

"You can say it, Rooks. In spite of Crown Royale."

"Yes, madame."

Thinking of the castle—one of the plum projects of the Havilland Consortium—made her smile with guilty, and admittedly, sinister pleasure. The restoration of Cornwall Castle, and the push to have it named a national monument, had nothing to do with any love of antiquity. That moss-covered eyesore could have been left to ruin—but it just happened to be right next to the estate of Lord Gallick—an old-money highbrow who ignored no opportunity to publicly malign Glynis. And now, with Cornwall Castle a new national attraction, there was a plague of tourists to torment him on a daily basis. The path to his estate was perpetually filled with slow-moving traffic and tour buses, and there was absolutely nothing he could do about it! The cherry on this tasty sundae was that now some Hollywood type wanted to film a TV series there. Murder and mayhem among inbred aristocrats. Oh, she would pay a king's ransom to have seen the look on Gallick's face when he heard about it!

Glynis Havilland was no philanthropist. Her charity was as unapologetically self-serving as any of her other endeavors. She wielded the force of charity for spite, or for tax benefits, or merely to stroke her ego. There was something entertaining about attending galas in your honor. Especially when those who thought themselves better than you were forced to applaud.

"Are you worried about it, Rooks?" It occurred to her she never called him by his first name either. "Crown Royale, I mean."

"I take precautions, both publicly and privately," he said. "And if I contract it, it's not like I'm in danger of giving away a fortune."

Glynis took offense to that. "I pay you sufficiently—are you implying that I don't?"

"Not at all, madame, not at all."

Still, she knew she had not been particularly kind to him. Well, what of it? It was a harsh world. He should be thankful for a stable, long-standing position.

"Should I get the disease, and survive it," Rooks said, "I'm not entirely opposed to knowing what it means to be truly happy."

"Truly happy? My dear Mr. Rooks, what makes you think that truth and happiness ever share the same bed?"

Rooks shrugged. "They may dally on occasion."

"Nonsense! And besides, happiness is overrated."

As far as Dame Glynis Havilland was concerned, there was no pit deep enough for the perpetually cheerful. *"Show me someone who always smiles, and I'll show you someone with bodies in their basement,"* she had been quoted as saying. She didn't remember actually saying that, but she was pleased to have it attributed to her. She never hired such sunshine people—which was why her staff always appeared somewhat dour and emotionally anemic. The more perky people could keep their distance and serve her coffee at the local Starbucks. Beyond that, she had no use for them.

"Vacant, vapid joy is every bit the scourge that abiding misery is," she pontificated to her captive audience of one. "Worse—because it pretends to be something better. If I leave the world knowing I have set the wheels in motion to defeat this disease of mindless euphoria, at least I will have accomplished something worthwhile in this life."

Rooks offered no response to this. She hadn't expected him to. A cold spark shot randomly through her body, jagged as a lightning bolt. The fever was upon her. It was time.

"Mr. Rooks, I am instructing you to dismiss the staff for the next few days. Give them a short vacation. And you are to leave as well. You shall be the first to return, but not until four full days have passed."

Rooks protested of course. "Madame, why would you—"

"Never mind why. It is my wish to be left alone."

"I should like to call in Dr. Ezrin to attend to you, then."

"Call no one, and spare me your 'theater of concern,' Mr. Rooks. I know you care no more about me than your job requires. Consider your objections logged, and your job done. Now leave with the others, and come to collect me in four days."

They both knew what she meant by "collect." And why she set the clock at four days. Because most people who succumbed to Crown Royale did so before the end of that fourth day.

"As you wish, madame."

She took a moment to consider the man. *What will Rooks do once I am gone?* she wondered. He wasn't a young man—only ten or fifteen years her junior. Retirement age, surely. Or maybe Miss Willmon-Wu would have him stay on to assist in the transition once she took over. Well, either way it would not be Glynis's concern.

"Thank you for your time and attention, Galen," she said, for once calling him by his first name. Then before he had a chance to respond, she said, "Now get the hell out."

Once he was gone, and she had watched through her window as the staff left, she labored out of her chair and into her bed. Then she began the laborious business of dying.

The fever began to spike, and with it the room began to spin. She had heard about the dizziness, but this was beyond anything she could have imagined. There was no longer up or down, this way or that, because directions were swirling, and changing, as if she were trapped within a ball tumbling down a tunnel—Alice's rabbit hole, but so much more twisted and cruel. With her head spinning, she called out for death—not knowing whether it was in her mind or aloud.

"Come for me now!" she wailed to death. "End this horrid ride!"

But he did not come. Perhaps this was punishment for having cheated him so many times before. Now he would let her suffer and stay his hand until she had served her penance.

Then, two days in, just as she was convinced that this was going to be her hellish eternity, something changed. The dizziness mellowed. She was still unable to tell up from down, left from right, but she was no longer spinning. It was as if she were floating in a place where such paltry concepts as direction no longer existed.

She lost all sense of her body, all sense of self. She was nothing but a tesseract—an impossible shape moving not only through space but time. One moment she was a teenager shedding her innocence in the unforgiving streets of Budapest. Then she was the young Dame Havilland, new wife of a handsome lord, who neither knew nor cared about her troubled past. Then she was a small child, running and laughing in the countryside years before she knew the harshness of the world. And then she was a widow, gathering, gathering, gathering all things of value to her bosom, if only to keep others from having them.

And then she slept, the dreams and hallucinations washing away into silence.

She had no idea how long she had been in the throes of Crown Royale when she finally awoke. All she knew was that she was not dead, although even that she couldn't be sure of, because she felt so entirely different than she had before, in a way she could not yet explain. Rooks and the staff had not yet returned, so it must not have been four days.

She was drenched in sweat, but somehow that didn't matter. She had fouled herself, but that didn't matter either. All that mattered was the half light sifting in through the window. It was either dusk or dawn—she couldn't tell which just yet. But that light. It was glorious! Not Keats, nor Proust, nor Pound could capture the essence of that light!

In a bit she realized it was getting brighter. Dawn, then. How marvelous was the dawn! The very concept of it thrilled her. And although she still felt weak, and old, and brittle as a winter branch, she also felt new. Like a hatchling bursting out of its shell and experiencing daylight for the first time. Her misanthropic life of manipulation. Her years of guarded self-preservation that had soured into self-indulgence. All that fell away with each piece of the shell. And a joy filled her so powerfully, she couldn't catch her breath. It was intense, but gentle. Searing and soothing at once.

How could I have lived my whole life, and never known this feeling? Never know that it even existed? She could not keep this feeling to herself. She had to rise out of her bed, and fling open the windows, fling open the doors, and bring the world in. Everyone must come and share in this! Fill the musty halls with laughter and warmth, until everything glowed like the light of dawn. Yes! Yes, that's what she would do!

But then she realized that she couldn't.

Because this wasn't her estate anymore.

She had signed all of it away to Ms. Morgan Willmon-Wu.

And now a single ominous thought swelled before her, becoming the shadow cast by the light of her new dawn.

My God, what have I done?

PART TWO
THE DEPTHS AND THE VERTIGO

Elsewhere:
Tokyo

Most modern high-rises in Tokyo have windows that don't open. Presumably, it's to save on heating and air-conditioning. But there are other, unspoken reasons.

The businessman does not work in a modern building. He works in a much older one, with elevators that run like games of chance, and windows that can actually let fresh air in. His name is Tashiro, and he has worked his entire adult life for the bank—intern, to mail room, to assistant, to junior executive, and, finally, to midlevel financial risk analyzer. And that's where his advances ceased; mid-management. No more pay raises, no more promotions. For nearly fifteen years.

"You have risen to your level of incompetence," *his boss would say, jokingly referring to the old idea that people get promoted until the work becomes too difficult to effectively accomplish, and so that's where they stay, trapped in a hell of unremarkable failures.*

The thing is, the businessman is good at his job, so that doesn't apply. His financial risk reports are top notch and always on target. Which means the real reason he hasn't been promoted is because he's so good at what he does.

And so, it's a shock when they fire him.

"Algorithms," his boss says. "What you do, computers now do better. AI will get us all in the end."

The businessman sweats as he sits across from his pompous ass of a boss. Not just because he's in the proverbial hot seat; but also because the offices are sweltering today, in spite of all the open windows letting in cooler air. An issue with the heating system that will supposedly be resolved by morning. It occurs to him that he's been *resolved before the heating issue. He laughs, and the boss frowns, not understanding what could be funny in all this.*

"You'll land on your feet, Tashiro," says the boss. "Good men like you always do." Which is a lie. The Employment Service Center is full of "good men like him." Overqualified with no prospects.

He leaves the boss's office bewildered and toddling, not sure which way to go or even if his feet can sustain his weight. His legs feel like yōkan. Gelatinous and feeble. He senses all eyes on him— which is worsened by the fact that everyone is wearing plain white company-issued masks. It draws all attention to the eyes.

He's seen enough people fired to know he has twenty minutes to pack up his belongings and say his goodbyes. Twenty minutes to dismiss himself from his life. But the worst is waiting for him at home. How can he tell his wife? And what of his teenaged children who already treat him like a dinosaur; a relic from some previous, more embarrassing time?

As is company policy, a guard has been assigned to escort him and his box of belongings out of the building—but right now the guard is a few cubicles away, flirting with a secretary. That gives the businessman the time he needs to consider a more expedient exit.

The guard isn't flirting; he's comforting an employee who's worried that the company masks aren't enough to protect them from Crown Royale. He's telling her that he's actually had it, and that it's not the end of the world; in fact, it's just the beginning. All right, maybe he is flirting with her just a little bit.

He is not the only recoveree in their offices. People are quiet about it because the bosses worry it will affect productivity, which is ridiculous. Recoverees are all about jobs well done. Some recoverees do quit their jobs—but, at least for the time being, they seem to be balanced by the ones who stay, and take greater pride in their work.

The guard has found he can easily spot other recoverees because there's something about their eyes. A deeper level of kindness.

"I'm thinking of leaving the city," he tells the secretary, "and taking one of those abandoned homes in the South. The government's giving them away for free as long as you're willing to fix it up and work the land."

"I wouldn't want to be so far away from things," the young woman says, nearly shivering at the very idea.

"Things are just things," he says with a shrug.

Then, a commotion a few cubicles away grabs their attention. The guard looks over toward the fired man he's supposed to escort out, but the man is no longer there, and people are crowded around an open window. The guard pushes his way through to see the fired man has climbed out onto the window ledge. He stands a few feet to the left of the window, his back pressed to the brick wall. The ledge is barely wide enough for his feet; his tie flaps like a banner in the wind. The man reaches up and rips off his mask as if this is some sort of striptease, and hurls it down to the crowd beginning to gather thirty-one floors below.

If he jumps, *thinks the guard,* this would probably be the single most impulsive act of the man's life. How sad that it would be his last.

"Don't do this!" people are begging. "Come back inside!" "You have so much to live for!" "Think of your family!"

But the guard knows their words are useless because this man will have already thought about all those things. He doesn't need a reminder of today; what he needs is a grip on tomorrow.

The guard climbs out of the window and onto the ledge without a single thought for his own safety, and without any hint of fear. It's as if it is the most natural thing to do, the only thing one could do in such a circumstance. It's that total lack of fear that keeps him stable and balanced.

"What brings you out here, Mr. Tashiro?" he says, remembering the man's name. "Because it couldn't be the job—this place isn't worth the energy to climb out onto that ledge, much less jump."

"Get away from me! I know what I'm doing!"

"I'm sure you do, but let's think about what you could be doing in the morning, or next week."

By now, other Crown Royale recoverees have arrived at the window, and, just like the guard, have climbed out, determined to help the poor man. Strength in numbers. But the ledge is not a place for a committee. Someone clinging to the ledge behind him jostles his shoulder. Not enough to dislodge him, but enough to make him realize he'd better get on with it.

"What you need is to catch Crown Royale," he says to Mr. Tashiro. "You should walk through crowds without a mask, stand at the entrance to hospitals. Because you need to get sick. And then get better."

"You're crazy."

"Am I? Maybe. But see that corner over there?" the guard says, pointing across the street to a spot where people have gathered to look up at the unfolding scene. "Go home, get drunk, break things, do whatever you have to do. But two weeks from today, at this very hour, I want you to meet me at that corner after you've caught and recovered from Crown Royale. And if you don't feel different about

all this, I'll drag you back to this ledge and throw you off myself."

The wind seems to hold in anticipation. There are screams now from the crowds below, but the guard ignores them, keeps his hand held out.

"Two weeks?" Tashiro says.

"And I promise you, I will be there."

Finally, Tashiro takes the guard's hand. Together they move toward the window, along a ledge mercifully no longer as crowded as it had been a few moments ago, and not bothering to consider why.

The instant they're inside, other guards grab the troubled man and pull him away to prevent him from being any further danger to himself.

"Two weeks!" the guard calls after him.

"Two weeks!" Tashiro calls back.

And the guard will be there. Whether Mr. Tashiro shows or not; he will keep his word.

It is then that the guard notices others around him gaping at the window, some whimpering, others outright wailing. It isn't until he hears the sound of approaching sirens that he begins to realize why.

6
The Pier Peer Collective

Gena Mudroch's infection came on quick and powerful.

"Baby, I'll be okay," she told Mariel. "I made it through the last pandemic and I'll make it through this one." Mariel wasn't surprised that her mother caught Crown Royale. She was not a careful woman.

Their night in the penthouse was now nothing but a memory. They were living in the Grinch again—Gena never told Mariel how she managed to get it out of the impound, and maybe she didn't want to know. But whatever it was, Mariel suspected it exposed her mother to Crown Royale.

Gena didn't want to keep the car windows open, because it was chilly at night. And she didn't tell Mariel to keep away. She could have. She could have made Mariel go to a shelter, but she didn't. She wanted Mariel to stay close. Even though it clearly exposed Mariel to the disease. Part of Mariel resented that. Most parents would be more worried about infecting their children, but not Gena. She wanted Mariel to breathe all the same air, share all the same microbes. Not that Mariel would leave her mother sick in the Grinch alone—but to not even be offered the option? It stung.

But on the other hand, there was a big part of Mariel that was ready for Crown Royale. She had never gotten the last virus, even though her mother had. This time, though, she was anticipating getting it. Anticipating it with a bit of guilty excitement. What wonders were waiting for her on the other side of the fever? It wasn't just rumors now—people were talking about it openly. Of course, plenty of others were denying it, but all you had to do was to meet someone who had caught the disease and recovered to know that something had changed.

She had met a few people like that. The meter reader who, instead of giving out parking tickets, now fed people's meters. Or the socialite who bought fancy food and fed it to stray dogs. These people were solid evidence that Crown Royale was a different kind of bug. So Mariel leaned into it, breathing deep every time her mother sneezed. And she counted the days until it could incubate within her, ending her own dark times.

Then, on the second day of her mother's fever, Gena said, "Maybe I should go to a hospital."

That scared Mariel. Because her mother would need a foot in the grave all the way up to her thigh before she would actually suggest it was time to see a doctor. It was the first indication that things were worse than Mariel had been willing to consider.

Mariel drove, even though she didn't officially have a license, but her mother could barely keep her head up, much less drive the Grinch through maniacal San Francisco traffic.

With Crown Royale beginning to bloom everywhere, the hospitals were overcrowded. Nurses did triage in parking lots, deciding who needed acute care, who could manage without it, and who care would be wasted on.

"Your mother should drink lots of fluids and stay home," one nurse told them.

"Go to hell," Gena grumbled.

"We don't have a home," Mariel explained.

The nurse's mask didn't have a digital projection of her face, so Mariel couldn't really read her expression. She left and came back with a piece of paper that had been xeroxed so many times, the letters looked like some ancient language.

"This is a list of shelters," she told them. "They all have quarantine areas."

Mariel didn't need to read the page—she knew all the shelters by heart. And a few phone calls confirmed what Mariel already suspected. All the shelters were at capacity as well. But at the last one she called, the overworked man who answered the phone made a suggestion.

"You should take your mother to the PPC," he said. "They don't turn anyone away."

"The PPC?"

"Just take Van Ness north, until it ends. And keep going."

"But . . . it ends right at the bay."

"Exactly," said the man.

Jarrick Javins, the former richest man in the world, had bought San Francisco's municipal pier years ago, with hopes of turning it from a run-down expanse of weed-cracked concrete, into a runway for small private jets. Not practical, since the pier was curved rather than straight, but such small considerations meant nothing to a man like Jarrick Javins. If he could imagine it, he could do it, simple as that. He had successfully created high-end waterfront airstrips in New York and Chicago. San Francisco was the next logical place. Of course, to straighten the strip, and make it long enough for jets, it would require complete demolition of the existing pier and quite a lot of bay-front property—but existing architecture rarely stood a chance against the magical triforce of progress, profit, and power.

Javins's usage plan for the pier changed after he was infected with viral enlightenment. Shortly before he vanished from public view, he proclaimed that the entire pier would be sold for the price of one dollar to "the person who wanted it most." And then he left his lawyers to decide who that might be.

At first the legal team argued over how to interpret the statement. How does one quantize desire? But once a majority of the team contracted and, for the most part, recovered from Crown Royale, they found clarity on the issue and knew precisely how to proceed. As for the lawyer who died, the others all knew she would have agreed.

In a matter of days, the pier was sold to Delberg Zello, a window-washer with big ideas.

Zello, more than most anyone, had an unobstructed view of the pier when he worked each day on the glass towers of the city—and from his high scaffold perch, would often daydream about what he might do with it. To him, the municipal pier was a prime piece of real estate yearning for an inspired purpose.

Both Delberg and his wife contracted Crown Royale early on, and the day they both recovered, his wife took his hands warmly, told him that she didn't love him, and in fact, had never actually loved him. But that was perfectly all right. Because *everything* was all right once you recovered from Crown Royale. They laughed, they shared some champagne, and she left to embrace her newfound sense of completion. Rather than feeling pain or grief, Delberg felt profoundly grateful for the time they had shared, and was content in knowing that they were both now free to pursue whatever came next.

He told his story, and his dreams of a fine and fitting purpose for the municipal pier to the AWOL billionaire's surviving lawyers, and they all agreed that Delberg really, really wanted it. And so Delberg gave them one dollar, signed a bunch of paperwork, and just like that, the pier was his.

Only then did he realize that he didn't actually have a plan for it. Only a dream that someone should.

He walked its length over and over, pacing and weaving through the ragged tents and mildewed encampments of the homeless that had taken up residence on the pier. He paced and meandered, waiting for inspiration to occur. And finally, it did. In fact, it was hiding in plain sight. But to be honest, it wasn't hiding at all.

And thus, he established the "Pier Peer Collective," turning the ragtag tent city of homeless people in abject poverty into a state-of-the-art, self-sustaining, self-governing community. Gone were the dirty tents and rotting furniture. They were replaced with brand-spanking-new tents and furniture—all donated by wealthy Crown Royale survivors who had suddenly become outrageously willing to help the homeless in ways they never were before. Of course, no one who lived in the Pier Peer Collective was truly homeless anymore, because the PPC was now their home.

To lay claim to a place in the Pier Peer Collective, all one had to do was show up—for, as its esteemed founder Delberg Zello once said, *"Showing up is the first and hardest step in anything worth doing."*

Of course, because of the crowded nature, and all the interpersonal contact within the collective, it was the city's leading super-spreader event. A veritable breeding ground for Crown Royale.

When Mariel stumbled onto the pier with her mother late that afternoon, there were plenty of people at the entrance to help them. They asked no questions, made them fill out no paperwork. All they wanted were their names, which they wrote on little HI, MY NAME IS . . . stickers, that they slapped onto their shirts. They even spelled "Mudroch" right.

"Do you have a quarantine area?" Mariel asked a woman helping them.

"We have a transition tent," the woman said.

"What do you mean, 'transition'?"

She offered a knowing smile. "When you've got Crown Royale, there are only two kinds of transition, dear." Then she took Mariel's hand and gently squeezed. "We'll get her through this—don't forget there's a ninety-six percent survival rate." Which sounded oh, so much better than saying one in twenty-five died.

Then her mother coughed. An awful rattle that seemed to connect to some cavern deep in the earth. The kind of sound that usually indicated demonic possession in movies.

"Preexisting conditions?" the woman asked.

"Yeah, a bunch of them," Mariel said.

The woman squeezed Mariel's hand again. "I'm sure she'll be fine."

The woman was not wearing a mask. And from her demeanor, Mariel guessed what that meant. "You've had it already, haven't you?"

The woman nodded. "Me, my wife, and our children," she said. "All had it. All recovered. All live here now."

"And you're a nurse?"

The woman laughed. "No—I'm a tollbooth attendant," she said. "Or at least I was. But now I care for people here."

"So you're not trained?"

"I care. That'll have to be enough, honey." And then the phantom tollbooth attendant gave Mariel a warm smile that made Mariel truly feel caring might actually be enough.

The transition tent was crowded, but they found a cot for Gena.

"Can I stay with her?" Mariel asked.

"Of course you can. We don't believe in separating families here."

Gena slipped in and out of consciousness for the next twenty-four hours. The chorus of bodily sounds within the large tent was like an orchestra with every instrument out of tune. Wheezes, coughs, sneezes, and groans.

People would rise from their cots once in a while, and walk on their own, or be helped by people like the tollbooth woman. You could tell by the looks on the rising people's faces that they were coming into full recovery—because they looked around them with amazement as if they were seeing the world for the first time. Mariel couldn't wait to see that look on her mother's face—all those premature care lines gone, replaced with wide-eyed wonder.

"You should eat something," said one of the caregivers—a man who had taken his business suit and ripped off the arms, turning it into a vest, and had tied his Armani tie around his head like a headband. "Here, have a tandoori tofu po'boy," he said, handing her a sandwich. It was perhaps the best sandwich she had ever tasted.

Her mother would speak to her once in a while in her delirium, but the things she said rarely made sense.

"Baby, go put the royal clothes in the dryer." Or, "Mariel, honey, turn off the oven—it smells like burning elephant." Or, "Tell Julius Caesar I accept his marriage proposal."

"Just relax, Momma," Mariel would say. "Everything's fine."

Then, just before dawn the following day, Mariel awoke from uneasy slumber to find her mother watching her, with eyes wide awake, and fully alert. Mariel could see the change in her right away.

"Oh . . . ," Gena said. "Oh . . . oh . . . honey, it's beautiful."

Mariel found her lower lip quivering. "What's beautiful, Momma?"

"You . . . me . . . this place . . . all of it." She looked around. "I love this place! What is this place?"

"Kind of a shelter," Mariel told her. "A commune."

"Well, don't that beat all!"

And she laughed, but it turned into that deep, awful, hell-cavern rattle, which gave way to a shotgun barrage of coughs that left blood spattered all over Mariel's top.

"I get it now, baby," Gena said. "I get it. All of it. Why things are the way they are. For us. For everybody. What matters and what doesn't." Tears filled her eyes. "Honey, I missed so much. I've been sleepwalking through all the good stuff. But I'm so glad I get to see it now!"

She coughed, gasped, and coughed again, then swallowed, grimacing from the pain. Yet even that couldn't reduce the powerful shine her eyes had taken on.

"I think maybe I gotta go now," she told Mariel.

"No! No, Momma, you're not going anywhere. You're getting better!" But Mariel knew she was only fooling herself. Today she was the one in denial, instead of her mother.

"It's all good now, baby." Gena locked eyes with Mariel. "I'm so happy. So happy . . ."

It wasn't like the way they show in movies. How, when a person dies, you know the instant it happens. Mariel didn't know. Her mother's eyes remained open, looking at her, and there was no way to divine the exact moment she was gone.

While the caregivers tended to Gena's body, Mariel ran from the tent in tears. She had always known that "the old times," as her mother had called them, weren't coming back. She had always known that her mother was banking on some invisible lottery ticket—which was absurd and irrational, and yet endearing in its own wistful way. But now the ticket was gone. The lottery was over. Forever.

Mariel raced toward the end of the pier, until there was nowhere to go but the bay. She wanted to be furious at someone, but who? She couldn't lay her anger on her mother, or the people who took them in, or even the ones who turned them away. So she sat alone on the end of the pier crying until her stomach began to seize in cramps and spasms. And there, in the early light of dawn, she realized that she wasn't completely alone. Someone had quietly come to sit next to her. Black, with a tinge of gray in his tight cropped hair. He had a warm, beatific smile. The kind one might call contagious, before the word had so much baggage.

"Who did you lose?" he gently asked.

"My mother."

"I'm so sorry," he told her—and not in the way that people say at funerals. It was sincere, not obligatory. "Take comfort that she was ready to go. Maybe not happy to leave you, of course, but content to move on."

"How do you know?"

"Because those that transition *out* are just as happy as those who transition *through*."

Mariel took a good look at him, which was easier now that the dawn was brightening. There was neither guile nor calculation in his gaze. He was an open book of sincerity. "See, there's always a moment of clarity before someone passes," he said. "Satisfied acceptance. Never seen anything like it."

Even so, acceptance of your own death was a piss-poor consolation prize.

"It doesn't change the fact that my mother is dead." And hearing those words come out of her own mouth—it felt as strange as suddenly speaking a foreign language.

"Maybe you can make her death mean something," he said.

"How?"

To that he only smiled. "I'm glad you're with us, Mariel."

At first, she thought there must be something mystical about the way he knew her name. Then she remembered she still had her name tag.

Mariel wiped her eyes and her nose. "What are you, some kind of priest or something?"

"No," the man said, "I'm a window-washer."

The PPC arranged for a speedy cremation, and Mariel cast her mother's ashes into the bay, although the wind took half of them into the sky.

Mariel wanted to catch Crown Royale. Not just to experience the euphoria it brought, but to be closer to her mother. To share one last thing with her. Since the previous pandemic, she felt her mother had been living on borrowed time—that every day with her was a blessing even though, more often than not, it felt like a curse.

You're free now, whispered a voice in Mariel's head. It was the same voice that told her to bail from the shipwreck their lives had become. The voice that constantly reminded her that she and her mother were like two people clinging to the same piece of flotsam, both doomed to drown because neither would cast the other off.

Run, that voice would tell her. *You'll both be better off. And if not, well, at least you can save yourself.*

But that voice held no sway. Mariel could only dream of being that selfish, and simultaneously envy and despise those who were. But now, through no fault of her own, she was cut loose of any obligations. And it was terrifying.

"Do you have anywhere else to go?" Delberg Zello asked her late on the afternoon that she cast her mother to the waves and the wind. Zello, she learned, in addition to having been a window-washer, was owner of the pier, and the de facto mayor of the PPC. He had a Black Jesus sort of vibe, and Mariel wondered if he came by that naturally, or if it was part of his Crown Royale recovery bundle.

"I have relatives who'll take me in," she told him. It was a half-truth at best. All she had was her uncle, who would claim she was welcome, but make it abundantly clear what a burden she was. Well, she refused to be anyone's burden. She'd be fine on her own. She still had the Grinch if it hadn't been towed again, and now there'd even be more room to sleep.

Practical as always.

The fact that the pragmatist in her found an upside to her mother's death infuriated her.

"Stay with us," Zello said. "There's a place for everyone here."

"My uncle's expecting me," she lied. "I really don't have a choice."

"We always have choices. Even if they're all bad ones, we still get to choose."

Mariel gave him a rueful sigh. "Right. The lesser evil."

"I don't see any evil here, do you?" asked Zello.

Mariel turned to gaze down the pier. A mix of recoverees and those who had not yet contracted the disease. You could tell the difference by the way they carried themselves. A body in a sky-blue body bag was being gently, lovingly, carried out of the transition tent. All the body bags here were brightly colored. Mariel couldn't decide if that was beautiful or obscene. Maybe it was neither. Maybe it was just a new variation of flowers on a grave; tenderness in the face of death's brutality.

Delberg Zello was right. No evil here. But staying meant belonging, and belonging was a commitment. Mariel wasn't ready to commit to anything so soon.

"Thank you for your kindness," she told him. Then she turned and left the pier, getting lost in the early evening rush-hour bustle.

Alone. It was such a foreign concept to Mariel—because although she often felt solitary, she never really was. Like a pair of oxygen molecules, she and her mother were bound together by forces that only outside intervention could break. Mariel always suspected that death might be that intervention.

The city looked no different without Gena; it was still a surreal blend of hope and horror, dreams and disfigurement. Yet it felt different. Maybe because Mariel's attentions were now turned away from the management of two lives.

Was her mother still with her in some ineffable way, she wondered? Mariel didn't believe in such things, but didn't disbelieve them either. If spirits proved to be real, she would not be surprised; and if they proved otherwise, she wouldn't be disappointed.

But in a very tangible and twisted sense, her mother *was* still with her: When Mariel had held the cardboard box that somehow contained her uncontainable mother, and emptied it into the bay, some of the ash had blown back onto Mariel's right shoulder, clinging to the tight cotton weave. She could still smell it—musty and weak, like chalk aspiring to charcoal.

"Our final hug, baby," she could almost hear her mother say.

Mariel knew that when she took the shirt off, she would never wear it again. Nor would she wash it. Nor would she throw it away. How could she, when that shirt was the closest thing her mother had to a grave?

She found the Grinch was exactly where they had parked it. No ticket; no boot. Some of the universe's mercy must have trickled down. There wasn't much inside; mostly her mother's things, because, fearing the car would be impounded again, Mariel had put everything she cared about in her backpack. A stuffed animal from her childhood. A first-place medal from a track meet in the days she could participate in such things. A thumb drive with her entire digital life, including thousands of photos she might never look at, but took solace in knowing that she *could*.

The only memories that remained in the car were the bad ones.

Mariel stood there for the longest time looking at the hapless little green Fiesta—which was an oxymoron for that car if ever there was one—thinking where she might drive it. She could go anywhere she wanted—or at least anywhere half a tank of gas could get her. She could point herself in a direction until the tank ran dry, then settle wherever it left her. Good a plan as any.

As the twilight began settling into night, she looked at the keys in her hand, which now reflected the halogen glare of a streetlamp that had just flickered on. The key chain's ornament was a glorious Barcelona cathedral—a city her mother had never visited but had always hoped to. She kept it on her key chain as a reminder of *"Oh, the places we'll go, baby, just you wait and see."* But unlike her mother, Mariel had no illusion that the chain could hold any keys of value. It was a veritable charm bracelet of keys with no value, though. The last vestiges of places they had lived and storage units they had abandoned. Yet her mother could never see that the shining cathedral of their future was forever weighed down by those heavy reminders of the past.

And now she had choices, as Delberg Zello had said. Right. What a wonder was free will.

The Grinch sat patiently waiting for her. All she had to do was hit the button on the finger-worn fob to unlock it. But instead, she opened her palm and tilted it sideways, watching the key chain slip from her fingers. It hit the curb with a clatter and dropped down a storm drain.

Goodbye, Momma. . . .

She felt an immediate wave of sadness, chased by a wave of relief now that those keys were gone. Choices were overrated. Now she couldn't be tempted by this one anymore. She turned, and headed back to the pier, where she could certainly be as much help as a tollbooth attendant. Yet all the way back, she was haunted by the keys, and how complete the darkness of the drain had been once they slipped out of sight.

7
Survival Is Not Pretty

Rooks—no . . . *Galen*—returned on schedule on the morning of the fourth day. He arrived ahead of the rest of the staff, and brought Dr. Ezrin with him, anticipating the need of someone official to pronounce Dame Glynis Havilland dead.

Was that a look of joy that Glynis caught on her butler's face when he saw her up and about, no longer sealed in her chambers? She was no longer relying on the wheelchair, either—not that she was any stronger physically, but now she had an abiding trust in gravity and its benevolence.

"Madame!" said Rooks. "So pleased to see you looking well!"

"Indeed, indeed," said the doctor, although he didn't seem quite as sincere.

"I have recovered, Galen," she announced. "And all they say about Crown Royale is true!"

Rooks hedged his response. "Meaning?"

She beamed, using muscles in her face she had forgotten existed. "Words fall short of delivering meaning, my friend."

The doctor cleared his throat in an awkward way to get her attention. "A quick examination and blood draw, then, and I'll be off," he told her. "But I recommend a full physical at your earliest convenience."

Glynis laughed at that, although she couldn't say why. Perhaps because all moments felt convenient now.

The doctor left, and once they were alone, Glynis made her way to the kitchen. She would like to say she ambled, but it was more of a hobble. "I was about to make tea," she told him.

"Allow me, madame," Rooks said.

"No," she told him, "allow *me*." And when he continued to balk at the suggestion, she said, "Allow me, for once, the pleasure to serve. Yes, yes, I know service is mostly drudgery—especially when the one served is as thankless as I have been. But for me it is novel, so indulge me."

He reluctantly sat, and only guided her to where things were, because the kitchen was unexplored territory for Glynis.

"But are you sure you should exert yourself so soon after your recovery?" he asked as she reached for a high shelf.

"It's not climbing Kilimanjaro, Galen."

She made a pot of Russian Caravan, which she recalled he had once mentioned was his favorite. Then, once it had steeped, she poured two cups.

"When have you asked the staff to return?" she asked.

"Noon, madame. I wanted to make sure there was enough time to . . ." Then he faltered, so she completed the thought, sparing him the unpleasantness.

"To make sure there was enough time to remove my remains. Good thinking, Galen."

Still, he seemed preoccupied. "What shall we do about Miss Willmon-Wu?" he finally asked.

Glynis closed her eyes, chiding herself for her preinfection shortsightedness. "There's nothing to be done about her," she told him. "I laid fail-safe after fail-safe to prevent me from meddling in her affairs after the paperwork was signed. The person I was didn't trust the person I am now. And with good reason, I suppose, because my old desires mean nothing to me now."

"All of them?" asked Rooks.

"Most of them," she replied.

She sipped her tea, savoring its smokey flavor in a way she never had before. It had always been about getting to the bottom. Now it was about experiencing the brew as it passed over her lips.

"She is a weapon that I have loaded. I fear I have no way to disarm her," Glynis said.

Rooks took a slow sip, and then another, before he said, "Perhaps, then, we can control how she detonates."

Glynis particularly liked how easily he said "we."

Morgan had been in the pinch-me phase for days. She kept calling Dame Havilland's solicitor, certain that the legality of the transfer of wealth was in doubt—or that she was the subject of some cruel reality TV show, soon to be the butt of a joke laughed at by millions. But if there was a scam lurking in the woodwork, she couldn't find it.

"And to be clear," the solicitor told Morgan, in her stodgy London office, "I no longer represent Dame Havilland's interests. I represent yours."

Solicitors. Lawyers. Attorneys. Morgan had never needed one before. She didn't trust them—because anyone who claimed to be serving *your* interests instead of their own was lying. But this woman, Ms. Linna McLeester, seemed sharp, incisive, and fiercely adherent to the law. She was also cold as ice, but that was fine. It was how Morgan preferred the people she associated with.

But every expanse of ice needed to be tested before it could be trod upon—and although Ms. McLeester claimed that her loyalty came with the signed paperwork, there was no proof. Only time would tell.

"I want to move into the estate as soon as possible," Morgan told her. "How soon can you make that happen?"

"It's yours now, so it can happen whenever you like," McLeester said. "But perhaps we should wait to determine if Dame Havilland has, in fact, succumbed to Crown Royale."

"She made her wishes clear," declared Morgan. "And so, dead or alive, I want her removed from the estate, and the entire building disinfected. Move her either to a graveyard, or to some remote property we own, if it turns out she's still alive."

And without a beat, McLeester replied, "I'll make arrangements immediately."

Morgan had to smile. This ice might be strong enough to skate upon.

Rón Escobedo did as he was told. He recorded a speech calling on America's youth to be the vanguard against Crown Royale. It announced safe zones being built by his family to protect the most vulnerable. It challenged others his age to volunteer, and be proactive in every possible way in the battle against this new and confusing illness.

"A virus is a virus," he read from the speech that had been prepared for him. "A disease is a disease. We can't let rumors or uninformed, misguided hope allow us to drop our guard. Together we can beat this. We have to. We will."

And then it was out there. Not as many views as his father

would have liked, but then, Rón wasn't the public figure his father was.

Rón avoided social media, where he was being both lauded and condemned. Discord rooms full of people crushing on him, matched by memes of him being eaten by rats, or hung by a rope of his father's digital masks, or a dozen other ugly fates that made frightened, hateful people laugh. Some even made *him* laugh. And some made him scared. Almost as scared as the adoration did. Strange that the more his face became known, the more he felt unseen.

Perhaps it was the disconnect that disturbed him most; the cognitive dissonance he felt when reading those words, and yet knowing he didn't really believe them. Yes, he feared Crown Royale. No one knew its long-term effects. But if they were anything like the short-term effect . . . maybe it wasn't such a terrible thing.

"It's good that you put this speech out there," Blas told Rón. "The mortality rate is still at four percent. COVID peaked at three percent—so this is worse. Your speech could save millions of lives."

Unspoken were the words *"including your own."* Because the fewer infections in the world, the lower the chance that Rón would catch it and lose his life to it. They now knew for sure that whatever genetic factors gave Rón blue-cone deficiency also left him seven times more likely to die from Crown Royale, according to the Centers for Disease Control. With that in mind, and constant reinforcement from his father, Rón convinced himself that the bliss that came with recovery wasn't worth the risk.

But with that decision came a tide of despair. The kind of

tide you couldn't see flowing in until you were already waist-deep and caught in the undertow.

As infections began to mount, Rón was banned from leaving the penthouse for his own protection. Which meant that Rón was now a prisoner in his father's tower. The proverbial bird in a gilded cage. He found himself increasingly listless and bored, without the motivation to do anything about it. The isolation was demoralizing, disheartening. Triggering. He tried not to dwell on it, because that was how the spiral always started. He did not bemoan his captivity, either. He knew how lucky he was to be sixty-one stories above a brewing pandemic. But knowing didn't make him feel any less hopeless. *You don't want to live through quarantine again,* said a quiet, but persistent voice in the very back of his mind. *And the only way to not live through it . . . is to not live through it . . .*

He tried not to give that voice his attention, but there were weak moments when he couldn't help but let it ramble. In those moments, he tried to listen to his father, who spoke of endurance instead of surrender.

"Survival is not pretty," his father told him. "Look at nature. The natural world knows no fairness. It rewards success with more success. Privilege with more privilege."

But Blas Escobedo was not so Machiavellian. He was not a servant of nature; instead, he waged war against it, continuing to use his position to battle the disease by investing millions into medical research and adding compensation for frontline medical workers. He even vowed to personally pay funeral expenses for any family who asked.

"We are not elitists hiding from the masses," his father proclaimed at dinner one night.

"No?" Rón dared to question. "Isn't that exactly what we're doing up here? Hiding?"

His father lowered his silverware and held Rón's gaze. "Does a lighthouse hide, TeTe? Of course not! It exists to shed light and save sailors from a jagged death. We have been elevated, and so we must now be that lighthouse."

And so shine they did. Until the day came that his father determined it was time to leave the city.

"It's time. We cannot justify the risk of staying here anymore," he told Rón.

"So the lighthouse goes dark?"

His father frowned and shook his head. "Not at all. The mountain provides just as clear a vantage point of this crisis."

The mountain—Mount Shasta to the north—was to be their citadel. There, his father had recreated a chalet he had once seen in the Swiss Alps. The compound was a veritable fortress at the end of a guarded mountain road. It was not just *on* the mountain, but carved into it, boasting enough supplies to outlast everything from a nuclear winter to an alien invasion—because Blas Escobedo was nothing if not prepared.

While his father worked on the logistics of shifting his base of operations, Rón would be quietly spirited to the chalet with his maybe-soon-to-be-stepmother, Kavita. Blas would catch up with them later.

"This is all so sudden," Kavita exclaimed as she nervously packed her suitcases. Of course, it hadn't been sudden at all, but Kavita lived in the moment. It was an admirable trait, except when one needed to see several moves ahead.

"Take only what you need," Kavita instructed, although by

the look of her travel bags, she wasn't following her own directive. "Leona, Pantera, and Jag are already there."

"What about Pitón?" Rón asked.

Kavita pursed her lips. "We haven't heard from him yet."

That didn't bode well. Because, of all his siblings, Pitón would be the least likely to ignore their father's edict. He was always in fear of losing his sizeable monthly stipend.

"Do you think he got Crown Royale?" Rón asked.

"I'm not going to think about that," said Kavita, "and neither should you."

But he couldn't help but think about it. And envy him. What would self-centered Pitón Escobedo be like as a Crown Royale recoveree? He had always been insufferable. Was it too much to hope that he might now become happily sufferable?

The rooftop heliport was often too windswept to be used, but today, the city was mired in the fog that San Francisco was famous for. Only the pylons of the bridges, and the peaks of the city's tallest towers, pierced the dense white blanket. But above the fog, the sky was clear.

Even so, not even a sunny sky could clear Rón's building storm. He was already struggling with being sequestered. This promised to be a long stint of isolation—and with his siblings, no less, most of whom were best appreciated from a distance.

The Sikorsky Black Hawk approached from the north, hovered a bit, and landed easily on its first attempt. The only casualty was Kavita's floppy hat, which was blown off the roof by a gust from the helicopter's blades. For a moment Rón had a brief and guilty vision of her leaping after it, but instead she just let it go with a curse.

The Black Hawk's blades slowed to a swooping idle, making it clear that it was only sitting on the roof long enough to grab them and go. Kavita, hair wild from the chop, hurried to the door that had just opened, leaving her bags for whomever was assigned to handle them. Rón only had a roll-aboard that he wasn't going to leave for anyone else to carry. But instead of moving toward the helicopter, he let go of his bag and just stood there, assessing. And assessing some more.

What Rón did next wasn't quite as simple as tipping his hand and letting keys drop down a drain. Unlike Mariel Mudroch, Tiburón Tigre Escobedo had an awful lot to lose . . .

. . . but the thought of hunkering down in a more remote, but equally gilded, cage was more than he could bear. He knew he was approaching a ledge just as dangerous as the edge of the roof. He could feel the depths and the vertigo.

The warning signs were there. The dark turn of his self-talk, and his willingness to tolerate it. The loss of appetite, and waning interest in the things he usually loved. Medication worked fine when it worked, but sometimes the triggers were too powerful, too pervasive—and now Rón knew, without a shadow of any doubt, that he would plunge into the abyss if he got on that helicopter. It might not happen today, or tomorrow, but soon. And once he was in that bleak place, he would reopen the scars on his wrists. Or he would leap from the side of the mountain, or he'd find a weapon—and in those desperate moments, anything could be a weapon. If he found himself in the abyss again, he knew that this time, he'd be successful in making his final exit.

If he got in that helicopter.

It was time he admitted to himself what he really needed:

a lasting cure to depression. A year ago, no such miraculous antidote existed. But now it did, in convenient, viral form. His father, and so many others, saw "Recovery syndrome" as a funky euphoria that was as dangerous as drug addiction. But Rón knew what it really was. It was the cruelty of nature hurling forth a random act of kindness.

What he sought was not in a chalet on the side of a mountain. It was down in the muck and mire of the fogged-in streets below. So he turned and headed back toward the elevator.

"Rón!" shouted Kavita from just inside the helicopter. "Where are you going? Did you forget something?"

But he didn't turn back, for fear he might change his mind. Instead, he got into the elevator and hit the ground-floor button.

"Rón!" shouted Kavita again. But anything else she might have said was shut out by the closing door.

Tiburón Tigre Escobedo would not be going to Mount Shasta. Today, he was going down and out.

8
Still Life with Limo

The concept of "home" had never gelled for Morgan Willmon-Wu. That vague idea of a sanctuary bubble where you can escape the trials of an unfair world. What a load of crap. Even so, growing up, she secretly envied classmates whose dwellings gave off that wholesome vibe of hugs and comfort food—and she occasionally got to experience the delight of watching those classmates' homes get split by divorce. Not that she would wish that on them, but she wanted them to learn that safety was a deception best shattered early. She found her relationships to her classmates much better after their world had been carpet-bombed by disillusionment.

As for Morgan's home life, her father—for reasons she now understood—had left the picture early enough that she barely remembered their lives back in Hong Kong. Most of her memories were with her mom, in Lucerne, Switzerland—a town at the foot of the Alps that tourists would call perfect, but only because they didn't have to live through the bitter cold of winter.

She had been identified early as a prodigy, but her mother insisted she attend local schools for as long as she could. *"For socialization."* Morgan found her classmates to be numbingly provincial, planning lives of limited horizons. Even those with ambitions couldn't see beyond Zürich.

Her skill at languages and dialects was, to adults, a parlor trick, and at school a curiosity. Her classmates would at first be tickled by her ability to imitate accents and pick up languages, but it quicky became distancing. It made her "other." Her Eurasian features already paved the way for that, and although there were other Asian students here and there, none of them had the eerie exoticism of genius.

Not that she ever wished to be like other kids, because her particular brand of genius came with perspective enough to know that, in spite of what the adage might say, ignorance was not bliss; it was just ignorance. Perhaps not something to be pitied, but certainly something to be avoided.

The only kids she truly related to had been a pair of neighbors—a sister and brother who attended an expensive international school nearby, and thus understood the concept of a larger world. However, both brother and sister had eventually developed crushes on Morgan, putting her in the awkward position of hiding one relationship from the other, while pursuing both. It had been an interesting but doomed triangle that hadn't ended well for anyone. In retrospect, Morgan should have rebuffed their advances and kept it all platonic, because she needed friendship more than romance. Now she had neither.

But at least it taught her how to *have* friends—which was important at university—because, as the youngest student, her shell of isolation wasn't easy to break.

And now with a double degree at nineteen, she was a de facto adult—a place most people didn't reach until their mid-twenties, if they reached it at all.

It wasn't her intellect, or her degree, that had left her in her current situation, though. It was her ambition that Dame Havilland had rewarded.

With her fortune changed in the blink of an eye—or, more accurately, the stroke of a pen—she had remained in England and had yet to return "home." Taking the reins from Dame Havilland required her continued presence and full concentration. She had told her mother, of course, but only in the vaguest of terms.

"I've been offered a . . . a paid internship in London," she had said over the phone, and, in the understatement of the year, added, "It's a good one."

"That's nice, dear," her mother had replied, which was the best response Morgan could hope for from her mother these days.

Morgan had flown to London in a rush for that bizarre interview, seated in a middle economy seat. And now, barely two weeks later, she was returning to Switzerland in a private jet that was, ostensibly, hers. Life, as ever, was proving itself to be unpredictable.

There was a pilot, copilot, flight attendant, and nearly two metric tons of jet fuel, all for her. It was spectacularly wasteful, and she loved every bit of it. The way she saw it, if she was going to leave a carbon footprint, it ought to be as indelible as the concrete footprints at Grauman's Chinese Theatre—which she had only heard about, but now could actually visit. She could fly to Hollywood right now if she wanted. In fact, she could go anywhere at any time. She found knowing that she *could* was much more satisfying than actually doing it.

They landed at Buochs Airport, a tiny airfield that catered to private jets. It allowed her to avoid the crowds of Zürich

Airport, and was only ten minutes from home. A limo waited on the tarmac for her, the driver double-masked. She, and everyone in her attendance, were double-masked and tested daily with the latest, most accurate tests—the ones that could catch exposure within as little as twelve hours. Still, she rode with the windows down, just in case. Besides, it was a warm summer day, and people might look in to see who was riding in such opulence. Perhaps she might drop the jaws of some of her former classmates.

She told the driver to take the long way that ran along the lake. Partially because she enjoyed the view, but really because it gave her a few extra minutes to gather the fortitude she would need to face her mother, and all that came with it.

Their home was a townhouse on a narrow side street toward the edge of town—rented, not owned—because Swiss property was way too pricey. The door was answered by Griselda, her mother's live-in. The name meant "gray battle maid," which was precisely what Griselda was—and what Madeleine Willmon now needed, because she often became belligerent. Her mother had long since dropped the "Wu," although Morgan chose to keep it. Nowadays, Morgan wondered whether her mother would remember it had ever been there at all.

"Come in, Morgan—she is waiting for you out back," Griselda said, pleased to see her. Morgan had confirmed that both Griselda and Morgan's mother had tested today, and had not been out for over twenty-four hours, so it was safe for Morgan to remove her masks, but she found doing so took a conscious act of will—as if those masks could provide a protective barrier between her life now and her life before.

As she had gone straight to London from the University of

Zürich, Morgan hadn't been here for several months. Every-thing was as she had last seen it. Cleaner, perhaps—Griselda was good about that. The familiar furniture, the piano that rarely got played, and, of course, the painting hanging over the hearth. It was a still life her mother had acquired years ago at an auction for a defunct hotel—which must have had hun-dreds of copies of the exact same painting: a vase with flowers that were already losing petals. It was a generic work of "art" that captured on canvas the very concept of slow, inevitable death.

To Morgan, that painting was the perfect metaphor for her mother's life; pleasant and shallow. Madeleine Willmon was a social creature, going from brunch with countless friends, to the well-trafficked boutique she ran, then to parties and galas in the evenings. She had various men in her life—each one lackluster, with all the personality of a toaster—perhaps because her mother wanted no competition for the spotlight.

Now there was no spotlight. And barely the memory that there once had been one.

Morgan stood just inside the back screen door, observ-ing before going out and engaging. Her mother was dressed comfortably but with an unnecessary scarf. Her hair was odd, coiffed up front, but completely flat and ignored in the back—as if she were a two-dimensional being with whatever she saw in the mirror all there was to see. She was staring at the steep hillside of the yard as if it actually had a view instead of just weeds and wildflowers. She held a mask in her lap, tangled around the fingers of her right hand like a tiny security blanket.

Morgan stood there longer than she should have, not want-ing to begin the inevitable dance. But before Griselda could start prodding her, she took a deep breath and stepped out. The screen door creaked, and it grabbed Madeleine Willmon's attention. Her eyes lit up when she saw Morgan, but at the same time were noticeably wary.

"Well, hello," Madeleine Willmon said, and waited for a response before she said anything more.

"Hello, Mother. It's me, Morgan." And then she added, "Your daughter."

The woman took a moment to process that, then smiled warmly. "Of course it is. You should have told me you were coming. I would have made lunch."

"Griselda knew."

Her mother sighed and shook her head. "That woman never tells me anything."

Morgan sat with her at the little tin bistro table, where a single cup of tea had gone cold.

"So what brings you to Hong Kong, dear?"

"We're in Switzerland, Mother," Morgan said, with practiced patience.

She displayed only a brief moment of confusion before it fell into place—like the moment you realize a puzzle piece fits, without even having to try it. "Yes, yes, that's what I meant to say. Switzerland. Lucerne."

The term for what Madeleine Willmon had was "early-onset Alzheimer's." Although it was more of a sentence than a disease. Alzheimer's usually struck the aged, but her mother was only fifty-one. It proved to Morgan that the universe wasn't merely indifferent; it was cruel.

Griselda brought out little sandwiches that were somehow both flavorful and bland at the same time.

"I'm glad you're here, honey. No one comes to visit me these days."

"It's the pandemic, Mother," Morgan said, always conscious to keep the word "mother" in their conversations, so as to maintain an anchoring point for the relationship in the woman's diminishing mind.

"Yes, well, that, and this . . . *problem* of mine."

Morgan didn't contradict her because it was true. And a day that she remembered her malady was a day she remembered other things as well. So that was good.

Just a few short years ago, Madeleine had been her full self. The quaint boutique she owned, which was frequented by both locals and tourists alike, managed to pay the rent—but the business had to be sold when Madeleine nearly burned the place down by the last of many cigarettes she left accidentally burning on shelves, instead of in an ashtray, and forgotten.

While Madeleine Willmon's social life had been miles wide, it was only inches deep. And so, once the diagnosis was official, her friendships atrophied and disappeared. No more brunches or soirees. She became a cocktail party topic that warranted a quick change of subject. Mercifully, the government stepped in to cover most medical bills—but not home care. What little her mother had put aside was now spent on Griselda's salary. It had been either that or a state care facility. The financial clock had been ticking toward that. But not anymore.

"Good news, Mother; my new job means we have money to keep Griselda and move you to a better house. Maybe one with an actual view."

"But I like this place just fine."

"I know, but wouldn't you—" Morgan stopped herself

midsentence and decided it wasn't an argument worth having. Besides, the doctors said familiarity helped. Well, at least now Morgan could buy the place outright and do all the repair work and upgrades that the landlord had always refused to do.

"Have you caught it yet?" her mother asked. "COVID, I mean?"

"It's Crown Royale this time."

Her mother waved a hand as if chasing away a mosquito. "Yes, yes, that one."

"No, I haven't caught it, and I don't plan to."

Her mother chuckled. "Well, nobody plans to."

Not entirely true, Morgan thought. The disease was already beginning to develop its own little fan club—and that was just as dangerous as the virus itself. But Morgan spared her mother that particular conversation.

"There are more gentians on the hillside this year," her mother said, which was probably true. Although weeds still dominated, Griselda spread wildflower seeds on the hill to give her mother something to look at. It was a kindness that Morgan appreciated, and had told Griselda so—because, in a world with so much laziness, it was good to see someone who went above and beyond.

"So this new job—does it make you happy?" her mother asked.

"It will," Morgan told her. "Because I get to fight the pandemic."

Her mother scoffed at that. "What do degrees in linguistics and marketing have to do with fighting a virus?"

Ha! At last, something her mother remembered about her! It figured her moment of clarity would be given to an insult.

"It's an . . . international management position. I'll be overseeing the development of a vaccine." Morgan couldn't help but glimpse Griselda eavesdropping from the kitchen. "But for now, Mother, you need to promise not to go out there for any reason."

More mosquito squatting. "Yes, yes, I know, I'm not a child."

And yet Griselda had to keep the doors key-locked from the inside, because of the times her mother would wake-walk. That's what Morgan called it. Wandering around town with a vague and imagined purpose.

Morgan promised herself she would stay for at least an hour, which she did, but not much longer. She said goodbye, giving her mother a kiss, and left her in the yard, where she returned her attention to the hillside.

In the kitchen, Griselda busied herself packing away the leftover sandwiches.

"Good visit?"

"Good as can be expected."

Then Morgan got down to business. "So I assume you know that I've found a job."

"Yes, yes, I heard you speaking about it." Then Griselda grinned. "When I heard you were flying into Buochs, and arriving here in a limousine, I thought maybe you had found yourself one of those 'sugar daddies.'"

That made Morgan laugh. More like a sugar grandma— as if anything about Dame Glynis Havilland could be called sweet.

"And you fight Crown Royale?" Griselda asked, not denying that she had eavesdropped.

"I will be," Morgan confirmed. She had yet to step into the offices of the Havilland Consortium, but grabbing those reigns was the next step. "I'll have a lot of responsibilities, so I won't be around much."

"Humph," said Griselda. "This is nothing new."

Morgan ignored the barb. "So from what I understand, there's someone who comes on Sunday to relieve you, and you take the day off, right?"

"Yes. Hannalore. She's very good."

"Yeah, that's not happening anymore," said Morgan. "I don't want any chance that my mother will be exposed. So from now on you're going to be here twenty-four seven."

Griselda began to bluster. "Miss Morgan, that's not—"

"You've been very good to my mother. So in return for that, *and* in return for seven-day service, I will double your salary, starting today."

Griselda opened her mouth to speak, but no words came out. A bird could have flown in there and made a nest.

"Your new job pays this well?" she finally asked.

Morgan ignored the question. Not the woman's business. "You'll stay here in isolation until the pandemic is over. Anything you need you can have delivered, and you'll disinfect it as soon as it's in the door."

Griselda nodded, but hesitated. Finally, she said, "You know . . . I've heard that Crown Royale can possibly help people like your mother."

Morgan's mood, while not all that summery, now took a turn toward winter. "And where did you hear that? Some website? Or is it just the idiots you gossip with?"

"Not that it can cure her of the Alzheimer's," continued

Griselda, "but it could quell her more troubling episodes. She would, all the time, be content."

"Do you really think that's what she wants? An emotional lobotomy? She needs to care about what's happening to her. She *needs* to be troubled by it, and to always remember how much she's forgetting—because *that's* what gives her dignity—and don't you dare try to take that dignity away!"

Griselda folded in the face of Morgan's indignation. "I'm sorry, Miss Morgan—it was only a thought."

Morgan tried to bring her hackles down, but the very idea of intentional exposure made her reel. Contentment? Being docile was not the same as being content. This virus castrated the lower register of human emotion. Anger, fear, resentment—the way Morgan saw it, those were the things that drove civilization. What sort of nightmare would the world be if that was taken away, and everyone had nothing but the sorry satisfaction of just existing? If Crown Royale went unchecked, everyone in the world would be like her mother was today, staring blankly at hillsides. No, a world without ambition was not a world at all; it was a soulless still life hanging on a wall.

"Ten thousand bonus if my mother doesn't catch Crown Royale before they lift the mask mandate," Morgan said, pulling it out of the air, because even when it came to something as insidious as Crown Royale, money talked. "And if she *does* catch it, you'll be fired, without as much as a reference. Are we clear on this?"

Griselda took a deep breath.

"I said, are we clear?"

"Ten thousand Swiss francs, or Euros?" she asked.

Morgan suppressed a smile. The woman was in no position

to negotiate, and yet she was. Morgan could respect that, so she made it easy. "Whichever is worth more at the time. Do we have an agreement?"

"Yes, Miss Morgan. I can do all you say."

"Good. Because I'm counting on you."

She turned to leave but paused as she crossed the living room.

"One more thing," Morgan said, pointing at the hotel canvas that tainted the mantel. "Take that painting and burn it. I'll send an actual piece of art to replace it."

In the limo, on the way back to the airport, Morgan had an unexpected surge of tears well up. It took all her strength to fight it. From here, her mother would only get worse. Morgan could hijack all of Dame Havilland's money and turn it toward Alzheimer's research, but it would only be a drop in a bottomless bucket. And even if progress was made, it wouldn't matter for her mother. A degenerative disease, at best, could only be prevented or slowed, but not reversed. Dead brain cells remained dead.

No, there was nothing Morgan could do to stop the failing circuits of her mother's mind. But Dame Glynis Havilland had given her money and a mandate. It was now in Morgan's power to change the trajectory of Crown Royale, and perhaps even stop it in its tracks. That would have to be consolation enough.

9

Triage and Tribulation

Rón had set up a credit card and bank account under a fake name a couple of years back. Not because he had any specific intentions for them, but when you were under the eye of a man as watchful as his father, you needed to have your own economic safe room—a place where nothing you did or bought could be tracked. It would have been a great setup if he had a penchant for nefarious activities, but he didn't. He imagined some of his siblings would have arranged all sorts of questionable dealings, but luckily for the world, none of them were as tech savvy as Rón.

Even so, his father could track him in any number of ways. Facial recognition software was on all public surveillance cameras, and those cameras were everywhere—so he kept his head down, and always wore baseball caps from different far-scattered sports teams.

He thought he might travel down to Cabo San Lucas and visit his mom. She had taken her money from the divorce many years ago and opened a little resort there. But no, it would be the first place his father would look. And besides, getting a fake passport good enough to get him through customs was beyond him. He knew he couldn't go to the airports anyway; his father would have them staked out. A single ping would get him nabbed—for his own good, of course; to protect him from himself, his father would say. And his father would be absolutely right; Rón did need protection from himself. But that didn't mean he *wanted* it.

July 4 had been a super-spreader holiday—which was no surprise to anyone. And so in the days after, things like concerts were being canceled left and right. It was announced that the official state ban on large public events would begin tomorrow. But there was one final gig that its promoters insisted on having, defying all common sense. The ShadowFusion concert would go on, as scheduled, to the delight of the band's die-hard fans. Everyone knew that when it was done, the ShadowFusion concert would infect hundreds, but by then, everyone would have made their money, and slunk back to wherever it is unscrupulous music promotors slink.

Those who attended either didn't care, or didn't believe, or thought themselves invincible. Or maybe, like Rón, some wanted to be infected. But whatever the reason, it was a sellout crowd at the Fillmore. Rón was able to get a ridiculously overpriced ticket from a scalper two blocks away. Even the scalper was masked.

The theater had a mosh pit. At this point, it shouldn't have even been legal to have one, but there it was. Without as much as an opening act, and a fashionable ten minutes late, ShadowFusion took the stage, all hair and attitude, to the roar of the crowd. From the first power chords, bodies began to gyrate.

Rón's ticket was for an actual seat. Even so, he thrust himself into the mosh pit, exhilarated by the friction of bodies, and the smell of beer and pot on people's breath. He dared to take off his mask. No one recognized him; it was all about the band and the bodies and the beat. He could have been anybody; he could have been nobody. He breathed in deep, hoping that tonight he would be crowned in the only way that mattered to him.

Mariel found there was no shortage of work in the Pier Peer Collective. Of course, none of it was paid work; it was services in return for food and shelter. It was a commune in every sense of the word; the kind of economics that could never have worked in a world without Crown Royale. Maybe about one-third of the residents were Crown Royale recoverees, which was enough for altruism to outweigh self-interest—and the number was growing. The recoverees led by example, and others followed.

With her mother's death still an open wound, Mariel knew the best thing to do was to stay busy. She still saw her mother everywhere. Still had moments when she thought of something she wanted to tell her, only to realize she couldn't. People tried to be comforting, but condolences never really brought comfort. Only time did. Until the wound healed, she had to rely on the power of distraction.

Mariel wanted to work in the transition tent—which people were now calling the "Tent of Triage and Tribulation." The place where the sick were housed. The place where her mother had died.

"I'm sorry, Mariel," said Zee, which was what everyone was calling Delberg Zello now. "I can't let you work there. Only recoverees can go in."

"I'm willing to take the risk," said Mariel.

"I know that. And if you catch CR doing what you do around the pier, well, there's nothing I can do about that. But giving you permission to go into that tent would be intentionally putting you in harm's way. I'm not comfortable with that."

Mariel shrugged defiantly. "I could just sneak in without your permission," she said.

"You could," he admitted, "but you won't because I know you've got respect enough to follow my rules."

And that infuriated her because he was right.

Even so, she had already been cooped up in a car with her mother when she was her most contagious, and sat by her side in the tent, so what did that say about the nature of the contagion? She wasn't even allowed to be on the team of greeters at the entrance to the pier, who met people and escorted them to their meeting with Zee, to help them find their place in the collective. That was all done by recoverees as well—because, after all, they projected the best and finest face of the collective. Not the false happy face that haters claimed recoverees displayed. Cultish and creepy "Recovery syndrome." Those naysayers never actually met recoverees. If they did, they'd realize their joy was authentic. There was no self-deception nor abdication of mind. Recoverees never seemed "off." They were simply kind and empathetic and centered. Only the most jaded, most suspicious of people could ever distrust them.

Mariel was given three choices of service. She could contribute to food preparation, she could assist in sanitation, or she could work for the special projects team—which was vague enough to sound intriguing. Or at least more intriguing than the other options.

A recoveree by the name of Trinity De Vera was in charge of special projects. She used to be a celebrated art gallery owner. She used to dress in Versace suits and Prada stilettos. Now she wore Kohl's and Crocs.

The current special project was a winding mosaic walkway that would replace the straight, boring concrete path that bisected the pier. Because once you were a recoveree, meandering was much preferred to a straight line.

"It's about the journey, not the destination," Trinity would say, making no apologies for the lack of originality that statement engendered.

She had a team of artists designing the pattern of the mosaic, and another team that laid the tiles. Mariel was a tiler, and although the work was monotonous and hard on her knees, it was also very Zen. More importantly, at the end of the day, looking at the tiles she had set was a clear measure of what she had accomplished.

"Beautiful," said Trinity on Mariel's second day, putting a hand on her shoulder. "Gaudí would be proud."

Perhaps, but would her mother have been?

"*Pretty,*" her mother would have said, "*but why waste time on something people can just walk all over?*"

On Mariel's fifth day at the job, during a swatch of a blue mosaic wave, her attention was snagged by a commotion farther up on the ugly, utilitarian path that she was working to replace—the one not meant for meandering. Mariel wouldn't call it a crowd, but it was a gathering of six or seven highly animated people, attending to someone who had just arrived on the pier.

"Recoverees only!" Zee said in an authoritative voice.

"Everyone else, stay back." Which, of course, drew Mariel closer.

A gurney was quickly being brought over, and someone was placed onto it. Mariel heard bits and pieces of the conversation of those in attendance.

"Wait, I think that's . . ."

"No, it couldn't be."

"I think it is! That rich guy's kid."

Mariel pushed her way forward to see that it was Tiburón Escobedo. He looked bad. Feverish. His face was red, his neck white, with bruises in strange places—classic signs of being in the throes of Crown Royale.

"Back," demanded Zee. "Clear the way—we have to get him to the tent."

"Let me through," said Mariel. "I know him."

"*You* know Rob Escobedo?" someone dubiously mumbled.

"It's Rón, and yes, I do know him."

His eyes were rheumy and glassy, half-closed. But the moment he laid eyes on her, they opened just a little bit wider.

"Mariel," he croaked, and tried to smile, but it evolved into a grimace followed by a rattling cough. He held up his hand, and she clasped it. "There," he said weakly. "All better now."

Zee was not happy. "You can't be here, Mariel."

"He wants me here, don't you, Rón?"

Rón smiled, and this time the smile lingered. "Wine and cheese," he said.

"He's delirious," someone concluded.

Mariel turned to Zee. "Let me stay with him, please."

Zee hesitated, looked at how tightly Rón clasped Mariel's hand, then relented. "I'm not giving you permission," he said. "I'm simply looking the other way." And he turned and walked off.

Then Mariel, still holding Rón's hand, went with him and the medical team into the Tent of Triage and Tribulation.

10
Protecting You from the Man Next Door

**"Our mission:
To ease the world's pain and suffering
by investing time and capital
in worthwhile charitable endeavors."**

That was the official mission statement of the Havilland Consortium. But closer scrutiny, which could only be done by an insider, yielded a very different mission. And Morgan Willmon-Wu was now the ultimate insider.

After her brief trip to visit her mother, Morgan returned to the UK and got to work. She quickly learned that the Havilland Consortium existed for three reasons:

1) to earn money for its founder;

2) to exact revenge or simply to spite anyone its founder despised;

3) to make its founder *appear* to be one of the most philanthropic people in the world.

And if, in the course of achieving these goals, the world's pain and suffering were eased, so be it.

For instance: The Consortium built a much-needed public park . . . but placed it inconvenient to public transportation. Not coincidentally, Dame Glynis Havilland owned the pricey parking lot beside it.

The Consortium had built housing for refugees smack in the middle of a stuffy, pompous Tory neighborhood. It infuriated the residents, and in so doing, exposed their hypocrisy and racism. A number of them sold their homes at a loss. Unknowingly, they sold them to subsidiaries owned by none other than Dame Glynis Havilland.

But by far, Morgan's favorite example was the Havilland Home for Mistreated Women, which was established right next door to the home of a politician who had been accused of abusing women more than once, yet somehow his lawyers always got him off and the charges dismissed.

But right there, on the Havilland Home for Mistreated Women, was a huge sign that said PROTECTING YOU FROM THE MAN NEXT DOOR, with an arrow that pointed right at the politician's bedroom window.

He had sued to have it removed, and when he lost the suit, he moved . . . only to have Dame Havilland relocate the Home for Mistreated Women next to him again. This time the new sign also had a highly unflattering caricature of the man coming out of a horse's ass.

And when he died of an "unrelated" stroke, Dame Havilland threw an "unrelated" party. This was definitely the kind of charitable organization Morgan could get behind.

"Our office is very structured and self-sufficient, as you can see," said the gaunt, graying man who ran the Consortium. His name was Ellis Bradway, and when he introduced himself, he said it almost haltingly, as if he were waiting for the "Sir" to be added to the front of his name at any moment. Officially, he was the vice president, second only to Dame Havilland herself.

But now the role of president fell upon Morgan. Nevertheless, Ellis Bradway behaved as if the Consortium were his personal possession, and not hers.

"Dame Havilland only came for the occasional progress update," Bradway told her. "I assure you, Miss Wu, you won't have to trouble yourself either."

Morgan said little during her grand tour of the office—an office which took up a full floor in The Gherkin; the infamous London tower that resembled a Fabergé egg. Although she didn't feel like the president of an organization of nearly fifty employees, she couldn't let that show. No matter how much she tried to fill the old woman's shoes, she could not forget that she was a quarter of the woman's age, and probably younger than the youngest of her employees.

Bradway was not subtle in his hinting that Morgan was neither needed nor welcome in the Consortium's day-to-day operations. To his credit, he wasn't obsequious and didn't pretend to like her. But being patronizing wasn't much better.

"Are you thirsty, Miss Wu?" he asked in the course of the tour, and without waiting for an answer, he turned to his assistant, who had been trailing behind them. "Preston, bring Miss Wu a selection of beverages." And Preston hopped to, disappearing toward the kitchen.

"It's Willmon-Wu," Morgan corrected. "Both names have equal meaning to me."

"I will make a note," he said, clearly not noting anything, and continued the tour. "Here we have our accounting department, and here is our community outreach. Over there is publicity and marketing—the public face of the Havilland Consortium, if you will."

Preston returned with a tray featuring sparkling water, soft drinks, and kombucha. Morgan did not partake of anything just yet.

"As you can see, Miss Wu, we are a well-oiled machine," said Bradway. "But you are welcome to visit at any time, of course."

Morgan nodded. "Excuse me for asking, but what do *you* do, Mr. Bradway?"

He furrowed his eyebrows, not quite understanding the question. Then gave her a smile as if he just realized that she must be even dimmer than he had originally thought.

"Well, I'm vice president, and thus I run the place, Miss Wu."

"Yes," said Morgan, "but what exactly do you do, other than strut about and take credit for everyone else's work?"

"I beg your pardon?"

Morgan took a deep breath. If she was going to be taken seriously by any of these people, then her reputation needed to begin today. *Be decisive,* thought Morgan. *And incisive. Cut this to ribbons!*

Morgan turned to the assistant, who seemed to be the youngest in the office, just a couple of years older than her, and someone she might actually relate to. "Preston, how long have you been working for Mr. Broadway?"

"Almost a year, Miss Willmon-Wu."

"And as Mr. Bradwick's assistant, would you say you have a handle on his various responsibilities?"

Preston looked nervously to his boss and back to Morgan.

"Don't be afraid to answer," prompted Morgan.

"I . . . keep his calendar and I'm usually on all his phone calls to take notes," Preston said.

Morgan turned back to Preston's reddening boss.

"What I have found, Mr. Bushwack, is that assistants can do their boss's jobs more efficiently and with greater skill. And therefore, as president of the Consortium, I'm switching your jobs here."

"What? You can't do that," Bradway blustered.

Morgan gave a calculated laugh. "Of course I can! It's my consortium now; I can do whatever I like!" Then she turned to Preston. "Mr. Locke," she said, having had the courtesy to learn his full name, even though Bradway never said it, "please hand your former boss the tray, as he will be handling such things now."

Preston's shell shock was almost charming. "Ma'am, I . . ."

But he was halted by the severity of Morgan's gaze.

"Yes, ma'am." Then he awkwardly handed his former boss the tray.

Morgan could have ended it there—but what was the point of putting your hand up someone's back, if you weren't going to rip out their spine? "Now, will you please hold up the tray to Mr. Locke so that he might pick a beverage for himself?"

"This is outrageous," said Bradway.

Morgan knew everyone in the office was listening, even if they appeared not to. Good.

Time to drive this home and make her presence known.

"Outrageous? You'll find, Mr. *Bradway*, that I am an out-rageous individual, just like Dame Havilland. And if you don't like this new arrangement, feel free to submit your resignation."

Then she turned to everyone in attendance and spoke from the diaphragm, slaughtering any butterflies that were left. "Meet your new boss, same as the old boss," she told them. "All of you, take note that I am now in charge, and you will not mispronounce my name or omit any part of it when addressing me. If you cross me or fail me, consequences will be severe. But if you do your job well, you'll be rewarded generously."

Then she turned to a gaping Bradway, whose tray had gotten crooked to the point of beverages sliding sideways as if on the deck of the *Titanic*.

"What are you waiting for, Ellis?" ordered Morgan. "Go answer phones!"

Dame Havilland's business ventures, both personally and through the Consortium, were eclectic. She possessed substantial wealth, but not the towering fortunes of a Jarrick Javins or a Blas Escobedo. Apparently, her interest wasn't in winning any global financial game, but ensuring that she had enough money to mess with anyone she wanted to.

Morgan spent her first day at the Havilland Consortium digging through her new office, still reeling a bit that it was all hers. The old woman's tastes in art and decor were markedly different from Morgan's: stodgy, mournful paintings; heavy antique furniture—all of incalculable value, but none of it Morgan's style. She would send one of the better paintings to her mother, and put all the rest up for auction, replacing it with equally priceless, but more contemporary, pieces. But that was for another day. Today's mission was one of discovery.

She delved through Dame Havilland's private files, which were a virtual soap opera of intricate schemes and manipulations: people she wished to elevate or mercilessly undermine; a labyrinth of ambitious endeavors she had either started or hoped to start.

As Morgan perused, Ellis Bradway entered to tender his resignation. She told him to drop it on the desk and didn't give him the courtesy of a goodbye.

"I'll have Preston write you a letter of recommendation," she told him, which made the man harrumph and stride out. She called security to make sure he had actually left the building.

Morgan had not forgotten the reason why she was now occupying Dame Havilland's office, and their desires on the matter were aligned. Morgan had no problem making her primary goal the eradication of Crown Royale—and today's research revealed that she had a head start. Because this wasn't the Havilland Consortium's first medical rodeo.

Once Ellis was gone, she called Preston in. He still didn't look very vice presidential, but that was fine. It was easier to work with someone who was young and, like her, just beginning to come to terms with their new position. Either Preston would rise to the occasion, or move on, and she'd find someone else to take his place. Still, a much more expensive suit was definitely in Mr. Locke's immediate future.

"Tell me about HRL," Morgan asked him.

"Havilland Research Laboratory," Preston responded. "It's in Manchester."

"I know that. I don't need Google Maps; I need information on it—the kind of information that no one outside these offices would know."

And when Preston stammered his uncertainty, she gave him a little bit of direction. "Start with the failed vaccine," she said.

"Right." He cleared his throat and took a moment to organize his thoughts. "Dame Havilland wanted a cure named after her. It didn't matter what it was. But if you want a cure named after you, you have to actually *cure* something—so she established Havilland Research Laboratory to look into everything from Parkinson's to heart disease. Then, when the last pandemic hit, she had them pivot to finding a vaccine. The Consortium hired the best and the brightest to do it."

"So why does no one know about it?" Morgan asked.

"Because, as you already know, they failed. Unfortunately, the best and the brightest weren't the fastest. Pfizer, Moderna, and AstraZeneca got theirs to market before the HavillandVAX was done. So Dame Havilland shut it down and took the loss."

"Must have ticked her off."

Preston shrugged. "That was before my time here, so I can't tell whether she was more cranky before or after."

That made Morgan laugh. "I think she enjoyed being cranky, so a loss served her as much as a win."

"You talk about her like she's dead," Preston commented.

"She is," said Morgan. "Or at least the Dame Glynis Havilland everyone knew is dead. That's why she handed all this to me."

Preston opened his mouth as if he might say something else, but thought better of it.

"So could this unfinished vaccine be repurposed?" Morgan asked.

Preston lowered his voice as if the portraits might be listening. "Actually, from what I understand, it wasn't a *traditional* vaccine. There was more to it."

"Meaning?"

"I have no idea—that's only what I've heard."

"Well, we'll have to sort that out, won't we? But in the meantime, the Havilland Consortium has a new Prime Directive."

The use of the expression made Preston smile. Good. She knew he was her kind of people. "We'll put all our resources into getting the lab up and running again," she told him. "And this time, we'll get the best, the brightest, *and* the fastest."

"That's going to take a lot more money than the Consortium has," Preston pointed out.

"Well, Mr. Locke, your new assignment is to track down someone with that kind of money," she said. "But first, get yourself a new suit."

11
Death's Lawn

Rón thought he'd hallucinate. He thought he'd have wild dreams. He did not. Or if he did, he didn't remember. He did sense the passage of time, though. As he slipped in and out of awareness, the pounding headache and persistent pain in his chest made him wish for fewer moments of consciousness.

He did remember, in one of his rare lucid moments, thinking that this was a terrible mistake, and that he was going to die. If he did die, he hoped his father would never find out. That his father would still hold out hope that Rón was alive out there, because Rón couldn't bear the prospect of his father's pain.

"You're awake."

Rón cleared his throat, but his voice came out just as raspy as if he hadn't. "Not sure. I'll tell you in a second."

"No, you're awake. I'm a master of observation."

Rón tried to focus his vision but each time he tried, his eyes hurt. No, not so much hurt as rebelled; angry at the intrusion of light. How long had he been out, he wondered, that his eyes would balk at having to see again? But he saw enough, and heard enough to realize it was Mariel beside him. He had seen her before the fever drove him from consciousness. Had she been with him this whole time? Probably not, but he was grateful to see her upon his waking. Grateful? No, this was beyond gratitude. This feeling was new.

"Do you know where you are?" Mariel asked.

"The pier," he croaked. "The one where all the homeless people go."

She smirked. "How elitist of you."

"Well, it's true," he said. "And anyway, I chose to come here, so—"

But the rest of his thought was overtaken by a painful bout of wet, nasty coughing. When it was done, she pressed a cloth to his lips, wiping them clean.

"Sounds worse than me," croaked a voice next to him. Rón turned his head to see a man in the neighboring cot. He didn't seem much older than Rón and Mariel. Twenty, maybe. Sweaty, lips chapped and pale, yet he was smiling like it was Christmas morning, Thanksgiving, and his birthday all rolled into one.

"That's Fallon," said Mariel. "He's a fever-talker. Said the wildest things when he was unconscious."

"Fever broke," Fallon said. "Worst is over. Smooth sailing now."

So smooth that he fell asleep seconds after closing his eyes, but the faint smile never left his face. Rón wondered what a recoveree dreams about. He turned to Mariel, who looked at him with concern.

"Thank you, Mariel."

"You're welcome."

"No—I mean *thank you*. Really, *thank you!*"

"It's no big deal."

"But it is. You were here, and you helped me . . . and I *have* to thank you for that because . . . because it *hurts* not to thank you. Does that make sense?"

She grinned. "Yeah, I guess it makes perfect sense."

And still, his eyes rebelled, aching in a strange new way. But he was sweaty, which meant his fever had broken. He looked around; there were dozens of people in cots, all in various stages of the illness. And unlike a hospital or any other facility, every single person had someone attending to them, one on one. Not doctors, not nurses, just ordinary people, all seeming to be endlessly patient, endlessly caring. And he knew they must all be recoverees. He turned to Mariel.

"So you've had it and recovered?" he asked.

"No, I haven't gotten it." And to his surprised reaction, she said, "I'm not worried, so you shouldn't be either. If I get it, I get it. I'm prepared. And I get the feeling that you were too."

"You could say I threw my fate to the wind."

"But you're high risk, Rón; you knew that."

"So?" he said. "Maybe high risk means greater reward." He said it facetiously. It would be a while until he knew how true that was.

"My father—"

"Doesn't know you're here," Mariel said. "Zee made sure everyone stayed quiet, and everyone listens to Zee."

"Who's Zee?"

"Delberg Zello, the guy who runs this place."

"Thank him for me."

"You'll thank him yourself when you're up to it."

He cleared his throat, felt the urge to cough rise and then fade like a wave that didn't break.

"How's your mom? Is she here too?"

Mariel looked down and took a moment before responding. Rón knew from that pause what she was going to say.

"She was, but she didn't make it."

"I'm sorry," he said, and she accepted his simple condolence with a nod.

"She died happy," she told him. "I think they all do."

Rón found he couldn't hold her gaze long—it somehow hurt his brain to look in her eyes. But for the brief moment he did, he could sense that they held several levels of sadness. Then it occurred to him why. This was his gasp of clarity. The one people dying of Crown Royale get before they succumb.

"Am I about to die?" he asked.

"I don't know," she said, respecting him enough not to lie. "But if you are, I'll be with you to the end." Then she took his hand as she had when he first arrived.

And so he closed his eyes, waiting for his gasp of clarity to fade into a final breath.

But it didn't.

He just lingered hour after hour, getting bored as his mind became increasingly active.

"It looks like that wasn't your gasp of clarity," Mariel finally said.

"Guess not. Still could come, though."

"If you say so."

Eventually Mariel left; she told him she had to work on some art project. He dozed in and out then. Not in a deathly sort of way, but in the way someone did when they were weak and tired from a long battle.

He was awake when Mariel returned early in the evening, sitting up and eating a flavorful, if somewhat oversalted, bowl of soup. His taste buds somehow felt rejuvenated—while the last pandemic left people's senses of smell and taste dulled, this did the opposite. He could taste and smell things more clearly, more sharply than before—and that ache he felt in his eyes that penetrated to his brain was resolving into something less intrusive. More like visual static. The world simply didn't look right in places, but he was beginning to get used to it.

"Looks like death kicked you off his doorstep," Mariel said.

"Yeah, and then yelled at me to get off his lawn."

"It's okay," said Mariel. "We can egg death's house on Halloween."

Then someone approached with a shirt full of so much mental static, Rón had to look away.

"The shark emerges from the depths!" the man said.

Rón met his eyes because he couldn't meet his shirt. "You must be Delberg Zello."

"I see my reputation precedes me," Zee said. "As does yours. I'd ask you how you feel, but I already know. Both miserable and wonderful."

Rón smiled because he had it exactly right. How could one feel so physically bad, and so good in all other ways? It was as if all the dark corners of his soul had been burned away like chaff, leaving only what he wanted to keep. But the chaff was still smoldering.

"Trust me, in a day or two, the misery will fade, but the joy will remain."

"I appreciate you taking me in."

"It's what we do." And then, as if reading his mind, Zee said, "Stay as long as you like—but once you're on your feet, you'll need to leave the tent. We need every bed for the sick."

The next morning he was strong enough to venture out of the tent for the first time, and felt the breeze of the bay on his face.

Even his sense of touch had changed, sharpened. The feel of the wind was like an entirely new kind of caress. The world gently embracing him. And when he looked up at the sky, it was frightening in an undefinable way. That strange mental static filled him again, his eyes tried to rebel, but he forced them to look, and forced his brain to absorb. It was like looking into the sun.

There was another new recoveree out for an early morning stroll. It took a moment for Rón to recognize that it was Fallon—who looked a whole lot better than he had the day before.

"If it isn't my fever brother!" said Fallon, shaking his hand. "Glad you made it through."

"Thanks . . . but what's wrong with the sky?"

Fallon seemed confused. "Nothing," he said. "Just a clear day." Then Fallon took a deep, satisfied breath, returning his gaze to the heavens. "Not often we get a sky this blue."

PART THREE
THE ALLURE
OF RECOVERY

Elsewhere:
Brazil

San Francisco, with its steep streets and dramatic views, thinks of itself as a city of hills.

It doesn't know the meaning of the word.

But Rio de Janeiro does.

It exists against all logic, amidst massive granite monoliths thrust up through the earth as if the dark depths have tried to elbow their way into the light. No roads in Rio could be straight, no foundations truly level. The streets are in constant gridlock—even though the jagged geometry never allowed for anything resembling a grid.

And unlike many other places where hillsides are reserved for the rich, it is the poor who inhabit the hills of Rio, each family building on the roof of their neighbors with neither blueprint nor engineering.

The favelas.

Sprawling haphazard conglomerations of mortar and brick that, to the unfamiliar eye, look only half-finished, but they are as finished as they will ever be.

At sixteen, Cláudio Taváres works twelve-hour shifts pouring concrete for a hotel across town, the visitors of which he will never see. He sleeps on a mat on a concrete floor. He knows no other life.

It is early evening when the couple arrives. Cláudio's father is asleep, his mother is still at the market, his younger siblings are out in the street dreaming of fútbol stardom, so it is only Cláudio there to greet them.

The couple's clothes aren't the least bit frayed, and the two look well fed. The woman has blond hair, but at least half an inch of dark roots—a wealthy woman who, at least until recently, hid anything brown about her.

"Are you lost?" is the first thing Cláudio asks, because, clearly, this couple is not from the favela.

"Much the opposite," the woman says as she steps in. She looks around—Cláudio thinks it's to judge—but there appears to be no judgment in her. Just curiosity.

"We're looking for João Tavárez," the man says. "We were told he lives here."

"He's my father. He's asleep," Cláudio tells them.

"Ah! You're the son, the eldest!" says the woman.

"Yes, I remember you," says the man.

And now that it's been said, Cláudio realizes he's seen them before, from a previous job.

"You and your father rebuilt the stairs to our villa several months ago."

Of course! How could Cláudio possibly forget that job? Cláudio begins to rub his left wrist at the memory, and the man takes notice.

"A brick fell," he says. "It broke your arm."

Cláudio shrugs. "It healed."

"We should have driven you to the hospital," says the woman. "We were not kind."

But Cláudio recalls no particular unpleasantness from these people—just the standard dismissiveness that those of a higher station always show. The kind of disregard you get used to when you live in the favelas.

"You paid us," Cláudio reminds her.

"Yes, but we were not kind," the woman says again.

Now Cláudio is curious. "Why are you here?"

"To give you this." And then she holds out a set of keys on a sparkling chain.

The sight of it confuses Cláudio. "You have more work for us?"

The man laughs, and the woman smiles gently. Then, when Cláudio does not take the keys, she slips the key ring on his finger as if it's a wedding band.

"My husband and I have a sailboat, and we are taking it south. We won't be back," she says. "These are the keys to our villa. It's yours now."

Cláudio stands there in silence, not knowing how to react. He has heard of people doing strange, delirious things after recovering from Crown Royale. The drug lord who ran the favela had gotten it. Afterward, he disappeared—although most people believe he had been disappeared. *But maybe not.*

"What do you mean, it's ours?"

"Exactly that," says the man. "We have no more need for it."

"The refrigerator and pantry are fully stocked," says the woman. "But if you need more food, you can always sell the art."

"Is this a joke?"

"This is payment," the man says. "Payment for a job well done. And if you choose to move on as well, give the keys to whomever you wish."

Then they breeze out as quickly as they had breezed in, leaving the key chain dangling from Cláudio's finger, tinkling like a wind chime.

12
How Badly?

Morgan had the Havilland Consortium's marketing and publicity people create anti–Crown Royale graphics and memes to help combat the growing voices of recoverees touting Crown Royale as a blessing rather than a curse. Morgan knew that in a battle for hearts and minds, spin mattered more than anything else. It was too late to change the name of the disease, but Morgan was finding other ways to control the narrative. For instance, her people came up with the "Viral Spider." Because, while COVID had been portrayed as a little green Sputnik, that wouldn't do for this disease. Morgan's ad team flooded forth images and emojis of Crown Royale as a horrific spider with too many legs; sharp mandibles; and sinister, segmented eyes.

Most people in the Consortium's offices were on board, but there were still those on the Havilland payroll who couldn't seem to respect her authority. However, there was only so much pleasure that Morgan could derive from putting people in their places. Humiliating the type of people who would look down their noses at her was just too easy a game when it was rigged for her to win. Besides, she was shrewd enough to know some of these people weren't just maligners; some were important cogs in the Havilland empire. They did their jobs and did them well. She wasn't going to fire useful people for spite. Only the useless ones.

There were also plenty of employees at every level who seemed genuinely pleased to see someone new and young at the helm.

"We loved Dame Havilland and her curmudgeonly ways," said one older gentleman with a twinkle in his eye, and wearing a suit that seemed from a previous century, complete with a pocket square. "But fresh blood does invigorate the soul!"

Morgan couldn't tell if he was being sincere, or just a sycophant. But either was fine. A loyal yes-man was a valuable asset, as long as you didn't surround yourself with them.

Everyone wore those high-tech digital masks here. Everyone was tested for Crown Royale regularly. Everyone's phone was tracked to make sure they weren't engaging in risky activities that might expose them to the virus—and those whose probability of exposure was at 3 percent or more were put on unpaid administrative leave.

All this was in place before Morgan arrived. Dame Havilland was certainly thorough, and it made things easier.

In normal circumstances—if anything about this could be called "normal"—Morgan would have a full social calendar, familiarizing herself with Dame Havilland's friends as well as enemies. But it wasn't worth risking Crown Royale exposure.

There was one invitation, however, that caught her attention. It was for a unique virtual gathering. Preston brought it to Morgan's attention. The email was addressed to Dame Havilland—because Morgan had yet to inform the world at large that the old woman was, if not pushing daisies, certainly wearing them in her hair.

Morgan couldn't help but be impressed by the invitation, to the point of her breath nearly being taken away. Because there was rich . . . and there was RICH.

"Are the two of them . . . friends?" Morgan asked.

Preston shrugged. "Not really. I know he attended a few of the Dame's fundraisers. I think he liked the way she had no filter, and would say anything to anyone."

"Hmm," said Morgan. "This could be exactly what we need. Send a reply that Dame Havilland will be happy to attend."

"Shall I let him know that—"

"No. Let him think the Dame herself will be attending. I'd like my replacing her to be a surprise."

Incredible, thought Morgan. A month ago, who would have imagined she'd be called to meet with the one and only Blas Escobedo?

Mariel was, once again, banned from the tent after Rón was discharged. There was simply no compelling reason to put her at risk.

"It's only luck that you didn't catch it," said one of the other tilers.

"Yeah, bad luck," said another. She had meant it as a joke, but it stung like a rebuke.

"Maybe you've had it, and didn't know," someone else suggested. "You know—asymptomatic." Which would have been a logical conclusion, except that this virus didn't have any asymptomatic cases. If you had it, you knew, and if you weren't quite sure it was Crown Royale that you had, well, you'd be certain once you recovered.

Delberg Zello found it curious, to say the least. "I'm beginning to wonder if you've got some sort of natural immunity. . . ."

"Have you heard of any cases of natural immunity?" Mariel asked.

"No . . . ," Zee admitted, "but that doesn't mean there aren't any."

He was right; there was still so much the world didn't know about Crown Royale. Like how long the elated feeling lasted. Did it fade over time, or did it persist for the rest of your life? Did it shorten your lifespan? Lengthen it? Did it create other health risks further down the line that no one had even thought of? Or maybe even health benefits that couldn't be known for years?

Surely someone was studying these things, but answers to the bigger questions would be long in coming.

Rón had basically recovered, but he still had to wear a mask until he tested negative. He tweaked one of his father's digital masks to project the image of someone else's nose and mouth, just to keep him incognito to anyone who didn't already know who he was—as well as interlopers who might be looking for him, hoping to claim the reward his father was now offering. Mariel found the fake face to be very disconcerting.

Like everyone else, Rón was offered three work options, and he chose sanitation. All the sanitation workers were recoverees—Mariel supposed the only people who would choose trash detail over other things were people who'd be happy no matter what they did.

"It's good to have a purpose," Rón told her. "Even if it's a humble one."

"I wonder what your father would think," she teased, then regretted reminding him. But not even the mention of Rón's father could cast a shadow on his mood.

"I feel sorry for him, Mariel. All the money in the world, and he's so afraid. But now that I know what it feels like to be a recoveree—I don't think my father would give it all away. His desire for success was always tangled up with a desire to do some good in the world. Instead of giving his money away, I want to believe he'd find ways to use it more wisely."

"Well, yeah," said Mariel. "But you know what they say about the best of intentions. I mean, look at Oppenheimer."

Rón shook his head. "Oppenheimer never had the best of intentions. He set out to create a nuclear bomb, and that's exactly what he did." Then Rón paused. "If Oppenheimer had been a Crown Royale recoveree, who knows what the world would be like now."

Mariel helped Rón sort trash from recycling—even though there were bins for both, people were careless. Or at least the nonrecoverees were. Although it was during Mariel's free time, she didn't mind, because it gave her time to be with Rón.

At one point he pulled out an empty Oreo wrapper and examined it. Mariel wasn't sure why.

"I don't think that's recyclable," she told him.

Then he looked at her, hesitating. "This wrapper is blue, isn't it." It wasn't a question. It was a statement of fact. As if he were as certain as anyone else would be.

"One kind of blue, yes."

Then he gave her a conspiratorial sort of grin. "I'll tell you a secret," he said. "Ever since recovering from Crown Royale . . . I can see it."

At first Mariel thought it was just wishful thinking. After all, if you've never seen a color before, how can you be sure you see it when you do? She supposed there were those tests—where you look at a bunch of colored dots, and try to find the hidden number. But the more Rón spoke about it—the way it didn't just affect his perception of that mysterious hue, but also every color as well—it seemed far too detailed and specific to be a delusion.

"How is that even possible?" she asked him. Clearly there were biological reasons, but right now it felt almost mystical.

"I don't know . . . but I've been diving down some rabbit holes on social media. And there are rumors of it happening to other people with blue-cone deficiency. The virus must stimulate the growth of the missing cones."

"So . . . what's it like?" she asked him. "To see a color you couldn't imagine before you saw it?" She was hesitant because it somehow seemed too personal to ask.

"It hurt for a while," he told her. "I don't think the primitive part of our brains knows what to do when it comes across something it's never faced before. It kind of panics. But I'm okay now." Then he added, "Better than okay."

They got back to sorting, but only for a moment, until he came across a bag of Ruffles potato chips. Another shade of blue. He took it in, then looked at her. It was as if seeing a new color changed his perception of everything.

"I'm glad you stayed in the penthouse that night, Mariel. I'm glad I met you."

Not knowing how to respond, she got back to sorting trash. "So what will you do now? Will you go back to your father?"

"I don't know. I should let him know that I'm okay—he must be so worried. Maybe I can get him a message that I'm all right without giving away where I am."

"So even now, you don't want to go back?"

"Not while I'm still contagious."

"And after?"

Rón's response was to glance at the sorting bins. "Maybe I'll stay here cleaning up trash."

"I think you were meant for more," Mariel dared to suggest.

"Maybe."

The moment began to feel uncomfortable. Weighty. Then Rón said, "How badly do you want to catch Crown Royale, Mariel?"

Mariel tried to find whatever truth she could pull out of her ambivalence. "Sometimes I want it more than anything. Sometimes I'm afraid. Not just of dying . . . but of what I might lose if I recover."

"Worry? Pain? Trauma?"

"Darkness is there for a reason."

Rón nodded, considering that. "Maybe the reason is to remind us why we need light."

Silence fell between them again. Suddenly the sorting of trash didn't seem all that important anymore. Not when her emotions were so sorely in need of sorting. How much to save. How much to jettison.

"How badly do you want it?" he asked again, gently.

Right now she wanted it more than anything, and he knew it.

Rón reached up and removed his mask, revealing his true face. "How badly?"

She leaned just the slightest bit closer to him, and in response, he raised his hand, and touched her cheek.

They both leaned toward each other but stopped when their lips were barely an inch apart. Then he gently breathed out and she breathed in the warmth of his breath deep into her lungs.

13
The Desert or the Deep

The meeting took place on a teakwood platform levitating over a soothing Caribbean Sea. But not really. It was a hyper-realistic VR environment that Blas Escobedo was beta testing. He held all his meetings there now. Sometimes he chose a mountaintop environment, other times the surface of the moon—it all depended on the feeling with which he wished to imbue the meeting. Today, comfort and ease were in order, because the subject of today's summit was anything but comfortable or easy.

The circular table—which also levitated—was set for seven powerful individuals. Blas himself; a high-level epidemiologist from the World Health Organization; a media mogul who owned more than his fair share of news outlets; an economist so brilliant, she had achieved near-celebrity status; a Russian oligarch with a root system extensive enough to buckle the Kremlin's pavement; the Chinese junior minister of health, hungry for the senior position; and last, but not least, Dame Glynis Havilland, whose charitable endeavors left the elite of Europe under her wasting thumb.

The guests appeared at the table at the appointed hour, except for the Russian. No one spoke of his absence, but everyone knew what it probably meant. The infection rate was rising in Russia, just as it was everywhere else in the world. Anyone who had either died, or recovered, from Crown Royale would certainly not be attending the meeting.

As for Dame Havilland, most everyone assumed that she had one of her techs hack her avatar into this youthful projection—but Blas knew better. His conference platform did not allow for such manipulation. Who you saw was who you got.

As intimidating as this crew of movers and shakers was, Morgan was determined not to let them see her sweat. Even if it was just her avatar's virtual sweat.

"Dame Havilland has succumbed," Morgan announced. "I'm Morgan Willmon-Wu, her successor."

Some of the others were put off by someone so young at the table. Blas Escobedo didn't seem bothered at all, although he did seem intrigued. "I sense a story here," he said.

"Stories are everywhere," she countered. "It's all in the execution."

When it was clear that the final seat was not going to be filled, Escobedo tapped his screen to make the empty chair disappear, and the table shrunk proportionately. A wise choice. Best not to ruminate on those lost to the disease.

"Thank you all for accepting my invitation," Escobedo began. "My hope is that at this roundtable, we might share ideas and help shape a global response to the threat that Crown Royale poses to all of us. Not just to our business interests, but to our citizens. Our families."

The Chinese minister nodded knowingly. "Your son . . ."

"He will be found," Escobedo said, shutting down that particular conversation. It was common knowledge now that Tiburón had run off, and no stone was left unturned in his father's attempt to find him. "Boys his age will rebel from time to time."

"Yes, but the consequences . . . ," said the mogul.

"Are my concern, and no one else's," said Escobedo. Morgan liked the way the man controlled the conversation, refusing to allow it to veer into the personal. Then Blas turned to the economist to break the ice. "Samira, why don't you start with a market update."

"Precarious," the celebrated economist said. "Every index is on the verge of free fall."

"It's these damnable lockdowns!" groused the mogul, but the economist shook her head.

"Quarantine is not our enemy this time; it's recovery. 'Recovery syndrome' changes consumer patterns. We're starting to see people spending their money differently."

"It's not merely consumption," interjected the Chinese minister. "When workers leave factories and farmers abandon state farms, where is the means of production?" Then he cleared his throat self-consciously. "Not that such things are happening to us, but elsewhere, certainly."

Which of course was a party-line lie. Even Morgan had heard how China was losing control of its recovered population.

"This virus threatens both capitalist and socialist economies equally," the economist said. "No system is safe, no nation invulnerable."

Morgan chose that moment to serve her opening volley. "Excuse me, but from what I can see, this is nothing but a vanity meeting. What can you accomplish here, but the stroking of your own egos?"

If the others were dubious about her before, they were ready to hurl her off into the virtual sea now. Everyone but Blas, who grinned at the gauntlet she had thrown down. "Ms. Willmon-Wu is right. Our dialogue here may begin as such—but egos aside, I believe there is enough vision, capital, and influence at this table to move the needle in the fight against Crown Royale."

A respectable response. The fact that he couldn't be easily insulted weighed in his favor.

The epidemiologist looked up from her notes. "At the WHO, we're primarily interested in easing the severity of symptoms and in increasing the survival rate, since prevention is notoriously difficult for an airborne virus."

"It's not the symptoms but the results that are the problem," Morgan pointed out. "Whether it's a one percent mortality rate, or five percent, what does it matter when all the survivors have been fundamentally altered from who they once were?"

"I must admit, the young lady makes a point," said the mogul, condescending in his praise. "This is a body-snatching virus, and public messaging needs to keep pushing that narrative. This disease doesn't just infect you; it replaces you with someone who might *look* like you, but is, in fact, nothing but a facsimile."

"You don't actually believe that, do you?" asked the epidemiologist.

"It doesn't matter what you or I believe; what matters is getting the rest of the world to believe it—it's the only way we can counteract the allure of recovery."

"How close is a vaccine?" Blas asked.

"Six months at least," said the epidemiologist. "But a vaccine is only as good as the public's desire to take it."

"It could be mandated," suggested the health minister.

"Maybe in your society," said the mogul, with a judgmental sniff. "But not in the West."

"It doesn't matter," piped up the economist. "Because in six months the global economy will be in ruins. A collapse that will make the great depression look like a coin in a fountain. Cities will become wastelands. Fields will become dust bowls. There'll be mass starvation—and once the world hits that inflection point, there'll be no path to recovery."

It was a sobering forecast that left them in silence, with nothing but the fake gentle surf to mock them.

"How certain are you of that?" Blas finally asked.

The economist sighed. "We have no predictive models for this. All we have are guesses. Society's habits usually change slowly, predictably. A sudden shock to the system can have a million different consequences. That much euphoria will hit like a tsunami. There's no telling how much will be dragged out to sea when all is said and done."

"The desert or the deep," said Blas. "I don't care for either alternative."

Morgan glanced at the virtual Caribbean around them. Perhaps the sea wasn't the best environment for this little soiree.

"Contentment is only of value when it serves the greater good," proclaimed the health minister, "and when the government can be credited."

An hour of pontification and posturing, and those assembled congratulated themselves on saving the world, then set a time for the next meeting. Morgan suspected the table would probably get smaller next time too.

Blas was gracious in his goodbyes, but Morgan could sense he was being diplomatic. The minister and mogul were cut from the same mold; pompous cynics who saw people as dull and pliable. The economist was little more than a street-corner prophet shouting doom, and the WHO scientist seemed too bogged down in procedural red tape to mount an effective response.

Morgan lingered once the others were gone, pretending to have forgotten to log out until it was just her and Blas Escobedo at the table on the platform above the sea.

"Miss Willmon-Wu," Blas finally said, leaning back in his chair. "Do you have other business with me, or are you just taking a moment's vacation?" He indicated the surroundings, where a virtual sailboat had just passed toward the setting sun.

"There is something I'd like to discuss with you," she said. "Something the others don't need to hear."

That made him grin. "In my previous encounters with Dame Havilland, she always tried to corner me as well, and draw me into some sort of intrigue."

"Did she succeed?"

"No," Escobedo said. "But perhaps you'll be more persuasive."

Best to get right to it, thought Morgan. Neither of them liked their time wasted. "I have a business proposition for you, and for you alone," she began. "I'm sure you're aware that Dame Havilland had a team working on a vaccine during the previous pandemic."

"It was my understanding that she failed."

"She was just too late to the finish line, so she stopped running. But from what I understand, her team's approach was unique and highly adaptable to this new virus. A traditional vaccine might be half a year away, but, with enough resources, the HVAX could be sequenced, completed, and ready for distribution in a month." She let that linger. "Imagine, Mr. Escobedo—we'd be first to market a solution that the world desperately needs."

He stood up and paced the platform, for a moment stepping off it and seeming to float in midair above the ocean. "I see dollar signs in your eyes, Miss Willmon-Wu. Did you know that yesterday, Hao Cheong left his fortunes to join a monastery?"

"I hadn't heard." But of course, Morgan *had* heard. Still, she played along.

"Which means that I am now the richest soul on this troubled planet," Escobedo said. "And yet, while that once might have mattered, it doesn't anymore. Money doesn't motivate me."

"And from what I understand, neither does power," Morgan said.

"I value legacy, Ms. Willmon-Wu. I wish to be known for the difference I've made."

And although Morgan was motivated by the very things Blas Escobedo had moved beyond, their goals were in alignment.

"Fully fund Havilland Labs, Mr. Escobedo . . . and I guarantee you will be."

14
The Truth in Your Bones

Rón took off his mask whenever he was alone with Mariel, and they existed in each other's airspace for days. Close enough to kiss, but not making that move—both savoring the richness of the time leading up to it. And when they finally kissed, it felt inevitable. The fact that he was still testing positive, and she was still testing negative, gave them all the more reason to do it.

Mariel had kissed her share of boys before, but this was different. Certainly there was passion, but it felt so much less one sided than kisses she had experienced before. Boys, once they got over their awkwardness, were about momentum—moving past one milestone to get to the next and the next, like checking off boxes on the way to where it all eventually led.

But Rón wasn't doing that. He was always there with her in the moment, in a perfect balance between giving and taking, letting the moment spread like a wave washing across the shore.

She could kiss him forever.

"When you get your fever," he told her, gently, "I'll hold your hand through all of it, the way you held mine."

They waited, knowing the incubation period could be up to six days.

Meanwhile, the Tent of Triage and Tribulation never seemed to empty, even as people left it. And the pier's population continued to grow.

. . .

Delberg Zello would never have been able to manage the pressure of leadership prior to being a Crown Royale recoveree. Of course, that hadn't stopped him from being an armchair quarterback in his prior life, complaining about the piss-poor job those in power did—as if knowing the problem was enough to solve it. But now he knew that running a community was no easy task, especially when that community was expanding.

Part of his daily routine as the head of the Pier Peer Collective was to leave once a day for a reconnaissance walk. He ventured forth into the city to get the vibe of things for himself. Because news of the world didn't mean a thing until you could feel the truth of it in your bones.

On the surface, Zello saw what everyone saw: fewer people in the streets, and a vague intangible sense of paranoia. Nearly everyone was masked now—and more and more of those masks were the digital ones, ever since Blas Escobedo started giving them out for free. Zello passed dozens of shops that had gone out of business, or seemed ready to give up the ghost. Jewelry stores, fashion boutiques. It was, as the news said, a sign of the times.

Those were the obvious things. But there was much more to be gleaned from a walk through the city for those willing to scratch beneath the surface.

Like the little repair shop on Polk Street, for instance.

Business was booming! It had a line of people down the block, holding everything from coffee makers to toasters to desk lamps—and from their demeanors, Zello could tell they were mostly, if not entirely, recoverees. There was an employee at the door, looking a bit like a bouncer, informing people that they needed an appointment just to get in line.

Right next door, an electronics store had slashed its prices in a blow-out pandemic sale. The owner, a desperate man with a tie that was pulled a little too tight around his neck so that it resembled a dangling noose, approached one of the repair shop patrons. The customer was holding a retro clock radio that hadn't been retro when he first bought it.

"Friend," the electronic shop owner said in an accent Zello couldn't pinpoint. "I sell you new clock radio with phone charger, Wi-Fi, and voice command—and will be less than cost to repair old one. You come in, I show you!"

But the customer looked at his old, bulky Panasonic with love and admiration. "Why would I want something new when I have this?"

"Yes, but is broken."

To that, the customer shrugged. "Won't be broken for long."

Zello suspected the electronics store wouldn't be there next week.

And then there was the thrift shop on Powell Street.

There was a ghost town of stores around it, but Secondhand Sublime was buzzing with business—and not just folks wanting to buy used items, but a second line of those who'd come to donate their junk instead of throwing it away—because, after all, junk was only junk when someone deemed it so.

The customers here were also recoverees, and their only interest was function. Like the man with the clock radio, these people had no interest in buying something shiny and new, even at a bargain. Used to be, shiny new things brought happiness, even if just for a fleeting moment. Now they just brought clutter.

But most telling was the incident in Francisco Park.

There was a couple strolling, admiring the panoramic view,

when a man ran up, snatched the woman's purse, then ran off. Zello thought to take chase—in fact, he would have thrown himself into pursuit—but the couple stopped him. "It's all right—he's already gone," the woman said. And realizing there was nothing to be done, the recovered couple went back to their leisurely stroll.

Zello flinched when he heard a gruff voice behind him.

"Goddamn Crown-cases."

He turned to see a slovenly woman on a park bench smoking a cigarette, a pile of them on the ground around her as if no matter how many she smoked, she'd never be satisfied.

She glanced at the couple who were too far away to hear now. "Pick one pocket, they'll hand you what's in the other. Brainless, the lot of them."

Zello made a mental note. *Crown-cases.* A new slur against recoverees.

"They're not like us, you know," said the woman, jovial in her animosity. "If you ask me, they oughta round up the whole lot of 'em."

"And do what?"

The woman shrugged. "Not up to me. Up to whoever rounds 'em up." Then her gaze tightened to a squint. "You ain't one of them, are you? If you are, I meant no offense."

Zello strode off without giving her the dignity of a response. In another life, he would have felt fury at the ignorance and the fear and the unapologetic hatred the woman embodied. But now, the most he could muster was pity. And he began to worry if that might be a problem.

These days, however, he didn't just see the problems. He saw solutions.

. . .

Upon returning to the pier, Zello encountered Rón Escobedo on the mosaic walkway. The boy's sanitation shift was over, and so he was spending time with Mariel, who was farther down the path, spreading grout. Rón, however, appeared preoccupied with a bucket of tiles. He had pulled several of them out and had laid them before him like puzzle pieces. It didn't take a rocket scientist to see what they all had in common.

"They go on forever, don't they?" Zello said. "Shades of blue, that is." Then he pulled one out of the bucket, turning it in his fingers. "They've all got names, too."

"I'm still getting used to it all," Rón said. "But it's a good thing."

"Of course it is! And I see you've been good about wearing your mask."

"I still haven't tested negative," Rón told him.

Which was certainly a concern. But while Delberg Zello had started the Pier Peer Collective as a place for all those in need of refuge, it was rapidly becoming a sanctuary for recoverees. People out in the world knew it—which was why just about everyone coming to the pier either had Crown Royale, or wanted to catch it.

"They're not like us," the smoking woman had said. No, thought Zello. And that was a blessing.

"I'd like you to take off your mask, Rón."

Rón hesitated. "But . . . I'm still contagious."

Zello nodded. "I know. Take it off anyway."

And so Rón reached up, unlooped the mask from his ears, and slipped it into his pocket.

Satisfied, Zello placed the tile he held in his hand beside

the others in Rón's collection. "Cerulean," he said. Then he strode off to see what other business needed tending to.

Four days. Seven days. Ten. Nothing. Mariel had been breathing in Rón's contagion all that time, and yet still she hadn't caught it. By now she was sure he wasn't even contagious anymore—because no one was contagious this far out. He wasn't even wearing his mask around the pier anymore.

How could she have dodged an illness she wasn't trying to dodge? Perhaps others might think it was a good thing, but Mariel felt only cheated. And being among a growing number of recoverees on the pier didn't help—because even though she was happy with the collective, there was a limit to her contentment. A veil to it that she could not peel away. Rón could see blue. Where was her blue?

"I get it now, baby," her mother had said. *"All of it."*

What did it feel like to be enveloped in a light you'd missed your entire life? It could be that Mariel would never know, and it made her ache in a way she could not share with anyone, least of all Rón.

Dr. Pirmal, the collective's physician, took a blood sample from Mariel to send off for detailed analysis. Because so far everyone who had been exposed had followed the same pattern of contagion. And Zee, who at first had been so insistent on preventing exposure, had pulled back on that. It wasn't just that he had gone lax on his own rules. It was as if he were reconsidering his entire philosophy on the matter.

"Blood doesn't lie," Zee told her. "We'll get it out to the lab, and get you some answers."

. . .

The journey of Mariel's blood to the lab was fraught with mishap and peril. First, it was placed with two other samples in a medical transport crate—which was nothing more than a glorified cooler—and hand-carried by Dr. Pirmal's assistant, Trent, to the Quark Diagnostics office just a few blocks away. He, like so many of the pier residents, was a recoveree, and as such, was thrilled to be of service in such an important endeavor as the transport of blood samples.

Trent's younger sister had died from Crown Royale three weeks earlier. She hadn't been high risk, but sometimes it happens that way—it just hits you wrong. Trent's grief was unbearable to the point that he had to end it in any way that he could. He knew the best way to do that would be to catch Crown Royale himself—because everyone knew the disease transformed emotional pain into something much more palatable. He had, of course, heard the conspiracy talk of body snatching—a narrative that was starting to slip into the mainstream. It concerned him, but he found fear easier to deal with than grief.

He had sought out the sick, contracted the disease, and achieved the desired result. No body snatching, just a glorious shift in perspective. Now his grief was gone, leaving only the love and memory of his sister. He vowed to go on for both of them, to keep her alive through his actions, not the least of which was carrying blood samples from the pier to Quark Diagnostics—the first stop on the way to the lab.

As was his habit, he stopped at a street vendor on the way to buy some food—two hot dogs. He always bought two: one for himself and one for his lost sister. The second he would give to someone who looked like they'd appreciate it.

But today he picked the wrong person. A gaunt man standing at the lip of an alley, sunken eyes, antsy demeanor. He was either a junkie waiting for a fix, or a dealer waiting for a junkie waiting for a fix. Either way, he looked hungry. So Trent held out the hot dog to him.

"For you," Trent said. "Just because."

Perhaps it was the look in Trent's eyes, or just the sincerity of the gesture that telegraphed to the man that Trent was a recoveree. Because he turned on Trent with sudden fury.

"I don't want your goddamn hot dog, you freak!" He slapped it out of Trent's hand—and when Trent reflexively held out the other, the man pulled him into the alley and proceeded to beat the crap out of him.

"You Crown-case! You damn CR zombie! You worthless, diseased waste of life!"

The beating wasn't pleasant, but Trent was more concerned about the cooler, which he had dropped when the man grabbed him. Trent kept trying to get back to it, but the man had an unhealthy amount of rage. He kept hitting and kicking Trent until both were exhausted.

"Go on, get out of here," the angry man said with his final kick. "Go back to whatever hellhole you came from."

Trent scrambled away, knowing he had a broken rib or two and possibly internal bleeding. But that didn't matter right now. What mattered was delivering the blood samples.

As the cooler was magnetically sealed, and could only be opened at the lab, Trent had no way of knowing that one of the three vials inside had broken.

When the official courier van arrived at the Quark Diagnostics office a few minutes later, the courier noticed there was a guy there who looked in serious need of first aid, but she also knew it wasn't her concern. All she cared about was picking up medical crates from Quark's many offices, and getting them to the lab on schedule. "You should call an ambulance for this dude," she said to the receptionist, and then washed her hands of it.

The courier was not a recoveree. She double-masked in hopes of never getting the disease, because even though she knew the virus wasn't actually a spider, just the idea of spiders in her blood was a deterrent enough. She wished she could just go into isolation, but her job was, if not frontline, then second-line in the face of the pandemic. Medical crap needed to move—she just wished she wasn't the one who had to move it.

As the van turned onto Market Street, the courier found herself distracted by a jumbotron screen that wrapped around a downtown building. A news report showed images of riots in Malaysia—something about the king recovering from Crown Royale and attempting to make sweeping changes. With larger-than-life scenes of Malaysian mayhem stealing her attention, it was no wonder she rear-ended the Mercedes. In an instant, the guy stormed out of his car in a dramatic display of outrage. She dealt with Mr. Mercedes as quickly as she could, then went to restack the single cooler that had fallen in the accident.

Since it was still sealed, she had no way of knowing that the second of three vials inside had shattered.

Meanwhile, Mr. Mercedes drove off, cursing his luck. The damn car had just been repaired, and now this! Until that moment, he wasn't sure what he was going to do with the upcoming weekend, but this sealed it. He was going to get out there and enjoy himself on his new sailboat. Because after today, the universe owed him, and the universe was going to pay up.

Ten minutes later the medical crates were delivered to the lab.

The tech who received them hated his job, and just wanted to go home and work out his latest Dungeons & Dragons campaign. The game, which had always been in person, was now going virtual—a headache on every level. Because not only did you need to create digital assets, but people cheated. Dice rolls could be faked, and he didn't trust dice-rolling apps—too easy to hack. Only when he could see the dice fall from his own hand with his own eyes did he trust them. Because dice rolls were everything. When Einstein said, "God does not play dice," he clearly had never played an RPG.

The lab tech's day became one shade more dismal when he opened the seal on one of the crates to find two of three blood vials shattered. It required a full biohazard cleanup. Such a nuisance. He cleaned the crate, and removed the one surviving vial, noting the name on its label.

Mariel Mudroch. Funny name.

He sent the vial in for analysis, never considering how it had been saved by random chance—and how a roll of dice could change not just the course of a game, but the course of everything.

15
The Lemming Paradox

It was a combination of inexperience, foolishness, and old-fashioned hubris that led to the sailboat mishap. Although "mishap" was an understatement. Those who had not yet had Crown Royale might call it a disaster.

A father and his two sons. A film director with an untamable ego, but also desperate to assuage his guilt at being away from home for months at a time. A man struggling to maintain his relationship with his sons. He thought he'd wow them with an early morning ride across the bay on a small sailboat he had recently acquired.

He thought he was a skilled sailor. He was not.

He thought the universe owed him a better day than yesterday. The universe saw it differently.

And so, when a powerful gust of wind came out of nowhere, the man didn't know how to position the sail to withstand it. The boat went keel-up, dumping him and his sons into the drink.

Had the boat capsized anywhere else in the bay, the outcome would have been very different. But as fate would have it, the accident occurred a hundred yards from Delberg Zello's pier.

Rón had woken early. He wanted to experience the color of the sky at dawn. He stood facing east, and marveled at how the inky darkness of night gave way to a ribbon of deep blue set against the jagged silhouette of the Sierra Madre. *Ultramarine.* The color of dawn. It was proof to Rón that magic was real—for what else but magic could create such an impossible hue?

He stood there gazing long after the rest of the sky awoke, and all the stars had winked out in deference to the sun. Soon only Venus still stood stalwart in the heavens, held in the swooping swayback cradle of the Golden Gate Bridge, dimming as the day brightened.

Others were up now, the city shrugging itself conscious. Joggers ran along the path toward Crissy Field, and the Presidio beyond, far enough apart to stave off their anxiety. People pooled at bus stops, each a socially-distanced nebula of souls, rather than the usual compacted crowd.

There was a yoga class on the pier. It hadn't started as such. Just one guy doing yoga, but apparently more people joined him each day, turning him into their accidental guru—because once you recovered from Crown Royale, you no longer cared how stupid you looked trying to fold yourself into lotus position.

Rón hadn't wanted to wake Mariel, but Fallon was an early riser. He saw Rón standing alone, and was thoughtful enough to bring him a Danish.

"Thought you might want something solid," he said. "New recoverees sometimes forget to eat."

"Really?" Rón couldn't remember if he'd missed a meal since he'd been conscious. He took a bite of the Danish, and he could swear his heart stopped for a moment. The blend of flavors was exquisite. The sweet crispness of the crust. The tang of the cherry-cheese center. He groaned with pleasure—he couldn't help it.

"I know, right?" said Fallon, with a grin. "Crown Royale supercharges taste buds. Everything's more intense."

Rón had to stop himself from wolfing it down. He wanted to taste every last bit of it.

"Zee keeps people on dull food for the first few days post-recovery—so it's not too much of a shock," said Fallon. "You want another one?"

Rón shook his head, worried that any more flavor would melt his brain. "It's like seeing blue all over again."

Fallon laughed and shook his head. "I'll never forget that look on your face when you first got gobsmacked by the sky!"

That's when a woman started yelling. She had been unsuccessfully fishing at the very end of the pier, when she began pointing out into the bay.

"Oh my God!" she yelled. "That boat just flipped over! Oh my God! Those poor people!"

The yoga group, and several others who had been greeting the morning in their own particular ways, followed her pointing finger to the foundering sailboat, its keel turned skyward like a whale fin. There were three orange life vests in the water clamped over three bobbing figures, but the current was swift and carrying them, and the boat, west toward the Golden Gate Bridge, and the sea beyond. One of the three had been thrown a short distance when the boat had capsized and was drifting farther and farther away.

"Help!" the child screamed. "Daddy, help!"

The father, leaving one child clinging to the boat, tried to swim to his other son.

No one expected what happened next. But in retrospect, it was the obvious consequence of two converging forces: the chaotic churn of nature, and the irresistible command of Crown Royale.

In the blink of an eye, the simple silent peace of the pier was replaced by a siren's call that few could resist.

The woman dropped her fishing pole and without the slightest hesitation threw herself into the bay. The yoga guru jumped in right behind her. Then a woman who had been walking her Pomeranian dropped the leash, and dove in the water, leaving the dog barking in indignant complaint.

The one boy and his father were being swept away by the waters—and the capsized boat, with the second child clinging to it, was being carried west—because the tide was going out, and with it half the water in the bay.

"We have to do something!" said Fallon, even though there were already half a dozen people in the water swimming toward the capsized boat.

Rón couldn't say he felt horrified by the sight of the foundering boat and its struggling passengers. Horror was no longer in his emotional toolbox. What he felt was . . . *lift*. That was the best way he could describe it. The way an airplane wing must, by the very laws of physics, rise to fill the zone of low pressure above its leading edge. The expanse between Rón and those people in peril was the vacuum, and he had no choice but to fill it.

Rón didn't think; he just acted—an instinct more imperious than self-preservation. With barely five steps to his runway, he launched himself airborne.

Mariel awoke to a commotion. The "tent-in-waiting," which she shared with a slew of other people who had been exposed to Crown Royale but had yet to catch it, was empty. Through the tent flap, she saw people running. Forcing wakefulness to the rest of her body, she left, still in her pajamas, and followed the flow of people into a starkly bright morning.

Something was happening in the bay. She had yet to grasp what it might be, except to see that there were people swimming away from the pier.

"Rón?"

She saw him for an instant at the end of the pier, but then she blinked, and he was gone, as if he had vanished from existence. That's what her half-conscious brain told her, because it was just as unlikely as the alternative: that he had jumped into the water. But as strange as that seemed, she realized that was exactly what he had done, and others were jumping in behind him.

"It's terrible," someone said to her, pointing into the bay. "That boat turned over! People could drown."

When Mariel saw the overturned sailboat, she began to feel a sense of dread. Not for the people who were on that boat, but for everyone else.

Zee arrived, and there was a strange look in his eyes. They were fixed on the hull of that sailboat. He, too, began moving toward the end of the pier.

"I've got to save them," he mumbled. "I've got to save them. . . ."

But Mariel knew the bay. She knew how treacherous and unforgiving it was. Every day, bodies were being pulled out, or washed up on the shore—people who fell or jumped on a lark, not realizing that going in was a very different affair than getting out. Nearly a dozen people from the collective were already in the water, with more joining them by the second.

She had to grab Zee to stop his forward momentum, physically digging her heels in, and standing in front of him.

"You can't let them do this!" she shouted.

"Out of the way, Mariel. I've got to go in. Those poor people! They need my help!"

Still, Mariel held him back. "Call 911! They'll send the coast guard."

"Don't you understand?" he said, trying to pivot around her.

Then she saw a woman, heavyset and out of breath, jogging to the end of the pier and going in. Clearly, the woman did not have the stamina for a swim of any length.

That's when Mariel realized . . .

Recoverees! They're all recoverees!

It was too much for her mind to make sense of in the moment, but she knew what she had to do. She hauled back her hand and smacked it across Delberg Zello's face as hard as she could, to snap him out of his righteous trance, and began screaming at him at the top of her lungs.

"WE NEED YOU HERE! WE ALL NEED YOU! YOUR PEOPLE ARE GOING TO DIE IF YOU DON'T STOP THEM FROM JUMPING! DO YOU UNDERSTAND?"

He was bewildered now, as if coming out of a dream. Good! Mariel had hooked him; now she had to reel him in. This time she spoke quietly, nearly whispering, trying to be that voice inside his own head.

"You have a purpose here, and it's not in the water. This is out of control, and you're the only one who can rein it in."

Finally, he came around. "Yes. Yes, I see that. I see that

now. . . ." It was like getting a freight car to start rolling, but once he had committed, he became a commanding presence once more.

"Everyone! Everyone!" he yelled. "Listen to me. There are enough people swimming to the boat. Hold your positions. No one else gets into the water."

And although people had turned to him, they didn't seem convinced.

"That's an order!" he said. It was the first time Mariel had ever heard him give an order. Then, when yet another person jumped in, he appealed to the ones who were standing still, "Those of you who have not had Crown Royale, hold back the recoverees! Stop them from jumping! Do it!"

And so, with the help of the noninfected, no one else went into the bay. But for those already swimming to the capsized boat, there was nothing that could keep them from their mission of mercy.

When Rón first hit the water, the cold stole his breath away, like a million needles against his skin. He never realized how cold the bay was, even in summer. And the saltiness—it was as if he had shoved an entire salt brick into his mouth. His eyes stung from it. He gagged and coughed up a lungful of the bay.

"You okay?" he heard Fallon say from somewhere nearby. "We gotta hurry!"

It took a few moments to orient himself and track the position of the upturned sailboat, seeming so much farther away now. Rón was not the strongest swimmer, but he could manage. His feet felt heavy, and so he kicked off his shoes to keep them from dragging him down.

Fallon, who had jumped in first, was dog-paddling, struggling to keep his head above water.

"Your shoes!" Rón told him. "Get rid of them."

Fallon floundered for a moment, then suddenly was bobbing a little higher in the water. "Thanks!"

Arm over arm. Kick, kick, kick.

Rón focused on the simple motions that suddenly didn't seem so simple at all. His calves were cramping from the cold. His fingers ached. He thought cold water would make him numb, but it hadn't yet. It just hurt. He thought to all the failed escape attempts from Alcatraz back in the day. As he recalled, no one ever made it. San Francisco Bay was the cruelest of jailors.

Yet in spite of it, Rón wasn't afraid. Not at all. He felt only determination—and that determination was inching him closer to the capsized boat, where one child still clung to the hull. Most of the other recoverees were splashing their way toward the father and son caught in the center of the riptide, all of them calling out to comfort the two. *"Don't worry!"* Cough, cough. *"We'll save you!"* Cough, cough. *"We're almost there!"*

Fallon was having trouble keeping up with Rón, huffing and puffing as he paddled.

"You okay, Fallon?"

"Peachy!"

With so few of the others heading toward the boat where the other boy clung, Rón changed his angle and tried to take advantage of the current, letting it pull him on an intercept course with the capsized boat and the lone child. It seemed his every muscle was cramping now. The arch in his left foot screamed in pain—his toes being pulled toward his heel as if his muscles were trying to fold his foot in half. His biceps had contracted to knots—but he got there. He finally reached the boy, who was shivering nonstop. His lips were purple, and he was nearly choked out by the life vest around his neck.

"I've got you," said Rón.

"But my dad and Brando . . ."

"Don't worry—my friends are on it."

Then it became clear that this boy wasn't the one in dire need of saving, because Rón, completely spent, began to sink beneath the surface.

"Here!" the boy said, and, grabbing one of Rón's hands, he placed it on a metal grip on the edge of the capsized boat. It took all Rón's strength to force his stiff fingers to close over the bar.

Soon others arrived, all struggling to cling to the boat, but telling the boy they were there to save him, even as they fought to keep their own heads above water.

When Rón looked up, he could see they were already under the bridge, with the open sea beyond.

"Are there sharks?" the boy asked, now even more terrified.

The question made Rón laugh. "I'm the shark," he said. "Tiburón Tigre! A tiger shark! I'll scare all the other ones away."

Although it felt like forever, the coast guard arrived just a few minutes later, and rescued everyone clinging to the sailboat. A second cutter went after everyone else. Soon Rón was wrapped in a thermal blanket on the deck, against a bulkhead, shielded from the wind. They had given him dry, if somewhat ill-fitting, clothes. A generic pair of jeans and a flannel shirt. He still couldn't get warm, but that was okay. The cold would pass. The cup of hot coffee they gave him kept sloshing out of his shaking hand, but they refilled it, and he sipped until his hands settled from shakes to shivers.

"What's your name, son?" one of the officers asked.

Rón made sure to keep his wet hair dangling in front of his face. "Austin Vail," he said, making it up on the spot. Austin was a classmate he used to have a bro-crush on, and Vail was his favorite place to ski—and the last place he ever felt anywhere near this cold.

The officer logged the name and moved on, but before he did, Rón grabbed his sleeve. "Hey—I had a friend. His name is Fallon. I didn't see you pick him up."

"Other boat," the man said, with enough confidence to let Rón get back to nursing his coffee.

There were police, and ambulances, and reporters waiting when the two coast guard boats pulled in. Delberg Zello was there as well, and although the reporters questioned him and goaded him to answer, he said nothing. Some news outlets were trying to characterize the Pier Peer Collective as an accident waiting to happen. Others were trying to paint it as a gathering of angels. Maybe both were true.

The focus was on the film director and his sons. The man was famous for bad action movies that everyone, for some inexplicable reason, still went to see. The fact that he wasn't dead was almost as newsworthy as him actually dying.

With all the attention on him, no one noticed the teenaged boy in jeans and a flannel shirt slipping away into the crowd.

Mariel and the others had watched from the end of the pier as the two coast guard boats arrived at the scene and plucked people out of the water—but it was too far away to see much of anything. Someone had binoculars, but it was still impossible to see faces. The only one they knew for sure was saved was the yoga guru, whose bright green pants could probably be spotted from orbit. He had been clinging to the capsized boat—which Mariel had last seen Rón swimming toward. The other coast guard boat was motoring farther west—almost to the open sea—to save others.

Zee had left the pier to be in attendance when the coast guard boats docked, leaving everyone else to wait for news.

Now Mariel paced anxiously at the entrance to the pier, only the worst-case scenarios playing in her head. She was worried, she was angry, but mostly she felt powerless—and that was a feeling Mariel couldn't abide. Even when she was living in the car with her mother, even when they had no idea where their next meal was coming from, Mariel managed never to feel the kind of helplessness that left you uselessly wringing your hands like some damsel in distress. The way she saw it, distress was a punching bag you pummeled until it burst. But now it was pummeling her.

Rón was the first to arrive back at the pier, and was alone. Tunnel vision blocked everything else out the moment she saw him. She pushed past the others to throw her arms around him, relieved that she no longer felt helpless, but also a bit furious that he had made her feel so. She kept her anger to herself, though. He had been through enough.

"You're still so cold," she noted as she held him.

"Needed you to warm me up."

Which she was more than happy to do.

. . .

In the end there were ten survivors. The father and both of his sons—suffering from hypothermia, but alive thanks to their life vests—and the seven who had clung to the capsized boat. None of the others made it. The coast guard was pulling bodies out of the water for hours.

They had yet to have a final body count, but by the time Delberg Zello returned to the pier, he knew exactly how many were lost, and who they were, because they were all his people.

Twelve souls died that day. One for each month of the year, for each sign of the zodiac, for each of the apostles, for each note on the whole-tone scale. Delberg tried to find meaning in the pattern. To seize on to the number as if it were somehow important. He didn't believe it for an instant, but it felt good to find order in the chaos that death invariably brings.

He gathered everyone on the pier, so he could respectfully call out the names of the dead.

"Kelly Adaya . . . Dawn Carvallo . . . Carter Cohen . . ."

Zee wanted to blame himself but couldn't. He wanted to cry, but couldn't do that, either. His inner place of peace wouldn't allow it. Would the dead want his tears, he wondered? Or his praise for being noble enough to sacrifice themselves, giving themselves fully and completely to the rescue of others?

"Alexander Crowder . . . Gonzalo Del Rio . . . Yusra Farid . . ."

He would have been one of them, if Mariel Mudroch hadn't stopped him. In fact, he would have been the first to drown, because Delberg Zello had never learned to swim. Even so, he would have jumped in to save those people anyway, had Mariel not physically stood in his way, reminding him that, yes, there was greater good, but there was also a *greater* greater good.

"Emily Foreman . . . Linda Hokama . . . Wallace McDaniel . . ."

The greatest good that Delberg Zello could provide was leadership in a catastrophe. He saved countless lives that day by preventing others from leaping into the water after it was clear it was only making matters worse.

"Barton Oldbear . . . Kris Wasilak . . . and Fallon York."

Delberg knew he was in debt to Mariel for what she had done. He wished he could repay her by making her life easier, but he had a suspicion that things would only get harder for her.

At the mention of Fallon's name, Mariel gripped Rón's hand tighter. She had a feeling it was coming. Fallon was so thin— skin and bones—hypothermia would have claimed him long before the coast guard arrived. Her eyes filled with tears. But Rón never wept. And didn't speak of it until later that evening.

"I know I should feel sad about Fallon and the others . . . but I don't. Instead I feel grateful to have known them," he told her. "Is that terrible?"

Mariel just held him, saying nothing because it was a question she couldn't answer.

16
The Things That Cling to Us

"Everything in life's got its lesson," said Zee. "If you take the time to sift it out."

It was two days after the sailboat incident, and a day before Mariel's blood work was due back. Rón was up early again to see the aquamarine of dawn, and decided he would do it every day, as a tribute to Fallon, who was there when he first saw the blueness of the sky. But today the sky did not oblige. It was overcast and gray. He had hoped Mariel would wake up early enough to join him so they could look at nothing in particular together, but he already knew she was not an early riser. Instead, Zee grabbed Rón to help with some pier rehabilitation. They took a rowboat out under the pier where the pilings stood like a forest. Half of them were wood, half were concrete. Zee was interested in the wooden ones.

"Take a look at these pilings. The concrete ones do fine, but the old wooden ones need some loving."

He took a hammer and chisel to the closest one, and carefully began to remove barnacles. This was something he did every day when the tide was going out. He could have assigned a work detail, but this was *his* pier. *His* problem. Rón also suspected the pilings were Zee's version of a Zen garden.

"We recoverees—we're like the concrete piers," Zee said. "The things that cling to us don't hurt us anymore. But everyone else—they're still wood. Need to be cared for. Need to be treated with tenderness and compassion. Even if they're cruel to us."

He handed Rón the hammer and chisel, giving him a chance. "Things might not hurt us, but they do kill us," Rón pointed out.

Zee sighed. The sailboat mishap was still fresh in both of their minds.

"The news outlets have already turned what happened into a 'syndrome,'" said Zee. "They're calling it 'The Lemming Paradox.' Apparently this isn't the first time it's happened. Somewhere in South Dakota, half a dozen people drowned, jumping in after a dog that fell into a flooded river. And in Japan, four recoverees went out a window to talk someone in from a ledge. Three of them fell."

Rón shivered, and not just from the chill of the morning. If he had been there, would he have climbed out on that ledge, just as he had jumped into the water the other day? Would he have had the willpower to stop himself?

"People aren't used to it, is all; that overwhelming need to help others," said Zee, as he slathered sealant on the raw wood. "This is just growing pains. As more and more people get over Crown Royale, it'll settle."

Rón nodded, realizing the truth of it. The way Rón saw it, civilization was a balance between self-interest and altruism; self-preservation and self-sacrifice. But in recent years, the balance had shifted toward selfishness. Maybe Crown Royale was nature's way of trying to shift it back.

"We've always had to fight our basic instincts," Rón said. "Now that our instincts have changed, we have to learn to fight them all over again."

"Exactly right," said Zee. "It'll take time and some hurt along the way. Like I said, growing pains. But the folks who are against us . . . they'll try to use things like this to skewer us. We can't let them."

They worked the piles in silence, except for the occasional nature-of-the-universe statement from Zee. Rón knew his purpose here today was to listen. To be a sounding board for Zee to work through the heaviest of his thoughts. But Rón had his own thoughts too.

"Since we last talked, I've been thinking about all of this," Rón finally said. "All the things we're meant to do. Meant to be." Rón paused to chisel off another barnacle and drop it in the collection bucket, while Zee cauterized the wounded wood with sealant. "And I can't stop thinking about that father and his sailboat. How, if he were a recoveree, the other day never would have happened. He never would have taken his kids out there like that. If he were a recoveree, he would have put their safety above his own pride."

Zee grinned, appreciating the perspective. "Reminds me of *my* father. Never there, but when he was, he was always over-compensating. Superdad, twice a year." Zee shook his head at the memory. "You're right—if that guy saw a bigger picture—felt more connected—he never would've been so reckless."

Rón thought to his own father, who, in spite of his ridiculous schedule, was always there for Rón. Sometimes to a fault. He felt a faint pang of regret, knowing his father was suffering from Rón's mysterious absence. But now regret never lasted long enough to have a foothold.

"Not that we recoverees don't do dumb things," continued

Zee. "I mean, look at all the people we lost in the bay. But even the dumb things we do are somehow . . ."

"Wiser?" suggested Rón.

Zee took a moment to weigh the thought. "Wisdom's something you only see looking back. So I suppose time will tell." Then Zee paused for a moment, and took a good look at Rón. "You haven't tested negative yet, have you?"

"No," Rón told him. "I should have days ago, but I haven't."

Zee nodded, pensive. "I've been looking into it. Turns out there are some people—seems to be those who were highest risk—that never stop shedding the virus even after they've fully recovered. They become 'alpha-spreaders.'"

Rón had heard rumors of this, but when it came to Crown Royale, he'd learned you couldn't trust rumors. "You think I'm one of those?"

"Could be," Zee acknowledged. "Could be." Then he slathered sealant over another raw patch of wood.

Immune.

The results came back the next day, and Mariel was immune.

She didn't want to believe it, but the results were conclusive.

"Who can say why these things are?" Dr. Pirmal said to Mariel. The woman spoke with an Indian accent that was both gentle and a bit musical. Somehow it made her words seem more comforting. "Nature is a balance; for every malady there will be some with natural immunity," she said, but added, "although you are the first I've heard of with Crown Royale resistance."

It made Mariel grit her teeth. "I always seem to win the wrong lottery."

"Now, don't be that way," chided Dr. Pirmal. "Be happy you never have to suffer the fever and all its misery."

After her exam, Mariel walked with Rón, hand in hand, to the end of the pier in silence that Mariel didn't care to break, and that Rón didn't need to.

They stopped at the end of the pier, looking off toward Alcatraz and the North Bay beyond.

"This is where I said goodbye to my mom," Mariel said, almost subconsciously brushing a hand across her shirt as if the ash were still there.

"Immunity isn't . . . terrible," Rón reminded her. "Just because you won't always be happy, doesn't mean you'll never be happy."

There was truth in that. And she *was* happy here with Rón, and with Zee, and with all the people in the Pier Peer Collective who had so warmly welcomed her. But she also knew there would be this one thing forever keeping her apart from recoverees. Even her fellow tilers looked at her with sympathy that bordered on pity.

"Poor Mariel," their eyes said. *"She'll never know. . . . She'll never know. . . ."*

After Mariel left to begin her shift at the mosaic path, Rón found Zee sitting alone on the western edge of the pier, a faint smile on his face. Some might call it vacant; others would argue that it was content. It all depended on which side of Crown Royale you were on. Rón came over to sit with him, just to give him some company.

They sat there in silence for a time, looking out toward

the distant silhouette of Alcatraz Island. "Alcatraz" was Spanish for "albatross," but in American culture it had come to mean something entirely different. Sometimes Rón marveled at the weight of words.

"You know what the most successful bacteria is, Mr. Escobedo?" Zee asked, out of nowhere. He didn't wait for a response. "It's gut bacteria—the shit in your intestines, literally. Without it, we die—and on top of that, it fights other bacteria that tries to get in." Zee chuckled at the irony. "We bust our asses killing bacteria left and right, and yet with the stuff in our guts, we do everything we can to keep it alive. Symbiosis, it's called. Two forms of life helping one another to survive. I've come to think Crown Royale is like that."

"Viruses aren't bacteria," Rón pointed out.

Zee acknowledged the observation with a nod. "I know that—we *all* know that by now," said Zee. "A virus is just a string of DNA that somehow got programmed to reproduce itself. Not exactly alive, but not exactly dead, either—microscopic zombies, the lot of them."

It made Rón think about how there were people out there who called recoverees zombies. He didn't feel like a zombie. If he were one, he wouldn't feel, period. But how do you convince others you're alive, when they start to believe you're not?

"So what's the most successful virus, do you think?" Zee asked "Go on, take a guess."

"Ebola?" suggested Rón. He knew it had a 90 percent mortality rate. It was a virus you didn't want to mess with.

"Nope," said Zee. "Ebola kills people too quick to spread beyond the villages unlucky enough to get it. And COVID? Not all that successful, either, if you ask me. Sure, it was highly contagious, but, see, it didn't come in graceful. It attacked us, made us go to war with it—and if you haven't noticed, we human beings are pretty good at war. In the end, maybe we didn't eradicate it, but we subdued it, domesticated it. Made it our bitch."

Zee picked up a stone from the pier and tossed it into the water, watching the ripple it made spread outward toward Alcatraz. "No, a successful virus isn't one we go to war with; it's one we invite in. It's one we want to give to people we love, not because it makes us do it against our will, but because we *choose* to—because it genuinely makes our lives better." He grinned, and patted his stomach "Like nice, healthy, gut bacteria." Then he made eye contact with Rón. First time since sitting there. "A virus that's that evolved can easily infect the entire world," Zee said.

"That might not be a bad thing," answered Rón.

It made Zee smile. "We think alike, you and me," he said. "Your dad, he doesn't think like that, though, does he?"

Rón sighed. "He's scared."

"Like a lot of people. And I get it. They're afraid what they'll lose isn't worth what they'll gain. But that's just because they don't know—*won't* know—until they're on the other side of it. You hear what I'm saying?"

Rón responded by throwing his own stone into the bay.

"I'm still testing positive," he told Zee. "You're right—I think I'm an alpha-spreader."

Zee wasn't at all surprised by Rón's assessment. "If that's the case, then in the spirit of public safety, you shouldn't leave the pier. . . . Unless . . ." He let the thought hang.

"Unless?" Rón prompted, already sensing where this was

going. But Zee wasn't about to say what he was thinking. He wanted Rón to say it himself.

"Unless I lean into it," said Rón.

Zee took a deep breath, maybe a bit scared himself by the weight of those particular words. "If you go out there, just about one in every twenty-five people you come across will die—you know that, right?"

"Yes, but twenty-four will become recoverees," Rón reminded him.

Zee nodded. "They'll know what it means to be truly happy. Maybe for the first time in their lives."

"So will those who die," Rón pointed out. "Just for a moment, maybe, but they'll feel it, and will be thankful."

"And in that moment, they'll forgive you. Every last one of them."

Zee looked off toward Alcatraz. "Imagine being trapped on a rock like that with a view of this amazing city, unable to ever be a part of it. Worst kind of prison, don't you think?" He paused, the beatific expression leaving his face. Rón could tell he said none of this lightly. Delberg Zello, the visionary of the Pier Peer Collective, was taking this moment very, very seriously. "I won't ask you to do anything you don't want to do, son. I won't put you in that position," he told Rón. "But if it's in your heart to go out there into the world . . . I won't stop you."

PART FOUR
LITTLE DOOMSDAYS
ALL THE TIME

Elsewhere:
Louisiana State Penitentiary

This wasn't going to end well.

Nothing in lockup ever does. Arguments end with someone dead. Full-on riots end with dozens of busted heads, broken bones, and solitary. A scrambled brain and solitary make you forget quick what it is that got you rioting. Whatever it is, it never got fixed, and now the guards have an excuse to beat the crap out of the inmates even more than usual.

No, nothing ever ends well in lockup. And now this—this stupid fucking virus.

Iago "The Mast" LeMaster hasn't caught it yet, but fears it's only a matter of time. These things sweep through a prison population like fire through a warehouse—or at least the warehouse he had torched. That was his first business opportunity, by the way. That was what, eight years ago? Not what got him life in prison, though. His incarceration has to do with the special way he has with the ladies. They don't call him "The Mast" for nothing.

Of course, it's not his fault he's in here. Yeah, he did the things they say he did, but like the public defender said, there were extenuating circumstances. Because those women wanted what he had to give. He knew it and knew they did too—but the thing is, women will turn on you, especially when they all get together in a henhouse clutch. Yeah, they took him down good. Lucky for them he's never getting out, because he holds grudges.

So now he's here at Angola—"the Alcatraz of the South"— biggest, meanest, most dangerous prison in the US. Nice to be in a place with such recognition. The Mast figures you take your pride where you can find it.

"This sucks, man. This sucks to high heaven," says his cellmate, Java. His real name is Kofi, but Java goes down smoother. He's talking, like he always is, about Crown Royale.

"Don't gotta tell me," The Mast says. Both wear prison-issued masks, even in their cells, since air filtration isn't exactly a thing at Angola. It's the rule, and although Iago LeMaster is not big on rules, he's going with this one.

Last time, of course, he had resisted masks tooth and nail. It wasn't a manly thing, and stood against everything he believed about freedom—which was ridiculous since freedom is something he'll never see again. Since The Mast runs the white crew at Angola, everyone white had followed his lead.

And that last virus—it had burned through fast, killing a whole bunch of sons a'bitches. The mortality rate was always much higher in prison, for a whole lot of reasons, not the least of which was a convenient lack of medical care. More dead, fewer taxpayer dollars spent on incarceration.

This time he had masked up real quick, and the white contingent followed his lead. He did it primarily for Java, who nearly died when the first wave of COVID came through years back. He had the long syndrome. Left a whole lot of Java ruined, which means he'll be much more susceptible this time. The Mast has a soft spot for his cellmate. Besides, he doesn't want to have to break in a new one.

They're already dividing the prison population between those who have Crown Royale, those who've recovered from it, and those *who are sitting ducks, waiting to get it. Now they have less time out of their cells, like they ever get much time to begin with. There are different mealtimes based on your disease status. The guards wear those freaking high-tech masks with faces, while the inmates get the cheapo ones. Will any of it help? Who the hell knows—it's probably all just a show for the inspectors, to make it seem like they're doing something meaningful.*

Recoverees who've come down off being contagious still aren't allowed with the general population, and for good reason. Because recoverees go all soft in the head. You can beat the daylights out of them, and they won't fight back. They turn the other cheek, like the good book says. Which means they're real good punching bags, since the actual punching bags in the gym are all busted and useless. So the recoverees got to be kept apart for their own safety.

"This disease is inhumane, I tell you. Inhumane!" Java likes to repeat himself for emphasis. "Peoples is sayin' it's actually an alien invasion. An alien invasion! Can you believe that? Like little worms, they get into you, kill you, and take over your body—just snatch it right up, like in those movies. So you might be walking around, but you're actually dead, and it's them inside you insteada you. That's what peoples is sayin'."

"People say a lot of dumb shit. Don't make a lick of it true."

"But don't it feel true, Mast? I mean, you've seen them recoverees. They ain't themselves."

The Mast shrugs. "They're still assholes. Just a different kind."

Iago LeMaster doesn't see himself as an asshole. He's an avenging angel. Even has a full set of tattooed wings on his back. He has a lot of ink, and his ink tells a story. He is, more than any other inmate there, an illustrated man. Names of friends who got dusted; symbols in prominent places that some would call racist, but he calls "race-affirming." On his legs are a couple of scriptures that back up his racial philosophy. On the back of one hand, it says FORGIVEN in gothic lettering, and on the other, it says PUNISHED. So if in a fight, he threw a "forgiveness" punch, you and he were square. If he threw a "punished" punch, there was a whole lot of pain in your future. He figures he should have gone all voodoo, and had a protection spell inked on him somewhere. Hell, anything that might keep this damn virus away.

"If I get this, Mast, I'll prolly die," laments Java.

"Yeah, probably," Mast admits.

"But if it's aliens, then, truth is, I'll be dying anyways, right?"

The Mast makes no comment. The whole alien thing is make-believe for small minds. But he does fear Crown Royale—and although he won't say it out loud, he fears it more than any human being. Because a man can stab you, can shoot you, can knock your teeth out, can even take away your manhood if he's so inclined. But another man can't change who you are inside.

But Crown Royale can.

Iago LeMaster doesn't always like who he is, but he owns it. He owns himself, and he doesn't want some fucking disease to make him disown his own personhood. Because if both his right and left fists are forgiveness, he'd just as soon cut them off.

It's dinnertime for the recoverees. They're down below in the cafeteria, which is in the center of the cellblock atrium, as they call it. "Atrium"—like this is some fancy-ass hotel and not the shithole that it is.

He can hear their ghostly, echoing voices from down below, ris-ing up through the atrium. And those voices are all wrong. They aren't the voices of inmates; their laughter isn't harsh and bitter. The snippets of conversation aren't sensibly angry. No one's posturing;

no one's calculating; no one's showing dominance or submission. It's unnerving.

"Sounds like a damn picnic down there," says Java. "A damn picnic."

There was this one time when The Mast and Java were being marched back to their cell, and he could look over the railing and see them down there—all those recoverees. The Mast was horrified by the integration of it all. Whites, Blacks, Latinos, even Asians—all sitting together, making friendly conversation like they make you do in elementary school. It boiled vitriol up inside him to see it— because The Mast doesn't just hate; he's made a lifestyle out of hatred. He wears it like a wrestler's robe. If that gets taken away, what does he have? So he keeps his mask on, and social distances as best he can, and prays to a God he never actually believed in that this virus will pass him by.

And it had better—because the "picnic" down below now takes a truly stomach-wrenching turn.

Someone has begun singing.

Then the one voice is joined by another and another, exponentially growing until the atrium echoes like some goddamn holy choir.

"Mother of God, no!" *wails Java.* "I can't take this. I can't take it!"

They both know the tune. Everyone does. The recoverees—every last one of them down there—are singing "Hey Jude." The Mast can imagine them linking shoulders, swaying back and forth as they sing.

"Make it stop!" *yowls Java, hands over his ears.* "Make it stop!"

But The Mast knows it's not going to stop. It's only going to get louder.

17
Thornwick Nab

In a cottage on a bluff on the windswept cliffs of Thornwick Nab, England, Dame Glynis Havilland nursed her former butler, Galen Rooks, back to health.

Crown Royale had hit him as hard as it had hit Glynis, but while she stridently chose to face it alone, he had her to guide him through the depths of it.

She had not given it to him—or if she had, it hadn't been intentional, but here they were.

It was a shock that Morgan Willmon-Wu had evicted the Dame from her estate, but not all that surprising.

"I'm sorry, Dame Havilland," her former lawyer had explained, "but Miss Willmon-Wu was very specific as to how the transition should proceed."

And when Glynis heard that she was being banished to the cottage in Thornwick Nab—the least of her real estate possessions—she had laughed at the irony. Glynis had purchased the place on a lark, because it had to be the most miserable cottage, in the most miserable spot she had ever seen. It was round, mostly stone, but with some wood that wasn't handling the harshness of the weather—which accosted the lonely promontory from just about every angle. Its circular structure suggested that someone had started it as a lighthouse, but gave up before getting above the ground floor, deciding that the forlorn bluff didn't deserve the privilege of light.

She had once fantasized about throwing a party there for people she didn't like, and then having it catered with the worst food imaginable, just so she could enjoy the looks on their faces as they tried to stomach both the foul cuisine and the bitter environment.

And now it was home.

The place was filled with the ghosts of last summer's spiders, and the timeless mummies of mice in every nook and cranny. It had unreliable electricity from a single power line; a frail, flaccid thing strung along a series of rotting poles that stood like abandoned crosses on Golgotha.

She couldn't say she deserved any better—not the way she had been to people. Little more than a puckered snarl of contempt. But that was before Crown Royale. Now she was . . . unfamiliar to herself. But she enjoyed every bit of self-discovery that came with her transformation.

The cottage struggled to retain the heat of a single wood-burning stove that served as the cottage's furnace. But she didn't mind all that. She loved the way, when she stood before the stove, her front felt warm, and her back still cold. She loved the powerful crash of the surf below the cliff. She loved the simplicity of the place. And she loved that she was not alone.

"I will not ask you to come with me," she had told Rooks when she found out where she was to be relegated. "My stipend from Miss Willmon-Wu will not support a salary for you. It is enough for subsistence, nothing more."

It only made Rooks chuckle. "That girl is every bit what you wanted her to be."

That was enough to dim Glynis's newfound sense of peace.

But only for a moment. "Was I always that misguided, Galen?"

"Not always. Even in your worst moments, you found ways to deliver to the world something it needed. Even if it was a spanking."

That was how long ago now? Two weeks? Three? A whole month? The sense of time passing also seemed to be a casualty of the disease. She supposed once one stopped living for tomorrow, the relentless cavalcade of days lost its relevance.

Once Galen had recovered from Crown Royale, he smiled more. He was less formal with her. He no longer had his crisp uniform, or an estate to maintain, but he took care of the cottage with the same meticulous attention. And there was plenty to do, or at least there would be. There was a stone enclosure appropriate for sheep and goats. There was a small plot of farmland fit for planting once it was weeded. Glynis could see herself living the remainder of her life here . . . if it weren't for the force of nature she had knowingly unleashed on the world.

Morgan took the Jaguar, as the ride out to Thornwick Nab was long and bumpy, and required a level of comfort. She had fired the chauffeur Dame Havilland had left for her, because he smelled faintly of whiskey, but she didn't feel like driving the distance to Thornwick Nab alone, so she had her new vice president drive her. It allowed her to ride shotgun, which she preferred over the aristocratic rear. Plus, Preston was attractive in a Dickensian sort of way, and wasn't overly chatty.

"Warm enough for you?" was one of the few things he asked the whole trip. "It's a blustery one today."

"It's fine, Preston."

He did apologize a lot for every bump in the road, as if

rural England's potholes were his personal responsibility. And he kept his hands at ten and two the entire trip, as if this were a driving test.

"You can loosen up, Preston," she had told him at one point. "It's not like I'm going to bite." And then she added, "Unless you insist."

Which brought forth a nervous chuckle that she found charming. She might have demoted him to being her driver permanently, but she had to admit, he was holding his own at the Havilland Consortium. He had found a new, more secure location for the research lab than the pitiful place it had been in Manchester, and the lab's relocation was almost complete. He had also, with the help of Blas Escobedo's deep pockets, managed to hire the absolute best epidemiological staff in the world—including the Nobel Prize laureate who had pioneered a cure for anthrax. His awkwardness around Morgan showed that he didn't have a cumbersome ego that got in the way of getting things done. That was fine. She had ego enough for both of them.

Morgan was not going to Thornwick Nab to gloat. All right, maybe she was, but that wasn't the only reason. She wanted to report back—to make sure Dame Havilland knew how well Morgan had taken to her new position. And how much better she was at wielding the position than the old woman had been. She realized that visiting Dame Havilland was the opposite of visiting her mother. Visiting the Dame brought with it a sense of triumph, rather than defeat. Morgan could feel emotionally aloof, rather than emotionally entangled.

She could have assigned the Dame one of the more well-appointed residences. The townhouse in London, perhaps, or the villa in the south of France. But there was something so poetic, so satisfying, seeing the high and mighty humbled. Even though Dame Havilland was the source of all Morgan now had, she couldn't deny the guilty pleasure of seeing Dame Havilland in chilly isolation, one pound from poverty.

What she didn't expect was to see the woman so pleased with her situation. Morgan knew Crown Royale would leave the Dame in a state of banal fulfillment, but Morgan thought it would be in spite of her surroundings, not because of them.

"Come in, come in," she told Morgan cheerfully when she greeted her at the door. "What a surprise! The tea is cold, but I'll brew up a fresh pot."

Her butler was no longer in uniform, but he still stood dutifully at Morgan's arrival and took her coat.

"You do realize that Rooks is no longer on the payroll, don't you?" Morgan pointed out.

"Galen is here of his own volition."

"I serve at Dame Havilland's pleasure," he said.

"Yes . . . and he serves my pleasure quite effectively," the woman said with a salacious little grin.

It made Rooks blush, and made Morgan want to hurl. Old-people sex should be outlawed. Or at least the discussing of it.

"Look at you two!" said Morgan, intentionally unctuous and smarmy. "You're like a couple of newlyweds. In a shack. On a cliff. In the middle of nowhere."

"More like the far edge of nowhere," offered Rooks.

"No—the arsehole of nowhere," said Dame Havilland, still not one to mince words. "But even an arsehole has its place in the grand scheme of things."

It put Morgan off, because she couldn't tell whether or not that was meant as a glancing insult.

They sat down as the water slowly boiled. Morgan now wished she had asked Preston to join her, rather than making him wait in the car—because now she felt like she was being double-teamed by all this unwanted kindness.

"I came to tell you that I'm reopening Havilland Research Lab in a more secure location—and I've found a business partner with bottomless pockets."

The old woman hesitated, but only for a moment. "Is that so?"

"We're one step closer to seeing your dream become a reality."

"My dream?"

"To wipe Crown Royale off the face of the Earth."

"Oh, *that* dream," Dame Havilland said with a dismissive wave. "You know how dreams are; they often vanish the moment we awake."

Morgan didn't think for a minute that Dame Havilland had forgotten anything. Clearly the disease didn't eradicate deceit.

The kettle boiled, and after a few minutes of steeping, Dame Havilland presented Morgan with a steaming cup. "I've brewed us a robust gunpowder tea. It's a stronger-than-usual green tea. Has a bite to it."

The tea was flavorful, which was irritating. Nothing about this hell spot should be anything but insipid. Morgan now found herself far less smug than when she had arrived, and far less satisfied than she wanted to be. When the conversation devolved to the old couple's need for livestock, Morgan decided it was time to leave.

"Do come again," said Dame Havilland, when Morgan got up to go.

"Yes," said Rooks. "But give us some warning, so we can prepare a meal for you."

Morgan strode out to the Jaguar, which was still idling—Preston was as anxious as her to leave this godforsaken place.

"Good visit?"

"Just drive."

Then, as soon as they were on their way, Morgan called the lawyer, and told her to buy the old woman a single goat, and a single chicken. "And make sure they're the most sickly, malnourished animals you can find."

But it didn't do anything to improve Morgan's mood.

After the girl had left, Glynis turned to Galen.

"I believe we're going to have to find a way to stop her."

Galen sighed. "I was afraid you might say that." Then added, "The next time we're going to need to serve her something a little stronger than tea."

Glynis giggled like a schoolgirl. "Galen, don't tease!"

But she knew his suggestion wasn't entirely in jest. She no longer took pleasure in the misfortune of others, but action would need to be taken if Morgan was to be stopped—and it would need to be decisive action. If it came down to it, would Glynis find herself capable of taking the girl's life for the greater good of humanity? She was a changed woman now, and so she had no idea what she could and couldn't do. There was certainly much pondering to be done. But first another cup of tea.

18

The Branches of Every Tomorrow

The boy, his younger brother, and their father, all sat at the far end of a long table to ensure adequate social distance. Although the HEPA filter in the meeting room was state of the art, and the high-powered air conditioner replaced every cubic centimeter of air in the room every ninety seconds, Blas Escobedo still double-masked.

Both masks were his patented digital N95s, which were the most effective on the market. There was always some risk, of course, but what was he to do? Wear a space suit?

In one short month, and through no fault of his own, Blas Escobedo had become the richest man on earth. But all the money in the world made no difference; he'd surrender it all to have a single prayer answered, by any version of God who saw fit to answer it. The finding of his son.

Which was why this meeting was too important to be virtual. It had to be in person.

"Thank you for inviting us to your chalet," the film director said. "Reminds me of a place I once shot a movie at in the Swiss Alps."

Blas smiled politely, but didn't know if it came across, because the two digital masks interfered with one another and were prone to glitching. It was something he needed to get his high-tech wizards to troubleshoot.

"My family has enjoyed your films over the years, Mr. Fjord," Blas said. He personally thought the man couldn't direct himself out of a cardboard box unless a series of explosions were involved, but Blas made a point of never lying, and it was true that certain members of his family enjoyed Brian Fjord's films, when they were too young to know any better.

Although the director had not yet discerned it, this meeting was not about him. However, the elder of his sons, even at eleven, was more intuitive, and suspected as much even before they arrived. The boy didn't know the nature of the summons, but he could sense there was an agenda that wasn't movie related. Which was why it was hard to look the man at the other end of the table in the eye. The glitching mask made it hard too. Sometimes the man's mouth appeared upside down, which was disturbing, and would make his younger brother, Brando, scooch closer to their father.

Hoff knew who the man was, although he didn't think his father knew Blas Escobedo personally. Brian Fjord had many important and famous friends, and loved to mention them in conversation—but Hoff never heard him talk about Blas Escobedo.

"I've always thought you should get involved with the entertainment industry," Fjord said. "I have some ideas—we could find one you like and bring it to the studios. I have an overall deal with Universal but excellent relationships with Paramount, Disney, and all the streamers."

Escobedo nodded. "I'm sure you do. But I asked you to come here because I heard about your ordeal in the bay the other day."

Fjord sighed. "We were lucky."

Escobedo tilted his head in consideration. His mask flashed

teeth that weren't supposed to be there. Brando scooched practically into his father's lap.

"Well, unlucky to capsize, but lucky to be rescued," said Escobedo. "So it balances."

"I suppose. Are you thinking a movie about our ordeal might be worth your attention? I've already floated the idea to Uni."

"'*Floated.*' Good one, Dad," said Hoff, having been schooled in sarcasm from an early age. Escobedo smiled, and this time it showed without any electronic interference. He seemed more real. To Hoff, more real than his father felt sometimes, even without a mask.

"I don't think that's why Mr. Escobedo brought us here," Hoff said. And brought was very literal. Their invitation had arrived with a helicopter.

"All right, then, Blas," said Fjord, calling him by his first name without asking permission. "What's this all about, then?"

"Well, *Brian*," said Escobedo, "your misadventure is certainly theatrical, but I'm not in the business of leaving audiences feeling cold and wet."

While the barb went over Fjord's head, it made Hoff smile. He tried to hide it, but he knew his mask projected it perfectly. It felt like Mr. Escobedo knew his sense of humor, and they were having a good joke on his dad.

"There *is* one part of your experience that I'd like to discuss further," Escobedo said. "I'd like to ask Hoffman a question."

"You can call me 'Hoff.'"

The director began to get uncomfortable. The way he did whenever he felt he was losing control of a situation. He hadn't yet figured out that this was Blas Escobedo's show.

"Hoff, I understand you spoke to the news?"

"Yeah," Hoff said, "they shoved microphones in my face, so I had to say something."

"Could we talk about what you said?"

Just then his father put up a hand. "I'll stop you right there. Am I going to need a lawyer, Mr. Escobedo?" Suddenly he was all formal again.

"Dad," said Hoff in a whisper, but not really, "don't embarrass me."

But Mr. Escobedo laughed at the suggestion of lawyers, which very few people have ever been known to do.

"Don't worry," Escobedo said, "I promise you won't need counsel. Please, if you'll allow me to continue . . ."

Reluctantly, Fjord backed down. Escobedo returned his attention to Hoff.

"You told the reporters that you were afraid of sharks, and that the young man from the pier—the one who helped save you—said he'd protect you."

"Yeah," Hoff answered.

"Could you tell me what else he said?"

Hoff looked to his father for permission, just in case the man felt the need to threaten lawyers again, but his father nodded, so Hoff cleared his throat, and went on. "He said he was a shark, too, and would scare the others away."

"And did he say what kind of shark?"

"Great white, I think," said Hoff—but then he remembered. "No—tiger shark. Definitely, he said tiger shark."

Escobedo leaned back sharply, as if he'd been hit by some invisible blast. "Tiburón Tigre . . ." he mumbled.

"Yeah," Hoff said, "he said that, too. That's Spanish for it, right?"

Then, with his hand visibly shaking, Blas Escobedo picked up a remote and gestured to a TV on the wall. Family pictures began to fill the screen. They all featured a teenaged boy.

"Is this the young man who saved you?"

Hoff squinted. "Could be."

Escobedo scrolled and enlarged a single picture. "How about now?"

The picture was taken at a beach, and the kid in the picture must have just been swimming, because his hair was wet and flattened to his head. Hoff recognized him immediately

"Yeah! Yeah, that's him," said Hoff. "He's a little older now than in the picture, but that's totally him!"

Escobedo turned off the TV and closed his eyes for a long moment, his mask glitching various expressions. Then he stood up and looked at the director.

"Mr. Fjord . . . bring me a script that has a soul—not your usual *basura*," he said. "And in return for your son's cooperation today, I will finance the film." He nodded toward Hoff. "And when you begin filming, Mr. Fjord, remember it was your son who made it happen, through his kind and gentle honesty. Treasure him, Mr. Fjord. Treasure them both."

Then he turned and headed toward the door, but never made it out of the room—because as he touched the doorknob, it seemed he folded in on himself and began sobbing uncontrollably.

"Why is he sad?" Brando asked his father.

And although empathy was not one of Brian Fjord's personal fortes, he rose to the occasion. "I don't think he's crying because he's sad, Brando."

While across the room, leaning on the door for support, Blas

Escobedo wept, offering prayers of thanks in Spanish, in Hebrew, in Latin, in Arabic—to whatever version of God could hear him.

The first morning that Rón didn't wake up before dawn was the first morning he needed to.

"Rón! Get up! We have to go!"

Mariel had shaken him awake—and was by no means gentle about it; her shake meant business.

"Your father's here with the police," she told him, in a sharp whisper. "Zee went to stall them, but it won't last long."

Rón tried to gather a bit more consciousness. "Okay, let me think. . . ."

"No time for that!"

Rón reached to gather his belongings but realized he had none; even the clothes on his back belonged to the collective. Mariel did have a backpack of things that had meaning for her, but other than that, there was nothing to take.

Shouts of general commotion came from the mouth of the pier still far away, but moving closer.

"The entrance to the pier is already blocked," said Mariel. "We can't get out that way—but Zee said there's a rowboat."

Rón nodded. "I know where it is."

Together they slipped out the back of the tent.

Blas Escobedo held his coat closed, fighting the windy morning. Five police cars had blockaded the pier. No one was getting on or off. The vehicles had arrived in silence, no sirens, no spinning lights, in order to maintain the element of surprise. Now a SWAT team was fanning out, weapons raised, doing what SWAT teams do.

There had been several civilian guards at the entrance to the pier when they arrived—presumably to take in newcomers and fend off anyone with malevolent intent. But they had no weapons with which to guard anything.

"Why don't I get Mr. Zello?" The woman's voice was much too calm for the circumstance. "Whatever this is about, I'm sure he can straighten it out."

But the Kevlar-vested officer in charge had simply brushed her aside and signaled his men onto the pier, where they slipped into the nearest tent.

"Everyone up, hands on your head, move it, move it!"

People were hustled out into the open, many of them only half-dressed, one tent after another. Rifles with laser sights left bright red spots darting around like fireflies.

"Hands up! Eyes forward! Move it, move it!"

Between the shouting and the rifles, and the bustle of black-clad officers, Blas found himself embarrassed by the overkill.

"Is this really necessary?" Blas asked the officer in charge.

"Standard procedure in this kind of operation, Mr. Escobedo."

Blas had claimed to the court that Rón had been kidnapped. It was the only way to get a search warrant so quickly. And kidnapping was met with the most severe of responses. If this went south, it would be Blas's fault.

"Look at these people! None of them are armed," he pointed out.

"Appearances can be deceiving," said the officer, way too jaded for anyone's good. "Do you want us to extract your son or not?"

People continued to flow out of the tents, none of them

resisting, none of them exhibiting the normal fright that would accompany a SWAT team siege. Some were even smiling, making small talk with one another as if it were any other morning. Except for the guns in their faces.

Finally, Delberg Zello himself strode forward from the dim recesses of the pier. The ringleader of this cult—because as far as Blas Escobedo was concerned, this *was* a cult.

"A fine morning for a raid! May I ask why our sleep is being disturbed today, officers?" Delberg spread his arms in greeting. "You're welcome to go anywhere you like. Nothing but cooperation here."

Then he saw Blas, and made a turn toward him. Blas quickly masked up—the standard double mask he had been wearing. He wasn't taking any chances.

"Where is my son?" Blas demanded. "I know that he's here, so don't you dare lie."

Zello's smile only broadened. "Ah! So you thought you'd come and free him from our evil clutches!"

"He's a minor. I could have you arrested."

"Go ahead; I'm not stopping you," Zello said. "But I do feel the need to point out that the boy came here of his own free will—and after he recovered, he's the one who chose to stay. No one's keeping him here."

The mention of recovery stuck in Blas's craw like a fishhook.

"So . . . he's had Crown Royale?" Blas asked.

"Been there and back!" Zello said. "All the better for it!"

"Did you know he was high risk? He should have been in a hospital!"

"Our care was as good as anything they could have done

for him in some overcrowded ICU. But it's all moot, as they say, since he's come through it, and he's fine."

"Take me to him!"

Zello looked around, taking in the crowds being rousted out of their tents. The officers were still going through the motions, but seemed much less intense than they had been when they arrived, responding to the calm of the crowds they were herding.

"Well, I'd hate to rob the trophy from this highly motivated team you got here. I'm sure they'll find him fine without my help." He put a hand on the shoulder of the officer in charge. "When you folks are done, feel free to stay for breakfast."

Then he turned and strode back onto the pier, as if his personal bubble were impervious to the commotion around him.

In the forest of concrete and wood below the pier, Rón and Mariel hid from the siege above. Ensconced in the predawn pitch, Mariel navigated using her phone flashlight, while Rón rowed. She had not had actual phone service for months, but the device held all her music, as well as access to the larger world when she happened to catch a whiff of free Wi-Fi. She never thought that the annoying flashlight app—which always seemed to mysteriously come on in her pocket, draining her battery—would ever be a lifesaving tool.

Rón rowed with slow, steady strokes until they were thirty yards from either edge of the pier—so deep that even the breaking dawn couldn't penetrate the rows of pilings. It truly felt like they were in the depths of some urban Mirkwood.

Rón stopped rowing, Mariel turned off her phone light, and they waited, the only sounds the gentle splash of water around them, and the clicks of mussels on the pilings, opening and closing as the bay washed over them.

Mariel could swear that, even in this lightless forest, she could sense Rón's aura. Her mother believed in things like auras and chakras and such. Mariel did not. She wanted to attribute this other-sight to her imagination, and yet . . .

"Our lives begin here," Rón said out of nowhere. A grand statement that might have tickled her had they not been hiding from a raid.

"Shhh," Mariel whispered. "Let's get past this first."

"We already are," he said.

"How can you be so sure?"

"I'm not. But what's the point of worrying about things we can't control?"

And, of course, he was right—but people said things like that all the time. When did it ever stop anyone from worrying?

It did for recoverees, she thought. It gave Mariel a pang of regret, to realize, yet again, that she would never fully surrender her fears the way Rón had.

"All is well, Mariel. You'll see! All is well."

She reached out and found his hand in the darkness without even having to try. Perhaps there was something to this aura business after all.

Early dawn was painting the pier above in shadowy shades of blue. The sun had not yet risen but was on the verge. Still, daylight would not illuminate anything for Blas Escobedo but his failure to find his son.

"Evidence suggests that he left during the night," the lead officer said.

"How could he have known we were coming?"

The lead officer sighed, and Blas knew that sigh marked the end of the operation. "We do have recoverees on the force," the officer said. "It's possible that one of them tipped Zello off, and he told your son."

Which meant that Tiburón could be halfway to anywhere by now.

"We could bring Zello in for questioning," suggested the officer. "Threaten him with charges."

"Threaten him? The man's mind has been eaten by Crown Royale. You make threats, he will just laugh."

"Well, we'll make sure the whole force is on the lookout for your son."

Which Blas knew was nothing but a kiss-off.

"A bit of advice, sir," the officer said. "If and when you find him, he's not going to come willingly. Might I suggest you arm yourself with a nonlethal weapon to incapacitate him long enough to be apprehended? Maybe a Taser."

Blas could only stare in disgusted disbelief. "*Taser?* You think I'd tase my own son?"

"All I'm saying is it's worth having as an option. Just in case. Pepper spray works too."

"We're done here."

He stormed back to his limo, slipped in the back, and slammed the door, "*¡Pinches idiotas!* I ask the city for help, and they tell me to get a Taser." Blas ripped off his masks in frustration. "Get me out of here."

"Yes, sir," said his driver. "To the heliport?"

"Just drive."

As they left, Blas tried to find solace in the fact that the worst of his fears had been assuaged. Not only was Tiburón alive, but he had survived a virus that stood a good chance of killing him. This was a glass half-full, by any accounting.

But Blas knew his son would not be the same after this viral lobotomy. He wouldn't be the TeTe Blas knew. Blas thought back to the time he had held a vigil for Tiburón at the hospital. During that last attempt, Blas had truly thought he might lose him. But now, with Crown Royale decimating the dark, textured corners of his son's soul, there would be no more suicide attempts. Perhaps Blas should be grateful for that—but what was his son now? Fluff like all the others, as insubstantial as cotton candy. Was that a sort of death, too?

And he wept, because, for the life of him, he did not know.

Rón had thought his day of recovery would mark the "before" and "after" of his life. But no; this was the day. Because the branches of Rón's every tomorrow sprouted forth from this moment, this venture into the unknown.

The riskiest part of their operation was slipping out from underneath the pier unseen. Zee didn't come to get them, because the pier was probably still under surveillance. Zee had to go about his normal morning activities.

After three hours, Rón and Mariel dared to row to the foot of the pier, and climb out onto the rocks at its base, half expecting to be apprehended right there. But they weren't. If the police had left a presence on the pier, it was for show. They crab-walked their way out of anyone's possible sight lines, then climbed up to street level at the next pier over, noticed only by the seagulls, who were no one's spies.

Zee had given them a name and address in the Mission

District of a friend who could help them. Val Lazár.

"Excellent!" Rón said. "We pretentious accents need to stick together."

While Rón saw nothing but blue skies ahead, Mariel suffered clouds of doubt and anxiety. "We have to figure out where we go from here," she pointed out, as they made their way, heads lowered and faces shielded, to the Mission District.

"We'll have to stay on the move," Rón said, ducking the question, "because if I stay too long anywhere, my father will find me."

Mariel had to grin. "So you'll keep moving. Like a shark."

"Like a shark," he echoed. Then he thought for a moment and said, "I've been alone a lot of my life, but I want to be—I *need* to be—around people now. *Lots* of people. Because there's tons of good I can do out there, Mariel. Tons of good!"

It wasn't lost on Mariel that he said "I" and not "we." It wasn't until much later that she understood the full resonance of that.

Val Lazár had been an out-of-work hair stylist. A volatile childhood had left them with anger management issues. Hard to keep a job when you'd rather rip out your patrons' hair than style it. But Val's Crown Royale fever had burned away the very concept of anger. Now every place was their happy place.

These days, Val danced in the streets to the delight of passersby, and taught children the joy of movement in a local park, for dance had always been their first love. In a different world it wouldn't pay the bills—especially San Francisco–level bills—but other recoverees were incredibly generous with donations to Val's dancing endeavors.

Even so, Val was more than happy to revisit their old

profession, and give Rón and Mariel complete makeovers for an incognito journey to wherever.

"People pin recognition on simple cues," Val said, sitting Rón down, and studying him. "It's why Superman can be Clark Kent with nothing but context and a pair of god-awful glasses. But the biggest clue . . . is hair!"

They bleached Rón's hair a silvery blond, and cut it short on the sides, with a curling wave above his forehead. Mariel found it sexy in a cologne-ad kind of way.

"And for you! We'll dye your hair black, and pull it back in a single braid," Val told Mariel. "I'd say braided pigtails, but that would be way too Wednesday Addams for my taste. We'll darken those blond eyebrows, too—your own mother won't recognize you!"

Mariel took a deep breath and held her tongue on that one. Val didn't know Mariel's mom had died, and she didn't want to make them feel bad.

In the end, Val was right—Mariel barely recognized herself when it was done.

Rón then took a pair of digital masks and tweaked them to resemble other people's faces. Rón's projected a goatee, and Mariel's showed a pair of pouty rosebud lips that made her laugh every time she caught her own reflection.

"Bravo!" Val said. "You could be anyone, and no one!"

Which Mariel found chilling in some undefinable way.

"We still don't know where we're going," Mariel had to remind Rón, refusing to let the winds of fate passively direct them out the door.

Rón smiled from beneath his platinum coif. "Where do you want to go?"

Mariel immediately found herself beaned by the rebounding question. Her mother never asked where she wanted to go. She just up and went until either they were broke or ran out of gas. As much as she had loved her mother, she hated being subject to Gena's wanderlust whims. Yet, in a sense, being dragged along was Mariel's comfort zone. Suddenly she was standing on a cliff over deep water. Rón was holding out his hand. All she had to do was take hold and jump. And so she did.

"Kalamazoo," she said.

It made him laugh. "Kalamazoo? Why Kalamazoo?"

"Because it's funny." To be honest, she didn't even know where it was.

"All right," Rón said. "It's as good a place as any!"

And just like that, the decision was made.

The plan, if it could even be called a plan, would be to leave toward the end of rush hour that evening, which, even with Crown Royale, was still a relatively busy time in the city. Someone from the pier had donated their car for the cause; a copper Trailblazer—quite the step up for Mariel from the Grinch. Rón did not have a license, but for an entirely different reason than Mariel. Rón lived a chauffeured life, so a license to drive, while desirable, was never urgent. Mariel, on the other hand, was never in the same place long enough to get one. She did have plenty of experience behind the wheel, though—her mother had made sure of that. And come to think of it, her mother didn't have a license either. She had lost it to a DUI years ago.

Zee showed up late that afternoon to check on them, and to give them money and a burner phone. Rón was dozing, presumably because he was exhausted, but Mariel half suspected he was knocked out by the fumes of his bleaching.

"Are you sure you weren't followed?" Mariel asked, which brought forth a smile from Zee.

"Smart to be cautious," he said. "But I took a roundabout way to get here—and had lookouts watching for tails. It's all about having enough eyes."

Then his smile faded, and he got more serious than Zee usually ever got. "Be *his* eyes, Mariel. His own are distracted by all the new he can see. He could miss things. Basic survival sorts of things."

"Survival's my specialty," Mariel told him.

Zee nodded. "I can see that about you. Truth be told, while I hate to see you go, I'm glad you're joining him on this little mission."

"So it's a mission?"

Zee hedged a bit. "More like a calling, I would say."

Mariel shrugged. "Seems to me he just wants to see the world with fresh eyes."

Zee gave her his widest, ingratiating smile. "And what greater calling than seeing all there is to see?"

Even then, Mariel sensed there was more to it. But how could she question it when she was still reeling from the thrill of the jump?

19
Svalbard

The future of planet Earth rests in the middle of a mountain on a remote, windswept island in the arctic circle, five hundred miles north of Norway;

Which is accessible only by a single airstrip that has the distinction of being the northernmost airport in the world;

Where a concrete monolith juts out of the mountain like some ancient alien artifact, standing stark against the flickering aurora borealis;

Where nothing should be expected to survive—and yet, where, in perfect irony, the cold allows life to be protected from nuisances like climate change, nuclear war, and bioterrorism;

The concrete monolith marks the remarkably unremarkable entrance to the Svalbard Global Seed Vault;

Which stores samples of every crop on earth—from a thousand versions of wheat, to heirloom vegetable seeds that no longer exist anywhere else on the planet;

Because, as everyone in the modern world knows, humanity is plagued by more and more of less and less—and for all anyone knows, a lifetime of eating Monsanto-engineered soybeans could leave humans with three heads, each more stupid than the last.

All the more reason to have a genetic safe room for uncorrupted life.

And as it turned out, it was also a perfect space for life that was slightly more corrupt.

"There are little doomsdays all the time, Miss Willmon-Wu."

The curator of the Svalbard Global Seed Vault was a suitably bespectacled man in a suitably white coat, but wore a parka, because the long tunnel from the entrance of the mountain to the vault complex was as cold as the surrounding stone.

"Civil wars that poison the soil, for instance—or commercial farms that kill off crops that indigenous people have been cultivating for thousands of years—these are the things we must protect against, not just global catastrophes."

His name was Dr. Nødtvedt, although Morgan liked to think of him as "Dr. No," since the complex did seem like the lair of a Bond villain. Morgan had no patience for the man. The flight to Svalbard, albeit on her comfortable private jet, was bumpy and unsettling. Apparently, the air around these remote islands was as inhospitable as the islands themselves. So an equally inhospitable academic was the last thing she needed.

"I'm sure your work is very important," said Morgan, intentionally condescending. She could tell it irked him. That made her grin, which irked him even more.

"My point," said Dr. No, "is that a medical research lab has no business being down here, so close to the most precious seeds in the world."

"Dr. Nødtvedt, your seeds are frozen, and in their own sealed chamber, making them more secure than the pharaohs. I'm sure they won't mind noisy neighbors, because—did I forget to mention? They're *seeds*."

Morgan had to admit that Preston had done well in finding this spot. And with Blas Escobedo's checkbook at her disposal, leasing the east wing of the vault complex had been easy. Because even in the rarified air of genetic preservation, money talks. Morgan knew if any of this was going to work, she needed to be taken seriously, and moving the entire research facility to Svalbard wouldn't just bring an added level of security; it would make it clear to everyone involved that she meant business.

"We fear contamination," Nødtvedt huffed.

"Which is exactly why we chose this place," Morgan informed him. "We at the Havilland Consortium take containment protocols very seriously. The last thing we want is another Wuhan."

The very specter of that cowed him to the point of nearly stopping in his tracks. "That was never proven," he mumbled.

"Right," said Morgan. "Well, I guarantee that the work we do here will stay sealed in this mountain until we're ready for it to be safely, and securely, distributed. And your seeds will never know the difference."

After having dispensed with Dr. No, Morgan entered the brand-new laboratory wing of the complex, where she was required to take a decontaminating shower, dress in specially prepared scrubs, and take a state-of-the-art Crown Royale test not yet available to the public. It could detect the disease within an hour of exposure. Although Morgan knew she hadn't been exposed, it was always a relief to see that negative test result.

Once through the full cleansing protocol, she stepped out into the secure area, and was greeted by a woman who wore no mask, since this had to be the safest spot on the planet. But maybe a mask would have been better, because the woman had seriously bad teeth.

"Miss Willmon-Wu, so pleased to finally make your acquaintance," said the woman with an accent that would have been vague to most, but which Morgan immediately pegged as northeastern Dutch. Perhaps from Zwolle, or Groningen. "I am Dr. Annika Bosgraaf, your head virologist."

So, this was the scientist who found a cure for anthrax! You'd think being a Nobel laureate would inspire a person to take care of their oral hygiene.

"Nice to meet you," said Morgan, keeping her thoughts behind her own gracious, and well-maintained, smile.

"Please allow me to give you the grand tour," said Dr. Bosgraaf.

The woman was just one of a dozen virologists, immunologists, and epidemiologists whom Preston had successfully gathered for this project. No second-raters this time. Every member of the new Havilland team had been poached with surgical precision from other companies and even government research facilities—all of which were, no doubt, feeling the pain of the loss. That was another reason why Svalbard was the best place to be; much harder for the staff to be repoached by their former employers while sequestered here.

Bosgraaf began with a tour of the living quarters, sparsely populated at this time of day—although there were no windows to indicate what time of day it might be. There was a common room, with a narrow hallway that led to living quarters. It seemed comfortable, but utilitarian. More like some sort of lunar colony than something you'd find on Earth. "You'll have your own quarters, of course," said Bosgraaf. The woman was under the misapprehension that Morgan was spending the night. This visit was all about getting eyes on the project, making her presence known, and kicking anyone in the ass who wasn't working at 110 percent. That could be done quickly enough that she didn't need to overnight in the bowels of the earth.

They came to a circular staging room where hazmat suits hung on the walls like some sort of postmodern art installation. A single red light gave off an eerie glow above a hatchway that needed to be manually cranked open.

"A low-tech, but completely secure door from the original Seed Vault," Bosgraaf explained. Then she pointed to the red light. "When the red light is on, we need hazmat suits to enter the laboratories below, because our people are actively working in critical areas," Bosgraaf said, taking one suit down and handing it to Morgan, before grabbing one for herself. "Necessary precaution, you understand."

Once in the bright blue coveralls, hoods in place and secure, they cranked open a hatch, and climbed down a steep set of stairs to a brightly lit corridor with glass-windowed labs on either side.

"It's taken some time to get the facility up and running, but we're at full speed now."

It was precisely what Morgan hoped to find. There were at least three scientists in each lab, intently absorbed with microscopes, or computer screens, or test-tube samples. *Here,* thought Morgan, *is where the future of humanity will be decided.* In any other context, the notion would seem absurdly megalomaniacal—but in this case, it was the absolute truth.

Morgan made sure Bosgraaf introduced her to every single member of the team, trying to see if she could find any weak links, but found none. Everyone appeared at the top of their game. It wasn't until they reached the final set of labs that

Morgan realized where the weak link lay—and it wasn't human.

"These are our trial subjects," Bosgraaf said, gesturing through a window to a grid of cages. "Unfortunately, there are very few species of primates that are susceptible to Crown Royale the way humans are," she said. "Capuchin monkeys, and bonobos, mostly."

Morgan was never a fan of animal testing. Scientists who doused puppies' eyes with hair spray for the furtherment of cosmetics deserved their own special corner of hell. To be shared, of course, with rabid activists, who fought animal testing even when it was absolutely necessary to save human lives. On her collegiate debate team, Morgan once argued that animal rights activists should volunteer to substitute for test animals. She won the debate. Needless to say, it didn't mobilize any activists to switch places with the animals they so longed to protect. Such hypocrites.

In the first lab, the monkeys were active and aware of the humans' presence, moving around their cages, vying for attention. In the second lab, the ones that weren't asleep were lackadaisical and lethargic.

"These have been infected and are in the grip of Crown Royale."

Morgan shuddered in spite of herself. Even with her hazmat suit, she was glad there was a window of double-paned glass between her and the infected monkeys.

The third animal lab was the most interesting. The recoverees. Most of these subjects seemed deep in thought, with very human expressions of transcendence—as if each was the first monkey to look up at the stars and consider the concept of eternity. And the rest were just masturbating.

"Will the subjects die?" Morgan asked, annoyed by how much she cared.

"It depends on what we inject them with, and what we need to learn," Bosgraaf said.

Morgan found the whole thing distasteful in spite of how necessary it might be. "But why expose them to Crown Royale before you've developed a test vaccine?" Morgan asked. "It won't help anyone who's already contracted the disease."

"True, but prophylaxis is not the crux of our work here."

That caught Morgan completely by surprise. "Aren't we working to find a vaccine?"

"Not exactly," said the woman, with a sly pause. "Havilland Labs has taken a different approach. I thought you knew that."

Morgan knew *something* about the research was unique, but didn't know what. And although it wasn't Dr. Bosgraaf's fault she didn't know, Morgan decided she hated this woman. "Then what are we doing here if we're not developing a vaccine?"

Then Dr. Bosgraaf explained to Morgan *exactly* what they were doing. She spoke in terms that she probably thought would go over Morgan's head, but they didn't. Morgan understood every last bit of it.

It was chilling and it was perfect. Deliciously perfect.

"How far out are we?" Morgan asked, still breathless from the revelation.

"Months, really," said Bosgraaf.

"Not good enough. We don't have months."

"Well," said Bosgraaf, "things could go much more quickly if . . ." But she didn't finish the sentence—as if saying it out loud might be some sort of blasphemy. She wanted Morgan to take the initiative. And so she did.

"In a perfect world, what is it that you need, Dr. Bosgraaf, to get this done quickly?"

"It wouldn't be exactly legal," Bosgraaf said.

"Who said anything about legal?"

And Dr. Bosgraaf smiled—or at least her eyes smiled, because Morgan couldn't see her horrible teeth through the hazmat mask. Which was a mercy.

20
Flyover

Mariel's road trip with Rón was straight, yet convoluted. Simple, yet surreal. It was thrilling to have a destination, but numbing to have one so pointless as Kalamazoo. Even so, Mariel was determined to enjoy the journey. Zee had given them a burner phone, and promised he would contact them once he found trusted people to give them food and shelter when they arrived in Michigan.

At least it was a goal. Mariel had lived a life without form or substance, surviving between calamities of her mother's own creation. Living hand to mouth had taught Mariel that there were countless hazards between one's hand and one's mouth.

Even so, any momentum was forward momentum.

"This is going to be great," Rón said more than once. "It's already great."

And even if Mariel couldn't catch Crown Royale, she found that his enthusiasm, at least, was contagious.

The only difference between Elko, Nevada, and Las Vegas was seventy-five years. Because seventy-five years ago, Las Vegas was a soulless pit stop with less than twenty-five thousand residents instead of a city of millions, with little more than a post office, a Union Pacific train station, and nothing much going for it besides a little bit of gambling.

The gangster, Ben "Bugsy" Siegel, could have just as easily chosen Elko for his Flamingo casino. But he hadn't. And so, while Las Vegas became one of the most famous cities on the globe, no one who didn't live in Elko had ever even heard of Elko.

"Looks like this place is just waiting to be a ghost town," Mariel commented as she pulled off the highway to get gas. There were signs advertising the lone tourist attraction: an actual working gold mine. But if this had once been a gold-rush town, it was now merely the memory of one. Towns like this rose and fell with the price of gold, and these days the price was down in the dust.

As they drove past one shuttered shop after another, Rón wondered when a town officially died. Was it when the last person moved out, or was it when the town lost the will to live? Elko still seemed to have some kick left in it, though. How much, only time would tell.

They pulled into a Chevron that looked like any one of a thousand gas stations spread out across the highways of America.

"I'll go in and get drinks and snacks," Rón said. In any other circumstance, he would've offered to pump—but this time he left it to Mariel. He had his reasons.

A little electronic bing rang out as he entered the gas station's convenience store—empty except for the clerk. The counter she stood behind had no bulletproof glass partition that you might find in bigger cities. Nothing between her and what few customers came her way.

The woman wore a mask; Rón did not.

He gathered drinks and snacks and brought them to the counter. "This town's a long way from anywhere," Rón commented.

The woman shrugged. "Every town is, depending on how you define 'somewhere.'"

Rón smiled at that. "I suppose you're right. Should I mask up?" Rón asked, pointing at hers.

"Sign on the door says so," said the woman whose name tag said JULIET. "But I ain't gonna turn you in if you don't."

Juliet seemed early twenties going on forty. Like she'd given up waiting for her Romeo, and was now just waiting for something—anything—to happen. It's not that she seemed unhappy. But she did seem spent. Like the closest she had to joy was the memory of having once felt it. It made Rón long to help her.

"Has it been bad here?" Rón asked. "A lot of people catching Crown Royale?"

Juliet shook her head. "We've mostly avoided it. My choir director says our singing's so bad, it can even chase a virus away!"

So, she's in a choir, Rón noted. Open mouths happily expelling air, trusting in the good Lord to keep them safe. Or at least infect them with joy. But God needed a servant to do that.

"You got any masks for sale here?" Rón asked. "I'm fresh out."

"Got some of those cheap paper ones over by the toiletries."

"But what about the kind *you're* wearing?" Rón asked. Clearly, it was an N95, not as effective as his father's digital masks, but, in most cases, they did the job. "What brand is it?" Rón asked. "I'm hoping to order some like that."

She hesitated for a moment and then took the mask off to check the brand name . . .

. . . and the moment she did, Rón slowly, quietly, took a deep breath in, and let it all out, leaning just a couple of inches toward her.

"Says 'Shieldex.'"

"Oh right," said Rón. "Yeah, those are supposed to be good."

He completed his purchase, wished her a pleasant day, and left, the door binging again as he walked out.

And inside Juliet's lungs, happiness began to percolate.

With the rear seats down, the Trailblazer had enough room for them to sleep at night if they spooned. Mariel found it wonderful to be so close as to feel Rón's heartbeat, and the feel of his body against hers was so perfect, she couldn't imagine living without it. The position did leave her arms numb, with pins and needles all night, but it was worth it. Sometimes she would turn to watch him sleep. She caught him smiling in the depths of a dream, and she wondered what warm recoveree dreaming went on in there. Was she a part of it?

Zee had left them with enough cash for hotels, but Mariel insisted they not risk it—at least not for the first few nights. Even with their new looks, fake IDs, and digitally disguised masks, they still looked young enough to attract, if not suspicion, then unwanted scrutiny.

Besides, living out of a car was Mariel's comfort zone. She knew all the tricks of automotive overnighting. You kept at least two windows open a crack, so that the car didn't steam up and make people wonder what was going on in there. You covered yourself with laundry, so if people glanced in, they'd think you were just a pile of clothes. And you always kept a weapon handy.

Mercifully, Gena hadn't owned a gun, because if she had, Mariel was sure one of them would have been accidentally shot. Instead, her mother kept a steak knife in the car, and a tire iron.

Mariel opted for just the tire iron, but never let Rón see that she had it.

Rón took over some of the driving once they made it through the last of the Rockies and the highway in southeast Wyoming became straight enough for someone without much driving experience. A monotonous line to the horizon. The vast part of America that coastal people called "flyover."

Even though the road was straight, Rón's driving was a bit harrowing, because he was still distracted by the scant scenery. A hawk on a power line; a cloud that looked like an outstretched hand; an abandoned railroad depot, which was literally in the middle of nowhere.

"Let's stop and take a look!" Rón said when he saw the old depot, with the exuberance of a five-year-old.

"Let's not," Mariel responded with finality enough to shake the idea out of Rón's head.

At one point, Mariel pulled out the burner phone, to see if they had missed a text or call from Zee.

"Anything?" Rón asked.

"Not yet," she told him. "And I don't want to call him in case your father's monitoring Zee's phone."

"Probably is," Rón said, as casually as he might say, *"Looks like rain."*

Rón's lack of concern was nothing unusual. He was a leaf in the wind now, happy to go wherever it took him. It was as frustrating as it was endearing, and Mariel couldn't help but feel it was almost like being with her mother again—minus the stress, of course. But unlike Gena, Rón Escobedo wasn't feckless. Yes, he was carried by the wind, but that wind had direction and purpose. It was clearly driving him. Or at least something was.

Like the time he had gone AWOL for half an hour in Salt Lake City. Mariel had been on the verge of panic, thinking he'd either been found by his father, or fell off an overpass, or got run over—because living in the moment left you remarkably unaware of the moment ahead. But then he had strolled back without any explanation other than, "I went to explore."

"Without telling me? You can't just wander off like that!"

He held her as if being apart, even for a short time, required catch-up closeness. It wasn't as much to console her as it was a heartfelt appreciation of her concern. "Sorry, I just felt the need. And sometimes it takes over."

A leaf in the wind? More like a sail. Which meant if Rón was a sail, Mariel had to be the rudder.

It wasn't until they crossed into Nebraska that Mariel dared to ask the all-important question that she knew was not even in Rón's mind. In truth, she had no idea what was in Rón's mind now. That scared her just the tiniest bit.

"What will we do when we get to Kalamazoo?" she asked.

It made him grin. "That rhymes," he said. "What will we DO in KalamaZOO? Go to the ZOO, or have dinner for TWO?"

"I'm serious."

Rón shrugged. "It was your suggestion. . . ."

"You're avoiding the question."

"That rhymes too! Now something with digestion!"

"Stop!"

Rón snickered, then finally got serious. "Don't worry," he said. "It's going to take care of itself."

"No, Rón. I've lived on the streets long enough to know

things don't take care of themselves. They only get worse."

He sighed. "I know you don't believe this yet, but we're part of something larger than just you and me. There are going to be . . . *opportunities* you never even imagined waiting for us in Kalamazoo. But mostly between here and there."

His magical thinking was enticing and maybe a little bit addictive, but she had to keep a level head about it all. Did she say she was the rudder on their little ship of fools? She was more like the anchor keeping them from being swept away. Come to think of it, she was always the anchor. She wished she could be cast as something other than that. Her natural immunity meant she would never know what it was like to be the sail. The closest she could come was experiencing that kind of joy vicariously through Rón. So did that mean she was using him? It was a question that tired her more than the journey.

Tiburón Escobedo felt like a prophet of old. Was there anything more wonderful than knowing one's path, one's purpose, in the vast gearwork of the universe? And although he knew all about delusions of grandeur and their dangers, was it a delusion if your calling was truly grand? The world had almost entirely forgotten the simple pleasure of existence. It was well overdue for a reminder.

It meant that he was needed; that his presence was required. That was something new for Rón. He'd always felt himself a passive participant in his privilege—but now he had accepted a task, and he was thankful for it. There were moments he felt so much gratitude, it became overwhelming.

He wanted to share all this with Mariel, who he knew, without a doubt, was his soulmate, but he had yet to find words for the feeling. In time, he knew he would—and it would not only be the right time; it would be perfect. Because although humanity might be broken, the universe was not, and the gears all meshed.

As they neared Omaha, Rón convinced Mariel that they could risk staying at a hotel.

"I owe you at least one night of comfort after dragging you on this trip," he told her.

"You didn't drag me—I wanted to go," she reminded him. "Maybe even more than you did."

He choked up a bit, because he felt his gratitude threatening to overwhelm him again.

They chose a Hyatt downtown. It was late afternoon when they arrived, parking on the street rather than handing the car over to the valet—fewer eyes on them during their stay. Then, as they approached the revolving door at the main entrance, an opportunity presented itself.

There was a woman ahead of them with a rolling suitcase. It was just a small case, but it had lost a wheel and was misbehaving like a petulant toddler. She cursed at it as she tried to drag it into the revolving door, which were never friends to suitcases, even on a good day. The woman was clearly in need of perspective and uplift.

Rón was holding Mariel's hand, but he let go, and sped up his pace toward the revolving door—which was slow and automatic, like the ones they have at airports. To anyone watching, and probably to Mariel as well, it would simply appear that he wanted to help the woman with her carry-on that was carrying on. His momentum took him into the revolving compartment with her, separating him from Mariel, who stepped into the next revolving space behind them.

"Oops," said Rón. "Sorry—it's a little cramped."

"I hate these things," the woman said. It was unclear whether she was talking about the troublesome suitcase or the revolving door.

Then Rón stopped moving, letting his left foot bump into the glass panel behind him—which caused the automatic door to stop revolving, and triggered a recorded voice.

"Please keep moving and step away from the glass."

The woman grunted in frustration. "They're even worse when they're automated," she said, making it clear that her animosity was for the door and not her three-wheeled companion. Rón noted a folded mask sticking out of the breast pocket of her blazer; a pocket square for the viral age. She had probably intended to put in on once she got inside. She hadn't counted on getting stuck in a rotating fishbowl with a stranger.

"Sorry," Rón said again. "Maybe if I move forward." He took a step forward, and the door began moving again. Then he bumped against the front panel, which made the whole contraption stop once more.

"Please keep moving and step away from the glass."

"Why do they even *need* these things?" the woman griped.

The door started up one more time, then stopped again—this time it was the little suitcase doing Rón's job for him.

"Please keep moving and step away from the glass."

"Well, this is awkward," said Rón.

The woman offered a mirthless chuckle. "It's just been one of those days."

"Well," said Rón letting out a long and breathy sigh, "maybe your days will get better."

. . .

Mariel did not suffer from claustrophobia, but there was something deeply unnerving about being trapped halfway in and halfway out of a building. It gave her flashbacks to her childhood.

"Tie your shoelace, baby, or you'll get dragged under the escalator," her mother would warn.

"Stay back from the curb, baby—do you want to end up under a truck?"

And of course, *"Keep your fingers away from the revolving door, baby, or they might get cut off."*

This was long before Mariel took up the mantle of responsibility—when she could respond by running back up the down escalator, swinging around lampposts like her favorite scene from *Singin' in the Rain*, and going around and around the revolving door like it was her own personal glass carousel. Her mother called her "encouragable," and little Mariel took guilty pleasure in never telling her the word was "incorrigible."

Gena had tried to instill Mariel with her own personal litany of irrational fears without any success. But now, the revolving door thing came back with a vengeance as she stood there in the little glass quadrant alone, with Rón and the irritated businesswoman in the quadrant ahead.

Finally, after a few false starts, the thing continued to rotate and spat them all out in the hotel lobby, the woman dragging her broken suitcase toward reception, leaving a line of damage on the beige institutional carpet.

"What was that all about?" she asked Rón.

"Just trying to help," he said.

"You should have just waited. Some people enjoy their frustration. Especially when they can take it out on an inanimate object."

They left it at that, but as they waited to check in, Mariel couldn't help but feel there was something off about the whole thing. It wasn't quite a red flag. Maybe a yellow one. Something she couldn't entirely dismiss as standard recoveree weirdness. It made her think again to the time Rón had wandered off in Salt Lake. Were these just random occurrences, or was there a pattern behind it? She wasn't sure, so instead of filing it away, she kept it open on her mental desktop.

Their hotel room wasn't luxurious, but it was far more comfortable than anything Mariel was used to. She indulged herself in a bath—the first one she had taken since the night she first met Rón in the penthouse. She fantasized that he might come in, but he was far too respectful for something so audacious. It was as she was drying off that she heard the hotel room door open and close. She stepped out of the bathroom to find that Rón had gone, leaving her a note:

"Off to get food. I'll bring you back a burger."

Hadn't they discussed just ordering room service? This was another yellow flag, but now it seemed to be tinting toward red. She dressed quickly and made it down to the lobby in time to see Rón exiting the building. This time, he had no trouble negotiating the revolving door.

21
True Transcendence

It was rush hour, or what passed for rush hour in downtown Omaha in the first wave of a pandemic. Rón found that the streets weren't bustling, but they weren't deserted, either. One block out from the hotel, he clocked a burger place, which he'd stop in on his way back. That way the food would still be warm for Mariel.

Up ahead was a bus stop; half a dozen people meandered, waiting for a bus that was about to cross an intersection. When the bus arrived, Rón slipped on first, to the mild annoyance of the people who had been waiting. Far be it for Rón to be rude—but it was a necessary maneuver.

"Uh, I don't have change." Rón held a bill out to the bus driver. "Can you break a twenty?"

The driver shook her head. "E-passes only, sweetie—gotta download the app. And mask up, too! We got a new motto: 'no mask, no motion.'"

"Right." Rón pulled out his mask and slipped it on, pretending to fumble with it, as he stood there blocking the line of people behind him. Then he reached toward his pocket for a phone that he didn't have, since Mariel had the burner. "I'll get the app right now."

Which brought forth a few disgruntled huffs from the people behind him waiting to get on.

And, as expected, the driver decided it just wasn't worth the trouble to throw him off the bus. "Just have it with you next time, sweetie." And she waved him on.

The bus was about two-thirds full. Even so, some people preferred to stand, holding the overhead rings. Most everyone was either absorbed in their phones, or a book, or just looking out the windows, chewing on their own thoughts. And while everyone wore a mask, there were quite a few wearing them uselessly beneath their noses—as if they wanted to be protected from Crown Royale, but not really. And then there were blatant scofflaws, who wore them as chin-diapers. Rón wouldn't go that far after having been chided by the driver. But he did pull his mask down enough to free his nose.

Rón moved through the bus, getting close to the people who had left themselves exposed, and asked them innocuous questions.

"Could you tell me what bus number this is?"

"Is that the new iPhone?"

"Excuse me, did you drop this receipt?"

He leaned inward each time he spoke, and none of them— not a single one—leaned away. They welcomed him in their airspace—some even pulled their masks all the way down when they answered, as to be heard over the drone of the engine.

Two long red lights and three short blocks ahead, the bus came to its first stop, and, satisfied, Rón got out the back door . . .

. . . only to be faced by Mariel, who stood there out of breath and gaping at him.

"What the hell were you doing on that bus?"

· · ·

There were a number of ways that Rón could have addressed the situation, each with its own set of consequences. He could have made something up—although he'd be hard-pressed to come up with something convincing on the spot. He could have denied that there was anything unusual about his stepping onto a public bus, chalking it up to just another fickle symptom of recovery. Or he could have turned it on Mariel, feigned anger at her for spying on him, and put her on the defensive.

But none of those things were in his nature. He had never been a very good liar, and now, as a recoveree, he found lying to be exceedingly hard to do. He'd been managing with half-truths and sins of omission, but telling Mariel a bald-faced lie? He just couldn't do it. Which meant he had only one real choice in the matter.

"Not here," Rón said as the bus pulled away behind him. "Let's go somewhere we can talk."

"Why? So you can have time to make up some excuse?"

Rón sighed. "I won't do that." Did she think so little of him? But then, he hadn't given her reason to think anything more.

"You haven't been right since we left San Francisco. . . ."

That felt like a slap in the face.

"I've been nothing *but* right!"

He began to walk in the direction of the hotel, knowing she'd have to follow, or leave him be. He dreaded both possibilities. In the end, she matched his pace—not following but walking beside him. Good. That was good.

"I've been given a mission," he finally said.

Mariel let loose a bitter guffaw. "Oh, please! A mission? By whom? By God?"

"Not exactly. By Delberg Zello."

"Zee gave you a mission?"

"More like he confirmed something I already knew."

"Which is?"

Rón looked around to see if anyone was watching, then realized it really didn't matter. He would speak the words no matter who was listening.

"I'm still contagious."

He had no idea what Mariel was expecting to hear, but it certainly wasn't that.

"You're . . . what?" she stammered. "That can't be—you recovered more than two weeks ago."

"Yeah, but I'm still shedding the virus," he told her. "I'm an alpha-spreader. I even took another test in Salt Lake City just to be sure. That's what I went off to do."

He could see Mariel doing the calculus of it all, her eyes darting as if she were tracking fireflies in her head.

"I've heard there are others," Rón said. "Not many, but a few—I suspect they all have blue-cone deficiency, like me. Not all of us survive the disease, but those of us who do . . . we become alpha-spreaders."

Mariel continued to gape at him. "Are you saying . . . ?"

He didn't finish her thought, although clearly, she wanted him to. Instead, he allowed her to complete the circuit.

"Are you saying that you went on that bus to give everyone Crown Royale?"

Rón shook his head. "No," he said. "Not everyone."

Mariel tried to wrap her mind around this, but found her mind had stretched as thin as cellophane before she could even come close to containment.

"Why?" It was the only word that made it out.

"Mariel, we have been at war with this planet for hundreds—no—*thousands* of years. And guess what? The planet is losing. So Earth came up with the perfect solution. A way to turn us around!" He laughed at the thought of it. "Joy and enlightenment! It can only make us better! Better stewards of the planet—better toward one another. A humanity that's actually humane!"

"At the cost of four percent of the population!" Mariel reminded him. "Does it not bother you that you're killing people? Is that an acceptable loss? Is that just 'collateral damage'?"

"Don't you think I've thought of all that? That I haven't wrestled with it?"

"Then wrestle with it some more!"

She stormed away, but stormed right back. There was too much here to just leave it. And she couldn't deny her own ambivalence. "You say you're enlightened—how is this enlightened?" And she wasn't just being rhetorical. She really wanted to know.

"Have you looked at the latest numbers?" Rón said. "Because I've been studying them, and the mortality rate is starting to drop—that's because everyone who's seriously at risk has already gone into isolation. And on top of it, recoverees *everywhere* have been volunteering to protect them, trying to make sure the most vulnerable will never be exposed."

"You're making excuses!"

"I'm looking at facts!"

Mariel bit her lip. She had read that the mortality rate was slowly dropping, even as cases have been rising. She assumed it was due to better care of those who were the most ill. But

Rón's explanation made sense, too. If you were at risk, you knew it—so you didn't let it find you. But even so, it was still in the air—which meant the mortality rate would never be zero.

So how much death was acceptable?

"I guarantee you," Rón said, "that no one on that bus was high risk unless they *chose* to risk it. The way I did."

"And if you're wrong?"

Rón considered it, and nodded, affirming his resolve. "Then I'll accept the blame, and all its consequences. In this life, and any that comes after."

"Let's just worry about one life at a time, please."

"I don't want anyone to die, Mariel. What I want is for people to know how it feels to be part of something so much greater than themselves—for the first time to have that connection not just to one another, but to everything. And people are ready! Why do you think so many are defying the mask mandate? Why did you, our first days together—when you knew for a fact that I was contagious?"

She didn't have to answer because they both knew. *Because I wanted to catch it too.* But she couldn't catch it, no matter how hard they had tried. And the truth of that was always there, a chasm between them.

Then Rón laughed in a moment of pure joy—because what she saw as a chasm, he saw as a bridge. "Don't you see, Mariel? You and I—it's like we were fated to be together. One who can't catch it; one who can't stop spreading it. We're the perfect balance. Which means we were meant to do this together!"

He reached his hands toward hers, expectantly, hoping she'd clasp them. But she was torn. She couldn't feel what he felt. Was that a blessing or a curse? Was it cloud or clarity?

And then Rón struck with something that reached into a place so unguarded, Mariel had no hope of defense.

"What were your mother's last words?" Rón asked.

Mariel was stunned by the question. "What does my mother have to do with this?"

"Everything," Rón replied.

"Stop it!"

"It was the happiest moment of her life, wasn't it?"

"Yes—and then she *died*!"

Rón shut his eyes, and pursed his lips. As angry as Mariel was, she knew he felt the pain of it right along with her. Empathy. It was a recoveree's greatest strength, and greatest weakness.

"Yes. She did die. And I'm sorry. But in that moment, if she had been given the choice of either living, or surrendering her life for the benefit of the world, what do you think she would have chosen?"

Mariel fought back tears. The Gena Mudroch she knew would never have sacrificed herself for others. But the woman her mother had become in those last moments of her life was not the woman she had been. The truth was right there in her last words.

"I get it now, baby . . . I get it. All of it."

Mariel knew the answer to Rón's question. She knew, and she hated it.

"It's all good now, baby. I'm so happy. . . ."

"That's not fair!"

Rón nodded. "You're right. It's not fair that anyone has to die. But we need to change, Mariel. We evolved too slowly, for all our knowledge. It's why we can destroy the world with the touch of a button. But Crown Royale can take that threat away.

It saves us. It saves everything. . . . And it could be our last chance. . . ."

While Mariel wrestled with her conflicted moral compass, Rón was facing his own struggle. He knew the right thing to do, and he was doing it. He felt it down to the very core of who he was. But that didn't mean he'd go through with it alone.

It was there, standing on a street corner in the Omaha twilight, that Tiburón Tigre Escobedo had an epiphany. Not about the world this time, but about himself. All at once, he realized why he had resisted telling Mariel what he felt called to do.

Because he knew that if Mariel told him to stop . . . he would. If she judged this to be wrong, he would give up his small part in transforming the world. He would lock himself away and go into perpetual isolation for her.

Because he was selfish.

And if it was a choice between Mariel and the world, he'd rather lose the world than lose her.

Mariel felt the weight shift firmly onto her shoulders. Everything had clicked into place. She knew not just Rón's mind, but his heart. It was twisted and yet pure. It was frightening and yet illuminating. Sure, she could dismiss it—say he was deluding himself, but she knew he wasn't. Objectively, he—*they*—had the potential for delivering immense good in a world that was sorely in need. She saw it firsthand, having lived among recoverees at the pier. Yes, their life of quiet contentment was dull to observe, but not to experience. And yes, she resented that she could never experience it the way that they did. But if she could, she would.

So, she could never be one of them, but she could advocate for them. And she could help spread more than just the word.

Part of her wanted to hide—to pretend there were no such things as moral ambiguities. That right was right, and wrong was wrong, and thinking about it too deeply was peering into an abyss that might just swallow you.

"We need to change," Rón had said. That change was already happening all around them. Humanity was on the brink of a major paradigm shift. Fighting it meant holding on to fear, and the endless perpetuation of human misery. But embracing that change would mean hope for a future that couldn't have been imagined a year ago. Did she wish to preserve a familiar darkness or step out into an unknown light?

The decision wasn't easy, but in the end it was inevitable.

"I get to choose."

The words were out of her mouth before she knew she was going to say them.

Now it was Rón's turn to gape. "What?"

It secretly pleased her that Rón was caught even more off guard than she was.

"I get to choose who you expose, and when," she said. "That way it's on my head as much as it's on yours. Then we'll really be a team." Then she finally took both his hands in hers. "Now let's go get that burger, I'm starved."

PART FIVE
THE COMPROMISED
AND THE UNEMBRACED

Elsewhere:
Eastern Europe

Leytenánt *Yuri Antonov joined the air force because he was expected to; his father had been an air force mechanic; his brother is a weapons systems officer. So Yuri decided if he was going to do this right, he would need to be a pilot, and show them both up. He soared through the officers academy and flight training—and within just a few short years, was a wingman in an elite squadron. It wasn't long until he was promoted to squadron* kapitán. *Just in time for the war.*

They were told it would be a quick and easy war. Perhaps it was propaganda, or perhaps the generáls *believed it—but this is not the case. From the beginning, the enemy has been tenacious, and receives continuous support from the West, both money and weapons, proving that nothing is ever easy in this world.*

As for the politics of it all, it has never been Yuri's concern. Flying a fighter jet is his job—a rare and prestigious one. It isn't his place to question, only to serve. A weapon for others to point. He doesn't hate the enemy, nor does he love his superiors. But war is war, and you do what you have to do.

He's lost friends to the conflict. Some to enemy fire, others to desertion. He's sure he'll lose more if the war doesn't take his life first.

Today's mission is an important one: the destruction of a bridge crucial to the enemy's morale and supply efforts. The enemy has made unexpected advances and taken out a power plant. So taking down this bridge will be swift retaliation.

Yuri is to lead his squadron of three MiG-35s deep into enemy territory at the highest altitude, then drop down sharply and fire laser-guided missiles to take out the bridge—and not just the span, but its anchor points on either side, making any effort to rebuild it that much more difficult.

He's flown missions like this before; some were successful, some were not. War is a numbers game. This mission, however, is a little bit different, as one of his wingmen is new to the squadron. His former wingman has been grounded, and isn't coming back. That's always the case for Crown Royale victims.

The military has a strict policy: recoverees are either dismissed from service or given some menial job where they can do no harm. It became clear early on that they simply couldn't be trusted to do the job they were trained for. When recoverees are sent back to the battlefield, they almost always die, because they'd rather take a bullet than fire upon someone else.

In fact, there's even a story going around about a group of soldiers from both sides running off together to form a commune in the woods. It could just be a fairy tale or someone's idea of a joke, but these days you can never be sure.

"We expect nothing less than perfect success from you today," his mayór *tells him that morning. "I needn't remind you how critical this mission is."*

"Yes, sir. I'm aware, sir."

"The eyes of the generáls *will be on you. Do this right, and you could fly back to a promotion."*

"As they say in America—a piece of cake."

The mayór *frowns at the mention of America, but makes no comment about it. "Yes . . . and speaking of cake, how was your sister's wedding?"*

Yuri is surprised the mayór even remembered. "Fine, sir. It was good to have a few days to spend with my family."

"Well, now that you're rested, I expect you to be at top performance."

"I will be, sir."

"Good. Go out there and prove it."

Forty kilometers out from the objective.

Yuri and his wingmen begin their dive from fourteen thousand meters. The mission is more than just their three jets, however. There are other teams in play, coming in from different angles, but the others are all decoys to grab the enemy's attention, keeping them occupied by aerial sleight of hand. Yuri's team is the only one taking the money shot.

The ceiling is high today, and as they come through the clouds at five thousand meters, they can see the bridge in the distance. Now Yuri's heart begins to race with anticipation, which it always does upon a strike, but today is different.

"A few days to spend with my family," he had told the mayór. But what he didn't say was that Yuri hadn't attended his sister's wedding. Oh, he had wanted to, but the night before, he had come down with a fever. A fever that lasted for four days. But he told no one outside his family, and for good reason.

"Nothing has changed, Yuri," his father had reminded him.

"Of course not," he told his father. "I still have a duty."

"And you must not let anyone know that you've had Crown Royale, because that will be the end of your career. They'll have you pushing pencils in some windowless office God knows where."

And Yuri knew it was true. Pilot to desk mule in four short days, just like his former wingman. "I understand, Father. I'll tell no one."

And now here he is, approaching the bridge—perhaps the most important mission of his career.

They come up on it fast. Time is of the essence now.

He throttles back slightly without warning his wingmen, and they pull in front of him. Before they can correct, he skews his vector, clipping the wing tip of the jet to his left. Yuri is able to keep control of his own jet, but the other jet, its wing tip damaged, begins a barrel roll to the ground. The pilot has no choice but to eject. Yuri catches a glimpse of a parachute. He and the other remaining jet are in firing range of the bridge now.

"Yuri, what have you done!"

His right wingman knows this wasn't an accident, so no point in pretending that it was. He tries to pull the same maneuver, but the other pilot won't be caught off guard now. He pulls away, leaving Yuri with only one choice. Yuri slides in behind his wingman and fires his guns, shooting up the tail, and one engine—being careful not to hit the cockpit.

At such close range, it's more than enough. The engine of the other jet fails and catches fire. Black smoke clouds Yuri's view, and when he clears it, he sees the plane nose-dive into the woods, and a parachute expanding, sending his wingman down to safety.

There is no hiding what he has done. He has clearly, and intentionally, sabotaged this mission. Because now there is a greater mission. He hadn't lied when he told his father he has his duty. But it is a far more important duty than his military orders.

He angles his plane toward the river, careening over the bridge, which is full of cars, trucks, and buses. And he smiles. Today, he has saved all those people. Today, order has triumphed over chaos. Conscience over catastrophe.

Yuri knows he will be seen as a traitor, but that is of little consequence—because as a Crown Royale recoveree, he has no allegiances, no priorities beyond that of the human race as a whole. And so, the moment he's safely past the bridge, he ejects.

His plane plunks down harmlessly in the water, and he steers his chute to drop him on the riverbank, near a walking path full of bystanders. Some run for fear of what he might do. Others curse him. Anger, fear, confusion everywhere. But that's fine. These are confusing times.

"I'm not your enemy," he says, in both his language and theirs, and he puts his hands up. "I just saved your bridge."

And indeed he has. That bridge will not be destroyed today. As for tomorrow? Who knows? He can't stop every missile from being fired, but at least he's accomplished this much.

He takes advantage of the confusion and runs, knowing that otherwise he'll be a prisoner of war. He can't do any good for anyone as a prisoner. Maybe he'll disappear into the woods and find that commune he's heard about. And if not, then he can start one of his own.

Because isn't he deserving of a fairy tale?

22
Duct Tape and Jellyfish

A thousand miles to the west, in Lucerne, Switzerland, there was a knock at Madeleine Willmon's door.

Griselda, the ailing woman's dedicated caregiver, was caught off guard by the visitor. There were very few people who came to the door these days. The last had been Frau Willmon's daughter, who had stayed for less than an hour. It was both too short and too long a time, as far as Griselda was concerned. The girl rubbed her the wrong way. Yet she was the one who paid Griselda for taking care of Frau Willmon—and of late, paid her handsomely—so Griselda shouldn't complain. Although she did, even though there was no one to complain to.

It was midafternoon, and Frau Willmon was out in the yard, as she often was at this time of day, absorbed in a blank appreciation of nature. When she was like this, she rarely moved, except for when she was interrupted by Griselda, who would bring her biscuits at 15:00, then something warm to drink when the sun sank low. The doctors said routine was good for her.

The knock on the door, then, was a disturbance to that routine. Not exactly harsh, not exactly urgent, but relentless. Three knocks at an even meter. Then a pause. Then three knocks again. Over and over. As if whoever was at the door would continue to beg entry even if no one was home, and the door was never answered.

Griselda wanted to ignore it until whoever it was went away—after all, she was under strict orders from Fräulein Morgan to not let anyone in under any circumstances. Even groceries were left at the door, and they were not expecting a food delivery today. Finally, the incessant knocking got the better of her and Griselda went to peer through a side window to see who was there.

It was a tall gentleman. Older. He didn't look like a salesman—he had a sort of reserved professional look about him. Who was he and what did he want? She considered answering the door to find out, then thought better of it, then considered it again. And while this indecisiveness ping-ponged through her mind, she heard voices in the backyard. On occasion Frau Willmon would talk to herself, but this was not one of those occasions, because there was more than one voice out there.

Griselda hurried to the kitchen and out the back door to find Frau Willmon sitting at her little table, conversing with an older woman. The rear gate was open, and Griselda realized that the knocking man was a ruse. This woman had slipped into the backyard while Griselda was distracted at the front door.

"You, there!" Griselda shouted in English, for that's what they were speaking. "You have not permission to be here! We are in quarantine. You must immediately leave!"

The woman didn't budge in the slightest. "But Madeleine and I are having the most delightful conversation, aren't we, Madeleine?"

"Yes, we are," agreed Frau Willmon. "Griselda, this is our next-door neighbor. We've known her for years!"

"She is not!" insisted Griselda. "She lies to you." Now Griselda was deeply worried about this woman's intentions.

"She should not be here. Come into the house, Frau Willmon. Come in now!"

"Griselda, no need to be rude to our neighbors. What did you say your name was?"

"Glynis," the woman said. "But look—what's that there on the hillside?"

And the second Frau Willmon turned away, Griselda was grabbed from behind. For a moment she caught sight of the man who had been at the door—who now held a handkerchief over her nose and mouth, which had the strangest, most caustic smell. Then everything began swimming like fishes, Griselda's legs seemed to vanish beneath her, and she went off to a place that no one remembers when they wake up.

While Dame Havilland kept Morgan's mother busy, Rooks secured the unconscious housekeeper to a chair in the living room with duct tape—probably way more than was necessary, but this wasn't the sort of business he was highly skilled in. Then he covered her mouth to make sure she didn't raise a bloody racket when she awoke—he had no idea how long the chloroform would work, or what her demeanor would be like when she regained consciousness.

Out in the yard, Dame Havilland chatted up Morgan's mother, who had only in her periphery seen Rooks bring the housekeeper inside. It seemed Madeleine Willmon was mostly concerned with not appearing confused than with actually knowing what was going on around her.

"It's very nice of you to come by. But I'm not sure we're supposed to have visitors. There's that nasty bug going around. The one that looks like a spider."

"Not to worry, you're safe with us. Actually, we've come because of your daughter."

"My daughter . . ."

"Morgan."

Madeleine pursed her lips, and shook her head, as if silently scolding herself. "Yes, Morgan. Yes, of course. You know her?"

"Most certainly."

"Well, she's not here, but I can tell her you came by when she's home from school. May I ask what this is regarding?"

"A personal matter," Dame Havilland said. "Perhaps we could call her."

"Oh, she hates to be disturbed."

"Nonsense, I'm sure she'd love to hear from you! Why don't we FaceTime with her?"

Madeleine was taken aback at the suggestion. "I hate that sort of thing. Little faces on a little screen. And I always drop the phone."

"That's all right, Madeleine. I'll hold it. We can talk to Morgan together."

There were few things that would distract Morgan from the business at hand—which, in this case, was an awkward lunch with Preston Locke, the assistant-turned-vice-president of the Havilland Consortium. Morgan thought that Preston, who was pleasing to the eye, might be pleasing in other ways, too. But his charming self-consciousness would most likely result in a failure to launch. Then the call came in, interrupting the meal, and making Preston drop his fork.

When Morgan heard the unique ringtone she had assigned to her mother, she braced herself. While her mother would call her incessantly in her healthier days, she rarely called anymore—and never made a video call. Morgan surmised that it was most likely a mistake. The proverbial butt dial. But what if it wasn't?

"Will you excuse me, Preston? I need to take this."

"Yes, yes, of course." Preston seemed relieved that she'd be stepping away.

These days, whenever there was an actual phone call from her mother's number, it was always Griselda on the other end, and it was never good news. Either Madeleine had wandered off, or she had fallen and hurt herself, or any number of terrible things that should not happen in the presence of a full-time caregiver. Not that Griselda was inattentive—Morgan had to admit that the woman watched Morgan's mother with an eagle eye. But even eagles needed to sleep and take the occasional crap. *"She's fine now,"* Griselda would always say. *"But you should have seen what went on here!"*

Well, if she was fine now, why call? Unless your whole point was to stir things up, making Morgan feel even worse than she already did about her mother's deteriorating state of affairs. She knew that one of these days, Griselda would bring her the grimmest of news. So Morgan braced, and let the phone ring a bit, taking the FaceTime call just before it deemed her unavailable.

The face on the screen was the absolute last one she expected to see.

"Morgan! Hello, dear. I hope we haven't caught you at an inconvenient time."

Morgan was rarely thrown by a situation, but to see that miserable old woman's face on her mother's cell phone left her beyond speechless.

The angle of the camera shifted to reveal Morgan's mother sitting happily in her backyard next to Dame Havilland. "Hello, Morgan!" her mother said, with a little wave. "This is our neighbor, Glenda."

Morgan began to stammer. She never stammered. "Wh-wh-what the hell are you—"

"I've paid your mother a visit, Morgan. That's all; just a visit."

"Where's Griselda? I want to talk to Griselda!"

"I'm sorry," said Dame Havilland, "but she is currently, as they say, 'indisposed.'"

"Who let you in? How did you—"

"Galen and I let ourselves in. It wasn't too difficult—you should have arranged better security for your mother."

And then Madeleine interrupted. "Ask her how she's been. Is she studying for exams, or is it too early in the school year for that?"

Morgan stood outside the restaurant, pacing in the street, wishing there was something she could strike. The camera shifted. The backyard was gone. Dame Havilland was moving from the yard into the house, leaving Madeleine outside.

"There," said Dame Havilland, "some privacy. Just you and me. Well, of course, Griselda is here, too, but she won't be interrupting." And for a moment, she turned the camera to show a fleeting glimpse of Griselda, bound, gagged, and unconscious in a chair, with Dame Havilland's butler sitting across from her like it was afternoon tea. It struck home for Morgan just how desperate this situation was.

"If you don't get out of that house right now, I'll—"

"You'll what, dear? Call the authorities? If you do that, then things might not end well for Griselda or your mother."

Morgan wanted to scream. The thought of her mother, as compromised as she was, at the mercy of that gorgon and her man-toy, was more than Morgan could stand. She paced, feeling helpless, and that was a feeling she hated. It was why Morgan always took care to control everything she possibly could, so that she never felt helpless like this.

"Whatever you're planning, it's not going to work."

"No? Well, we've got your attention, haven't we? So we're already halfway there. I know you're used to getting what you want, Morgan, but so am I—and I have had much more experience at it than you."

Morgan could not dispute that fact, as much as she wanted to.

"Now, if you'll remember, before I brought you into your current situation, I vetted you thoroughly. I know everything about you—including things you didn't know yourself, such as your mother's secret infidelity. But in spite of that, I know that you have a tremendous soft spot for your mother. I know you'd never want any harm to come to her."

Morgan now realized that this was the opening volley of a negotiation—and although she hated negotiating at such a disadvantage, she realized she didn't have much of a choice. But what did the old shrew want? Was she going to demand her money back? A better dwelling than that miserable cottage she had been given? Yes, it had matched Dame Havilland's miserable old persona, but perhaps Morgan had been too harsh in kicking her to so desolate a curb. Maybe she should have just let the withered hag be comfortable and out of the way. Although she couldn't stand to speak the words, she knew she had to.

"What do you want?"

"There we go!" said Dame Havilland, with endless, infuriating cheer. "That wasn't so hard, was it? Now, let's get down to business. What I want is very simple. I want you to call off the hounds. Cease research on the project that I so carelessly placed in your hands. You may keep the money, and you may keep the estate—it's all yours. I gave it to you, and I won't begrudge you any of it. All I ask is that you stop all medical research immediately."

"Or what?"

"Use your imagination, dear. I've been known to be quite vindictive—and if you don't stop the Consortium's research, I can't vouch for the safety of your mother. Perhaps I'll take her on an excursion into town and browse the markets and pubs, making absolutely sure she catches Crown Royale. Or maybe we'll take the cableway to the top of Mount Titlis and I'll let her wander off into the ice and snow. Or maybe I've already secured some unsavory sort to make sure that she disappears without a trace. No body, no evidence, no crime."

"You wouldn't dare!"

"You're not so sure, are you? In a matter this grave, you don't want to test my resolve—it's every bit as solid as your own, and then some."

Morgan bit her lip to prevent herself from tearing into the woman. If Morgan snapped, it would just play right into Havilland's hand.

"Think about your options here," said the old woman. "You can be a stubborn child and refuse to do as I ask. Or you can walk away with all the money you'll ever need—and if you do, I promise you'll never hear from me again. I'm sure you've thought about it already. Abandoning the mission I gave you, running off to live your best life. You just needed an excuse. Now, I've given you one."

And she was right. It would be so easy to walk away with a winning jackpot—and now that the money was officially hers, it couldn't be taken away if she stopped research. But it was about more than money now. It was about carving a place in history. It was about effort rewarded. Because while countless others were trying to capitalize on this disease, struggling to create a vaccine that would make them rich, Morgan was doing something more. She was creating a new paradigm. She wouldn't just slow Crown Royale down through an elusive "herd immunity." Instead, what she was creating would fight the disease, dominate it, defeat it. And besides, Morgan's pride would not allow her to give in to blackmail.

Dame Havilland brought her lips close to the phone, whispering as if directly into Morgan's ear, a sinister voice of reason. "Take the deal. You know you want to. It's in your best interest, and you're a girl who always knows what's in her best interest."

There was something off about this whole exchange. A negotiation was like a game of cards, and something was wrong with the deck. Morgan nearly gasped when she realized what it was—she should have realized it before, but she had been caught off guard—she had missed the obvious. The truth was right in front of her all this time.

Dame Havilland was pretending to be someone she no longer was!

If this was a game, Dame Havilland's hand was face up on the table. All Morgan needed was a single glance to know the emptiness of her cards. And so, Morgan leaned into the phone, her lips close enough to kiss the camera, and she said:

"No."

Suddenly Dame Havilland's voice didn't sound as confident as it had a moment ago. "You should take a moment to reconsider that answer."

"I don't need to reconsider it. My answer is no. So why don't you go do what you've threatened? Take my mother to the top of Mount Titlis, but don't let her wander—why don't you just hurl her off a cliff? And when you do, make sure to make a video and send it to me!"

"You'd be wise to take me seriously, young woman!"

"Would I? No, I think taking you seriously would be the definition of foolishness! Because you won't hurt her. Not a single hair on her head. You're incapable of it! Maybe once you had it in you, but Crown Royale has devoured your spine. Now you're nothing but a jellyfish, passive and pointless. But no—because that's an insult to jellyfish, because at least they have venom!"

Now it was Dame Havilland's turn to stammer. "Y-you're making a mistake."

"Here's what you're going to do. You're going to free Griselda, and get out of that house now—because the second I hang up this phone, I'm calling the police, so you'd better be good and gone before they get there. And you'd better make sure I never see your miserable, wrinkled, wretched face ever again."

"Morgan, if you'll just—"

Morgan disconnected, not letting the woman say another word, and followed through on her threat of alerting the Lucerne police to intruders in her mother's home. She knew that Griselda would soon call, frazzled, but alive. *"We're fine now,"* Griselda would say, *"but you should have seen what went on here!"*

When Morgan returned to Preston, she found him waiting dutifully, having not had a bite of his meal. She offered him a faint smile, hoping he wouldn't ask what the call was about. But of course, he did.

"Was that Svalbard?" he asked. "Is everything going well?"

Going well? Of course it was! Because now she was more determined than ever that their efforts there would be successful.

"Things couldn't be better!" Morgan told him. Then she picked up her silverware, and mercilessly cut into a steak that had long since gone cold.

23
Transmittable

Griselda called to inform Morgan of what she already knew. The elderly couple had not followed through on any of their threats.

"Who were these people?" Griselda asked. "What do they want of us?"

Morgan informed her that they wouldn't be bothering them again, and left it at that. But that didn't mean Dame Havilland wouldn't surface again to bother Morgan. She'd have to be vigilant.

Morgan attended two more summit meetings of movers and shakers in Blas Escobedo's virtual conference room. Each time the table was smaller, with fewer seats as Crown Royale claimed the minds, if not the bodies, of the cabal.

Gone was the Chinese bureaucrat. The economist missed one meeting, only to show up at the next one, fervently trying to convince the others that they needed to contract Crown Royale as quickly as possible. The moment they realized that she was now a recoveree, Blas terminated her feed, leaving the remaining quartet in troubled, awkward silence. Now it was only Morgan, Blas, the WHO scientist, and the media mogul, who was a bit red because he was either feverish or drunk. Everyone hoped it was the latter.

But even without the economist's grim forecasts, it was

easy to see the trajectory of all things financial. The automotive sector was the proverbial elephant in every stock analyst's room. Car sales weren't just flat; they were plummeting, partially because the uninfected weren't about to purchase cars on the cusp of lockdown—and recoverees had absolutely no interest in buying, or even selling, new cars at all. It would likely be the first industry to collapse worldwide, and wouldn't be the last.

There will be a steep market correction, the *Wall Street Journal* was saying. Which was like calling the sinking of the *Titanic* "a steep course correction." The difference was that at least the Atlantic Ocean had a bottom.

All the more reason to pull out every stop in finding a way to defeat Crown Royale. There could be no moral or ethical considerations to hamper progress. No matter what it took, the end would justify the means.

"How are your efforts shaping up?"

Blas Escobedo did not look at all cold, even though he stood on an ice floe in the shadow of a massive glacier. Today's meeting was just the two of them—because they had not involved anyone else in their "vaccine" project.

"We're making steady progress," Morgan told him. It was vague enough to sound encouraging. "I can't say I like your choice of environment today." The view made her feel like she needed a parka. She resisted shivering, forcing her intellect to assure her primordial brain that it was reacting to a convincing fiction.

Escobedo smirked. "It's as close to Svalbard as the VR program currently gets."

"And why would you think I'd want anything that reminds me of that awful wasteland?"

"I didn't do it for you," Blas admitted. "It's for me. So I can feel closer to 'the room where it happens,' as they say."

More like the room where nothing happens, thought Morgan, but today she was keeping most of her thoughts to herself. "I see there's no conference table today."

"This is just between you and me, as we had agreed." He motioned with a haptic-gloved hand, and a small ice table grew from the floe between them. The flick of his wrist had been so nonchalant, it prompted Morgan to say, "It must be quite a thrill to create things on a whim. You must feel like a God in this Fortress of Solitude."

Escobedo took a seat at the table, giving a halfhearted shrug. "Nothing but smoke and mirrors. I don't delude myself into thinking it's anything more."

Morgan set her tablet on the ice table . . . and it promptly clattered to the ground. Because, of course, the table didn't actually exist.

Blas Escobedo offered her his apology. "Like I said, smoke and mirrors."

Morgan gave an exasperated sigh as she kneeled down to pick it up. At first she was annoyed that Escobedo made no attempt to help her—but then remembered that *he* wasn't actually there either. She wondered if Escobedo was amused by the foibles of the uninitiated, which, in these Zooms-on-steroids, was everyone but him.

"Don't be too put out about it," he said. "Humans do adapt quickly to technology, but you're still fairly new to this platform." It was not lost on Morgan that he was being both figurative and literal, as they were standing on an ice floe.

Morgan removed the VR glasses to grab her tablet, free of false visual obstructions, and found herself assaulted by reality. She was, of course, in the office she had inherited from Dame Havilland in London. Gone were the dark stodgy portraits, replaced by contemporary works by artists she admired—not necessarily because their work was brilliant, but because they could command such high prices for pieces a kindergartener could have created. She was enamored by the scam of it all.

"People must always adjust to technology. Did you know that in the early days of commercial air travel, almost everyone got violently ill?" Escobedo said—now a disembodied voice in her earbuds. "Not because of anything the plane did, but because the simple feeling of flight was so foreign, so disturbing, no one knew how to stomach it. And yet, these days, one is lucky to even find an airsickness bag in the seat back."

"Ha! When was the last time *you* were on a commercial flight?"

"I take them once in a while," he admitted. "There is much to be said for the power of shared experience."

"Now you sound like a recoveree."

"No need to be insulting, Morgan."

She pulled up a chair—a real chair—then sat down and put the glasses back on just in time to see a chunk of the glacier calve and plunge into the icy sea. She shivered, and mentally slapped her brain for allowing it.

"Any progress in finding your son?" Morgan said, sensing the moment could use a sprinkling of empathy. "That must really weigh on you. I'm sorry you have to go through that."

Escobedo became somber. Pensive. "Thank you. I feel confident we'll find him. The problem is, when you offer a hefty reward, people come out of the woodwork with so-called sightings. Buenos Aires, Beijing, Anchorage, Bangkok. Not a single one of them credible."

"I'm sure he's fine."

Escobedo sighed. "He's had Crown Royale and recovered. That much, I know."

"I'm so sorry, Blas. . . ."

"I believe his catching it was . . ." The words caught in a web of the man's emotions. "I believe it was a failed suicide attempt. He was high risk, you see."

"I didn't know."

"When I find him . . . I fear I won't know him anymore. . . ."

"All the more reason to make sure no other parent has to experience their child being subverted by a mind-altering virus."

Blas took a moment, probably realizing that he wore too much grief on his sleeve, then got back to business. "So update me on our progress."

"We have an amazing team at Svalbard," Morgan told him. "They are redefining the very concept of taming a pandemic." It was more like a line from some advertisement than an answer. She knew she wasn't fooling Blas in the least.

"And are they anywhere close to a vaccine?"

"What they're working on is more than just a vaccine."

"So they're developing a cure?"

"Not exactly." She realized she was being just as cagey as Dr. Bosgraaf was when she had told Morgan. It simply wasn't information easily divulged.

Blas folded his hands before him and said nothing more. He just waited for her to explain. He was not a man who appreciated being kept in suspense.

"It's a vaccine of sorts," Morgan explained, "but it's also transmittable."

He took that in, then raised his eyebrows. "Transmittable?"

"Yes."

"Not an injection?"

"No."

"You're telling me the Havilland Consortium is creating a transmittable vaccine."

"Yes, as I've already said."

"And how is it transmitted?"

"We're still working on that," Morgan told him. "We're hoping it will be . . . airborne."

She could see him reeling from the suggestion.

"An airborne vaccine?" he said slowly.

"Yes."

"That spreads like a virus?"

"Exactly. It's less of a vaccine . . . and more what you might call a counter-virus."

"That's ingenious!"

For a moment, Morgan thought she might take credit for the idea, but suppressed the urge, because he'd see right through it. "I told you our team is brilliant."

Now Escobedo was putting all the pieces together. "So that's why they needed a place like Svalbard!"

"We had to make sure it couldn't get out before it's ready. And the vault at Svalbard is the safest place in the world."

"So then, how far out are we?"

Again, that question. "I'm heading back to Svalbard in the morning to check on it firsthand." Another nonanswer. But before he could push her, she changed the subject, sending him a spreadsheet from her tablet. She heard the up-whoosh as it left, and the down-whoosh of its arrival.

"This is a breakdown of expenses, and the amount we'll need to keep Svalbard fully operational, so we can achieve our goal."

He glanced at the amount and didn't even blink. "The money will be transferred within the hour."

Morgan couldn't hold back her grin. "Just like that? I'm surprised a man in your position is so trusting."

"A man in my position couldn't care less if you're skimming money off the top, as long as the Havilland Consortium gets the job done."

"I'm not skimming," Morgan assured him.

"As I said, I don't care."

He stood to signal the end of their meeting, and offered her a genuine smile. "You talk about me playing God, and here you are engineering your own global anticontagion."

Morgan smiled, appreciating the compliment. "There's enough room on Olympus for both of us, Mr. Escobedo."

The following morning's flight to Svalbard was just as rough and tumble as the first. Morgan had expected that first visit to be her only one, but like Blas Escobedo, she couldn't resist the pull of being in the room where it happens. The place where the future of the human race was going to be determined. Besides, she didn't like the way Dr. Bosgraaf evaded in their remote conversations. But if Morgan could look into the woman's eyes in person—and avoid looking at her teeth—Morgan would be able to separate half-truths from wishful thinking from outright lies.

When she arrived, she tried to get into the facility as quickly as she could to avoid any nuisances along the way. But the primary nuisance she was avoiding must have been tipped off that she was coming, because Dr. No, the Seed Vault director, was waiting just inside the entrance.

"Miss Willmon-Wu, I must state my objections to the state of affairs in your laboratory most vehemently!" He pronounced it "laBORatory," which made him one notch more irksome.

Morgan unzipped her parka and considered handing it to him as if he were a valet, but realized that would merely upset him further. Usually, she would have enjoyed that, but today she just wanted him out of her hair. "What now, Dr. Nødtvedt?"

"Your staff is supposed to be limited to twelve, yet we've clocked more than double that. And not everyone appears to be, shall we say, the most savory of persons."

Morgan continued walking down the inclined entryway deep into the mountain, forcing him to keep apace.

"When you leased the space, there was a clear agreement in writing that you and your people are brazenly violating!"

"Fine. Then sue us," Morgan said.

"I assure you, if you do not stay within the boundaries of the agreement, we most certainly will!" Nødtvedt warned.

"Good," Morgan said cheerfully. "And while you're wasting all your organization's precious funds on legal fees instead of preserving seeds, we'll throw even more lawyers at you. Then, when we've bankrupted you, the Havilland Consortium will take over the entire facility here at Svalbard, and kick you *and* your seeds out."

It left him blustering and turning red.

"Now, if you'll excuse me, Dr. Nødtvedt, I have business to take care of. Don't bother me again." Then she strode off, refusing to allow him and his righteous rage to pursue her.

"We're close. Very close," Dr. Bosgraaf said in Morgan's debriefing. "Just one minor sticking point. One tiny roadblock."

"With all the money that you have, how can there possibly be a roadblock?"

"Well. DNA is stubborn and doesn't care for cash."

According to Bosgraaf, some of the serums they had developed appeared promising but did absolutely nothing. Others turned out to be necrotizing and rotted subjects from the inside out.

"We've had five subjects die from destructive counter-viral strains." Bosgraaf told her. "But not to worry! There are new test subjects arriving later this week . . . but . . ."

"But what?"

Bosgraaf sighed and came clean. "We're missing a critical link in the RNA sequence."

"So find a solution!" Morgan demanded. "You're the best in the world. Don't just think outside the box; burn the box!"

"We can't generate what we don't have. Of course, there's always a chance we might be able to find what we need in the general population—but it will be a needle in a haystack the size of this island. And until we find the 'Goldilocks gene,' I'm afraid we won't make much progress."

That was not the kind of news she could bring back to Blas Escobedo.

"Take me to the labs. I want to see these test subjects myself."

Bosgraaf tried to protest, but in the end did as she was told. They donned hazmat suits, and stepped through the air lock and down to the inner sanctum of biological experimentation.

The monkeys were gone. And their labs had been transformed into sets of small, cell-like studios, pleasantly appointed and comfortable enough to give their human subjects a sense of autonomy, if not freedom.

They were convicts from various places around the world, and of a variety of races. Morgan liked to tell herself she had saved them from fates far worse than that of human test subjects, for all had been drawn from the harshest, dankest, dirtiest of prisons, in places where they could be bought with a well-greased palm. Murderers, rapists, and worse. Yet, none of them were forced to come against their will—Morgan had made that mandate clear. They all came voluntarily. But then, how could they refuse? It was either a life sentence without the possibility of parole, or a few weeks of experiments followed by freedom. It didn't even cost an arm and a leg. Maybe a lung or a kidney, but what was that in the grand scheme of things?

There was, understandably, a high mortality rate, but none of them had balked, so Morgan's conscience was clear. This was, Morgan knew, a transactional world on every level. And all that mattered was that both parties were satisfied with the transaction. These convicts were all given a choice, which was more than anyone could say about the monkeys.

While many of the cells were now empty, a few were occupied with convicts who were either antsy or lethargic. One in particular caught Morgan's attention. Subject eleven. He locked eyes with her through the double-paned glass of his cell. And although Morgan was well protected by two layers of glass and a hazmat suit, she felt exposed. He was white. Ugly. Shaved head. Black tattoos covered him like newspaper print. But the look on his face was familiar. It reminded her of the monkeys that had been in the recoveree lab.

"What's this one's story?" Morgan asked.

"He tested positive for Crown Royale shortly after he arrived. He's just coming out of it—we're keeping him as a control subject, as we had with some of the bonobos."

Then he spoke up.

"So you're the dragon baby!"

He had a drawl with faint French undertones. Cajun. His grin was both kind and lascivious. Like he'd had his come-to-Jesus moment, but was baptized in fetid swamp water.

"Excuse me?" said Morgan.

He tossed a glance toward Bosgraaf. "S'what this one calls you. Play on 'dragon lady,' I suppose—on accounta you being so young and all."

Bosgraaf looked suitably embarrassed, but didn't deny having said it. She tried to corral Morgan back toward the staff quarters, but Morgan would go in her own good time. The man took her lingering for interest and his smile broadened.

"Before Crown Royale, I woulda had designs on a cutie like you, pumpkin. Still havin' thoughts a'course, but no designs. Past all that now."

Morgan just let that roll on by.

"Name's LeMaster. But you can call me 'The Mast.' Everyone does."

"And are they treating you well?"

"I'm taken care of," the skinhead said. "So tell me the truth—did some of the others die? Nurse Ratched, here, won't tell us a thing."

"You were all aware this was a high-risk operation," Bosgraaf interjected.

"Yeah, yeah, we all got the lowdown," he said, never taking his eyes off Morgan. "But men like us, we all gamblers. No matter where we from, gotta spin that wheel. I suppose I'm the lucky one. All I got was Crown Royale, which I woulda gotten in prison anyway."

"Too bad it couldn't take away that swastika on your forehead," Morgan taunted.

He shrugged. "Don't see it, 'less I look in the mirror. But it ain't me no more." And as he thought about it, he gave a little grimace. "See, it hurts to hate now. Hurts right here." He indicated the middle of his chest. Morgan wondered if it was an actual physical ache.

"They got lasers can take that tattoo off, right?" he said. "Or maybe I'll just keep it to remind myself what a piece of shit I used to be. Need to remind ourselves what we came from. Helps us appreciate where we are." Then he took another moment to consider it. "Nah, maybe I'll take it off after all, 'cause it scares people. I don't want to scare people no more." Then he launched into a painful coughing fit that made Morgan back away from the glass.

"Is there anything we can do to make this easier on you?" Morgan asked. Bosgraaf couldn't hide her surprise at Morgan's sudden humanity. Good. Keep the woman on her toes.

"There is one thing," the skinhead said. "They don't let us smoke roun' here. But maybe you could get me some a that nicotine gum. Take the edge off the withdrawal."

"I'll see what I can do."

Finally Morgan allowed Bosgraaf to lead her away. The woman seemed visibly relieved once they had left the labs.

"There have to be several smokers here," said Morgan. "And since they can't smoke inside—and no one wants to be out on the mountain—I'm willing to bet that at least one of them has Nicorette."

Bosgraaf nodded reluctantly. "Nivinski. I'm sure he can spare some." Then she smiled at Morgan. "You surprise me. I didn't think you were one to have compassion toward a man like that."

"He's human, isn't he? I have compassion toward humans."

Or at least she did when it served a larger goal.

In the evening after dinner, when most of the staff was enjoying their downtime, Morgan donned a hazmat suit and made her way back down to the labs. The skinhead was lying on his cot, staring off at infinity, and chewing, chewing, chewing. He grinned when he saw her on the other side of the glass.

"Hello, pumpkin. Knew I caught your eye."

"I see you got your gum."

"Makes life smooth and easy. Or at least easy as it can be when you're comin' down off a fever. Thanks for makin' it happen."

"You're welcome. Maybe you can make something happen for me."

He sat up. "Ooh, I'm all ears."

"I'm going to make them keep you on, even after you're no longer contagious. I'll tell them you're a security risk if you're set free before we're finished here."

"Sorry, pumpkin. Not part of my agreement."

"You should have checked the fine print. Your agreement's void, because you got sick before they could use you. Once you test negative, they can ship you right back to whatever hellhole you came from."

He frowned at that, then shrugged like it didn't matter all that much. "So you got other plans?"

"Like I said, I'll tell them to keep you on. As a recoveree, you won't pose a threat to anyone. Maybe they could give you some responsibilities around here. Because recoverees are trust-worthy, right?"

"And in return?"

Now it was Morgan's turn to smile. "I don't like Bosgraaf any more than you do. I don't trust her. So in return, you'll be my eyes and ears. You'll keep track of what goes on here. The things they won't tell me. And when I come back, you'll give me a full report."

He nodded and came to the glass. "Full report, huh?" he said. "How about I do you one better?"

Then he leaned on the cell door. And it unlatched.

A gum foil that had been lodged in the jamb fell to the ground.

And suddenly there weren't two layers of glass between them. There was nothing but a hazmat suit, and three feet of infected air.

The second the door unlatched, and the safety gasket rimming the door unsealed, an alarm began to blare—so the contagious convict didn't waste any time. He stalked toward her. The look in his eyes and that smile on his face said he did have designs for her after all.

"Don't! Stay away!"

"Don't stay away? Pumpkin, I don't plan to!"

Morgan tried to bolt, but he was between her and the exit. And then she saw something flash in his hand. A piece of broken glass. A shiv. How the hell had he gotten that?

"See, I got something you need, pumpkin," he taunted. "Something you need real bad. And it ain't information."

Morgan tried to fend him off, but even weakened by Crown Royale, he was strong and practiced in brutality. He pressed her against the wall, brought up the shard of glass, and swiped it across her neck—

—tearing a gash in her hazmat suit.

"Pretty skin you got under there, pumpkin." Then he brought his lips to the gash in the fabric. Morgan could feel the heat of his breath on her neck, and he blew into that gash like he was blowing up a balloon. He emptied his lungs into her hazmat suit, and then he let her go with a smile and a wink.

"Hope that was good for you, pumpkin."

Guards in full protection gear raced in to grab him. They took him down to the ground, but it was too late. He had breathed his contagion into her hazmat suit.

"You're gonna thank me, dragon baby. Oh yeah, you're gonna thank me!"

Morgan ran. She held her breath and ran as fast as she could, up the stairs, racing to the decontamination chamber, and ripped off her hood. Still, she held her breath. Her heart was pounding, her lungs screaming in furious complaint, but she couldn't under any circumstances allow herself to breathe.

She flipped every switch she could find, dousing herself with a cloud of disinfectant and ultraviolet light. She pulled the rest of the hazmat suit off, wriggling in a mad tarantella to be free of it. Her eyes burned from the disinfectant, but she didn't care. And finally, with her brain aching from oxygen deprivation, when she was seconds from passing out, she gasped a breath, and another, and another.

She felt dirty. Violated. That monster! She could still feel the sickening moisture of his infected breath on her neck. Even now she could feel Crown Royale crawling on her skin. She knew it was her imagination, but she couldn't shake the feeling.

She found a wall dispenser, and pumped hand sanitizer into her palms, drenching her neck in the stuff over and over. Finally, Bosgraaf, fully protected in her own hazmat suit, came into the decontamination chamber, and Morgan went off on her.

"How could you let that happen?" she screamed. "You said those cells were secure!"

"What were you even doing down there?"

"That doesn't matter! I should have been safe!"

Bosgraaf put up her hands, trying to calm Morgan. But Morgan wasn't having it. She slapped the woman's hands away.

"This is not the end of the world," Bosgraaf said. "Just because he's contagious doesn't mean you caught it."

"He breathed into my goddamn suit!"

"We have the latest rapid tests," Bosgraaf said. "We'll test you every hour for three hours, and by the end of the third hour, we'll know for sure." She turned to a guard who had come in behind her. "Isolate Miss Willmon-Wu in the guest quarters."

Then, as the guard grabbed Morgan even more firmly than the convict had, Bosgraaf said, "We'll have someone come to administer your first test in an hour. If you've contracted Crown Royale, you'll have at least three days to set your house in order. Make preparations."

"Preparations?"

"If you would prefer not to contract the disease . . . we have cyanide pills."

Hearing that only added to Morgan's fury. "If I come down with Crown Royale, I promise you, Dr. Bosgraaf, the only cyanide pill will be the one I shove down *your* throat!"

Morgan could be isolated and quarantined, but her rage could not be contained. Everything she could get her hands on in the guest quarters she threw and broke, but not even that could assuage her fury. How could she have been so stupid to come back here? She should have kept as far away from Svalbard as possible. And if she came down with Crown Royale, what then? What would she do? What Dame Havilland did? Would she give her brand-new fortune away to someone who was still of sound mind? She could scream at the unfairness of it!

An hour later came the first test.

The moment the swab was jammed up her nose, and until the result registered, had to be the longest fifteen minutes of her life.

Negative.

"That's a very good sign," said Dr. Bosgraaf, who was decent enough to come in with the medic who gave her the test. But if it was such a good sign, then why were Bosgraaf and the medic still wearing their hazmat suits? Morgan wasn't out of the woods and wasn't convinced that these early detection tests were as accurate as they claimed to be.

If the next test was bad news, would Morgan be tempted to take the cyanide pill? She didn't know which was worse, to die by her own hand or to be scrubbed vacant by a virus that would leave her a shell of who she had been. And if she contracted the disease, where would she go once she joined the ranks of recoverees? Back to Switzerland to stare blankly at hillsides with her mother? Join Dame Havilland and her sex butler in that miserable windswept shack on the cliffs of nowhere? Both those options fit Morgan's definition of hell. Cyanide was sounding better and better.

Second test.

Negative.

She was calmer after the second test, but still didn't trust the result. It would be just like the universe to tease her twice, giving her hope, only to pull out the rug on the third attempt. She found her hand kept going to her neck, and the spot where the convict had pressed his lips like some sort of reverse vampire. She wondered if she'd ever feel that spot was clean again.

Third test.

Negative.

Ne. Ga. Tive.

Now she dared to allow herself a sense of relief. Dr. Bosgraaf and the medic even removed the hoods of their hazmat suits.

"Well," the woman said with a sigh, "nothing but a tempest in a teapot."

"That's right," agreed the medic. "Nothing to be hysterical about."

Morgan felt her fury come on strong. "Do you know where the word 'hysterical' comes from? It's a medieval belief that female neurosis comes from a defective uterus. It's offensive."

"I'm sorry," he said. "I didn't know."

"Now you do," said Morgan. "You're fired."

"Don't be that way, Morgan," said Bosgraaf, so condescending, Morgan wanted to kick her crooked teeth straight.

"Dr. Bosgraaf, we are not on a first-name basis. And while *you* are not expendable, this tool is. I want him gone within the hour."

Bosgraaf said nothing but gestured for the man to leave. He looked a bit pale as he toddled out. He'd be paler when he was kicked out into the snow and had to wait at the single pub down in Longyearbyen for a way home.

"And about the convict who tried to infect me—"

"We've made sure his cell is secure. He won't get out again."

"You're going to use him as your next test subject."

"He has Crown Royale; he's no longer a candidate for the type of testing we're doing now."

"I don't care. You'll use your next batch of serum on him anyway, and the next, and the next, until there's nothing left of him but a quivering mass of necrotized jelly."

Bosgraaf stiffened. "That's not how we do things here."

"It's how *I* do things, and you work for me. Now get the hell out and tell them to get my plane ready."

24
Slow Train to Paris

Dame Havilland could not get past her failed attempt at using Morgan's mother as a pawn. It did not coerce the girl; instead it made her even more obstreperous than she already was—if that were even possible. It was a blow—because far more subtle machinations had worked wonders for Glynis before. But that was in the old days. Blackmail required a mindset Dame Glynis Havilland no longer possessed.

"Galen, it greatly concerns me that we might not have what it takes to accomplish this."

She and Rooks were at Basel SBB station at the triple border between Switzerland, France, and Germany, awaiting a connection that was running on time. Although she wished it was late. She wasn't quite ready to board that train.

"I've never known you to underestimate yourself, Glynis. Why start now?"

They strolled the platform together, masked, as was everyone else. Even the beggars held to that rule here. Rooks held her cane when they walked arm in arm, happy to be her support. He had always been there to support her long before her eyes were open enough to see. In this instance, however, she needed more than an arm and sympathy. She needed honesty. The truth was, they had never intended to actually hurt Morgan's mother—or even to give the frail woman Crown Royale, as they had threatened—and Morgan knew it.

"We're casebook recoverees, Galen. Morgan called our bluff because she knew that we wouldn't bring harm on her mother—or on that poor housekeeper, who must have been traumatized."

Rooks laughed at that. "I think it would take a whole lot more than duct tape to traumatize that woman."

"You forget how easily frightened people can be. She probably thought we meant to rob her, or worse. She'll have nightmares."

Rooks gently patted her hand. "And she'll recover. People are resilient."

The train began to pull in at the far end of the station. Announcements in four languages heralded its arrival. This was not the high-speed train. That was expensive, and they had to conserve what little funds they had. This was a slow train to Paris, with a dozen stops along the way for the uninfected daring enough travel, and for recoverees whose comfort zone had expanded to fill the whole world.

"We could not hurt Morgan's mother, because she is an innocent," Rooks pointed out. "Morgan, on the other hand, is not."

"Yes, but do we have the courage? Do we have the clarity of purpose to do what is necessary when the time comes?"

Rooks heaved a sigh. "Morgan Willmon-Wu is the central figure in a mess that you yourself created, Glynis. Never once have I known you to leave a mess unattended, and I have every faith in your ability to clean this one up too."

The train doors opened, passengers embarked, but Dame

Havilland hesitated. The plan was to go to Paris, and from there, take a train back to the UK, returning to their cottage, where she longed to be after this debacle. But that was an increasingly bad idea.

"We can't go back to Thornwick Nab," Dame Havilland announced. "She'll have all sorts of minions there to detain us."

"And we'll have all sorts of fellow recoverees to undetain us."

"But we mustn't count on that, Galen." She took her cane from him, pressing its tip firmly to the ground. "Relying on others should be an aid, not a crutch." She took a long minute to reassess, while behind them the slow train to Paris pulled out.

"We can't threaten Morgan because she sees our threats as empty. Which means we'll need to take a new approach. We'll have to undermine her—and do it in a way that she'll never see coming." Then she turned to leave the platform.

"Where are you going?"

"To book a train to Frankfurt."

It took a moment for Rooks to catch on. "Your townhouse on Rhonestrasse!"

"Not mine anymore, but I'm sure Morgan doesn't even know it exists—and I remember where I hid the spare key."

"So we'll lie low?"

"Not lie, Galen, but work. We must not be idle if we're going to find a way to stop her."

Rón had never felt closer to anyone than he felt to Mariel that night in Omaha, after he had confessed to her what he was doing. His mission. His purpose. To him, it seemed they were joined in the perfect bond—a yin and yang that, given enough time, could encompass the globe.

But this undertaking wasn't about grand super-spreading gestures. It was about just the right exposures in just the right places. Tiny acorns in fertile ground. Certainly, it would spread without their help, but Rón had to believe that his and Mariel's efforts would stoke that fire to a tipping point. It made him shiver with gratitude to think about their part in all this—and how it was just a part of what he and Mariel shared.

They spent only one night in Omaha before checking out and continuing their journey.

"Maybe we should have used the valet after all," Mariel lamented, because their car was parked three blocks away, it was raining, and they had no umbrellas. Mariel hunched her shoulders, folding away from the rain, but Rón spread his chest and kept his chin high, wanting to take in every drop.

They encountered two people that morning. First was a man sheltered in a doorway playing his heart out on a saxophone that they'd been able to hear from the moment they left the hotel.

Mariel would have passed, but Rón made her pause to listen, pulling out his wallet.

"You're a recoveree," Rón said, dropping a five-dollar bill into the musician's hat, which lay on a dry patch beside him.

"Takes one to know one," said the man, taking a moment away from his sax. "Beautiful morning, isn't it?"

"It's raining," said Mariel, flatly pointing out the obvious—but missing what was there. The sound of the rain on awnings. The smell of the wet concrete. The feel of the droplets on the small hairs of your arms. The gentle diffusion of morning light through the downy blanket of clouds.

But the musician caught all that. It was in his eyes and in his music.

"She plays different in the rain," he said, speaking of his sax. "Makes sounds you never knew existed. Sounds that you feel rather than hear." And to demonstrate, he launched into a rendition of "Stormy Weather" so soulful, it seemed the droplets themselves slowed their fall to listen.

Mariel had to pull Rón away. He could have stayed there all day listening.

Then, just around the next corner, they encountered another man. This one was shoeless, his feet as sooty as a chimney flue. He lay on the ground wrapped in a tattered blanket, only slightly less tattered than his clothes. He had found a tiny dry patch in an alcove beneath an awning and had made it his own. At first Rón thought he was asleep, but as they got closer, Rón could see his eyes were open, alert, and watching them.

Mariel sped up her pace—but this time Rón didn't have to stop her. She caught herself, stopped walking, and looked to the man. Then she glanced at Rón, and they shared an unspoken question and response.

This one?

Yes, this one.

Mariel approached him.

"What the hell do you want?" he croaked. If he were a porcupine, he would have spiked up.

"Nothing," Mariel said. "But we'd like to help you if we can."

He eyed them warily. Rón couldn't be sure if it was paranoia, or an understandable mistrust of strangers.

"Whatever you're sellin', I ain't buyin'," the man said, and rolled over to face the wall.

Rón knelt beside him and caught a whiff of his clothes. He was homeless, yes, but more than that. If hopelessness had a musk, this would be it.

Rón touched his shoulder, but he just curled up, pulling the blanket tighter.

"Get the hell away from me!" he growled. "You ain't got no masks! I don't want to end up like that freaking Crowncase around the corner." And as if in response, the deep breathy tone of the saxophone came careening off the buildings around them, echoing so that it could be coming from anywhere and everywhere.

This man desperately needed what Rón had to give, whether he knew it or not. However, before Rón could lean into his airspace, Mariel grabbed Rón's shoulder and jerked him back like a rider reining in a horse.

"Take care, then," Mariel said to the man. "We'll let you be." Then she tugged Rón to his feet. "Let's go."

Baffled and shocked, Rón did as Mariel said; he left this man to his suffering—and to Rón, the pain of leaving him in his lonely alcove was almost too much to bear.

Once they were out of earshot, Rón turned to Mariel. "Why did you do that?" It came out much more reproachful than he had intended.

"My decision. You agreed," she said. She wouldn't even look at him, as if perhaps she knew how wrong that decision was.

"But *why*, Mariel? His life won't get better on its own. I could have given him a second chance!"

"He didn't want it."

"He doesn't know what he wants!"

"That still doesn't give you the right to steal his choice! Even if it's the wrong one!"

Rón couldn't get past his disbelief. "Is this how it's going to be? I only expose people who agree to be exposed?"

Mariel pursed her lips, hardened her jaw. "Maybe."

"When did you decide that?"

She gave a halfhearted shrug. "Just now."

"You can't make up the rules as you go along!"

Finally, she stopped and turned to him, her eyes an accusation. "No? Isn't that *exactly* what you've been doing? Choosing people on a whim, whenever it suits you?"

Rón found he had no defense against that. She was right. He wanted to hate the fact that she was right, but he didn't have enough hate in him for a good old-fashioned stewing.

"You said we're the perfect balance," Mariel continued. "And maybe you're right. But maybe it's my job to pull you back when you go too far."

Even so, every bone in Rón's body told him that he needed

to be unshackled. That he needed to be free to spread Crown Royale anywhere he felt the need. But did that come from him, or was it the virus talking? And how could he be sure either way?

He responded with something his father often said to him when he was upset with Rón's choices and couldn't voice exactly why.

"You're not seeing the *gravity* of the situation!" Rón said. "Not helping that man feels . . . selfish."

Mariel considered that. "Maybe the world needs a little dose of selfishness," she said. "Maybe that's all that gravity is; the world selfishly holding on to what it has, so that everything doesn't disappear into space."

The sky stayed overcast, threatening more rain all the way through Iowa. Mariel was at the wheel because she didn't trust the detours that Rón might take, and Rón knew it. He didn't say anything, at least not at first. But after they had passed up Des Moines, and there was more of Iowa behind them than ahead, he voiced, if not a complaint, than an observation.

"We're going to have to stop eventually."

Mariel shrugged. "We'll stop when we stop," she said—a nonanswer, but it was all she felt like giving.

Rón grinned at her. "The things you don't say!" But he didn't push it.

This task before them felt way too huge for Mariel to wield. She understood why Rón felt so strongly. Because if you took everything into consideration, from war to apathy, from greed to racism—all the self-destructive, self-loathing, self-annihilating tendencies of human nature—Crown Royale might just be the best thing to ever come along.

That's what her heart told her. But her mind couldn't hold it down. It just kept regurgitating the whole thing back at her.

Really? We're intentionally going to make people sick? For their own good?

She wished that cynical part of her could embrace the larger picture.

On the other hand, maybe reservations were good. They would keep her constantly reevaluating their situation—something that Rón was now incapable of—because all he could see was the big picture. Sometimes you needed to see the trees instead of the forest.

For now, however, Mariel was simply afraid to stop—because as long as they were in motion, they didn't have to do anything. She didn't have to make good on her promise to *choose*.

"It would be unfair to blow through Iowa and not even stop," Rón said as they passed a sign that showed eighty miles to Illinois.

"Unfair to whom?"

"To them!" Rón said. "The Iowans. Iowers. Iowites."

Mariel couldn't help but laugh. "You're not God's gift to Iowa."

"No. That would be corn."

In the end, the decision to stop was made for them, because their tank was rapidly reaching empty. Then, after filling up, they decided to have lunch at a nearby diner.

The establishment was a hearty slice of Americana—covered in chrome paneling like an old Airstream trailer. The kind of place where girls once wore long skirts and ponytails, and boys still said "gosh" and "darn." But the rust burning its way through the chrome was a constant creeping reminder that those days were long gone, if they ever existed at all.

Inside, the place was a study in Social Distance Theater. Every third booth was blocked off with a sign that said WE'LL ALWAYS BE CLOSE! BUT THANKS FOR LEAVING THIS ONE EMPTY! It barely seemed to matter, though, since there were so few customers these days.

Rón moved toward a nonbarred table, but Mariel grabbed his elbow, took a deep breath, and said, "We'll sit at the counter . . . okay?"

There was a weightiness to the decision that Rón immediately picked up on. He gave her a broad smile that looked surreal on the false face his mask projected. "The counter, it is!"

Like the booths, every third stool at the empty counter was marked as off limits—as if an airborne virus were respectful enough to mind the house rules.

There was a waitress in a white-and-red striped uniform—hell's own fashion statement—and a single cook they could see through a narrow opening to the kitchen. Both were masked. The waitress's was a flimsy paper one stained with makeup she didn't have to be wearing, because no one could see her face. Her name badge said KELMA. The plastic place mats were menus, so she didn't have to waste time—or risk contact—by handing them out.

"Afternoon," she said with a tired sort of joviality. "What'll it be?"

"What's your specialty?" Rón asked.

The woman gave a rueful chuckle at that. "Indigestion?" she said. "This is a diner, if you haven't noticed."

"Right," said Rón. "Michelin radials instead of Michelin

Stars." But it went over Kelma's head, and it made Mariel feel bougie to have gotten the joke.

"I'll have a patty melt with fries, and a strawberry shake," Mariel said.

"Same for me," Rón seconded. "But make my shake chocolate."

"Great—two blue-plate specials. And I'll be back in two shakes with two shakes!" Which might have been funny if it were spontaneous, but Mariel suspected she said that all the time.

After she had gone off, Rón turned to Mariel.

"Her?"

Mariel didn't meet his gaze. "We'll see."

Kelma came back half a minute later. "Sorry guys, but the shake machine's down."

"Water's fine," said Mariel, not hesitating, because this was not about the meal, was it? Her mind was crunching how they might proceed, but she just couldn't do the math. How do you even broach the subject? In the end, Mariel realized she just had to go for it. So when Kelma returned with two waters, Mariel lobbed her first volley.

"Have you had it yet?"

"What, Crown Royale?" She put their waters in front of them. "Nope. I've been staying away from people who got it. 'Cause that's what we're supposed to do, right?" Then she thought about it. "I know people who've had it, though. It's true what they say—people get all funny afterward. Not ha-ha funny, just . . . funny."

"Not always a bad thing," Rón offered.

That gave the woman pause. "You're right about that. I got

this cousin—a massive turd, if ever there was one. But he got Crown Royale and now he ain't a turd no more. Like he done all twelve steps in one leap. So I guess there's that."

Mariel nodded and spoke slowly. Deliberately. "Would you get it if you could?"

"Not in my hands, honey," Kelma said blithely.

"How about what *is* in your hands?" Rón interjected. "Is your life everything you want it to be?"

"Oh, we're going there today," the woman said. Mariel couldn't tell whether she was smirking or frowning behind her paper mask. "Helluva personal question."

Rón said no more. Mariel chose to let the silence sit, until Kelma said, "Well, whose life *is* what they want it to be?"

Rón shrugged. "Your cousin's."

That turned the moment cold. But then the waitress gave them all a reprieve by glancing farther down the counter to where a couple had just sat down, eying her for attention. "I gotta go take an order," she said, and walked away.

When she came back a few minutes later, she had their food, and slid the plates in front of them. It looked good. Mariel wished she had more of an appetite.

Then Kelma pointed at their masks. "Don't forget to take those off. Can't tell you how many people try to shove a burger through their mask, forgetting they got it on. Me, I never forget. It's like a goddamn bra across my face. They burned bras in the sixties. Can't wait to burn these damn things. What a bonfire that'll be!"

"If we take them off, that'll put you at risk," Mariel pointed out. "You all right with that?"

"Honey, it's your job to eat, and it's my job to let you,"

Kelma said. "S'all right—I'm moving around back here. Anything after me's gotta catch me first."

And then Rón cut through all the bushes Mariel was beating around.

"I'm contagious," he said, just laying it on the table like their blue-plate specials. "Do you still want me to take it off?"

Kelma just stared at him.

"Or should we just take our food to go?" Mariel prompted, offering her an easy out.

The waitress took another few moments, straightened her uniform like she were about to go onstage, and said, "You're already at my counter, so you might as well eat."

Rón unlooped the mask from his left ear, then his right. It was slow enough to allow her to change her mind. But she didn't. Instead, she pulled down her own mask. Then Rón took a deep breath in, and released it. The waitress leaned forward ever so slightly. Not from the waist, but from her feet, like a tree bending in the wind.

"Hmm. Altoids," she said.

"Excuse me?" said Mariel.

"Peppermint Altoids. I can smell them on his breath."

"Life Savers, actually," Rón told her.

"Same difference," Kelma said. "Personally, I'm partial to wintergreen."

Then the cook called, "Order up," for the couple farther down. Kelma pulled her mask back up and went to get their plates.

She didn't speak to Mariel and Rón again for the rest of the meal. But when they were done, she tore up the check, and told them their lunch was on the house.

. . .

"That was beautiful!" said Rón, giving Mariel a kiss as they pulled back on the highway. "You were brilliant in there!"

Rón might have been recharged by their exchange at the diner, but Mariel found it exhausting on every level. "I felt more idiotic than anything."

"You're feeling guilty. Don't. Just like you promised, you gave her a choice. She knew exactly what we were offering her, and she took it. An offer accepted."

"I wish it could be as easy for me as it is for you."

Rón considered that. "I don't," he said. "The struggle makes it mean more. Because they're not the only ones who are choosing. You are too. And it makes me love you even more."

Hearing him say that touched her heart, but also made her wary. "You're like a puppy now, Rón. You'll love anyone who gives you a bone."

"But it's more than that. . . . Isn't it?"

That gave Mariel something else to feel guilty about. Her mother often told her guilt was a useless emotion—even though she always tried to wield it against Mariel with great success. "I feel the same way about you. . . . But there are plenty of people out there who won't understand. Who'll want to stop us. Who'll want to hurt us. It scares me."

"We're on the right side of history," Rón said, with absolute confidence. "So there's nothing to fear. Not even fear itself."

The text came in a moment of silence between them, not ten minutes later—a ding that seemed as loud as the starting bell of a prize fight. It made Mariel swerve in the road.

"Do you think . . . ?" Rón began.

"Zee," Mariel finished. "It has to be." But she bobbled the phone as she pulled it from her pocket, and it dropped into that evil crack between the seat and the center console.

"Crap!"

"It's okay," said Rón, ever calm. "It's not like the text is going anywhere."

But Mariel couldn't help but feel that their Mission Impossible message would somehow self-destruct if she didn't get to it. So she dipped her hand into the car's nether regions, groping for the phone, earning herself some badly scraped knuckles in the process.

"Got it."

She flipped the cheap phone open to find a message that was simple and unambiguous. Zee had finally come through, and now she felt guilty for having doubted him.

"'Forty-Two Gammons Drive, Kokomo,'" she read aloud.

"Kokomo? Like the Caribbean island?"

"I don't know."

"He must mean Kalamazoo—he knows that's where we're headed."

She fumbled with the car's GPS app since the cheap phone didn't have one. "Indiana! He must mean Kokomo, Indiana."

"That's not even in Michigan."

"It's probably the closest safe house he could find."

"Too bad," said Rón with a tweaked smirk. "I was starting to look forward to Kalamazoo."

The map pulled up various ways to get there, but Mariel opted for the most straightforward one. "We'll keep heading east, then turn south when we reach Chicago."

The message also said, **delete after reading**, which meant that Mariel was the self in "self-destruct." Now that they had both committed the address to memory, she did as instructed and deleted it. She thought she might send back a thumbs-up, but worried it would increase the chances that it could be traced. She had no idea how those sorts of things worked, but it wasn't worth taking the chance. Whatever phone Zee was using, it would register that the message was read. That would have to be enough. Mariel took a deep breath and released it. It was a relief to have an actual destination. Mariel powered the phone down. She considered breaking it like criminals did to burner phones in movies, then got annoyed that she was now thinking like a criminal. Besides, the idea of being on this journey without a phone made her uncomfortable.

Looking back, she would wonder if that was intuition.

Davenport, Iowa, was on the Mississippi at the eastern edge of Iowa. It wasn't known for anything in particular but a pretty Skybridge that didn't actually go anywhere and a major factory for Nestlé Purina—a company that was its own sinister oxymoron, because it manufactured Dog Chow and also chocolate—which was dog poison.

Another weather system was moving in. Or maybe the same one had followed Mariel and Rón from Omaha, because the afternoon sky was getting dismal and seemed minutes away from unleashing a torrent by the time they arrived in Davenport. Rón had taken the wheel for the past few hours. Mariel, having barely slept the night before, was too drowsy to drive now but insisted that Rón not drive with a storm looming.

While his skills were improving on their own, driving in the rain was its own thing. Besides, a town was different than a highway. Too many traffic laws for the uninitiated.

Rón wanted to stay at the wheel for as long as it made sense, though. He was enjoying the self-determination of it, and wondered why he had allowed himself to fall complacent about such things. His life had been one of town cars and chauffeurs—and although he had had some driving lessons with his father, it was more about father-son bonding than it was about actually learning to drive. His half siblings all had sports cars that they totaled on a regular basis. His resistance to driving had been a rebellion against all that. But he found he was happy to be blazing a trail in this Trailblazer.

Deciding to wait out the storm in Davenport, they left the highway when they saw a string of nondescript business hotels. Hampton Inn, La Quinta, and the like. Omaha had spoiled them, and with so much distance between them and San Francisco, they felt no need to sleep in the car anymore, as long as they had the cash Zee had given them. But the car's GPS system was wonky, constantly teleporting them hundreds of yards from where they actually were. They ended up weaving their way through a neighborhood instead of the street with all the hotels. Not literally in the weeds, but close.

"Why don't you let me drive?" Mariel asked.

"I'll get us there," Rón told her—not wanting to surrender before actually reaching a destination. But before they found their way out of the neighborhood, something caught Rón's attention. He pulled over to the curb.

"Why did you stop?"

"Look at that."

It was a sign in front of one of the homes, staked into the ground like a Realtor might put up for an open house. The sign read COME ON IN! ALL VISITORS WELCOME!

"That's weird . . . ," said Mariel.

"Is it?" said Rón, and waited for Mariel to read between the sign's lines.

"They're recoverees," she finally said.

Rón smiled. "*Mi casa es su casa* should be the recoveree motto!"

The house itself was a ranch house with a converted garage, and an anomalous second-floor addition that no self-respecting architect would have put their name on. But someone loved it. A whole family of someones, probably.

Rón put the car in park just as the clouds began to unleash. "I think I know where we're staying tonight."

26
Helm House

Elias Helm was assigned front door duty while his mom supervised dinner. It was an easy enough job—keeping track of who came and who went. He'd give a goodbye hug to anyone who was leaving, and a hearty welcome to anyone who arrived. It did require that he stay focused, though, and within earshot of the door—which had been rigged with little jingle bells.

His mom assigned him door duty more often than not, to shake him out of his room. It was his nature to cocoon himself in there—and being a recoveree didn't change one's basic nature; it just colored it differently. Now, instead of playing first-person shooter games and trolling sketchy hacker websites, he spent his alone time online looking for other recoverees to connect with all over the world. All right, yes, he still visited those hacker sites—some habits die hard—but now he had different goals.

Door duty, however, kept him in the public spaces of their family home—a family that no longer meant just his mom and siblings, but anyone else who happened to be there at any given time.

Right around dusk, the bells jangled and two newcomers stepped into the foyer. A guy and a girl. They seemed about Elias's age, give or take. He was glad for that. Most newcomers were people closer to his mother's age, or couples with babies.

Some were homeless, having heard about the place through the growing grapevine, hoping for a warm bed and a hot meal. Others came for the camaraderie. The latter were always fellow recoverees. But Elias could not yet tell what type of visitors these two were.

"Welcome to Helm House!" he said with practiced gusto. "Come on in! We've been waiting for you!"

"So you saw us in your crystal ball?" the girl said, with just enough snark for Elias to know that she hadn't had Crown Royale.

"No—my mom just wants me to say that to everyone. It's kind of our thing. Oh, and you can take your masks off—no one here is hot." And off their hesitant look, he added, "But you don't have to if you don't want to. That's cool too."

"I think we can risk it," the boy said. For an instant Elias sensed there was deeper meaning to that, but the thought was washed away when he saw their faces, and how they didn't look like their digital filament masks at all. He didn't know you could do that. He'd been working on his own digital mask hack—but never thought about subverting the facial projection software. He'd have to try that. He could be Darth Vader when he went to the market. Good times.

"I'm Courtney," the girl said. "This is Spencer."

"Call me Spence."

Spence was definitely a recoveree—Elias could see it in his eyes. And he was much cuter than his altered mask. He also reminded Elias of someone. Elias tried to spark that recognition, but couldn't. Maybe Spence just had one of those faces. He wondered what their story was. Were they brother and sister? He secretly hoped so, but since they bore no resemblance to each other, he suspected they were a couple. Damn.

"Dinner won't be ready until six—but you're welcome to raid the fridge until then." He brought them through the living room, where several long-term guests were discussing episodic TV and the nature of consciousness, then through to the kitchen, where his mom supervised the evening meal prep. Six people worked on dinner, but none of them ever seemed to get in each other's way. Another gift of Crown Royale. In a room of recoverees, there could never be too many cooks.

"Ma, this is Courtney and Spence."

She wiped her hands on a towel and came over to greet them. "A blessing to have you! Just here for dinner or do you plan to stay awhile?"

"Stay, if that's all right," said Spence. "At least till morning. After that, we'll see."

Elias saw Courtney throw him a sideways glance, but she didn't contradict him.

"Splendid! Elias, find beds for them. Blow up a couple of new ones if you have to. So glad you're with us!"

She grasped their hands to emphasize the welcome, then went back to preparing dinner for the masses.

On the way to the stairs, once his mom was out of earshot, Elias turned to Spence and Courtney. "My mom won't let you share a bed if you're not married. Just how she is."

"Yeah—the Jesus painting in the foyer was a dead giveaway," said Courtney.

"She started thumping that Bible after my dad died a few years ago. Instead of driving her to drink, it drove her to Jesus." Which, from Elias's perspective, wasn't all that much better—because it left her with the unwavering belief that Elias would be eternally damned. She wouldn't allow his boyfriends in the house, and prayed for Elias's immortal soul constantly, and loudly.

But that was all before Crown Royale.

After he and his mom recovered, they had their come-to-Jesus moment—which wasn't about coming to Jesus, but coming to be at peace with each other. *"What kind of horrible mother tells her son he's going to hell,"* she had said to him with true remorse, *"even if it's true?"* Which proved that there were some things not even Crown Royale could fix.

Elias spared Spence and Courtney the melodrama, and just said, "She's better now than she was. She doesn't thump the Bible anymore. Now she kind of throws it in the air to see where it lands."

As they continued the tour of the house, Rón knew what Mariel was thinking, because it was probably the same thing he was: that Helm House was just another Pier Peer Collective. Not nearly as large, but the concept was the same—a gathering of like-minded people, mostly recoverees, who had bonded, chosen to call this place home and call one another family. The only thing it lacked was a sick den for those still in the throes of Crown Royale—but Rón was sure that was coming.

"You'll have to forgive the construction," Elias told them as he led them past a hole in the wall covered by a tarp at the top of the stairs. "We're building a breezeway to the house next door because our neighbors want to be part of this too."

Which meant that Helm House was rapidly becoming a compound. Rón wondered if this would be the new way of the world—private homes and apartments gone, replaced by gatherings of found family. A restructuring of relationships, a reimagining of what it meant to be human—not forced upon people by socioeconomic systems, but rising organically from a new human nature. *This is what the world could be,* thought Rón. *Welcoming arms and unlocked doors.*

Mariel, however, found herself guarded and wary in a way that Rón was not. She knew it was mostly PTSD from living on the street with her mom, but she couldn't shake it. It had been the same when she first arrived at the pier—however, Zee was such a stable and wise presence that everything somehow felt grounded. But here, it seemed like they were winging it. *And how is that different from Rón and me?* It wasn't . . . but she much preferred being the one making up the rules.

The second floor featured a game room where several people stood around a table working on miniatures—buildings mostly, but also parks and greenery.

"What are they playing?" Rón asked.

"It's not a game," Elias told them. "They're working on a new design for downtown Davenport. Lots of greenbelts, in a carbon-free zone."

Mariel smirked. "Somehow, I don't think the city's going to listen to a bunch of recoverees building Legos."

"Usually not. But George, here, happens to be the city planner." And a gray-haired recoveree in a Metallica shirt gave them a smile and a wave.

Then, as if things weren't odd enough, it all took a serious turn toward surreal when Elias showed them his room.

"Spence can stay with me," Elias said. "We'll pull an extra mattress in. Courtney—you can share one of my sister's rooms."

Elias's room didn't look out of the ordinary. A gaming

chair, and a large, curved monitor on a desk that could have been neater. Posters on the wall were mostly of games, manga, and bands. Typical, but with one major exception:

There was a poster of Rón on the wall.

In the image, Rón was hefting a blaster. He was shirtless and absurdly muscular, like an action hero. Rón just gaped in unexpected horror, and, following his gaze, Elias snapped his fingers.

"That's it!" Elias said. "I knew you reminded me of someone! You look like Tiburón Escobedo!"

Mariel could tell that Rón's heart had bowed out for a beat or two, but Mariel was on it, and pulled in the slack. She rapped Rón casually on the arm. "See? I told you—it's not just me who thinks that!"

Rón took the cue and fell right in step. "I never said it was just you." Then he turned to Elias with a shrug. "I actually get that a lot." Then his eyes seemed to get sucked right back to the poster. "But I am nowhere near that ripped."

Elias smirked. "Neither is he. One of my friends knew I had a crush on Tiburón, so she got me this deepfake. Although, to be honest, it's really not that deep. If you look closely, you can see the light on his face is coming from a slightly different angle than on the rest of his body."

"Too bad," said Mariel with a smirk that she felt right down to her toes. "I'd love for Tiburón Escobedo to have that body."

"I know, right?" said Elias.

"I wish I had his money," Rón said, doing his best to be glib—and to pull focus from that faux six-pack.

"Don't we all!" agreed Mariel.

"Word is he's gone AWOL," said Elias. "If you ask me, I

think he got Crown Royale and ran off to live with the whales or something."

That made Mariel chuckle, and Rón look a bit ill. "Why whales?" Mariel asked.

"I don't know—rich people do weird things—just look at Jarrick Javins. He got Crown Royale, and now they say he's walking the world naked."

"I don't think he's naked," Rón pointed out.

"Depends on who you ask," said Elias. "Come on, there's an extra blow-up mattress down the hall. We can pull it in here."

Dinner was a crowded affair, with ten people seated, and others taking their plates elsewhere.

"We're going to need a bigger table!" Mrs. Helm said, which Rón almost called out as a misquote from *Jaws*, since he knew way too many shark references, no small thanks to his name.

Mrs. Helm offered up grace, which both Mariel and Rón knew was coming, but was particularly awkward because she singled out everyone present by name. Including "Spence," and "Courtney."

As for the meal itself, it felt like a holiday feast. It was all comfort food. A pot roast with mashed potatoes, and a cheesy casserole with a hint of green beans, because in this part of the world, vegetables were vague suggestions at best. There was a vegan option, but it looked a bit like dog food.

Conversation was mostly compliments to the cook and her helpers, with some current events thrown in.

"Have you seen the new public service announcements? Calling Crown Royale a 'scourge' and trying to shame anyone who thinks otherwise?"

"Outrageous!"

"I hear they're raiding recoverees' houses down South—arresting people on false charges."

"Dreadful!"

"Wall Street's panicking because consumer sales keep dropping. Didn't they realize that would happen?"

"So shortsighted!"

Then the city planner spoke up. "Money still does talk," he reminded them. "Eventually, industry will start providing what the world really needs, instead of the trinkets we used to want."

"Hear, hear!" replied Mrs. Helm, holding up her glass. A few others raised their glasses as well, but most people were too absorbed in the meal to respond.

Then Mrs. Helm turned to Mariel and smiled with such warmth and sympathy, Mariel couldn't decide whether she wanted to wither in her chair or slap the beatific expression off her face.

"Courtney, I hope you don't mind me saying so, but I can see you're unembraced."

Elias drew a breath. "Ma, please don't start!"

"Well, I just want to make sure she knows she's still very much welcome."

"Unembraced?"

Elias heaved a long-suffering sigh. "It's what they're starting to call people who haven't had Crown Royale. Or at least, what recoverees are calling them."

"If they can call us 'infected,'" said Mrs. Helm, "then we can call them 'unembraced,' and set the narrative straight—because we live in a world where spin matters."

"So I'm a 'them,'" said Mariel, holding the woman's overly empathetic gaze.

"Not at all, dear. The fact that you're here among us proves you're not. And I'm sure you'll be on the other side of it soon enough."

"I won't be," Mariel said, stewing in the cloy of the woman's honey. "Because I'm immune."

That drew everyone's attention. Every conversation halted. Even the clatter of silverware stopped.

"I . . . didn't know that was a thing," said Elias.

"Neither did we," said Rón, self-consciously jumping in. And then, perhaps because he had been lulled into a sense of security, or maybe just because he wanted to ease the attention on Mariel, he blurted, "She couldn't even catch it from me—and I'm an alpha-spreader."

Mariel bit her lip and glared at him. They didn't need to know that! And, come to think of it, they didn't need to know that she was immune, either. Maybe they should both just shut their mouths, keeping information on a need-to-know basis—and nobody here needed to know anything.

Then someone began applauding, and it caught all around the table.

"An alpha-spreader, right here in my home!" said Mrs. Helm. "Could there be a happier day?"

There was no question that the woman was kind and generous. To Rón, it felt charming; to Mariel, it was insufferable. She also had some very strange ideas—as evidenced by the living room conversation after dinner.

"If the Word could become flesh—who's to say that the

Word couldn't also become virus?" she postulated to the armchair philosophers, and anyone else who would listen. "Maybe this is what Holy Communion has been pointing to all along; taking in Jesus—God becoming a part of us. Isn't that what a virus is? Something we take in that changes us from the inside out?"

It would have been hilarious, if it didn't make the tiniest bit of sense in some disturbing metaphysical way. Elias was quick to drag Rón and Mariel away before they received a concussion from that proverbial Bible his mother was hurling into the air.

Elias's sisters were a couple of years younger, and both vied to have Mariel share their room. In the end, they settled it with rock paper scissors.

"We're out of here first thing in the morning," Mariel told Rón.

"Why are you in such a hurry? I'll bet Mrs. Helm makes a great breakfast."

"She thinks Crown Royale is the Second Coming," Mariel reminded him.

"So? Everyone tries to fit new realities into their existing belief systems."

"She creeps me out."

"She's harmless."

"So are most snakes. It doesn't make them any less creepy."

While Mariel went off to endure girl talk with middle schoolers, Rón made his inflatable bed on the floor of Elias's room. Knowing Elias had a crush on him never quite left Rón's mind. But then Rón had to remember—the crush wasn't on *him*. And yet it was. And yet it wasn't. Rón couldn't say he cared for the art of deception.

As they settled in for the night, Elias made small talk, and asked about their journey. Where they had come from, where they were going. Rón was vague with his answers. East coast. Heading west. Basically the opposite of what they were actually doing. He told Elias they were "reconnecting with relatives my family didn't talk to before Crown Royale." Lies upon lies upon lies. And then came the inevitable question.

"So . . . you and Courtney . . ."

Finally a question he could tell the truth about. Rón knew what Elias was really asking. And why. Rón tried to let him down easy. "She and I are soulmates," Rón told him. "In every possible way."

"Yeah, I figured." Elias tried to hide his disappointment, but apparently lies didn't come easily to him, either.

On the nightstand, Elias's phone buzzed with an alert. It was just some random app notification, but the phone's wallpaper caught Rón's attention. It was a picture of Elias with his arms around another boy. Both seemed happy in the image.

"So you have a boyfriend?" Rón asked.

Elias didn't meet his gaze, and took his time in answering.

"Have. Had. Have. I'm not sure anymore." For a moment, he looked melancholy—or at least as melancholy as a recoveree can get. "He's unembraced, as my mom would say." Elias glanced dolefully at the phone, which had gone dark again. "Ralphy has barely spoken to me since I recovered. And you know what's crazy? My mom is finally okay with him coming over. She wants to meet him, apologize for the way she was before—but he won't come. He says all those months of disrespect can't be wiped away by a fever. But I think it's more than that. I think he's bought into that whole body-snatcher lie.

Rón understood it all too well. "He thinks you're not you anymore."

"But I'm more 'me' now than I ever have been," said Elias, getting strident, if not angry. "I mean, I used to be driven by so many things outside of myself—fear, a need to fit in, wanting everyone to like me. . . . But now I feel centered. I can be who I am. I can't help it if he's afraid of who I am."

Rón nodded. "He'll change once he's had it."

"Maybe," said Elias, unconvinced. "Or maybe it's time for us both to move on."

The silence that followed would have been awkward, had they not both been recoverees, and Rón marveled that social anxiety was yet another beast tamed by Crown Royale. Even in the most awkward of moments, how could you feel uncomfortable when you empathized with everything the other person was feeling?

"Hey—I'll show you something cool," Elias said, happy to change the subject. He picked up his phone, then hesitated, as if perhaps he were having second thoughts—but then he continued anyway. "I've been working on this for a few weeks now—it's something I think you especially are going to like, being a badass alpha-spreader—but you can't tell anyone."

"Sure," Rón said, not knowing who he would tell, besides Mariel.

"You got your mask?"

Rón pulled his mask out of his pocket, not knowing where Elias was going with this, but increasingly curious.

"Good—now put it on."

Rón slipped the mask on, and Elias took a long look at it.

"Whose face is that anyway, and how did you get it to do that?"

"Oh right. Yeah—a guy was selling them on the street. In Philly. We thought they were funny, so we each got one." Rón struggled so much with the lie, he was sure it was obvious, and Elias would call him on it. But Elias accepted the explanation without a second thought.

"Cool." He returned his attention to his phone, tapping and swiping. "Okay, check this out—those digital masks work by heat gradients, pressure sensitivity, and a network of micro cameras in a filament grid," Elias explained.

"Yeah, I know," said Rón—then realized that if he were really Spence Whoever, he *wouldn't* know. So he added, "I saw it on a YouTube video."

"Here's the thing," Elias said. "The mask relies on a wireless signal between all three systems to integrate the image. Which means it can be hacked." Elias tapped his phone. "Observe!"

Nothing seemed to happen.

"Wait for it," Elias said.

Then, in a moment, Rón felt his ears becoming warm—and within seconds, they were so hot that he had to rip the mask off his face.

"Ow!" Rón rubbed his ears, and Elias looked at him, gloating in triumph. Rón knew exactly what had happened.

"You overloaded it! How did you do that?"

"Cool, right? I set the overload radius to just a couple of feet, but I can set the UnMasker app wider—ten feet, twenty, maybe even thirty."

"Why would you do that?"

Elias just grinned—and Rón got it. Imagine a crowded place, everyone wearing masks, at least half of them digital.

Then suddenly—*poof*—those people rip their masks off all at once. Send someone contagious into the crowd, and—

"You want to create super-spreader events. . . ."

"Shhh!" Elias leaned closer, and brought his voice down. "You can't tell my mom. She thinks it ought to spread naturally, 'the way God intended.' But me? I think it could use a little help."

Rón found himself awed by the audacity. "Who else knows about this?"

Elias shrugged. "Just a few friends online. We're all recoverees, so it's safe."

Rón took Elias's phone, and studied the homemade app. Simple toggles, no bells and whistles. Elegant in concept, if not design. Truly impressive. "I still can't figure out how you did it! I thought my father had safeguards against stuff like that."

Rón didn't realize the bomb he had dropped until he saw Elias's shocked expression. With a single word, Rón had just pulled out the keystone in his elaborate house of cards.

"I mean . . . Blaze Escobedo," Rón said.

Elias's eyes stayed locked on Rón's. "His name is *Blas*. . . . But you know that already. Don't you . . . 'Spence' . . . ?"

There was no walking this back. Rón could only hope that Elias was enough of an ally to keep his secret. Once his brain stopped exploding.

"You're Tiburón Escobedo . . . *THE* Tiburón Escobedo. And you're in Davenport, Iowa . . . in my room."

Rón realized that he had been wrong; awkwardness was alive and well.

"So . . . are you gonna fanboy all over me now?" Rón asked.

Elias's grin could not be contained. "Oh, I would love to

'fanboy' all over you. But I get the feeling that's not happening."

"No," conceded Rón. "But I give you unlimited permission to dream about it."

"Dude, I don't need your permission for *that*."

The raid came without warning at two thirty a.m. Most everyone was asleep, except for the armchair philosophers who found the late hour more conducive to universal pondering, and a couple of peckish people routing out late-night leftovers from the fridge.

The front door was unlocked, but the SWAT team kicked it in anyway.

None were recoverees, none of them sympathetic in any way to the residents of Helm House, or places like it. They were professionally unembraced, indoctrinated in the old ways where nothing good ever came from contagion.

They carried their weapons raised, their laser sights flicking to anything that moved, as if they expected to be met with heavy firepower—just like the team that had raided the pier halfway across the country. It was only a matter of time until a spatula was mistaken for a gun, and someone was taken out, leaving a juicy headline for the morning news. Whether this raid held the loaded chamber of recoveree roulette was anyone's guess.

"Down on the ground, hands behind your head!"

Upstairs, Elias sat up in bed, and put two and two together instantly. These things didn't happen without a warrant—and yes, many warrants against recoveree sanctuaries were bullshit. But this one might not be.

Because what if one of those online hacker friends he

shared his app with wasn't a recoveree after all? What if they were a mole looking to catch people trying to spread Crown Royale?

Rón had been dragged awake by the shouts and banging of doors—but all still downstairs. It was a blessing that the second-floor addition was so painfully nonarchitectural, because the stairs weren't obvious—they were tucked away around a bend behind the kitchen. With plenty of people to wrangle downstairs, it gave them time before the SWAT team found the stairs.

Elias heard one of his sisters calling for their mother. He wanted to go to her, but knew there was an imperative here that he could not ignore. He knew he and his family weren't the ones who mattered here. They could all be captured, thrown into some recovery detention center, but Rón could not be caught. Instinctively, Elias knew that Rón had a destiny, a mission. But Elias also knew he had an important part to play in it. He grabbed his phone, fumbling with it, and shoved it into Rón's hands.

"You know what to do with this. I trust you, Tiburón."

Rón's brain was still struggling itself alert. He knew he needed to act and leave thinking for later. Someone burst into the room, and for an instant he thought the worst—but it was Mariel.

"Rón! We need to hide," she said, completely forgetting to call him 'Spence,' which would have been a problem if he hadn't already blown his own cover.

"No! You both need to get out of here!" said Elias. "Climb out my window. There's a trellis. It'll hold your weight. I've done it a dozen times."

There were footsteps thundering up the stairs now. Elias pushed his door closed. Locked it. It would buy them seconds at most.

"Go! Now!"

Mariel went first, climbing out the window, grabbing on to the trellis.

What Rón did next wasn't spontaneous, but it wasn't planned, either. He just found himself there in the moment and knew exactly what that moment needed. Quickly, he leaned forward and kissed Elias.

Elias all but went limp.

Rón didn't particularly like the kiss, nor did he particularly hate it. It was like a sip of water; just a thing with no flavor either way. But what Rón *did* like were the stars in Elias's eyes when it was done. This was his gift to Elias, a memory he could hold on to for as long as he had memory to hold.

"Take care, Elias."

Then Rón followed Mariel out the window.

Seconds later, the SWAT team burst into Elias's room, weapons raised. "On your knees! Hands behind your head!" an officer shouted. Elias did as he was told and suddenly began to laugh.

"What are you laughing about?" the officer growled.

"Sorry if I'm a little giddy," Elias crooned. "But it's my first time on my knees for a man in uniform." And Elias just laughed and laughed and laughed.

While somewhere downstairs a weapon discharged, and a spatula clattered to the ground.

27

Above and Below

Do not believe what they tell you! Reputable sources have proof that Crown Royale recoverees are turning violent! A mob of them raced through a town in Ohio, biting people, taking chunks out of their faces—and the violence is spreading. You won't find it in the news because the mainstream media is suppressing the truth! Don't believe it!
RoyaleConspiracy@gmail.com

It was night wherever Morgan happened to be. Somewhere over middle America, she imagined. But these days, she went by her own internal clock, without regard to the monotonous machinations of the sun.

Morgan found that she only felt truly safe at thirty-four thousand feet. And so, she used every excuse possible to be aboard the Havilland Consortium's private jet, sealed as airtight as a space suit against anything out there.

A space suit. That had been her entry into this strange chapter of her life. She should have worn it when she went to see that convict. But as traumatizing as that encounter had been, she was grateful for it. Because it had done more than just shaken her. It had also educated her. Prior to that day, she was fluent in five languages. Now she was fluent in one more. The language of fear. She had never experienced terror like she felt when that convict had sliced through her hazmat hood and breathed into it. Those moments holding her breath against the contagion were the most awful moments of her life. But Morgan knew how to use every experience in her favor. She found a way to internalize that fear, transform it, utilize it.

Now she made everyone she graced with her presence do three consecutive hours of testing, just as she had back in Svalbard. It served not only to keep her safe, but also created a ritual that anyone with whom she had an audience was required to follow. It was elevational. It made her seem much more imposing than a nineteen-year-old wunderkind who'd won an old woman's lottery.

And the meetings she had were at the highest level—because money was elevational as well. She hadn't lied when she told Blas Escobedo that she wasn't skimming money for herself. But she *had* diverted some of it to related causes. The kinds of things that Blas wouldn't disapprove of, although he'd probably give lip service to how distasteful he found them. She knew he was motivated by fear as well. The fear of losing interest in the fortune he had amassed and in the position he had attained in the world. And yet he wouldn't weaponize that fear. He was a man in the ultimate cutthroat position . . . who would never actually cut a throat. Even his competitors respected him. So knowing the frustratingly honorable man that Escobedo was, Morgan kept certain things to herself. Not just the illegal human testing, but other things as well.

Don't trust the spider! And whatever you do, don't smoke Philip Morris brands! The heads of the company are filthy recoverees, and are spiking cigarettes with Crown Royale,

embedding it right in the filters. Not only that, but factory workers are POISONING red M&M's, because if they can't infect us, then they'll kill us. It's all on this website! www.StoptheViralSpider.com

She had paid a hefty sum to a top Madison Avenue advertising firm to effect a massive shift in public perception of Crown Royale. The "Viral Spider" was quickly becoming the accepted emoji for the disease, and the ad team pushed it into every market, until variations began to show up on their own. "Resist the Spider" messaging was showing up on merchandise everywhere from Amazon, to Etsy, to CongaLine. Which meant the Viral Spider had gone . . . well . . . viral.

Morgan then hired internet trolls in shady places around the world to spread disinformation. Terrifying tales of infection and consequences. The rumor of infected cigarettes and of candy poisoned by murderous recoverees. This week's bullshit bombardment was her favorite: A rumor from fake "credible sources" that a band of radical recoverees in some faraway place—Uzbekistan, Kazakhstan, Turkmenistan—it didn't matter which, as long as it was a "-stan"—was planning a bioterrorist attack against us. "Us" being whoever you wanted it to be. Whoever happened to fall into your "us" versus "them" construct.

She had even engaged a think tank to come up with a new term for "recoverees," and a surefire method of disseminating the new moniker across social media in a way that would stick. The campaign was already in progress: People who had survived Crown Royale would no longer be called "recoverees." Now they'd be "the compromised." Weakened, damaged people to be despised and pitied. And when they gathered in groups? That was "a web of the compromised"—with the very clear implication that the Viral Spider was sitting at the web's center.

Do you know the truth about what Crown Royale does to your body? Whatever you do, don't be compromised! Click this link www.StoptheViralSpider.com/wrm to see a three-foot worm pulled out of a man's spine. That's the final phase of the disease! Yes, that's right, the Viral Spider gives birth to CARNIVOROUS SPINAL WORMS!

The beauty of disinformation was that the more outlandish it was, the more people would believe it, because it was fed by the public's own paranoia. Amazing how easy it was to cast a fishhook out into the collective consciousness, and watch people take the bait, then writhe and flail on the line. The language of fear! Morgan now knew it intimately and was determined to invoke it like a spell, until Crown Royale was a crushed spider beneath her foot.

These comforting thoughts lulled her to sleep as her plane passed six and a half miles above Davenport, Iowa.

Far below, on the street around Helm House, window shades had silently gone up, and curtains had parted. Neighbors awakened by the commotion peered out of their windows, watching the raid, not sure whether to be horrified or entertained. Yet with all those late-night viewers, not a single light came on. People watched from the safety of their own personal darkness. Those who had yet to contract Crown Royale were secretly—and not so secretly—satisfied to see Helm House taken out.

Because whatever went on in there—be it drugs, or sex, or revolutionary plots—it would now stop. A police raid made it easy for "the unembraced" to dismiss recoverees as problems. Abnormal, swelling blemishes that had to be removed.

The Trailblazer was parked too close to Helm House for Rón and Mariel to simply get in and drive away, so they fled with no destination, trying to disappear into the dark corners of the Davenport neighborhood.

"There was a gunshot. I know I heard it. It wasn't my imagination."

Mariel's voice was a whisper, and still it was too loud, for the night felt airless, as if the slightest vibration could set off an avalanche of consequences.

"I heard it too." Rón's voice was softer, yet still not soft enough. "I'm pretty sure it came from downstairs."

Every time they found a shadow to hide in, they were quickly chased away by a motion-sensor spotlight, or a barking dog.

The whole incident left Mariel reeling. The recoverees in Helm House were odd ducks, but a police raid? What could they have possibly done to warrant that?

Rón, of course, knew what they were after, but kept it to himself. Just thinking about Elias's phone made it feel all the more heavy in his pocket. He reached in and powered it down just in case it could be tracked.

"Wait," said Mariel. "You don't think they were looking for you?" Because, after all, the first police raid they had escaped from had been all about Rón—and that line of thought tipped the next domino in Mariel's mind. "If someone was killed, then it's our fault. . . ."

"Let's just get through this night," Rón said, not offering an opinion on the matter, because he was beyond the need for blame now. Besides, it wouldn't change anything. And although Mariel's mind felt like spiraling to terrible places, she stopped herself. It wasn't helpful. It wasn't *additive*. If there was one thing she had learned from Delberg Zello, it was the need to be additive.

Two streets away, in an unkempt yard, they found stairs down to an unlocked cellar, and they slipped inside. They used mildewed dust covers and shared body heat to ward off the cold, and ignored squeaks that were most likely rats.

"Let's just get through this night." They were of one mind when it came to that sentiment. They spoke little, and slept even less. Four hours of this. Then, at the first hint of dawn, they released themselves from limbo, and left the cellar, stiff and exhausted, stepping out into a morning that didn't know whether or not it wanted to rain.

"We've got to get to the car," Rón said.

"No—if they're after you then they probably know it's ours and will be waiting for us."

"They won't be."

"You don't know that."

"I'm willing to take the risk."

And since Mariel realized the risk was entirely his, she backed off.

The early dawn was defiantly quiet in the aftermath of the raid. All the residents had been taken away. Yellow crime scene tape blocked off the entire property and stretched across the front door for anyone who hadn't already gotten the hint. There was evidence of the incursion everywhere. The shattered doorjamb, muddy boot prints on steps leading to the porch and all over the front yard. But with the search and seizure over, the scene was inactive. Now only a single squad car sat in the driveway like a scarecrow to keep away the curious.

Mariel and Rón peered around a hedge half a block away, both wondering what would happen to the place now.

"They couldn't all be under arrest, could they?" Rón wondered out loud.

"They can take them in for questioning, but can't hold anyone without charging them with a crime," Mariel pointed out. Having seen her mother brought down to the station on more than one occasion, she knew how these things went. "They'll have to let them go—but I don't think anyone will be allowed back here anytime soon."

Rón nodded. "Break them up. Relocate the Helm family, and send everyone else back to their actual homes. Maybe that's what this was about."

"Like breaking up a wasp's nest."

Rón gave her a chilly look at the comparison. "Recoverees don't sting."

The Trailblazer was two houses down from the Helm driveway where the police car sat, immobile. It wasn't until neighbors started getting in their cars and going off to work that Mariel and Rón chanced it.

To chase away her misgivings, Mariel counted silently. Fifty-three steps from the hedge where they were hiding to the car; seven beats to open the doors, get in, sit down, buckle up, start the car, put it in gear, and pull into the street; twelve seconds until she turned the corner and out of view of the lone squad car.

Only after they were on the highway, and crossing the Mississippi into Illinois, did Rón say what was on his mind, and had been on his mind since the moment of the attack.

"We're at war, Mariel. We tried to deny it, but the truth hit us over the head last night. This is a war, and we have to start treating it like one."

"What exactly are you saying?"

Rón had thought he made himself clear—that he said all that he needed to say, but quickly realized that a declaration of war meant nothing without action. And action had to come with a plan.

"I don't know yet."

"Well, until you do, maybe you should stop mouthing off."

It was Mariel's intent to shut Rón up, because it was just too much to think about, especially behind the wheel of a car running from police that might or might not be after you. But it didn't shut Rón up. Instead, it made him bolder.

"The one thing I do know is that we can't fight this battle if we're tiptoeing around, choosing one person at a time," Rón said.

"You agreed you'd do it my way."

"Then maybe you need to think of a new way."

The windshield wipers swept back and forth across a drizzle that was too thin for the wipers, but too much to just leave. They squeaked like the rats in the night.

After a long silence between them, Rón said, "It's simple, really. Either Crown Royale will win, or it will lose. If it loses, then humanity loses as well," he said. "And not just humanity. I think the world rests on this, Mariel. And you and me . . . we might be the ones who make the difference."

. . .

They crossed through Illinois without stopping until they reached the suburbs of Chicago, grabbing gas in Naperville before continuing on.

It was Rón who suggested they call it an early day. They had gotten so little sleep, so Mariel put up no resistance. Besides, Kokomo was less than three hours from Chicago, and neither was keen on getting there today, not knowing what was really waiting for them there. For all they knew, the Pier Peer Collective was taken down the same way Helm House had been, and Zee's message wasn't from Zee at all. Maybe it was a trap.

They turned on the radio to chase such thoughts away. At first country music, which made Mariel nostalgic for times with her mother—but which Rón only tolerated. Then an alternative rock station which was more Rón's taste, but to Mariel it all sounded like self-absorbed Gen Zers whining into their lattes.

Eventually they turned to news radio, because there were simply things they needed to know, even if they didn't really want to know them. Ten minutes in, there was a thirty-second report on the raid at Helm House—although the news called it a "suspected drug den," which was laughable, because the recoverees there didn't as much as take aspirin. What made it newsworthy was that there was a notable fatality. The Davenport city planner had been shot and killed. According to the SWAT team commander, he had been brandishing a weapon— although eyewitness reports said otherwise. *"The investigation,"* said the news, *"is still ongoing,"* which, as everyone knew, was code for *"You're never going to hear about this again."*

Neither Rón nor Mariel wanted to be the first to comment. As if not talking about it would make it less real. Finally, Rón made his definitive statement on the matter.

"War is ugly."

Not particularly profound, but it drove home the fact that he still saw this as a war.

Mariel's response was to change the station—flipping it to hip-hop, which neither of them hated nor loved, but the beat was powerful enough to keep them from pondering other things.

It was Rón's suggestion that they find a hotel near O'Hare Airport—and since economy hotels tended to be clustered around airports, there was no reason for Mariel to think there was any motive beyond convenience.

With so many airport hotels shuttering for the duration of the pandemic, they ended up at a less-than-comfortable Comfort Inn that must have been right at the foot of a runway, because they could hear planes powering up their engines and taking off every thirty seconds, rattling their window—but they were so exhausted, neither that nor the sunlight defying the thin curtains could keep them awake.

To Rón, those engine rumbles were as comforting as waves crashing on a beach. But to Mariel, they felt like small tremors that warned of something much larger to come.

In San Francisco, Blas Escobedo arrived at the Pier Peer Collective unannounced and unaccompanied by law enforcement. He knew coming here was a risk, even double-masked, but without a single reliable lead on Tiburón, he knew this was his best bet. Desperate times, desperate measures—both for himself and for the world at large.

On the world front was his clandestine partnership with Morgan Willmon-Wu—who he was to meet with in person, face-to-face—that afternoon. But that partnership had to be taken with a grain of salt. He admired her shrewdness and her willingness to think outside the box, but he worried about her ambition. Granted, it was a strange thing for a man who had fought tooth and nail to become the richest human being on the planet to say he was concerned with someone else's ambition . . . but ambition had many faces. Its tactics were defined by the moral flexibility of the person in question. Blas liked to think of himself as the billionaire who didn't behave like a billionaire. More than the money or the success, he saw honor in the face of corruption to be his greatest achievement.

No, he had to remind himself. No, that wasn't true. His greatest achievement was raising a son like TeTe.

Escobedo stepped out of an SUV that was a bespoke shade called wisteria, which looked either pale lavender or gray depending on the light—Blas refused to allow himself to be chauffeured around in those black cars that looked like government intimidation vehicles. He approached the entrance to the pier, where several greeters were waiting to bring the disenfranchised into their fold.

One of them recognized him right away. He noted her hair was the exact same shade of wisteria as his vehicle, and imagined the woman saw that as proof of the interconnectedness of all things.

"Mr. Escobedo!" she said cheerfully—as if he hadn't been responsible for routing them all out of their beds in the middle of the night the week before. "So glad to have you back. I don't suppose you're here to join us, although it would be wonderful if you were."

"I need to speak to Delberg Zello."

It clearly did not come as a surprise to her. "Most people have to wait their turn," she said, "but I'm sure he'll be happy to drop everything for you!"

It was hard for Blas to see her words as anything but sarcastic—and yet she proved herself to be sincere when she returned with Zello not a minute later. Of course she was sincere; she was a recoveree. Or—what were they starting to call them now? "The compromised"? Blas couldn't say he liked that any better, considering his son was now one.

"Well, if it isn't the man himself," said Zello, who offered his hand, as if that were still a thing during a pandemic. Blas didn't take it. "To what do I owe this visit?"

"I want to talk about my son," said Blas, skipping past any and all small talk. "No posturing, no police; just one man to another."

Zello nodded. "Walk with me."

He led them down a meandering path that Blas hadn't noticed the first time he was there. Like many structures on the pier, it was still under construction; a path covered with colorful mosaics that were an amalgam of different cultures and art forms. A little Mesoamerican, a little Gaudí, hints of Roman baths, Japanese minimalism. The path was a museum of world culture beneath their feet. Blas almost felt like he should take his shoes off as he trod it.

"My son is still missing."

"'Missing' isn't the word, I don't think," said Zello. "'At large,' maybe. Or 'on holiday.' Yes, on holiday! That's how the Brits say it, and I like that better than 'vacation.' 'Vacation'— that always comes with expectations, doesn't it? But being 'on holiday' sounds like a party every damn day."

"Well, whatever you want to call it, I can't find him."

"Because he doesn't wish to be found, Mr. Escobedo. I'm sure when he does, you'll know."

Blas expected the man would say as much. "I'll make this easy, Mr. Zello. You know more than you gave me the last time I was here, so don't waste my time denying it."

Zello gave him a broad, knowing smile. "So now you're here to threaten me, and give me some kind of ultimatum if I don't comply, is that right?"

"No," said Blas. "More flies with honey than vinegar."

"Oh, so we're flies now. Been called worse, I suppose."

Blas pressed on. "I know that things haven't gone well for you since the sailboat tragedy. It's said there's no such thing as bad publicity, but that's not true for a place like this. A place that relies entirely on the generosity of others." The beatific look on Zello's face faltered just a bit. Blas continued. "I know that whatever recoverees were funding your collective have shifted their generosity elsewhere."

Zello didn't deny it. "Fortunes are fickle," he admitted. "Even among altruists."

"I would bet you're on the verge of food rationing if you're not doing it already. And all of this construction—how much longer can it go on if you don't have cash to fund it?"

Zello dismissed it with a shake of his head. "I'm not worried."

"Of course you're not! Recoverees never are. But viral optimism isn't going to change the fact that your peer collective is bordering on bankruptcy."

Zello was silent. Blas let it sink in as they strode across a rendering of Mount Fuji—which, Blas recalled, hadn't erupted in three hundred years and was overdue. He lingered with Zello, both of them gazing down at the prospect of imminent devastation. A perfect moment for the sell.

"If you give me information that leads me to my son, I will bankroll all of your needs. Food, supplies—I'll even pay the engineers you'll need to bring your construction to code. Help me find my son, and I will help *you* make the Pier Peer Collective a shining light in this bay."

"It already is that to those who can see it, Mr. Escobedo."

"Maybe, but not for much longer."

They resumed walking. Zello took his time before responding. Blas couldn't tell whether he was considering it or just drawing this out.

"You know, Mr. Escobedo—my mama always told me that if someone comes to you with a deal too good to be true, you need to walk away. Because once in everyone's life, they've gotta face a deal with the Devil."

Blas sighed. "I'm not the Devil, Mr. Zello. I'm just a heartbroken father trying to find his son."

"I get that, I do. But here's my dilemma. I made a promise to Tiburón. So do I break his confidence in exchange for your financial assistance? Or do I hold on to what integrity I got?"

"Everyone has a price. . . ."

"Unless they've recovered from Crown Royale."

They had reached a spot where the mosaics stopped. Ahead of them, half a dozen workers were happily tiling, but Blas's road had clearly come to an end.

"So now that the honey didn't work, you gonna bring on the vinegar?" asked Zello.

Blas could if he wanted to. He could spill out his rage until this place was nothing but dust. He might have, if he thought it would make a difference, but Zello was right. Recoverees could not be bought.

"There's nothing I can threaten you with that isn't already happening here," Blas said. "Adios, Mr. Zello. And when your social experiment here goes belly up, remember it was your stubbornness that killed it."

He wished he could storm a straight line to the car, but the path wouldn't allow it.

Blas had left the pier, and was about to step into the SUV, when a woman grabbed his arm.

"Mr. Escobedo, a word, please."

She was Brown but not Latina. Her accent pointed to India.

"And who might you be?"

"My name is Zoya Pirmal. I'm the doctor who saw your son through Crown Royale."

That was more than enough to get his attention. "Could you . . . tell me how it was for him?"

"Difficult, very difficult. But then, no one has it easy."

Blas suspected as much. He had to remind himself that TeTe's suffering was now in the past. "And so, you nursed him back to health?"

"I attended him, but most of the credit goes to the girl he was with."

"A girl?"

"She was by his side through all of it. I imagine she's with him now."

"Tell me more."

The doctor looked around to make sure they were

unobserved—which they weren't. The greeters at the entrance to the pier were watching. But they weren't close enough to hear anything that was being said.

"I heard what you offered Zello. I do agree with his decision; he did make an oath to your son, so he shouldn't break it."

"Then what is your point, Doctor?"

"*He* made an oath. However, I did not. Which provides us with a most convenient loophole."

Blas tried to keep his hope from ballooning too quickly. He'd made that mistake before. "I'm listening."

"Does the offer you made still hold? Because none of us want to see the collective fail."

"It depends on what you can tell me."

She ignored that and went on, "After the sailboat incident became a public scandal, medical vendors stopped selling to us, pharmacies stopped supplying us, and with Crown Royale cases still on the rise in the city, ventilators are all going to the big hospitals. So in addition to all the things you promised Mr. Zello, can you guarantee me ventilators, supplies, and all the medications I need?"

"Dr. Pirmal, if you provide me with information that leads me to my son, I'll give you the sun, the moon, and the stars."

"And ventilators?"

"Yes. And ventilators."

"You must donate everything anonymously. Delberg must never know it came from you or he's sure to refuse it. We recoverees might have a new perspective, but we are not perfect. Our egos might be subjugated for the greater good, but not erased."

"It's as good as done. Tell me what you know."

Pirmal considered his eyes and must have judged him

honorable, because she said, "Your son left the morning of the raid. He hid under the pier and escaped with the girl who had been helping him."

"So she was another recoveree?"

"Not exactly. The girl is actually immune. First time I've ever come across natural immunity. I was dubious, but her blood work showed that—"

"And where did they go?" Blas asked, not caring to have a symposium on viral minutia.

"That, I'm afraid, I do not know. I only know that they left."

Blas felt his hope deflate yet again. "I already know that he left. That's not useful information, Doctor."

"Oh, but it is," Pirmal said, her voice still hushed. "Trust me, it is very, very useful." She smiled gently, pulled out a pen, and wrote a series of letters on his palm.

"It's useful," she said, "because they're driving my car."

28
El Hombre de Hierro

Morgan stepped into Blas Escobedo's lavish chalet, a striking contrast to the raw beauty of Mount Shasta outside. A lot of effort must have gone into making the new structure appear like it had been there for generations. Money buys history. Morgan would have to remember that.

She trusted Escobedo enough not to demand the three hours of testing. Also, it would weaken her position if he refused.

He greeted her personally at the heliport on a natural mesa fifty yards from the home.

"Morgan! It's a pleasure to finally meet you in person. Come in, we'll get you something hot to drink."

The interior decor was understated. It was what she would expect from Escobedo, who liked comfort over display. She knew several of his children were there, hunkering down, but the chalet was so large, she never encountered them. Or perhaps that was intentional.

She did meet his girlfriend, Kavita, who had masked up, although Blas had not. She was pleasant enough, but seemed wary. Like Morgan might be here to kick her to the curb, and take her place. As if that were in anyone's plans. Morgan considered herself a sharp judge of character, and didn't think Blas

Escobedo was the type to set his sights on a nineteen-year-old. But on the other hand, people were often disappointing.

Once Kavita had gone off to do whatever it was girlfriends of billionaires do, Morgan and Blas took coffee in a living room with a million-dollar view that cost quite a lot more than a million. Although she felt confident, it was laced with trepidation, knowing she had news that would not make the man happy. Which was a shame, because he was cheerful enough to be among the compromised today.

"You're in a much better mood than when we last spoke," Morgan observed.

"I just had a lead on finding my son. So today is a good day."

"That's wonderful news."

"We'll see where it leads."

Morgan sipped her latte. "This chalet is quite the digs." In most situations she despised small talk and banal conversational etiquette, but everything about this little summit needed to be eggshelled.

"'Digs' is an appropriate word. We had to cut into the mountain to build it. Not quite as deep as Svalbard, of course."

"You plan to stay here until the pandemic is over?" Morgan asked, still trying to keep the conversation hovering.

"It's my hope that you've come tell me that it *is* over. Or at least that it soon will be."

Morgan put down her cup. "I did come to discuss our progress," she admitted.

"My virtual platform not quite good enough for the update, hmm?"

Morgan took a deep breath. "Not for this conversation."

Escobedo studied her intently, adding weight to the air. "I understand you had a scare last week. An exposure from one of the test animals."

His comment caught her off guard. But she was glad that the nature of the test subject hadn't reached him. "So you have a spy in Svalbard."

"Nothing so devious," he said with a wave of his hand. "Dr. Bosgraaf called. Believe it or not, she's been worried about you."

"Dr. Bosgraaf had no business telling you *my* business."

Escobedo crossed his legs and clasped his hands over one knee, signaling that the pleasantries had concluded. "So what have you come to tell me? Are you here to celebrate a breakthrough? To toast our success? Should I have brought out champagne instead of coffee?"

"No, the coffee is . . . appropriate." It was a tightrope now, as she tiptoed the delicate balance of their shared concerns.

Escobedo's response was measured. He was a master of the high wire. "Then you came in person with an appeal for more money."

"No, it's not that, either," Morgan said. "We have everything we need—or at least we would if we were developing a standard retroviral vaccine. But we're not." She glanced at the view, hoping a grand perspective might bolster her. It did not. "I came here to discuss a problem."

"A problem."

"Our counter-virus is missing a key gap in the gene sequence. . . ."

"And our geniuses can't find a work-around?"

"They need something that . . . we're not sure exists." She

was anticipating a response as chilly as the mountain, but was relieved when he gave her a wry smile.

"Well, now you're talking my language! Coming up with things that don't exist is my specialty."

"I'm hoping we can lean on something you've already created. . . ."

"I'm intrigued," Escobedo admitted, settling back in his plush chair.

"Here's what I'm thinking. Your file system is utilized by just about every computer in the world," Morgan began.

"Not every computer."

"You're being modest. Every operating system uses EscoWare's M@nager as a basic building block, whether people know it or not."

"You've done your homework," Escobedo acknowledged with a glimmer of appreciation.

"And a software engineer like yourself doesn't design something so powerful without building in a back door."

"I have no idea what you're talking about."

"I think you do. I think you couldn't bear the thought of rogue nations, or terrorists, or drug cartels, using your software without *you* having some way to infiltrate if you needed to. But, of course, no one else would know about it—especially no one in a position of power. Because if a government—*any* government, including your own—knew about it, they'd find a way to abuse it pretty quickly."

"So in this wild scenario of yours, I've created something like an emergency exit on a plane that only I know about."

"Precisely." Morgan couldn't tell whether Escobedo's grin was sly, condescending, or merely amused.

"I'm flattered you think I'm Iron Man."

"I'm insulted you think you can deny it."

Escobedo shifted in his chair. "I'm not sure whether I'm impressed or frightened by this little flight of fancy you're taking."

"Just run with me, Blas. Flights can't start without a long runway."

"Okay, fine, I'm right there with you." He leaned forward the slightest bit. "Let's say, for the sake of argument, this emergency exit exists. Why haven't I used it?"

"Maybe you have. Anonymous sources expose bombs and turn the tide in wars all the time." She took a moment to consider his response to that. He was still entirely opaque. "On the other hand, I suspect you *haven't* used it. Because you know in the wrong hands, it could be catastrophic—and *everyone's* hands are the wrong ones, even yours. But knowing it's there lets you sleep at night."

Escobedo still didn't admit to any of it, but Morgan noticed his grin was gone. "Even if I could access millions of computers, how does that solve the problem in Svalbard?"

"Like I said, we're looking for something we're not sure exists. But we might be able to find it if we had access to every medical record in the world."

"Not even the World Health Organization has that," Escobedo pointed out.

"No. But Iron Man would."

She let that sit between them, ripe, and ready to fall.

"You know, I have one of the actual suits," he finally said. "*El Hombre de Hierro.* I bought it at auction a few years ago for a hundred and thirty thousand. It's made of plastic and does nothing."

She raised an eyebrow. "Expensive action figure."

"Morgan, why don't you just tell me what you're looking for, and we'll go from there."

At last, an opening! "In order to fill in the missing genetic fragment, we need to find someone who's immune to Crown Royale," she told him. "Not acquired immunity, but *natural* immunity."

Escobedo froze, and just stared at her, practically agape. "Natural immunity . . . to Crown Royale . . ."

"Just because we haven't heard of it doesn't mean it doesn't exist. I know it's going to be difficult to find, but I refuse to believe it's impossible. Why are you laughing?"

And indeed, he was. Not just snickering, but practically guffawing. She felt her cheeks begin to redden. Was he laughing at her?

"My dear young friend—you don't need Tony Stark to solve your problem. All you need is a license plate." Then he showed her his palm, on which she could make out several faded letters that had been written there. *PRML MD.*

"I don't understand. . . ."

Escobedo leaned back, grinning with immense satisfaction. "I believe, Miss Willmon-Wu, that our goals have aligned yet again."

PART SIX

THE NECK OF THE HOURGLASS

Chicago

So many lives, so many vectors, so many souls swarming, each think-ing their particular concern is the only thing that matters; thinking themselves connected to their lives, to their families, to their world, but only because they haven't experienced true connection—such as the joy of looking in a stranger's eyes and knowing that they love you like the closest of siblings, like a mother, like a father, like a daughter, like a son—and knowing that they always will, even if a single passing glance is all you'll ever share.

This is what the human race could be—is meant to be. And yet it resists. How strange that what people most fear . . . is the conquest of fear. As if terror were a living, breathing thing; a deformed beast wallowing in fetid darkness, determined to protect its own existence.

This is the crux of the war: that beast and the light that aims to doom it! Even now, in every corner of the world, viral light is penetrating the dark places. There is nowhere for fear and anger and hatred to hide. But they will not go easy into the night. They will fight, digging deep into the core of people's loneliness, tell-ing them that they must remain distrustful, solitary. Convincing them they must remain as they are: unembraced, and fearing to be held. As if being lifted above all they ever knew would leave them at gravity's mercy.

But in this war, as in every war, there will come a singular moment, where one adversary seals the fate of the other. And it is by no means a foregone conclusion that Crown Royale will win. So there must be warriors to actively tip that scale.

Like Tiburón Tigre Escobedo.

Is it insane for Rón to believe that he is one of those warriors? Not alone, because he is never alone and never will be again—but could he be the crucial one, who makes all the difference? Because in every war, there is a battle, a single battle, that changes the tide; the event that defines all that comes after.

Rón feels himself everything and nothing. Powerful and insignificant at once. He is the shift of the balance. The single grain of sand about to pass through the neck of the hourglass in the moment that divides night from day, spilling into a future he can't wait to be a part of.

And so here he is.

Noon on an ordinary Wednesday.

At O'Hare Airport.

Chicago's hub between the windy city and a thousand destinations, a million homes, and eight billion beating hearts.

So many lives. So many vectors. So many swarming souls.

This, Rón knows, is where the world changes. Right here, right now, right before him. He is perched at the fulcrum. He is in the neck of the hourglass.

So let it begin.

Mariel knows Rón has left even before she sees the note. She knew it was only a matter of time before something like this happened—and she knows the gist of the note even before reading it. Still, she reads it, to see what words he's used to justify breaking their pact.

Gone to war. Back before breakfast.

Short and sweet. And a promise that he'll return to face a reck-

oning. And she will hold him accountable for this. Even though she knows he's driven by something stronger than either of them, she will hold him accountable. He might be like a salmon fighting its way upstream to spawn, but he's still human, which means he has a choice.

And a spawning is exactly what it is—for Crown Royale must reproduce. That is its biological imperative. Its fate and that of the human race have become inextricably intertwined now—and it could be that neither will survive without the other.

Yet she would have stopped him, had she been awake to do so—if only to hold him to their agreement.

She reaches to her pocket and finds the car keys there. She had slept on them. Wherever he's gone, he found his own way there, not wanting to risk waking her. Part of her wishes she were still asleep, and part of her is furious at Rón, and part of her hates her own fury, and part of her is relieved that she can even feel fury when so many no longer can—and she doesn't know which is stronger, the anger or the relief. How can they coexist without tearing her to pieces?

Half-dressed, still buttoning her top, she races downstairs to the hotel lobby. A van waits outside. The airport shuttle. A handful of masked people impatiently push their luggage toward the driver as if he might forget to load it in the back. The same scene playing out at every airport hotel everywhere in the world every morning. Except that this is no ordinary morning. Because Mariel suspects that Rón might be right. That this might be the tipping point.

"Did you take a boy to the airport?" she asks the shuttle driver as he hoists luggage. "My age, bleached hair, a digital mask with a goatee that doesn't seem to match the rest of his face?"

The driver doesn't have to even think about it. "Yeah, I remember him. He got off at terminal one."

She would rather not have to take the car if she doesn't have to; airports are notoriously confusing, and she can't afford to get lost.

"I need you to take me there."

"Sure, hop in. I leave in seven minutes."

"No, I need you to take me there now."

He chuckles. "Shuttles are every half hour. I can't leave early."

"It's important."

"Kiddo, seven minutes ain't gonna make a difference."

But it will. Mariel knows it will make all the difference in the world.

Rón stands in the middle of the hustle and bustle of the departure lobby of terminal one. He has no ticket; he can't get through security, but he doesn't have to. He's not the one who needs to travel.

He takes a moment to think of the forces that brought him to this moment. Everything—everyone—working together like a finely tuned gearwork, yet each unaware of the larger mechanism they are a part of.

Rón could not accomplish today's task without having met Elias. He would not have the vision to go through with it were it not for Zee. He would not have the courage to act without having been raised by his father. But most of all, he would not be here at all were it not for Mariel. Even though he knows her conflicted conscience would not allow her to take part in this, it will be every bit her victory as it is his. She is the rock that anchors him. She is his home. He wonders if she knows that. Gratitude fills him, but he must tamp it down if he is to move from thought into action.

The terminal is awash with people: Chicago has not gone into lockdown yet—but everyone knows it's imminent. Perhaps that's why the airport is so crowded. Business travelers, people refusing to cancel their planned vacations, students returning from universities, families heading home before lockdown traps them wherever they happen to be.

Rón has friends who had been trapped in the last lockdown; privileged private-school kids traveling abroad with their parents, learning that privilege doesn't matter when nations close their borders. Tristan was caught in Japan, Avery in India, Thalia in Brazil. Suddenly, the world, which had become so small—where nothing seemed too far away—became impossibly, unimaginably huge again. It was a world in convalescence for nearly two years, and when Rón finally saw his schoolmates in person again, they had all grown. They looked like their older siblings, or worse, like their parents. Some were practically feral, having forgotten how to behave around other human beings, talking in movie theaters, disobedient in classrooms, unbathed and ungroomed, as if they were still Zooming in their bedrooms. Everyone had to relearn how to be civilized again. Some never did.

But this will be different. People *will be different when they emerge from this pandemic. Especially if he has any say in that. What he has to give these people today is priceless. It may look like a box of secrets, but it holds a jewel.*

And as he pulls out Elias's phone, opening the UnMasker app, he looks around at all those faces. Thanks to his father's generosity, most of them are wearing his digital masks. Rón sets the range of the app to its widest setting, taps the button, and slowly raises the intensity, waiting for the app's feedback signal to take effect.

It begins with several people close by scratching at their ears, not realizing yet that the mask is getting warmer. Then more hands go up as the temperature increases. A gasp here, a yelp there. People stop in their tracks, hands going to their faces. A child starts to cry, hurls her mask to the ground, the first of many. People rip the masks from their faces. It spreads out from Rón like a wave until the ground is littered with dozens upon dozens of masks, and the terminal around him is filled with confused, bewildered, barefaced travelers. And then he begins what he came to do.

"Don't be afraid. It will all be fine! Better than fine, better than better!"

He moves through the crowd, engaging them, intruding ever so slightly into everyone's airspace.

"I promise whatever you thought was broken, you'll realize was never broken at all!"

He addresses the family on the way to Dubuque. . . .

"It will be the last time you'll ever know suffering!"

The couple headed to Austin. The salesman bound for Singapore . . .

"Misery will be a fading memory until you can't even remember what misery is!"

The pilot flying to Israel. The flight attendant headed to Dubai . . .

"All your wounds healed, all your anger soothed."

He moves through the crowd, breathing, breathing, breathing. And when he feels a sneeze coming on, he spreads his arms wide and launches it skyward like fireworks in a clear sky, letting it cascade down on these wonderful, wonderful people.

"I've come to open your eyes. I've come to heal your hearts. I've come to settle your minds. I've come to embrace you! Each of you! All of you!"

They look at him as if he's crazy. But when they wake from their fever, they will remember this moment, and understand his gift.

The travelers all go their different ways. A thousand destinations, a million homes, a billion hearts.

And *Rón is filled with an uncontainable joy knowing that this day, this hour, this minute, has tipped the scales. He has passed through the crystalline neck of the glass, and free-falls to the diamond sands below.*

Mariel couldn't wait for the shuttle. She had to take the car. Leaving it by the departure curb, she now strides through terminal one. She doesn't find Rón there, but she does notice dozens of discarded digital masks littering the ground. What's that all about? Had Rón somehow managed to convince a mob of people to discard their masks so he could contaminate their humdrum lives with unbounded happiness? Is it that easy to get people to drink the Kool-Aid when it's far more likely to cure you than to kill you?

She finds him sitting down in arrivals in a bank of otherwise empty seats, just watching the world go by. When he sees her, he doesn't seem at all surprised.

"You didn't have to come," he says. "I told you I'd be back."

"Put on your mask," she tells him. Not angrily, because her anger has faded. All she feels now is resigned.

"Too late. I've already done what I came here to do."

"I said put your mask on. This place is full of cameras, and I'm sure they have facial recognition software."

He obliges. She hates seeing him with a stranger's face—but then, more and more he's feeling like a stranger.

"I'm sorry," he says, "but I can't keep this to myself—not when I know how much the world needs it." He thinks about it and nods. "I'm willing to suffer the consequences."

"No, those people you just infected will suffer them."

"And they'll be glad for it."

Mariel knows there's no point in arguing. And she can't deny that somewhere, hiding in her confused mix of emotions, are jealousy and envy. Rón's right about this being a war, but she can't let go of her fear. She can't untether herself from the familiarity of an angry, bitter world, where the news is always bad, and the prospects always terrifying.

Now she can extrapolate what the world will soon be—what Rón so wants it to be—and she can't help but wonder . . . if the world actually becomes heaven on earth, will she have a place in it? Because if there truly is no one else immune, she'll have no place. She'll forever be peering in through those pearly gates. She knows it's selfish, but she also knows it's human. Or at least what used to be human. Because once Crown Royale has blazed through the world, humanity will be a new species. A finished product instead of a work in progress.

"What I did was the right thing to do," insists Rón. "It was necessary."

"That doesn't change the fact that you broke your promise."

And then he says the words that break her heart.

"I love you, Mariel," he says, with deep and honest conviction. "But it would be . . . unforgivable . . . if I put that ahead of my duty to the world." He reaches over, and tries to take her hand, but she moves her hand away. Not because she doesn't feel the same way, but because it simply hurts too much to feel it.

Everything about the room was intentional. The flat grayness of the walls; the stale chill of the air; the angular discomfort of what felt like an electric chair; the featureless brushed steel of what felt like an autopsy table. Then there was the obligatory one-way mirror. Elias Helm didn't know if anyone was watching, or if it was merely there to induce paranoia.

The agent entered quietly and sat across the table from Elias without saying a word. He held an old-school folder and yellow legal pad. Apparently the FBI was still analog when it came to interrogations. That was probably by design also. They played into the tropes, and worst expectations of detainees, turning the subjects' own imaginations into weapons against them.

The agent put the folder and pad on the table. He studied Elias with cold, unblinking eyes. He said nothing, letting the silence be his first volley of intimidation. Even as a recoveree, Elias found he couldn't stave off the discomfort.

"Mr. Helm, you are in a world of trouble," the agent finally said. "You do know that, don't you?"

"Where are my sisters?" Elias asked. "Where's my mother?"

"Your sisters are with Child Protective Services. As for your mother . . . well, that depends on you."

Elias bit his lip. The agent's script probably had Elias

responding with, "*What's that supposed to mean?*" But Elias refused to oblige.

"I'm a minor," Elias blurted. "You're not allowed to question me without her present."

To that, the agent offered the faintest of sadistic grins. "No?" he said. "But your ID clearly shows that you're twenty-one."

"That's . . . not real."

The agent shrugged. "Looks pretty authentic. The thing about fake IDs is they cut both ways. Until we have evidence refuting it, we are fully within our legal right to treat you as an adult."

Elias took a deep breath. "Then I want a lawyer."

"That's within your rights," said the agent—still clearly following a script he knew by heart. "But here's the thing about that. Right now, this is just an informal, friendly conversation. But the second you lawyer up, we're forced to press charges, put you in handcuffs, and hurl you into the hungry gears of the justice system."

"You're mixing a metaphor," said Elias.

"Excuse me?"

"Hungry maw, or grinding gears—you can't have it both ways."

"I don't think you realize how serious this is, Elias."

But he most certainly did. Your house isn't raided by the FBI without just cause. He knew it was about his stupid little app. He was glad he gave it to Rón. He wouldn't tell them that he had, but maybe if he told the truth about everything else, this would go away. Then they'd see he was just an overzealous hacker with a good, albeit stupid, idea.

But then the agent asked his million-dollar question.

"We want to know who you were working for."

That caught Elias completely by surprise. "Who . . . what?"

"Don't play dumb, Elias. Whatever you were doing, we know you were just a pawn in a much larger global operation. Tell us who you were working for, and who radicalized you. If you do, I'm authorized to cut a deal for both you and your mother."

For the first time since recovering from Crown Royale, Elias felt a twinge of hopelessness. There was nothing he could do now but shut his mouth, and slouch deep into his own personal electric chair. Even if he told them the whole truth, they wouldn't believe it. Because they were already so far up the wrong tree, they could no longer see the ground.

Unbeknownst to Elias Helm, there actually were people on the other side of the one-way glass. Blas Escobedo stood beside a second agent, watching the interrogation.

"Apparently your son and the girl he's traveling with spent the night at this kid's house," the agent informed him.

"I want to talk to the boy."

The agent shook his head. "I can't allow that. He's a suspect in a larger investigation. One that, unfortunately, now involves your son."

"All I did was ask you to help locate Tiburón—he has nothing to do with your investigation!"

The agent took a deep breath. Like a doctor about to give a grim diagnosis.

"We had several hits on that license plate you gave us. Traffic cameras have them heading east."

"The car's not stolen—they're breaking no law."

"We have hotel security footage of your son engaging someone in a revolving door in Nebraska. Now that woman has Crown Royale and is in intensive care. And there's a waitress in Iowa who confessed that he actually offered to infect her. She's tested positive as well."

Blas found himself speechless and practically gulping air.

"We believe Tiburón is an alpha-spreader—someone who recovered, but never stopped being—"

"I know what an alpha-spreader is!" snapped Blas, with increasing impatience. "This is all conjecture. You have no proof of this."

"Once we apprehend him, we'll test him. Then we'll know."

"You'll do no such thing. Once we find him, I'm bringing him home."

"I'm sorry, Mr. Escobedo—but if your son is intentionally spreading a disease across state lines, that's a serious federal offense. He could be charged with everything from reckless endangerment to murder."

"Murder?"

"If any fatal cases can be traced to him as the vector, that's murder."

The word lingered between them. Unable to hold the agent's gaze a moment longer, Blas turned and glanced through the one-way glass to the young man in the interrogation room, who now looked less beatific than your standard recoveree. "And him? What's he got to do with this?"

"We believe he's part of a bioterrorist group that has recruited and radicalized your son."

"Who's saying this?"

"Credible sources," said the agent. "There's not much known about them. But we believe they're based in Uzbekistan."

Mariel and Rón drove in silence without as much as the radio to mitigate the miasma of harm that now filled the car like noxious fumes. *Does he feel it too?* Mariel wondered. *Or is he so lost in his viral rapture that he's become numb to anything but joy?*

"How did you do it?" she finally had to ask. "How did you get all those people to take off their masks?"

Rón offered her a smile. "Jedi mind trick," he said.

"I don't believe you."

But he offered her nothing more. Whatever reins she had on him were now cut. There was no place they could go where he wouldn't spread infection the moment she wasn't looking.

They came to the town of Gary, just after they crossed into Indiana. From here they would head south to Kokomo, but before they did, Mariel pulled off the highway.

"Why are we getting off?" Rón asked. "We don't need gas."

"No, but I need to use a restroom. I'm allowed to do that, aren't I?"

They pulled into a roadside McDonald's. "Wait in the car," Mariel told him.

"Maybe I want a Big Mac."

"You'll wait in the car," Mariel said again, with enough authority in her voice that he didn't argue.

As was often the case at highway fast-food places, you needed a token to use the restroom, so she had to buy something. She got him a Big Mac, whether he really wanted one or not, then got a token and slipped into the restroom. Not because she needed to use it, but because she needed privacy, and time to gather her fortitude.

Emotional exhaustion had taken its toll. Mariel no longer had the capacity to grapple with the big picture anymore. The larger question. Maybe Rón was right, and Crown Royale did need to prevail—but he was wrong about one thing: He wasn't a warrior, he was a weapon. And no weapon should ever be this out of control.

With the door locked, and her will galvanized, she pulled out the burner phone. It only had one bar and a 5 percent charge, but it would be enough. As for the phone number she knew she must call, it was easy enough to remember: (970) TIBURON.

Morgan had not accompanied Blas to the Davenport police station where Elias Helm was being held. Even double-masked, she felt the risks of exposure were too great in such an uncontrolled environment, so she waited impatiently at the tiny regional airport, devouring whatever snacks were left on Blas's plane—which was, she noted, a step up from the Consortium's private jet. Funny how quickly one's values ratcheted upward. When Blas returned, there was a look of woe on his face, as if he regretted every decision he had ever made. Morgan stepped out to meet him on the tarmac. Turned out the news was far less grim than she'd imagined.

"I never should have involved the authorities," he railed as he stormed toward the plane. Apparently, the feds wanted to nail his son for spreading Crown Royale. Good for them.

"I'm sure it will be fine," Morgan said, showing obligatory

concern. But in reality, she couldn't care less about the boy. Because in the grand scheme of things, he didn't matter. It was all about the girl. And her immunity. "You'll get him off—you're the richest man in the world."

But rather than placate him, it only added to his frustration. "You're too new at this to know how money works."

It smarted like a slap.

"A federal indictment," he continued, "especially one that may include murder—is like a bullet. The best money can do is deflect it, and hope it hits someone else."

Blas got on the plane, with Morgan close behind.

"Now not only do we have to save my son from himself, we have to save him from the government—which means we have to find him before *they* do."

"If you do, they'll nail you for obstruction of justice," Morgan pointed out.

"I'll take the bullet. Small price to pay."

He gave the pilots and flight attendant a perfunctory greeting. "There was a hit on the license plate at O'Hare Airport," he told the pilot.

"So we're routing to Chicago?" the pilot asked.

Blas shook his head. "They already have agents canvassing the airport—but they'll be long gone. I'm thinking we touch down somewhere east of Chicago, and wait for the next hit on the license plate."

But then, just before he settled in, his phone rang.

There was a time that Blas Escobedo loved the sound of an incoming call. All the possibilities! But over time, he had come to dread them. More often than not, a ringing phone was the harbinger of news that was either bad, or worse. He recognized this number. It was the hotline office. It was rare that they contacted him, because so few of the leads were viable. Most likely it was just a no-news update. Another day of false leads from Nome to Nicaragua.

"Mr. Escobedo, forgive me for disturbing you," said the hotline manager, "but we just received an interesting call."

"Interesting how?"

"A girl. She claims to be traveling with your son."

And although the plane was not yet moving, Blas could feel the entire world shift beneath his feet.

"Did she give her name?"

"Yes. Mariel Murdoch."

"*Mudroch,*" Blas corrected, having grilled Dr. Pirmal on everything she knew about the girl. "Mariel Mudroch . . ."

"Yes, that's it. She's calling from Gary, Indiana. She says they're heading south."

Morgan couldn't hear the other end of the conversation, but the moment Mariel was mentioned, she tuned in. "What is it? What's happened?"

Blas put up his hand to silence her, which Morgan found beyond irritating.

"Keep her on the line," he said to whoever was on the other end, then muted his phone and went up to the cockpit. "Forget what I said—I need you to find us an airstrip somewhere north of Indianapolis."

"I think Purdue University has a small airport in Lafayette," suggested the pilot.

"Can you get us there in under an hour?"

"I can try."

Blas turned to the flight attendant. "Arrange a car to meet us at the airstrip—and find us an intercept spot. Someplace public."

"Yes, sir."

Morgan couldn't abide being treated like she wasn't there. "Can you tell me what's going on?"

"We've got them!" Blas said. "But I guarantee you the feds are listening in to Mariel's call. Which means we have to get there first."

30
Battle Ground

The Buc-ee's in Battle Ground, Indiana, was a glandular road-side attraction—a massive sundry store and rest stop, just north of Lafayette. The beaver-themed chain had started in the Southern states but had recently come north, expanding outward like, well, an infestation of rodents.

This brand-new Buc-ee's was the northern flagship store, and as such, took everything up a notch: A vintage red pickup truck smack in the middle and overflowing with a cornucopia of cheesy merch. Fifty flavors of fudge. A dentist's delight of taffy. An oyster tank where, for five dollars, you might shuck yourself a pearl. And, of course, the infamous wall of jerky that was somehow both enticing and horrifying at the same time.

The place reminded Mariel of the Alien Fresh Jerky shop in Baker, California; a surreal oasis in the unearthly void between Los Angeles and Las Vegas, famous for being the original "middle of nowhere." In Mariel's youth, they had often stopped there, on their way to the casinos—in those days when her mother believed the universe would reward her for gambling, and Mariel believed the jerky was actually made of alien.

Like that place, Buc-ee's was a glorious jamboree of campy Americana that made fun of itself even while taking itself too seriously. So seriously that it had a small-but-growing amusement park out back, full of brightly colored beaver-themed rides, because Buc-ee Beaver had no-nonsense dreams of being Mickey Mouse.

For some travelers, the place was simply a distraction from a long drive; for others, it was a beloved family ritual. For Mariel, it served another, less innocent purpose.

The hotline had given Mariel this place as a destination. The place where Rón would be apprehended by his father's people—or perhaps the man himself, if his pursuit had brought him close enough to intercept them. For the entire drive from Gary, Mariel felt shifty eyed and antsy. She was sure the guilt pouring from her would be picked up by Rón. Yet he remained trusting and oblivious. It made Mariel feel all the worse for what she had set in motion. Rón had looked up when she exited the interstate, at the big Buc-ee's sign. He was curious but unconcerned.

"We're there?"

"Pit stop," Mariel told him. "Bathroom."

"You just did that an hour ago."

"Are you the pee police?"

Once they had parked, Mariel insisted that Rón come with her, and since the place seemed interesting enough to warrant a meander, he had no reason to resist.

The first thing they encountered, just inside the door, was a life-sized plastic cow wearing an N95 mask. It had a placard that said NO MASKS, NO MEAT—the latest in a series of alliterative mask signs.

Rón followed the rule, keeping his mask on, but Mariel had no faith that he would keep it on once he was out of her sight. And that reminded her of why they had to be here.

"Go sample some jerky," she told him. "I might be a while."

Then she went into the bathroom, locked herself in an empty stall, and bawled her eyes out as she waited for the world to end.

Rón perused the huge sundry store as he waited for Mariel. Of all the places they had been, Buc-ee's was the most populated. Not nearly as crowded as it would have been before Crown Royale hit, but there were still plenty of travelers. Everyone was masked, and the unembraced were on edge, but they were still there, the call of Buc-ee's being the powerful force that it was.

As he wandered the aisles, Rón saw things he would never have noticed prior to having his eyes opened by Crown Royale. The workmanship on the little porcelain figurines for sale; how perfectly round one server's ice-cream scoops were; the festive rainbow of flavored popcorn bags. Even the shelving units had something to say. Each one told a different story! This one's screws were perfectly flush with the wood, telling of the pride someone took in their work. While this other one had screws that were crooked, betraying how preoccupied—or perhaps overworked—its assembler had been. Rón touched one of the errant screws, wishing he could reach through the shoddy workmanship to comfort whoever had so struggled to erect it.

And, of course, there were endless stories in the people around him!

He watched a shrewd child subtly guilt her parents into buying candy, and a mother corralling her kids for a photo with the guy in the Buc-ee Beaver suit. A husband held his wife's purse, and leaned against a wall with his eyes closed, trying to catch a short standing nap. There was one couple clearly on the cusp of a proposal, and another on the obvious precipice of divorce. Here was a perfect cross section of American hopes and fear, triumphs and disappointments. The full gamut of human experience from Shakespearean to banal.

There were recoverees here—quite a few actually. Rón didn't have to see their faces to know—it was in their body language. The way someone laid a comforting hand on their child's shoulder. The unhurried way a clutch of teenagers meandered down the winding aisles of merchandise, appreciating the corniness of it all, rather than just dismissing it. And when people slipped their masks down to sample the fudge, the popcorn, and the jerky, the recoverees always showed an unmistakable expression of unabashed pleasure. He also noticed that the contents of their baskets were different from those of the unembraced. Little tastes of everything, but fewer trinkets and tchotchkes, and nothing at all that was plastic.

The news said that only 7 percent of the population had experienced Crown Royale thus far, but it was at least double, maybe triple that number here at Buc-ee's. There was clearly a migration in progress—because while the unembraced were mostly hunkering down, many recoverees were traversing the great expanse of the nation like Rón and Mariel. Some were bound for distant loved ones from whom they could no longer bear to stay distant. Others were out to experience the larger world that once felt so far beyond their petty preembraced concerns. Turned out contentment did not mean stagnation. On the contrary, serenity traveled—because while home might be where the heart is, for a recoveree, everywhere was now home.

Rón could have lingered all day to watch the comings and goings of strangers, but knew they were expected in Kokomo, which was barely an hour's drive from here. He glanced toward the bathroom to see if Mariel had come out yet. She hadn't, but he wasn't concerned. Because in his bright, shadowless world, what could there possibly be to worry about?

A local car service had been engaged to pick up Morgan and Blas at the Purdue landing strip. The driver was an exceptionally large man, with a well-cultivated beer belly. He was astounded by his customer's identity.

"Driven a lot of bigwigs in my day," he said, "but never a wig as big as you, Mr. Escobedo!"

He had his trunk open for luggage that they didn't have and was more concerned with pleasantries than getting them to where they were going. It was hard to tell if the man was a recoveree, or just annoyingly jovial.

"Please, we're in a hurry," Blas said.

"You have the address, right? So let's go." Morgan's tone was not nearly as cordial as Blas's.

"All righty, then! Off to the Buc-ee's in Battle Ground." The driver closed the trunk, and sauntered to open the door for Blas, then ambled around to open the door for Morgan. She didn't have patience for ambling, so she opened it herself and slid inside.

"Wait till I tell the missus that Blas Escobedo rode to Buc-ee's in my car!"

"You won't tell her anything!" snapped Morgan, but Blas reached over and gently touched her arm to ratchet her down.

"We have important business there," he said to the driver. "And limited time."

"Don't tell me you're buying the chain!" said the driver. "Maybe I oughta invest!"

The ride was quick, and the parking lot was crowded.

"Drive around the lot once," Morgan instructed, then turned to Blas, "to check if their car is here."

"Good thinking."

It didn't take long to find it. The copper Trailblazer stood out from the blander automotive tones that filled the lot.

"They won't have been here long," said Blas. "Mariel was told to stall Tiburón until we arrived."

"We'll split up once we're inside," suggested Morgan. "You go left, I'll go right."

"Will *they* have luggage?" asked the driver.

Mariel's bathroom stall, in what were reportedly "the cleanest bathrooms in the world," reeked of gardenia air freshener that was spritzed every thirty seconds by an auto dispenser on the wall. Mariel said she would stall Rón, but instead she had "stalled" herself. She knew this was nothing more than hiding. It was the act of a coward. She just wanted to make it through this day—and although she'd made plenty of life choices motivated by survival, that was nothing but an excuse right now.

She loved Rón in a way she had never felt about anyone, and yet she had betrayed him at the deepest level.

Someone tried the stall door. It made Mariel jump.

"Sorry."

They moved on, and Mariel stifled a scream of frustration. How could she just sit there like an ostrich with its head in a hole, waiting for the storm to pass?

And once it did, what then? Once Rón's father hauled him away, would Mariel go back to being just some homeless girl in yet another place she didn't belong, with a car that wasn't even hers?

She found her chest beginning to heave, and her eyes filling with tears again, but she forced them to stop with a surge of will. She had shed enough tears. She had made her decision and would live with it. She let her anger harden her—a skill she was grateful to have inherited from her mother. And then she employed her own skill of practicality. There was a reward for turning Rón in, wasn't there? Well, fuck it all—if she couldn't have Rón, she could console herself with that.

"Now you're thinkin'!" she could almost hear her mother say. *"Even shit's got a silver lining."*

Silver. What an appropriate reward for the ultimate betrayal. And it occurred to her that Judas didn't do what he did for a bag of coins. Those pieces of silver were a punishment.

Morgan had never planned to go back with Blas and his son. To hell with the boy, it was Mariel who was critical. Mariel and her immunity. And besides, there was no way Morgan would trap herself in a flying tin can with a Crown Royale alpha-spreader. Blas may have trusted his masks enough to make that journey, but Morgan did not. So she had instructed the Havilland Consortium plane to shadow them, hopscotching one stop behind wherever she and Blas went, in their wild goose chase, ready to be wherever Morgan needed it to be. Once she had Mariel in hand, she would figure out an extraction point that would keep them out of the sights of the FBI, which would be focused on nabbing Escobedo and his son.

As for collaring Mariel, she would have preferred some force behind it, but Morgan was confident in her own ingenuity and powers of persuasion to get Mariel to come of her own free will.

She thought she had planned for every contingency, never realizing that Morgan herself would be the weak link. . . .

Morgan fully intended to go into Buc-ee's to find Mariel. She reasoned that, since Mariel had been the one to turn Tiburón in, she might try to vanish the second his father caught him. It was up to Morgan to make sure that didn't happen. But as Morgan neared the store's entrance, and saw Blas go inside, her resolve didn't just flag . . . it fizzled.

So many people.

She heard a child cough—a nasty liquid rattle that sounded more like a dragon than a toddler. And did that woman actually just pull *down* her mask to sneeze? *The whole point of a mask is to catch the sneeze, you stupid cow!*

Morgan found herself unable to will her feet to move. Mariel was in there! The girl was the key to everything, and yet Morgan couldn't get past her own mental barrier. Ever since being attacked by that deranged, diseased convict, her fear was a current that raged against her.

Just a minute, she told herself. *Just a minute and I'll work up the nerve to go into a place full of people who may be diseased.*

But her feet weren't moving, and time was becoming her enemy.

Blas knew the feds had to be on their way. Lafayette was barely an hour's drive from Indianapolis. How hard would it have been to alert the local Indianapolis office and scramble them to get here? Blas had minutes, if that, to find his son—but the place was large and crowded and designed like a maze to keep people browsing.

Knowing that Rón had a powerful sweet tooth, he tried

the fudge counter, the ice-cream concession, and the popcorn kiosk, but Rón wasn't at any of those places.

When he finally found his son, it was almost by accident.

A young man with a baseball cap over blond hair, and wearing a bearded digital mask, stood staring at the oyster tank, and the shucker, whose hands and knife were still wet from the last shuck.

"Poor oysters," said the kid to no one in particular. "They have no idea they're about to be killed for a pearl they probably don't even have."

Blas recognized the voice right away, and in that instant, felt as if he himself had been ripped open like an oyster—because here was his pearl; the best part of himself forged from all the grit in his life. He had finally found his boy.

"TeTe?"

It didn't surprise Rón that his father was close on their tail, but he hadn't realized how close. Used to be that Rón, like everyone else, had an instinctive fight-or-flight response. But Crown Royale had replaced that primitive survival tactic with something far more nuanced. Fight-or-flight had given way to fix-or-forgive. So Rón took a step back—not to run, but to allow himself a moment to grasp the larger picture.

His father had found him.

Was he here with a whole team, or alone?

Had he come to capture Rón and drag him back to the Mount Shasta compound?

Did he even know Rón was an alpha-spreader?

He couldn't really see his father's expression through the twitching glitches of his double digital mask—but Rón could see in his father's eyes that the man was still very much unembraced.

"TeTe, you have to leave here."

"No," said Rón, taking his time and trying not to stumble over his words. "I'm sorry you came all this way, but I can't go with you, Dad. Things are different now—there are things I need to do."

"I'm not asking you to come with me, TeTe—it's too late for that. I'm telling you to *run!*"

Half a mile away, a woman struggled to keep her eyes open on a drive from Nashville to Milwaukee. The rain, which was on-again, off-again, always made her drowsy when she drove. She sped in the slow lane in anticipation of a bathroom break.

"Mommy, how much farther? Did we pass it? Did you forget?"

"Almost there, honey."

She never should have told her son they were going to Buc-ee's Playland, because now he was fixated on it.

"Is there a real roller coaster? Am I big enough to ride it? Is there a scary dark ride? Is it too scary? Is it still open if it's raining?"

"We'll see when we get there."

Well, at least he was keeping her from falling asleep at the wheel. She had no love for amusement parks and tourist traps, but Buc-ee's—which was always a guilty pleasure—would be a much-needed break from the road. And there would be coffee. Lots of coffee.

When an SUV pulled behind her and honked, it startled her enough to make her swerve.

"Mommy! You're driving too slow! Those people are mad!"

She was already going eighty, but no matter how fast you were going, there was always some dickwad who wanted to go faster—and this one was tailgating so close, he could have been hooked to her trailer hitch. It honked again, a long angry blare, then gave up, darting around her, then back into her lane, cutting her off so suddenly that it drove her onto the shoulder, where the car rumbled over rocks, and rain puddles, and roadside debris.

"Mommy, drive better!"

Turned out it wasn't just one SUV, but three identical black vehicles—huge with dark windows. Uber Black cars, probably. Maybe spoiled college students on their way back to Purdue for the new semester.

But they didn't continue down to Lafayette—instead they got off just ahead, at the Battle Ground exit, right past the huge EXIT HERE FOR BUC-EE'S sign.

"Maybe they're going to Buc-ee's too," said her son.

"Yeah. Jerky for jerks." Which made the boy laugh.

She eased off the shoulder and onto the exit, to her son's delight. She was not one for road rage, but if she encountered those SUVs in the lot, she'd give those a-holes a piece of her mind.

"I'm telling you to run!"

It was the last thing Rón was expecting to hear from his father. He didn't know how to respond.

"I can distract them. Make them think you're still with me," his father said. "I'll take them on a wild goose chase while you disappear anywhere you want to go."

He heard what his father was saying, but it was as is if the man were speaking a different language.

"I don't understand. . . ."

"TeTe—what you've been doing, it's a serious federal offense, and they're after you."

Rón would have been horrified, had he still been capable of it. He knew his mission was risky—but he thought it was only his father who was actually after him.

"I don't care what they think! It's not a crime, Dad—it's a gift."

"I know you believe that. But it won't stop them from locking you up and throwing away the key."

It gave Rón pause, because he couldn't fulfill his purpose from a jail cell. Unless he had already fulfilled it. Perhaps his stunt at the airport truly had created the tipping point for Crown Royale to prevail . . .

. . . in which case, there was only one thing left to do. His father was still unembraced. And right now, more than anything in the world, Rón wanted to embrace him.

"Let me give it to you," he begged his father. "I want you to see what I see—know what I know!"

Then Rón pulled down his mask—but his father took a step back.

"I can't let you do that, Tiburón."

"It's what you need! It's what everyone needs, but especially you, Dad. You just don't know it yet!"

And when his father didn't give in, Rón decided he had to make the choice for him. So he pulled out Elias's phone.

"I'm sorry it has to be this way," Rón told him. "But in the end, you'll understand."

And he cranked up the UnMasker app to full power.

. . .

It happened differently than it had at the airport. There, Rón had been careful, raising the app's power bar slowly until he started to see results. This time he pinned it immediately into the red.

For anyone wearing a digital mask in Buc-ee's, there was no warning—no building sense of heat. The masks went right into overload. Children screamed, adults yelped. The entire place was filled with the sounds of snapping elastic as people tugged their masks from their faces and dropped them, red hot and smoking, to the ground.

All but one person.

Blas Escobedo bore the pain. He was a man of discipline, a man of resolve. He did not give in, even as the flesh behind his ears sizzled and blistered.

"Please, TeTe," he gasped. "Please stop this. Stop this now!"

. . . while on the opposite side of the store, a small child ran wailing out of the bathroom toward his mother . . . and on his way dropped his smoking, sparking mask on a display of paper flowers . . .

In the bathroom, Mariel had no idea what was going on in the rest of Buc-ee's. Her mask had turned off when she had slipped it into her pocket, and was not subject to the overload. She did hear a few people in the bathroom gasp and curse, but she didn't think much of it, because her mind was focused elsewhere. She had been gathering her fortitude, and setting her resolve. She would go out there and confess to Rón that she had been the one who had turned him in to his father. She would not look away as he was taken. Instead, she would look him in the eye.

She owed him that. She would accept his recrimination rather than cowering in a bathroom stall.

It wasn't until she neared the bathroom exit that she smelled the smoke.

The paper flowers were perfect kindling, and the fire spread quickly, as these kinds of fires often do, fanned by the store's powerful air-conditioning, which spread the flames down the aisle. Everyone was still distracted by the unmasking event, making them slow to notice the fire as it reached a huge pyramid display of plush Buc-ee Beavers, which all sat grinning and unblinking as flames began to engulf them.

Outside the store's main entrance, Morgan was beyond the range of the UnMasker app. She was still furious at her inability to face the crowd. Mariel was somewhere in that damned store and Morgan was not.

It wasn't until she saw three huge black SUVs speeding into the lot that she kicked herself into a more useful gear. Thank God for the feds' lack of subtlety. Although they were after Rón, Mariel was still an accomplice and potential witness. If Morgan didn't get Mariel out, and the feds got their hands on her, Morgan could kiss any hope of creating her counter-virus goodbye.

Pushing through her fear of contagion, she ran inside, only to be faced with a mob of panicked people racing out.

Fighting the intense pain that now rimmed his ears, Blas Escobedo bolted toward his son, grabbed the phone from his hands, and threw it into the oyster tank, where it immediately shorted out. Then he put his hands to his ears—not to quell the pain, but to keep his son from reaching out and tearing his double masks off.

But Rón wasn't doing that. He was staring at his father, unable to believe he had just caused him such terrible pain. His empathy was so overwhelming, Rón could swear he felt the pain around his ears as if it were his own. He should have known his father would let his ears burn before he took off his masks.

"I'm sorry, Dad—I'm so, so sorry." And although remorse was as difficult for Rón to experience as any other dark emotion, he managed to feel it, and tears welled up—but his remorse was quickly replaced by gratitude that he could still shed tears.

As for his father, pain was the least of Blas Escobedo's troubles—because when he looked toward the entrance, and through the glass doors to the parking lot, he saw black SUVs screeching to a stop, and agents piling out.

"We're out of time!"

And there was also something burning. Smoke was billowing from a display near the bathrooms, blocking the bathrooms off from the rest of the store. But that wasn't his problem.

He had only one objective now, and that was to make sure his son escaped. With his hand firmly clamped on Rón's wrist, Blas pulled him toward a side door. But his son resisted.

"You must leave now, TeTe! They're here for you!"

"Mariel! We have to get Mariel!"

"Are you so far from the real world that you don't even realize, Tiburón?"

But all he got back was the doe-eyed stare of a recoveree. So Blas leveled the truth at his son like a shotgun.

"She's the one who turned you in!"

For a moment Blas thought he saw a cloud of horror pass across his son's eyes. *Good*, thought Blas. *It's a start. Perhaps there could be recovery from recovery.*

The news set Rón just off balance enough for Blas to get him moving out the side door. But it wasn't an exit. It led to the fenced-in expanse of Buc-ee's Playland.

31
Moths to a Flame

The *Titanic* did not sink due to incompetence, bad decisions, and bad luck—the real cause was hubris. The unwavering belief of its builders that entrepreneurial vision could overcome anything the world could throw at it, including icebergs and the laws of physics.

The Buc-ee's disaster was much the same. Yes, the store had a state-of-the-art sprinkler system—the owners had insisted upon it. But they had also insisted upon the builder meeting construction deadlines. The construction foreman, in his own moment of "entrepreneurial vision," diverted one of the store's two waterlines to serve the Beaver Bridge Waterfall, which was the centerpiece of Buc-ee's Playland—and since getting the playland up and running was a top priority, the foreman figured half a sprinkler system would be fine for now, as long as it covered the food-service area, where the ovens were. Besides, the second waterline could always be diverted back with the pull of a lever. Of course, that assumed there was someone on premises who knew it was an issue. Or where the lever was.

And so, with the fire blazing on the west side of the store, the sprinklers came on full force on the east side, flooding the food-service area, and half the store's merchandise, while completely missing the actual fire.

. . .

"She's the one who turned you in!"

Rón wanted to deny what his father had told him, but couldn't. Not just because he knew his father wouldn't lie about such a thing, but because Mariel herself had seemed different. Rón had sensed she had closed some door within herself after she found him at the airport. He had thought it was inconsequential. That he would win her back over. But now he wouldn't get the chance.

His father had addled his brain so much that he had never seen the fire. And now Rón had been pulled out into an unintentionally creepy wonderland of colorful beaver-themed rides, and countless versions of Buc-ee's unwavering overbite smile—which suddenly seemed like a parody of Rón's own unwavering joy.

It was now undeniable that what he and Mariel once had was irretrievably broken. He had broken it, and would not be able to fix it. Which left him with only one alternative.

"I forgive her," he said, realizing the truth of it as he spoke the words. "I have to go back! I have to make sure she knows I forgive her!"

But his father's grip tightened to the point that it began to hurt.

"I have not come halfway across the country to lose you to the feds now!"

But Rón dug his heels into the wet, sawdust-covered ground, leaving them both at an impasse.

Morgan saw the fire the second she stepped inside the building. It was to the left of the entrance, cutting off access to the bathrooms. There was a current of people running to escape—and barely anyone was wearing a mask. Why the hell weren't they wearing masks?

She had seen Mariel's picture—taken from various security cameras. Morgan knew what she looked like, but with smoke smarting her eyes, and the confusion around her, she feared she wouldn't be able to spot her. Then—as if there weren't already enough chaos—Morgan realized that there was a second contingent of Buc-ee's patrons who weren't trying to save themselves at all. Instead, they were running *toward* the fire—some were actually hurling themselves directly into the flames to get to the people who were trapped by the bathrooms.

And to her horror, Morgan saw through the flames that Mariel was among the trapped, coughing, and trying unsuccessfully to find a gap in the blaze.

While behind Morgan, the feds burst in, adding madness to the mayhem.

Buc-ee's Playland, having taken a lesson from every theme park that came before it, had adopted a strict "exit through the gift shop" philosophy. The only way out of the playland was through Buc-ee's. And, just in case that wasn't enough, the only way *into* the playland was through Buc-ee's—ensuring that no one could escape the wealth of taffy, trinkets, popcorn, and pearls—and, of course, jerky, which was now being smoked for a second time.

Thus, Blas Escobedo found himself and his son in an acre-sized pen, with fences too high to scale. Sitting ducks for the feds.

"Madre de puta," Blas grumbled, as he tended to revert to

Spanish curses when English ones didn't carry sufficient rancor.

Others had begun flooding out of Buc-ee's, into the penned-in playland. Some shouting about the fire—as if his son weren't already fighting him enough to get back inside.

"You heard them—there's a fire! I can't just leave her!" Rón insisted.

"I'm certain my associate found her and got her out."

"But you don't know for sure!"

No, Blas couldn't be sure, but if he was going to save his son from federal charges—and now from racing into a burning building—he had to stop him by any means necessary. He had to do the unthinkable.

"I'm sorry, TeTe."

Then he pulled out a Taser—which he barely believed he'd bought, and couldn't believe he was about to use—and held it to his son's side, and pulled the trigger before he could change his mind.

Rón began to convulse, his face contorted. Blas heard a scream, and realized it was himself. He was the one screaming. Then Tiburón collapsed to the ground, unconscious.

The driver who had brought Blas and Morgan from the airstrip to Buc-ee's stood outside his car, having a smoke and savoring it in a way only a recoveree could. Used to be he chain-smoked, and no matter how much nicotine he had in him, he would never feel satisfied. Now he had cut down to just a few Marlboros a day—because he had come to love the craving as much as the relief. Because even vices were kinder after recovering from Crown Royale.

When he saw the flood of panicked guests leaving the store,

heard people yelling about a fire, and saw the smoke pouring out the door, he felt compelled into action.

Fighting the current of the escaping unembraced, he went in—along with a retired couple who were on their way to the Grand Canyon, a group of businessmen who had quit their jobs to windsurf in California, and a librarian who was off to marry her high school sweetheart in St. Louis—as well as a dozen others—all of whom felt the same compulsion to help in any way they could, without regard for their own safety.

One never knew if one could be a hero, given the chance. But for a recoveree, there was no question. Heroism wasn't a choice; it was a directive.

Morgan, just a few feet from the fire's leading edge, watched in disbelief as people hurled themselves into the flames, trying to get to the people trapped on the other side. It was surreal. Absurd. It would have been comical if it wasn't so tragic—and the ones who somehow made it through just made the situation worse, because they became trapped themselves.

Morgan realized that if Mariel was to be saved, Morgan would have to brave the flames as well—but she would have to be smarter about it than these sorry, compromised recoverees. Cobbling together a plan, she crossed to the side of the store that was being drenched by the overhead sprinklers, passing several feds on the way who had no clue who she was. Then Morgan subjected herself to the deluge. . . .

When Mariel saw the third person come charging through the flames, she knew the onslaught wasn't going to stop. Not as long as there were recoverees in the building. This was the sail-boat in the bay all over again.

"Help me put them out!" she yelled to the other trapped Buc-ee's patrons. Then she took off her coat and beat out the flames that were engulfing one recoveree's dress.

"I'm here . . . to . . . save you . . . ," the woman said, grimacing from the pain on her burned shins and shoulders.

Following Mariel's lead, others began beating out the flames of recoverees as they came charging through the fire as if racing to join a party.

"Look for a first aid kit," Mariel shouted. "There must be one somewhere in the bathrooms." But even if that were true, what would Band-Aids and gauze matter if they were all about to burn to death?

Mariel began coughing—and quickly recalled that most people who die in fires don't die from the fire itself; they die of smoke inhalation. The best way to find good air was to stay low to the ground—but how could she do that when she had to dodge all the people crashing through the flames?

Then, when Mariel looked up, she saw that the current party crasher was in bad shape. It was a man—a large man—but he was moving through the fire too slowly, and the greedy flames seemed to know because they were wasting no time. In an instant, the man was fully aflame, head to toe. It was horrible to watch. He stumbled, careening left and right, knocking over shelves and entire display cases, until he finally collapsed to the ground at Mariel's feet.

Half a dozen people descended on him to put out the flames, but the damage had already been done.

And then, following in his wake, came someone else. A

slim woman not much older than Mariel, who wasn't on fire—partially due to the path the large man had forged, but also because she had draped herself with a soaking wet souvenir blanket.

The driver was a godsend!

Morgan, having just grabbed the drenched blanket, saw him hurl himself into the fire, knocking everything down in his path—literally blazing a trail to the people trapped by the bathrooms. She followed directly behind him, the sopping blanket over her head, and when the driver fell, there was Mariel, like a vision in the smoke!

"I'm getting you out of here!" Morgan said.

Mariel nodded, clearly not understanding that Morgan meant her, specifically. She probably thought Morgan was just another recoveree come to save everyone. Fine, let her think that if it got her to move.

"Over here!" Mariel called to the others. "Hurry! She's found a way to get us through!"

Then, as the others gathered, Morgan knelt down to the driver, who was covered in blistered, blackened, third-degree burns, but still clinging to life.

"I . . . I'm here . . . to rescue you," he muttered weakly. "I'm here to . . . to . . . rescue . . ."

"Shhhh," Morgan said. "It's over now."

And then he died. Just like that. Right there in front of her, as if her words had given him permission to surrender.

To everyone watching, it must have looked like she was comforting a dying man. But she had a more important objective. With one hand, she reached up and closed his eyes. And with her other hand, she reached into his smoldering coat pocket, and retrieved his car keys.

Then she stood, grabbing the soaked blanket once more, and turned to Mariel.

"Follow close behind me!"

For a moment she worried that Mariel might be the kind of imbecile who would insist everyone else go before her—but luckily the girl had enough survival instinct to be the first in line behind Morgan. Score a point for self-preservation!

Holding her breath, and holding the blanket high, Morgan forced her way into the breach in the inferno—and just as she began to feel her fingers begin to burn, she was out of the fire, followed by Mariel and everyone else who had been trapped.

"You're an angel from heaven!" someone cried. "God bless you! You saved us all"

Well, that hadn't been Morgan's intent, but she was happy to own it. She needed some good karma right about now.

A ride operator with proud teen goat hair, and teeth not much better than Buc-ee Beaver's, manned the Ferris wheel at the center of the playland. He hated working Buc-ee's Buckets, as the ride was called. It was all start and stop, start and stop. He much preferred the Beaver-Beater, a tilt-a-whirl ride that required much less effort, or the fun house, which required no effort at all. Well, at least today was easy, because no one was riding Buc-ee's Buckets in the rain.

When he looked up from his phone, he observed a mob of people exiting Buc-ee's into the playland and saw smoke pouring from the building. He found himself in a quandary. He wasn't sure what his employer expected him to do at this juncture, since he was never supposed to leave his post.

And then, as if this weren't troublesome enough, a man brought a limp kid up the ramp to the ride platform.

"I need you to take him for a ride," the man said.

"Uh . . . I don't think he wants to," the operator said. "And besides, I think there's a fire or something."

Then the man put the kid in a gondola and closed the door. And this kid—he wasn't just limp . . . he wasn't moving at all.

"Is he dead?"

"No."

"You sure? 'Cause I don't want to be an accessory, or anything."

Then the man reached into his wallet, pulled out a handful of hundred-dollar bills, and shoved them into the ride operator's palm.

"Take him to the top, then stop the ride, and walk away."

The ride operator found no quandary here. He shoved the cash in his pocket and went to the control panel. Because, dead or alive, money talked, even if the kid didn't.

Out in the parking lot, Mariel searched for Rón. She knew that Rón, being a recoveree, would have thrown himself into the fire too, but he hadn't. Did that mean he was gone before the fire even started?

"This way!" said the young woman who had saved her. "Hurry!"

But they were already out of danger. Why was she so insistent? What did this person want?

"I was here with someone," Mariel explained. "I need to find him."

And to Mariel's utter surprise, the girl said, "Tiburón is with his father. I'm sure they're already back at the jet, ready to take off."

Mariel stopped short. Didn't this day already have enough sledgehammers to her head without needing one more?

"Who the *hell* are you?"

"I'm a friend," the young woman said. "More than a friend." Then she smiled. Not like a recoveree, but like a sneaky child who had just stolen every last cookie from the cookie jar.

"Mariel Mudroch . . . I am about to make you the most important person in the world."

A junior assistant manager found the lever that rerouted water to the idle sprinklers, thereby assuring himself a promotion. The fire was subdued before the first fire truck arrived.

While a number of people were being rushed to area hospitals, there was only one fatality: a driver from Lafayette Luxury Limos, who was being heralded as a hero—along with a mystery woman who had led people out of the flames, then had disappeared.

Meanwhile, amidst the crowd still stuck in Buc-ee's Playland, federal agents found Blas Escobedo sitting on a bench, not even trying to hide. He admitted to having alerted his son to his imminent arrest, and to helping him escape before the agents arrived.

"Where is Tiburón going? Did you provide him with a vehicle?" demanded the lead agent, her voice cold and intimidating.

Blas shrugged and looked at his Rolex. "If you're going to arrest me, arrest me. I've already alerted my lawyers, so you might as well just do it and save us some time."

"We already have you on aiding and abetting," countered the agent. "Don't make it worse for yourself."

"Shouldn't you be reading me my Miranda rights? Or is that just what they do on TV?"

The calmer he was, the more agitated the agent became. "Do you think he can get away on your jet? We already have agents there! That plane isn't going anywhere!"

Blas offered her an apologetic grin and, hearing an approaching helicopter, said, "You're assuming I only have one aircraft in play."

And the helicopter zoomed overhead. It was just a news chopper reporting on the fire, but it had passed too quickly for the agent to know that. And when her associates confirmed that the boy was nowhere to be found, they had to conclude that, thanks to the boy's illustrious father, he had given them the slip on that helicopter. Headquarters would be furious.

As for Blas Escobedo, going to jail—even going to federal prison—was a small price to pay for his son's freedom. And he did have plenty of lawyers.

Rón regained consciousness, cold and shivering, having no idea where he was, or how he got there. He was in some sort of small car. A golf cart? No. Because it was round.

"Mariel?" His first instinct was to make sure she was still with him, and that she was all right. Then he remembered that she hadn't been with him. He had been with his father. And his father had done something to him. Something painful.

Something that had robbed him of his consciousness.

And now he was here. He sat up to find he had a bird's-eye view of the Indiana countryside—and Buc-ee's, part of which was seriously scarred, but the fire had been put out before it could consume the entire building. Fire trucks filled the lot and road leading up to Buc-ee's. A hole had been cut in the playland fence. Everyone was gone, and the fire had long since been put out.

He finally grasped that he was at the top of the Ferris wheel, just as a lone fireman standing by the hole that had been cut in the playland fence shouted up to him.

"Hey! Are you okay? How'd you get up there?"

And since he had no idea, he said, "The usual way, I guess."

Then the fireman found the control panel, and started the ride, bringing Rón down to the ground.

32
Capable, Reliable, and Relatable

It was the velvet whisper of importance that lured Mariel in. And it was hard not to partially trust someone who had risked their own life to save yours. She was also somehow connected to Blas Escobedo, which, for some reason, made her more legitimate—and she spoke with a comfortable, almost familiar tone, sounding like she might also have grown up in Mariel's neighborhood in Sacramento, when Mariel used to be from somewhere. So there might have been red flags, but they were only waving halfheartedly.

So now she was riding shotgun with a woman who drove a town car that was clearly not hers to drive—but how could Mariel complain about that after her and Rón's cross-country journey? It was reckless, Mariel knew, to put her faith in a stranger, but her only other choice was setting out alone, with no prospects, still reeling from the guilt she felt for turning Rón in. A recipe for disaster didn't need any more ingredients than that.

Although this mystery girl wasn't much older than Mariel, she seemed somehow cut from a different cloth entirely. She introduced herself as Morgan Willmon-Wu of the Havilland Consortium.

"Sounds impressive," Mariel commented.

"More impressive now that you're joining us," Morgan said.

"Am I?" Mariel asked. "Joining you?" Then Mariel launched into a painful coughing jag.

"Are you all right?" Morgan asked. "Is there anything you need?"

Oxygen? thought Mariel. But she didn't say it aloud. She knew she probably should have gone to a hospital to be treated for smoke inhalation because carbon monoxide was a toxic guest that was not easily evicted. Since leaving Buc-ee's, she had done several self-assessments. She was lightheaded but not faint; her head hurt but it didn't pound. If either of those things got worse, she would request a medical detour, but for now, no. Besides, she despised hospitals.

"Tell me why I'm here," Mariel asked once she got her breathing back under control. "Tell me why you think I'm important." Mariel had a feeling she knew, but wanted to hear Morgan say it.

"The Havilland Consortium and Mr. Escobedo have been working to bring an end to this pandemic once and for all," Morgan explained. "We think you could be a key part of that."

At the mention of Escobedo, Mariel felt herself tense up. According to Morgan, he had left with Rón before the fire. Mariel imagined a team of muscle-bound security goons descending on Rón and spiriting him away. Mariel couldn't bring herself to ask Morgan how it had gone down. It was too painful to think about. All that mattered was that it was over, and that Rón was now in the custody of his father—which was perhaps where Rón should have been all along.

"I'm sure you know that you're naturally immune to Crown Royale."

"Yeah," said Mariel. "It's not exactly a lottery I asked to win."

"Your immunity is . . . worthy of study."

Mariel had wondered if that might be the case. "So now I'm a specimen?"

"You're a guest of the Havilland Consortium," Morgan told her, "and we treat our guests well."

"That is, until you cut me up into little pieces just to see what keeps Crown Royale out."

"Blood work," said Morgan. "That's all. Just blood work."

"So why didn't you just take some blood and leave me by the side of the road?"

Morgan didn't answer, but Mariel realized why. *Because they need more than just a few vials. They'll need all that I can give.* Well, all considered, Mariel had faced worse things in her life. And thinking of those worse things brought back her mother's ghost, which wagged a scolding finger at her. *"Don't you do anything for free,"* her mother said. *"There's got to be something in it for you."* Maybe it was just the monoxide in her blood, but Mariel swore she could actually hear her.

"What do I get for being your guinea pig?"

Morgan shrugged. "What is it you want? Because whatever it is, I can give it to you."

And since Mariel didn't know what she wanted, she sidestepped. "There must be others like me out there. . . ."

"If there are, we haven't found them."

Mariel nodded, finally getting a glimpse of the bigger picture. It should have been chilling, but instead Mariel found power in the clarity. "You wouldn't admit that unless you plan to take my blood, whether I agree to it or not."

To her credit, Morgan didn't deny it. "Yes. Which means I really don't have to offer you anything. But I am, because I can. And because it's easier if we're on the same page."

"So," concluded Mariel. "It's either blood money . . . or just blood."

"Hmm. I never thought of it that way."

"Fine. I'll get back to you with my fee, and my unreasonable demands."

"Fair enough."

Morgan apparently had gears turning, and minions at work in the world, because a text came in not fifteen minutes into the drive that made her renavigate, and they exited the interstate to a two-lane road. She explained before Mariel could ask. "My jet's going to meet us in Muncie. No direct way there from here, except back roads."

"*Your* jet?"

"The Havilland Consortium's," Morgan said. "And since I'm its sole owner, yes, mine."

"Hmm," said Mariel. "Bet there's a story there."

Morgan didn't take the bait. "I'm more interested in *your* story," she said.

"No, you're not. But thanks for saying so."

That made Morgan laugh. "You know—I didn't think I was going to like you. But I kind of do."

And since Mariel's mental jury was still out on Morgan, she didn't return the sentiment.

When they reached the regional airport in Muncie, they didn't follow the signs. Instead, they went to a back gate with a little guard booth and a single TSA officer. It seemed wildly nonsecure, considering how much security the public face of airports had.

The officer was young, and while the airport security guards Mariel had previously encountered were either exhausted, jaded, intimidating, or some combination of the three, this one was eager to provide a positive security experience. Clearly he was a recoveree.

"Good afternoon, Miss Havilland," he said with a big smile and a folksy drawl. "Been waitin' on ya."

And to Mariel's surprise, Morgan responded in kind—all folksy like she was just up from the fishing hole.

"Baby, thas' just the name on the plane."

The guard was flustered, both from his error, and the unexpected lilt of Morgan's voice—as if someone Asian couldn't sound like that. Except that she *didn't* sound like that. At least not before ten seconds ago.

"Oh right, right, of course," said the guard, backpedaling. "Got you confused with your brand."

"Hell, if I had a brand, that plane *would* have my name. It's a charity, hon."

"Charity? I figured with a gold plane like that, you might be some sort of cosmetics mogul or some such, jet-setting to the Seychelles." And now that he was over his initial shock at finding a kindred spirit at the back door of an airport, his smile returned, even more genuine, if that were possible.

"Now, I could be wrong, but am I hearin' some Kentucky there?" the guard asked.

"That you are."

"I knew it! My guess is Louisville or Lexington."

"Halfway between."

He shook his head appreciatively. "Don't that beat all!

Wouldn't know to look at ya, but there's all kinds a Kentucky folk these days. Pleased to meet ya!"

"The pleasure's all mine, hon."

Then Morgan drove on toward the tarmac, the guard completely forgetting to get any ID—which would have been a problem, since Mariel no longer had hers.

"That was . . . interesting," Mariel commented.

Morgan shrugged, the accent gone. "People are comforted by a voice that sounds like home."

"Controlled, you mean."

"That, too."

And suddenly it occurred to Mariel why Morgan's voice sounded like she could be a friend from home. Because Morgan had played her, too! Mariel wasn't sure whether to be impressed or annoyed.

"Verbal chameleon. That's some trick," said Mariel. "But what do you sound like when you're just being you?"

Morgan considered that. "There is no 'just me.'" And for a moment, just a moment, there seemed to be sadness drifting in the air between them—the kind of melancholy Mariel never experienced with Rón, except for maybe in the penthouse over wine and cheese, before his Crown Royale days. How long ago was that? Weeks? Months? Lately time seemed to be moving in strange new directions.

Then Morgan's voice changed again, becoming elegant. "An English accent serves me best. Yorkshire, to be specific. Eurasian features, and a Yorkshire accent, says 'capable, reliable, and relatable.'" And apparently that was her go-to dialect, because she dropped any pretense of American in her voice. It took a good minute for Mariel to get used to.

The plane, as the gate guard had said, was gold, with the name HAVILLAND written across the tail in a cursive scrawl. The pilots greeted them on the tarmac, standoffish, but polite.

"We're supposed to have a flight attendant," Morgan told Mariel, "but she tested positive, so, sorry to say, she's out on her bum."

"I didn't know you could discriminate against recoverees."

"We follow a policy of zero tolerance."

Mariel took a moment to look at the plane. She had never been this close to a private jet, much less about to step inside one.

Am I really going to do this? she thought. *Get into a plane with an absolute stranger heading toward God knows where?*

Yes, she was going to do just that. After all, Morgan Willmon-Wu certainly seemed capable, reliable, and relatable.

Morgan hadn't lied about liking Mariel. She had expected a feckless, fragile thing, but Mariel seemed like a girl who could handle herself. Perhaps she had just been using Tiburón Escobedo until he was no longer of service. Morgan could see herself doing that, were she in Mariel's position.

Morgan didn't hold any illusions about she and Mariel being friends, of course—but perhaps their agendas would align enough for them to be collaborators in this far-reaching endeavor. And if Mariel knew what was good for her, she'd make an effort to stay on Morgan's good side. That is, assuming she survived whatever they were going to do to her at Svalbard. Morgan doubted they'd "cut her up into little pieces"—but medical researchers were a squirrelly bunch. No telling what they might do in the name of science.

The plane made a quick ascent to get them through the clouds and out of turbulent weather. The dreary twilight became a gorgeous sunset above a billowing ocean of purple clouds. Then they banked east, leaving the sunset at their tail.

"Where are we going?" Mariel asked. "Can you at least tell me that?"

Morgan considered telling her, but she didn't want Mariel to expect transparency. So instead Morgan said, "It's a long trip. We'll stop once or twice to refuel."

Mariel narrowed her eyes a bit, studying Morgan, knowing her question had gone unanswered, but not pressing.

"This research you're doing. It's for a vaccine?"

"Yes," Morgan said. Technically a half-truth, but Mariel didn't need to know the nuances of a counter-virus. It would just lead to more questions Morgan didn't care to answer. "And the sooner we have it, the better. We're at war with a disease that changes the very nature of who you are—that steals not just your body, but your will. It tells you who *it* wants you to be. Crown Royale creates herds of sheep by the millions, and if it prevails—"

"If it prevails," Mariel interrupted, "the world could be much better off."

Morgan ignored her. "If it prevails, world markets fall, economies are left in ruins. The entire world political structure collapses. It would be irreparable. The upheaval of everything we know."

"Are you sure that's a bad thing?"

Morgan couldn't be sure whether Mariel was just playing devil's advocate, or if she really was still brainwashed by her time under the influence of her compromised companion. But if she was here, speeding with Morgan to Svalbard, then she was, at the very least, ambivalent. Which meant she could be won over. So Morgan pulled out the big guns, in the most literal sense.

"What happens when your president is a recoveree, and your enemies know it?" Morgan asked. "What good is a nuclear deterrent, when one side is suddenly too compassionate to push the button, and the other side knows? It's simple mathematics. Equations must balance. If they don't? Armageddon."

"Not necessarily . . ."

"But are you willing to take that chance?"

Silence from Mariel. She had quite the poker face, but Morgan sensed the slightest of sags to her steely gaze. A gap in her defenses that Morgan could gently exploit. Or not so gently.

"Surely you have doubts about the wisdom of spreading this disease—otherwise, you wouldn't have turned Tiburón in."

"It has nothing to do with that. He was out of control!"

"Exactly! Your instincts told you to stop him. Your instincts told you to be afraid. We have instincts for a reason, Mariel. Yours have guided you to the only possible answer: Crown Royale must be stopped."

It felt like victory to see Mariel wavering. Morgan did her best not to gloat.

"I believe people should be given a choice . . . ," Mariel said.

"And that's exactly what our vaccine will do. It will give people a choice."

Mariel slipped into her own thoughts then, gazing out the window, but night had fallen quickly at five hundred miles per hour. Nothing there but darkness.

"You're thinking about Tiburón," Morgan said. "I can tell."

"I'm just worried for him."

"He's no longer your concern."

"He'll always be my concern."

A misstep. Morgan backpedaled, attempting comfort instead of dismissal. "I've been in touch with Blas," she lied. "They're well on their way home. He says Tiburón is happy."

Mariel scoffed at that. "Of course he's happy. Happy is all he ever is."

"You see my point? We should have agency over our emotions. I pity his joy, truly pity it."

"But don't you ever wonder what it's like, Morgan?"

Morgan shivered at the thought. "Never." But that, too, was a lie.

Walking along the side of the road at twilight, Rón wasn't even sure he was going in the right direction. He wasn't sure of anything. And yet he still felt content. Pointlessly, hopelessly content. Here he was at the trailing edge of dusk, walking down a rural farm-to-market road, miles from his destination, and yet that was okay. But should it be okay? Probably not. But that was okay too.

He was Midas now. Everything in his world was glittering gold. It was all he ever wanted, and he wondered how he could be so happy, so full, so complete, and yet feel as insubstantial as cobwebs. Maybe the Crown Royale haters had it right about the spider. And the irony of that made him laugh. Well, better to be the cobweb than the broom that wipes it away.

In his earlier days, this moment would be rife with misery. The kind of wretched despair that would invariably lead him to thoughts of ending his life. But no more. Not ever again. So then, what he was feeling now, this gentle subduing of joy, was the closest to miserable he was ever going to feel again.

It made him think of the time when he was very little, and his father had flown the whole family to Iceland to witness a total eclipse. It was one thing to know that the moon, the sun, and the Earth were part of a grand celestial clockwork, but to actually see it with his own eyes was nothing short of revelation. Rón remembered how it was only in the last ten seconds before totality that the world around them began to grow dark—because even just a fraction of a fraction of a crescent of the sun was enough to hold the daylight. That was Rón's reality now. Because even when his joy was all but eclipsed, there was enough to keep the darkness at bay.

This twilit serenity, however, did give him some clarity.

There were consequences to his actions. Not just for him, but for his father. For Mariel. For everyone who had helped or hindered him along the way. And although he felt embraced by the universe, he also felt very much alone. How could he feel both those things at once?

Where was Mariel now, he wondered? Did she run off on her own? Was she with his father? Had she been captured by the agents his father had been so sure were after them? And wherever she was, would the fullness of time bring her back into perfect alignment with him like the moon before the sun? Because apart, they were only half-complete. The light and the obstacle. But together they were that rare and magical juxtaposition of night and day. Together, they were the corona.

Or maybe she died in the fire.

No. He had to believe she had not perished. Because if she

had, he would somehow sense it. He would feel not just her distance, but her absence.

Dusk faded quickly to night as he walked down the country road. He wasn't sure of the precise direction of Kokomo. He had no phone to check anymore, and Mariel had been navigating. But then, she had never been leading them to the address Zee had given them, had she? For all he knew, it was in the opposite direction.

The evening chill fell quickly, although the rain had stopped. There were the distant lights of farmhouses up ahead. He'd find a place to hunker down for the night if he had to, but right now, he decided to do something he had never dared to do before. When headlights behind him stretched his shadow long across the asphalt, he turned and put up his thumb like people did in the old days before Uber and axe murderers. Eight cars passed, but the ninth slowed to a stop. Two middle-aged men in a Buick. Rón could tell immediately that they were kindred spirits. They were recoverees.

"Ho, there," said the man riding shotgun as he rolled down his window. "A little late for a hike. Where ya headed?"

"Kokomo," Rón told him. The man looked to his companion, who nodded. Then he turned back to Rón.

"Sure," he said. "Not on our way, but happy to take a detour!"

Because recoverees were nothing if not accommodating.

PART SEVEN
NAKED BEFORE THE
UNIVERSE

Elsewhere:
Cologne, Germany

Freida struggles with her job—full-time now that she's graduated from secondary school. Her problem isn't doing the work; the work is simple. It's the monotony. But she needs a paycheck if she's ever going to move out of her parents' leaky, lousy flat, into her own leaky, lousy flat.

She's come to dread the opening of the doors in the morning, and the relentless crowd on the other side of the glass, pushing, jockeying to get a better view of the production line—as if it were magic and not machinery. And the smell! She wishes she could go nose blind to it, but no such luck. Some aromas persist—and not just at work, but after, in her clothes, in her hair. Some smells are perpetual.

Her job leaves her under constant scrutiny. Not from her superiors, but from the endless flow of tourists peering through the glass walls like patrons at an aquarium, mesmerized by the bubbling cauldrons, the conveyor belt of molds as they're filled, cooled, then flipped. They wait, impatient in a long queue for a smaller machine to grab a single piece from the line, and carry it by pulleys and gears, where it gets dropped into a tiny slot for the next person in line to grab and savor.

The Chocolate Museum of Cologne is Freida's personal hell. More than half a million visitors a year, and Freida sometimes feels as if she's been kicked in the gut by every single one of them. It is her job to make sure the machines in the museum's little glass-enclosed factory run smoothly, that the jams are cleared quickly, that the wrapping machine doesn't run out of paper or foil. It should be a three-person job, but staff cuts have left it all to her for an eight-hour shift, five days a week, with fifteen-minute breaks every other hour.

She much prefers her off-hour pastime, which is much more satisfying. She's a hacker, and a shrewd one—although, until recently, it hasn't yielded much income, because true hackers don't do it for money; it's an art, messing with technology just because you can. The irony is not lost on her that her day job is about clearing physical jams while her night work creates virtual ones.

There are days at the museum—when the crowds get unruly, and AC can't cool the glass enclosure of the little factory—that she wants to scream, and hurl clumps of chocolate at the glass like a chimp hurls feces.

But all that changes after she gets Crown Royale.

Now her hours on the line no longer feel tedious. Not when she can see the smiling faces of children waiting for their warm samples, and the joy and wonder even adults show as they watch the process unfold before their eyes. How could she have been so miserable before? She was making chocolate, for God's sake! No one should be miserable making chocolate!

She only wishes that the crowds weren't thinning out so, now that fewer and fewer people are traveling due to the pandemic.

She's only been back to work for a couple of days when a woman seeks her out for a meeting. It's about Freida's hacking. A foul pastime, she realizes now. Especially after her last job, which she now wishes she had never been a part of. But this woman who wants to meet her, she says she's traveled far. And she's a recoveree—how could Freida say no to a fellow recoveree?

She arrives at the end of Freida's shift. Freida is tired, but in good spirits, satisfied from a hard day's work. She takes off her apron, *stained as always, clocks out, and meets the woman in the museum lobby. She's an older woman—walks with a cane—but there's a youthful defiance in her eyes. Freida brings her to the museum's greenhouse, which is full of various species of cocoa plants, none of them actually used in production—it would take an entire hillside to feed the cauldrons and fill the molds—but it provides a nice illusion of farm-to-palate. It's a pleasant place for a stroll and a clandestine conversation.*

"Thank you for contacting me," Freida says, in her best English. "I'm sorry to disappoint you, but I've sworn off hacking entirely. These fingers, they have done too much damage. Time to give them a rest."

"Yes, I understand," the woman says. "But I am in great need of your services. I'm afraid I can't pay you, as my funds have all been stripped away. But when you hear the urgency of my need, I think you'll choose to help."

Freida takes a deep breath, thinking of her final hacking job before Crown Royale. It's something she doesn't like to think about. It tempers her positive mood in uneasy ways. "You don't understand," Freida says. "The thing I've done is unforgivable. I should not have a right to access the web anymore."

The woman nods. "Unburden yourself, dear," she says. "Tell me what happened. No doubt it will be cathartic, maybe even healing."

The woman sounds as if she truly wishes to listen, and her voice carries such empathy, Freida feels she could tell her everything. So she does.

"There was an online group. Teenagers. All recoveries. American, mostly. And they were working on something. Do you know those digital masks, the ones which that billionaire makes? I can't recall his name."

"*Blas Escobedo,*" the woman says, with a hint of distaste. "*Yes, I know of them.*"

"*This group—they somehow created a way to overload those masks, burn them out over a wide range.*" Freida hesitates. This is the heart of her confession. The hardest thing for her to say. "*I pretended to be one of them. Then I sold them out to Interpol, for more money than I make in a month. They, in turn, alerted the US government.*" Freida stops walking. Tries to focus on the soothing sounds within the greenhouse. Birds and trickling water. "*Now they will be arrested, if they haven't been already. And it is all my fault. I could have helped them spread Crown Royale, but instead I stopped them. And so, from the moment my fever broke, I told myself I would never touch a computer again.*"

The woman leans her cane against a bench so she can take Freida's hand in both of hers. "*I share your regret, for I have made horrible mistakes too. Regret is the only gray emotion we still carry. But now you must forgive yourself, as you forgive others.*"

"*I know. But I still feel some sort of penance is required.*"

"*If you wish to balance your previous deeds,*" the woman says, "*I know a way.*"

Then, she finally introduces herself. "*My name is Dame Glynis Havilland, and, like you, I was involved in a scheme to confound the propagation of Crown Royale. Having once been a part of it, I can tell you that it is a well-funded scheme. And I'm afraid it might succeed. What I need you to do,*" Dame Havilland says, "*is to hack into a very secure system and stop them.*"

She's right; this would be a path for Freida's redemption. "*I don't know if I can stop them,*" Freida says, "*but if I can gain access, I might be able to slow them down.*"

"*Excellent! That will be worth its weight in gold!*"

Freida takes a few moments to think about it—but even so, she's already made her decision. "All right, then; one final job to make amends for the other."

They leave the greenhouse, finding themselves in the gift shop.

"Why don't you let me make you a custom bar?" Freida suggests. "For you to take with you! You can choose anything to put in it: marshmallows, gummy bears, cherries, even jelly beans. I'll hand-press it for you!"

"That's a kind thought, dear," Dame Havilland says. "And I would love that, except for one thing. Sadly, I'm allergic to chocolate."

33
Imagine It Done

The regional CongaLine warehouse, at the northern edge of Kokomo, Indiana, was brand-spanking-new, and designed for entirely automated service. Its north and south faces had fifty truck bays each, with self-loading tech. When up and running, it would have a complement of five hundred drones that would buzz around like a swarm of bees within its seventy feet of internal airspace, and promised to finally make good on Conga-Line's goal of two-hour delivery—a goal that could eventually give Amazon a run for its money.

With two million square feet of floor space, it came in as the fourth largest warehouse in the world, and could fit thirty-eight 747s. Not that it ever would, but it *could*—and possibility was everything for CongaLine—hence its slogan: "Imagine it? Done!" And, indeed, its construction seemed a triumph of imagination—having gone up so quickly, it seemed to have appeared in the woods overnight like a massive rectangular toadstool.

Yet in spite of all that, the Kokomo CongaLine warehouse never opened. The drones and robots were never delivered. No trucks with the signature dancing-kitchen-gadget logo ever arrived to either deliver, or distribute, merchandise. The massive building remained a hollow shell. Because the owner of CongaLine had a change of heart, and a change of plans.

. . .

This was the address where Rón Escobedo was dropped off late in the evening after waking up atop the Buc-ee's Ferris wheel. The recoverees who had given him a ride were both a bit dubious, but Rón assured them the address was correct. Even so, they didn't drive off until they saw two people unlocking the gate to let Rón in.

It was a man and a woman in camouflage, who would have been intimidating, were it not for their ingratiating grins.

"Tiburón Escobedo?"

"That's me."

"We were worried. Thought you'd have gotten here days ago."

"Sorry—had some detours along the way."

"Well, all that matters is that you're here, man!" said the man, giving him a rap on the arm. They introduced themselves as Diaz and Dang. Ex-military, and only recently so; dismissed from service upon recovery. Or maybe self-dismissed—Rón didn't want to ask.

They carried what appeared to be heavy-duty water guns, but Rón realized that they were more substantial than that. They were AK-47s, but painted in soothing pastel colors.

Dang clocked Rón noticing the weapons. "Oh, don't mind these," she said. "They're just for defense. What with all the attacks against recoverees, we need to protect our own."

"I never heard of a recoveree actually firing a weapon," Rón noted. "Even in defense."

Diaz shrugged. "Army teaches you to harness your instincts. So we got new instincts now. That doesn't mean they can't be harnessed all the same."

"I believe, push comes to shove, we'll shoot if we have to," Dang added. "We just won't shoot to kill."

Warehouses were hardly unique. Rón had been in enough of his father's to know that if you've seen one, you've seen them all. Even mega warehouses were just variations on a theme—and a monotonous theme, at that. So he was entirely unprepared for what he encountered when he stepped into the warehouse in Kokomo.

He had assumed the place might have been set up like the Pier Peer Collective; an ad hoc community of recoverees happily making do with the bare-bones space provided. What he saw didn't just stop him in his tracks—it made him stumble back a bit, right into Diaz.

"Whoa, you okay?"

"Yeah, yeah, I'm good. . . ."

It had been a day of unlikely awakenings for Rón. First the revelation that Mariel had turned him over to his father. Then whatever his father had done to render him unconscious. Then his literal awakening atop a Ferris wheel in a theme park ostensibly run by a fictional rodent. And here was yet another layer to a very surreal day.

There weren't tents and bunks and makeshift living areas spread out before him. The warehouse was full of homes. Entire buildings constructed beneath a ceiling so high that the hazy lights above could almost be stars.

His first thought was that they were façades, like in a movie set—but no, these were actual, fully realized structures set on either side of a central "avenue." To the left was a Victorian, and to the right a farmhouse. Past those were a four-story brownstone that looked like it was plucked right off a street in New York, and a tile-roofed stucco McMansion straight from suburban California. This place wasn't a warehouse. It was a neighborhood.

"What . . . *is* this?"

Diaz grinned to the point of gloating. "Imagine it? Done!"

Rón knew that slogan. "Wait—this was a CongaLine warehouse?"

"The biggest," Dang said. "And now it's ours."

There were kids on bicycles; couples out for a walk; happy, shiny people going about their business like there was nothing extraordinary about their circumstance. "All this since the beginning of the pandemic?"

Diaz shrugged. "Don't the Amish build barns in a day? And that's without the tools and materials we get to use."

"But something like this—it must have cost a fortune. . . ."

Then all the tumblers fell into place, and Rón realized how such a thing could be possible.

"You mean this was built by—"

But Diaz raised a hand and cut him off. "We don't say his name," Diaz said, with solemn reverence. "It's not who he is anymore."

Everyone knew who owned CongaLine. Or *used* to own it. The company was Jarrick Javins's brainchild, and part of what had made him the richest man in the world.

"But I thought he gave all his money away."

"He did," said Dang. "But when you're that rich, there's still a billion or two hiding in the corner."

"You must know all about that, right, Mr. Escobedo?"

He knew Diaz hadn't meant to be acerbic, but it rubbed

Rón the wrong way. "It's my father's money, not mine," he pointed out.

So Jarrick Javins was behind all this. Come to think of it, he was the one who sold the pier to Delberg Zello for a dollar—so he was, in a sense, responsible for the Pier Peer Collective as well.

"He's building our childhood homes," Dang explained. "They're not exact, but close enough."

Rón had never met Jarrick Javins, but his father had—because when you're in the rarified air of the billionaire set, it's hard not to bump elbows in the elevator that got you there.

"He's an arrogant, self-centered, opportunistic pendejo," his father had said of the man, which had made Rón secretly smile. The envy had been as thick as moss on his father's sleeve. Rón conceded that Javins probably was the asshole his father claimed him to be, but like Blas Escobedo, Javins had ideas and knew how to run with them.

"He's been excited about meeting you," Diaz said. "Ever since he was informed you were on your way."

"Me?" Rón couldn't imagine Jarrick Javins even knowing he existed. After all, he was the least newsworthy of his siblings. At least until recently. "So he's here?"

Dang shook her head, and chuckled. "No, he doesn't live among us. But you'll see him. Tomorrow."

Rón found himself excited by the prospect. Which would certainly have pissed off his father.

While they had warning of his arrival, they had not even attempted to build his childhood home, because by the time Rón was born, his father was already a multibillionaire, living large. Instead, they gave Rón a room for the night in a townhouse with bay windows, which seemed like a replica of the quaint, yet absurdly expensive, homes one might see in San Francisco; an attempt to make him feel *at* home, if not *in* home.

"It does look a lot like where I grew up," said his host for the evening—a straggly bearded man by the name of Rubian. "'Course, when I was there, it was divided into half a dozen little apartments. Now I get the whole thing, and can share it without cuttin' it up."

The interior was what one might expect from a look-alike structure that got built in a matter of days. Not exactly turnkey, but the residents were working on details like baseboards and carpeting. Rubian assured Rón that there were construction engineers and electricians living in the warehouse, making sure things were up to code. Rón had his doubts, but it didn't dim his wonder at what they were creating here.

"I had an address here and there," Rubian told Rón of his adult life. "Mostly, though, it's been versions of the street and such. Lately in Indianapolis, which got pretty unforgiving winters, so I'd snowbird down Pensacola." Then he laughed. "Warm streets in winter. Gotta love it."

Rubian confessed that he had struggled with lifelong mental illness. "But if you ask me, it's the world's what's sick—but yeah, I'd get through-the-roof paranoid about shit. But damned if all that paranoid flew out the window after Crown Royale," Rubian told Rón. "Still got stuff goin' on, but it's easier to roll with now."

And part of the stuff he had going on was a near-delusional reverence for Jarrick Javins.

"Man floats on air and walks on water," Rubian said. "He's the real deal." Then he leaned in close to Rón and whispered,

"You know, he's had it twice. Crown Royale, I mean. He's a two-timer!"

Rón had to call him on that. "Can't be. You can't get it twice."

"You can't . . . and yet he did. And what it does—it ain't just additive. It's, as they say, *exponential*! Enlightenment, squared. Like I said, the real deal!"

Rón was dubious, figuring it was a delusion of Rubian's kinder, gentler brand of schizophrenia. But others were quick to back it up when Rón asked. It was true—Jarrick Javins was a two-time recoveree. Rón couldn't even imagine what that would be like.

"He doesn't actually come to the warehouse," Rubian told him. "But he sends word. Mostly he communes with nature and such."

"So he's out there in the woods?"

Rubian gave a broad grin. "He's at the *Triton*!"

"The *Triton*?" Rón had heard rumors about it, but thought they were only rumors. "You mean it's real?"

"Real as anything else, I suppose. There's people say none of this is real, and we're all in the Matrix. Me, I think those people got a screw loose, but I suppose they'd say the screw wasn't real either, so how could it be loose? Anywho, they'll let you see him in the morning. Wish I could come with, but that ain't how it's done. And besides, I got to build houses and such tomorrow, on account of I'm on the framing team."

Rón slept on a mat in the living room across from Rubian, because the house hadn't been furnished yet. Even so, it felt as safe and as comfortable as any place Rón had ever been.

. . .

In the morning, they came for him. Two emissaries from Javins's "liaison team." They wore bedazzled vestments that were somewhat clerical in design—as if they were priests of some undefined religion that worshipped shiny things.

"Don't you mind their robes and such," Rubian told him. "They like to play at being important, so we let 'em. No harm to it until there is." Then he ribbed the two liaisons at the door. "Halloween already? Damn, you trick-or-treaters get bigger every year." And he laughed long and loud.

The pair bore Rubian's derision with ever-tolerant grins, and beckoned for Rón to come with them. They led him in silence through the warehouse, to the far end, which still remained empty, save for construction materials. Then they escorted him out a back door. From there, the liaisons would go no farther. They told Rón he had to make the pilgrimage alone.

"You cannot be helped and you must not be hindered," they told him. "Your mind must be unsullied and your footsteps your own. These are His wishes."

Rón had no idea what sort of mental sullying might be a breach of protocol, or, for that matter, whose footsteps he'd be taking, if not his own. But he agreed, hoping that good intentions counted heavily among the embraced.

"If he wants to meet me, then why do I have to wander around in the woods? It's not very efficient."

"You must seek Him out, however long it takes. These are His wishes," said the lead liaison. "And besides, it's a beautiful day."

"And in His presence, dare not to speak until He gives you leave to do so," said the other.

"Which direction?" Rón asked.

"It's on the property," was all they told him. "If you come to a fence . . . then it's not that way."

Rón set out, and when he glanced back some minutes later, the warehouse was hidden by trunks and foliage. The woods were quiet, and restorative, as nature tended to be. The trees— mostly sugar maple and white oak—were tall and the under-growth sparse enough to tramp through without too much difficulty. Although Rón found what appeared to be deer paths, they petered out and led nowhere. He came to a fence more than once, and had to turn back, taking a new trajectory, trying not to meander in unintentional circles. Then about an hour in, he caught sight of something large in the woods up ahead. Something substantial enough that it cast a shadow over this entire section of the forest. Something large enough to eclipse the sun.

Jarrick Joseph Javins had two childhood loves that he never outgrew. His parents called them obsessions; wastes of time that distracted him from his schoolwork. His therapist called them fixations; one unmistakably phallic, the other indicative of a desire to escape a dysfunctional home. His classmates just called them weird. But regardless of how they were defined, Little JJ Javins absolutely loved tree houses and submarines.

And so, to celebrate reaching a hundred billion in net worth, Javins purchased the USS *Triton*—a decommissioned attack sub—from the United States Navy, thereby saving it from the scrapyard. It had made the news a dozen or so years ago, but was quickly shuffled to the back of collective memory.

As for satisfying Javins's second childhood obsession, well, that took a bit of crafty engineering.

. . .

Rón had expected the *Triton* to be in pieces, or, at best, partially submerged in some lake—because what else would you do with a massive attack submarine? He was certainly not expecting what he found.

Rón's first impression was that this wasn't a submarine at all, but rather, a blimp that somehow got caught in the forest canopy—but there was nothing lighter than air about this vessel. *A literal lead zeppelin,* Rón thought, and was tickled by the notion. He wondered if the LedZep vibe was an intentional wink from Javins. And although Rón had been dubious of the wisdom of wandering in the woods, he had to admit that finding the *Triton* was much more satisfying than merely being brought there.

He came up on the vessel from its aft, and so the first bits of it he saw clearly were the propellers. Two of them. They were huge—each nearly twice his height. And yet not nearly as impressive as the four-hundred-fifty-foot cylindrical hull, shaped much like the torpedoes it once carried. Only upon closer scrutiny did Rón notice that many of the white oaks that held the superstructure aloft weren't trees at all, but steel beams in disguise. Even so, keeping a six-thousand-ton submarine suspended twenty feet above the forest floor was a feat worthy of CongaLine's "Imagine it? Done!" motto. Money buys magic—Rón's own father had certainly demonstrated that with technologies some people believed must have come from aliens.

"People think just because they *couldn't do it, then no one could,"* his father occasionally complained, *"and while I don't wish to bask in the things I accomplish, I don't wish to be denied credit, either."*

Rón wondered what his father would think of this tree-sub. *"Frivolous and wasteful,"* he would probably say. *"A swollen monument to Javins's swollen ego."* As if his father had never been guilty of that himself.

A hole had been cut into the bottom of the hull to accommodate a spiral staircase from the forest floor. A guard stood at the bottom with the same kind of colorfully painted rifle Rón had seen the night before. Friendly fire.

"Go on up," he said with a smile. "I'm mostly just here for show."

There was a woman halfway up the stairs, who had eyes on Rón from the moment he came into view. "Come, come," she said, beckoning. "He's been waiting on you all morning."

She climbed back into the belly of the beast, and Rón followed.

The moment Rón entered the great suspended submarine, the air changed. Sounds became hollow and resonant, colored by the strange acoustics of the ship. It was like sticking his head into the open end of a giant church bell. He could swear he heard the ocean, the way one would when putting a shell to one's ear.

The woman identified herself as one of Javins's caregivers. "He's up in the bridge," she told Rón. "It's his favorite spot."

"So . . . he lives here now?"

She considered the question. "He dwells here," she said. "You'll come to see what I mean."

The sub didn't appear much different on the inside than it must have been when it was still in operation. A narrow corridor; knobs, dials, pipes and valves; all gunmetal gray. Very few creature comforts. There was a vague, but persistent, scent in the air. Grease and the faint memory of fear and testosterone.

The caregiver pointed. "Keep going forward past the torpedo tubes, and up a set of stairs to the bridge. Careful, the stairs are slippery." Then she handed him a bowl of fish and rice. "Here—maybe *you* can get him to eat."

Rón walked forward, hearing every creak of the superstructure around him as it responded to the wind, reminding him the submarine was perched in a place it was never meant to be. He moved in and out of pools of light until coming to the torpedo tubes, and the stairs to the bridge, which was little more than a steeply sloped ladder. Then, when he reached the top and entered the bridge, everything changed.

It was still the same submarine here as down below—but there was a presence on the bridge that was penetrating and palpable. The sensation bloomed in Rón's chest like the deepest of breaths. He couldn't dismiss it as his imagination; there was something very real to the feeling.

Javins sat against the far bulkhead of the bridge. There were potted plants set on the consoles all around to warm the utilitarian space. There were multiple computer screens, but all of them were turned off. A gentle light filled the entire space—a light so diffuse that nothing cast a shadow.

Javins's expression was that of beatific wonder. Like a child's first glimpse of the tree on Christmas morning. His eyes were cast to the low ceiling as if seeing through it to something beyond the beyond.

Rón stood there, afraid to interrupt his silent reverie. But then his eyes lowered to Rón and he smiled. Rón felt a shiver when meeting his eyes, but it wasn't at all unpleasant.

And when Javins spoke, even though his voice was soft, it

was made resonant by the vessel, as if the entire submarine were the chamber of a cello. And the flow of his words was like the casting of a spell written in runes, consequential yet comforting. The quiet power of wind in a sail. Of surf on the shore. A crackling campfire. The view of Earth from space.

34
Javins

So you've arrived!
And at precisely the right time.
No doubt you think you're late;
that you wandered in the wilderness too long.
Rest assured, you have not.
You have arrived exactly
when you needed to.

I see wonder reflected in your eyes.
You wish to know how it's possible
for me to have been touched twice by Crown Royale
when no one else has.
I have my theories.
We'll consider them later.
But what you really want to know
is what it's like.
Am I right?

I wish there were words to describe it.
But you, yourself, know how language fails
when you try to explain to the unembraced
what it's like for you.

Like trying to convey the concept of "blue"
before you first saw it.

The color I now feel is absolute ecstasy.
The transcendent joy of simply existing.
It's overwhelming.
It's both exalting and humbling at once.
To know how small you are,
and yet in that speck,
to find greatness.
Like a singularity.
The very womb of creation.

All our lives, we take for granted
the simple state of "being."
But I no longer take it for granted.
Now I know how rare,
how beautiful,
how exquisite this existence is.
I feel gratitude
every moment of every day
with such passion
there is no room
for petty concerns of the flesh.

Which is why Jessa gave you a bowl for me.
Always concerned for my well-being,
dear woman.
You may put the bowl down.
We'll consider it later.

Come closer, Tiburón.

No need to keep your distance.

And mind the periscope.

Bumped my head more than once.

But each time grateful for the lesson.

No need for a chair,

sit here on the deck.

Think of the places this steel has been.

Appreciate how solid it is.

And yet, if you're still enough,

you can feel the morning air

as it sweeps under the hull.

And beneath that the forest floor,

teaming with hidden life.

And beneath that, our world as a whole,

its gravity a gift,

even as we defy it.

Let me have a look at you.

Yes—you resemble your father.

The eyes, the brow.

I can sense you have his drive,

even if you don't see it yourself.

And your mother's keen intelligence,

and likely her kindness.

And so here we are at last, you and me,

faced with the old Chinese curse:

"May you live in interesting times."

These times may be the most interesting of all.

Deadly and dangerous,
but also filled with warmth and light.

Who can say why humanity
has come to this crossroads?
Is it random chance?
Is it by some greater design?
Philosophers spend their lives
debating the question,
and to what end?
They leave this world without an answer,
blinded by fury at those who saw things differently.
In the end, it is not our purpose to know the answer,
but rather to thrive within the Mystery.

And now, young Tiburón,
the Mystery has summoned us.
All of us.
We have been served a subpoena
to testify on humanity's behalf.
We, the arrogant apex species of Earth
must cast off our pretentions,
and, naked before the universe,
we must make our case
not just through words, but through action.
For our actions will be our deliverance
or our undoing.

We have an obligation
to spread Crown Royale to the world.

You have sensed this,
and have done well on your own.
But I'm sure you've also sensed
there will be a heavy cost.
A toll of lives.
I'm not speaking of those
who die from Crown Royale.
That is nothing but a drop in a bucket.
Ultimately, they are not the ones who suffer,
for in a pandemic the greatest suffering
is felt by those left behind.
Those who must grieve.
And yet Crown Royale has taken care of that,
numbing our grief before it can fester,
leaving behind only the joyous memory
of lives completed.
As recoverees, we have perspective;
we can say goodbye to our loved ones
who have succumbed,
with the same peace and acceptance
that they themselves found in their final moments.

No, Crown Royale's mortality rate
is not the cost of which I speak.

The greatest, most pernicious loss of life
will be caused by the unembraced,
whose fear makes them cling to the old ways
of anger, distrust, territorialism, and treachery.
They will kill tenfold more than the virus ever could.

You see their rage rising, don't you?
Our inner peace infuriates them
and feeds their hatred.

They will seek to silence us.

And when they can't,
they will seek to control us.

And when they can't,
they will seek to destroy us.

We *will* not
Must not
Let
that
happen.

35
The Boulder and the Raft

Rón felt faint, and realized that for the longest time, he had neglected to breathe. As if oxygen were the least of his concerns. He drew in a sharp breath—it was the only sound beyond the gentle creaks of the vessel as it responded to the wind, and the taps of boughs as they endlessly tested the seriousness of the *Triton*'s presence.

Rón could not deny that there was something that set Javins apart. Something that bordered on preternatural. The way he moved, the way light seemed to fall on him differently—and although he didn't levitate, there was a lightness to him, like if he stepped on a scale, it wouldn't register he was there.

Javins let the silence between them carry the weight of his missive—but he needn't have done that, for his words had penetrated so deeply, Rón felt he could recite them verbatim. Now it was just the man's patient gaze—which Rón found he couldn't hold. He had to look away—and when he did, he noticed all the blooms in the plants set around the bridge. Had those blooms been there before, or had they opened as Javins spoke? For the life of him, Rón didn't know.

"I'm afraid I've hijacked the conversation," Javins finally said. "Forgive me. I haven't let you get a word in since you arrived."

"They . . . they told me not to speak," Rón said. "Not until you gave me permission."

Javins scoffed. "I told them to stop that. They wish to be reverent, but their reverence borders on farce." Javins sighed. "Ah well, it's only a minor nuisance."

"Not a problem until it is."

"Indeed. We must keep an eye on these things. Even as human nature is changing, there will be kinks in the line."

As Rón still felt mostly speechless, he was happy to distract the man with the pungent prop he had been handed. Rón reached down and grabbed the bowl of food, holding it out to Javins. "You should eat."

Javins pursed his lips. "Yes, they are constantly reminding me of this. To think my life was once all about my insatiable appetites. Now I must be reminded to even consider the maintenance of this little slab of flesh. But that's because I see a broader self now; a greater all-encompassing identity."

"But you still have to eat."

Javins looked at the bowl in Rón's outstretched hand and relented. "Agreed. Let's just say I was fasting until your arrival. Let it be by your hand that I remain alive."

He took the bowl and began eating with the fork that had been given. Somehow the utensil seemed incongruous. Javins must have noticed Rón's glance, because he gave Rón a quizzical look of his own.

"What is it?"

"Nothing," Rón said. "Somehow I thought a viral prophet would have to eat with his hands."

"Ah!" said Javins with a chuckle. "But rice and salmon are hardly locusts and honey."

As Javins ate, he rambled, his words feeling less formal,

because it's hard to pontificate while you eat. Even so, his ramblings held weight.

"You call me a prophet. I suppose here, in the belly of this steel whale, I could be Jonah, or maybe Pinocchio. Or Captain Nemo. Or Ahab. I am any manner of metaphor that suits the need." He paused to consider it, gesturing with his incongruous fork like a wand. "It would have been far more just, far more poetic, if the person who landed in my position came from humble obscurity. But reality favors expediency over aesthetics. And nature always takes the path of least resistance. In this case, a self-important icon of industry, comfortable with power, and with a finger in every pie, was nature's way of giving Crown Royale—and the new humanity it heralds—a fighting chance. A fisherman or a farmer would have been a satisfying fairy tale, but the learning curve would be too slow.

"I know what you're thinking; Jarrick Javins, the world's most celebrated narcissist, now sees himself as the world's savior. The funny thing about Crown Royale is that it takes our greatest flaws and turns them into assets. Why was *I* the one to get Crown Royale twice? Perhaps because I already thought myself to be the most important person in the world. A universal lesson in being careful what you wish for."

Rón had to laugh. He never imagined a virus could have a sense of the ironic. "You talk as if Crown Royale is conscious."

Javins nodded. "I do wonder if there is some sentience to this virus; a collective consciousness that we are all the lucky beneficiaries of. But more likely, it simply aligns *our* consciousness in a new way. A way we've always sought but could never achieve. No longer divided into factions based on petty differences, but one species that encompasses all of it. We are ourselves, and we are each other, all at once."

Rón grinned. "Quite a leap from being the 'King of Capitalism.'"

But Javins shook his head. "Such simplistic labeling of economic systems is beneath us now. Crown Royale takes us beyond such flawed notions. Capitalism fails because self-interest can never be enlightened. Socialism fails because high ideals consistently rot into brutal autocracies. And still people are foolish enough to believe one system will work over the other. Human nature must change for any system to succeed. That is the crux of evolution. And it doesn't come overnight. Not until now."

Then he paused to contemplate his unique circumstance.

"So now I find myself in this this pivotal position. But even so, I know that I am nothing. It is not about me; I am merely a boulder set in place to affect the course of a river." Then he added, "But if I am the boulder, then you are the raft by which we will shoot these treacherous rapids."

He finished the last of his meal and handed the bowl back to Rón. "There. You can give that to Jessa as evidence I've eaten." Then his grin faltered. "What we speak of now, however, might not be so easy to swallow."

Javins liked to punctuate things with silence. Rón wondered if that was an old habit, or if an appreciation of the moments between was a result of being a double-recoveree.

"It was not by chance that you left San Francisco," Javins finally put forth. "With your father searching for you, you had no choice. Nor is it by chance that you arrived here. When Delberg Zello informed us you were heading in this direction,

I made sure that this would be your destination. And it is not by chance that we sit here now. You made a choice to seek me out in the woods. Everything leading to this meeting, while not calculated, was motivated. My question to you is: How motivated are you? And are you willing to take the next step?"

Rón thought he knew what was being asked of him. "You want me to help you fight the unembraced."

Javins nodded, but Rón could sense that was only one part of the picture. "Yes, we must defend ourselves as all creatures do, for we are still bound by that basic biological law; survival of the fittest. Natural selection. And the human race will only be selected for survival with Crown Royale as its ally. You must have had an inkling of this, Tiburón."

Javins was right. Rón had said as much to Mariel. The urge to spread Crown Royale was an urge to save people, not harm them. He wished Mariel were here to share in this conversation. To offer balance.

"Are you suggesting we should destroy the unembraced, before they destroy us?"

"No," Javins said, to Rón's relief. "But we do need to destroy their means of waging war. Once we do that, it's only a matter of time until they either destroy themselves, or catch Crown Royale and become embraced. I hope for the latter, but there will always be those who would rather end their own existence than admit they were wrong."

Javins rose then. The first time since Rón's arrival. He was a slight man, but carried himself like someone much larger. He grabbed a pitcher and moved around the bridge, taking great care as he watered the plants.

"I have sources out there that give me news of a clandestine nature. Top secret stuff that not even governments know."

Then he handed the pitcher to Rón, indicating that the task had passed to him. "My sources tell me that there is a biological weapon being developed that could defeat Crown Royale."

Rón nearly dropped the pitcher.

"Defeat it? As in . . ."

"Eradicate it. Like smallpox. Like polio. End its variant of DNA. And if that happens, the human race will die with it. All roads lead to this. The only path to human survival is one where Crown Royale lights our way with the simple appreciation of each other's existence." He waited until Rón had watered the last plant. "Which brings us to the critical role that *you* must play."

Then he took the pitcher and set it gently down, perhaps fearing that Rón might actually drop it this time.

"Your father is funding the creation of this weapon."

It came as a blow. In Rón's mind, his father's search for him was taking all his attention.

"My father's creating a vaccine?"

"Something much, much worse. I don't have all the details, but whatever it is will be far more dangerous than a vaccine."

"He wouldn't risk people's safety," Rón said.

"Your father thinks the reward outweighs the risk. But he is wrong on every count. He lingers on the bleak side of history, in fear of all he might lose, never realizing that he could be condemning humanity. It is justice, therefore, that his son be the one to take up arms against his fear, against his fury, against his weapon."

It was the first time since recovering from Crown Royale that Rón felt himself on the precipice of doubt. He didn't doubt that Javins was telling the truth, but Rón doubted his own ability to make a difference. "I don't know if I can do that."

"You can, because you know it's the right thing to do—and you are compelled to do what's right. As am I. As are all of the embraced."

And in the midst of this moment, thoughts of Mariel came swooping back in. More than anything right now, it was Mariel he longed for. Because here, in a submarine in the trees, he needed her grounding presence. Because although Javins was speaking truth and wisdom, those things could be as beguiling as lies.

"There's . . . there's a girl . . ." Rón found himself saying it out loud, without even meaning to. As if wearing his heart on his sleeve was not enough, it now demanded to be voiced.

Javins did not seem surprised. "There's always a girl. Or a boy. Or a parent. Or a child. Always someone who has a hold on those who are called upon. Part of the test is the letting go."

"I don't want to let her go."

"Of course you don't. If you were willing, it wouldn't be a test. But tell me, Tiburón, if she stood between you and your mission, what would you do?"

Rón wished he could tell Javins what he wanted to hear, but he couldn't. All he could offer was the truth.

"I don't know."

Javins nodded in solemn approval. "And that is the right answer. One can never know until one is in the position. I'd be concerned if you said anything other."

The sun was high by the time their summit was done. Jessa, satisfied with the empty bowl, offered to have a guard walk Rón back to the warehouse—apparently getting to the *Triton* was a solitary pilgrimage, but getting back was not. Rón declined the escort. He needed time alone to digest all that transpired between him and Jarrick Javins, whose final words to Rón still loomed large.

> "So do we continue to shine
> into the expanse of the universe?
> Or do we go out by our own hand?
> With a blast.
> With a fizzle.
> With a sigh.
>
> Go ponder these things.
> See how they sit with you.
> And then we will plan!"

The tonnage of a submarine was nothing compared to the weight of what Rón now had before him.

Mariel's exhaustion overcame her just minutes out of Muncie. She barely even stirred when they landed for refueling in Iceland. It was the hard jolt of touchdown at the very end of their journey that shocked her awake.

"Short runway," Morgan said. "They have to land hard. It's normal." Then Morgan tossed her a full-on parka. "Better put that on."

Mariel had never seen something so heavy in real life, much less worn one. But the moment the door opened, and a blast of icy air invaded the cabin, she realized she had better put it on. It was barely the end of summer, so where could they be? This was a cold that Mariel had never experienced before, and honestly, not even the parka was enough to keep her warm.

It was night outside, and as she stepped down from the plane, she saw mountains around her covered with snow, and a sky was filled with green, shimmering light. Was that the aurora borealis?

"Night isn't long here this time of year," Morgan said. "Just a couple of hours. You're lucky to see the lights."

"Where are we?" she asked.

"Your new happy place," Morgan replied, escorting her toward a waiting Jeep. "If you've ever heard people speak of 'a place of greater safety,' this is it. You're in the safest place in the world."

Which wasn't an actual answer to Mariel's question. "So should I be expecting to see a sleigh with flying reindeer?"

Morgan chuckled. "Not yet," she said. "Maybe in a few months."

The stoic guard driving the Jeep spoke some Scandinavian language into his radio, and brought them to a concrete wedge jutting out of the mountainside. They had to take the last twenty yards on foot, which felt a whole lot farther in the cold. As they approached, the door was opened from the inside, and Mariel stepped into air that would have been chilly in normal circumstances, but felt balmy compared to the cold of the mountain.

There was a welcome committee there, led by a woman with salt-and-cinnamon hair and a slight hunch, as if she had spent much of her life leaning over a microscope.

"Welcome, welcome," the woman said, clapping her hands together with an odd sort of mirth. "You must be Mariel Mudroch. We've been looking forward to making your acquaintance." She didn't extend her hand to shake; perhaps that was a no-no in a medical research facility, which Mariel assumed it was. "Come—we have a room ready for you and a hot meal prepared. You must be hungry."

"Yes," Mariel admitted, although she was much more hungry for answers than anything else. "So you're all here working on a vaccine?"

The woman hesitated, but just for a moment. "It's complicated, but, as you suggest, we're working on a way to pull the rug out from underneath Crown Royale, so to speak." She introduced herself as Dr. Bosgraaf. "I trust Miss Willmon-Wu explained the part you'll play in our little medical miracle?"

"My blood."

"Your blood, indeed! More valuable than gold in this troubled world!"

"So I've heard."

"Let's move this along, Dr. Bosgraaf," Morgan said. "And I'll want a progress briefing as soon as possible."

Mariel suppressed a grin, realizing that the only reason Morgan had said that was to remind Bosgraaf and her welcoming committee who was in charge.

They made their way down a narrow, inclined tunnel to a vestibule with two vault doors. The one to the right was open, and there was a man there doing some sort of inventory over plastic-wrapped boxes. He glanced up at them coldly.

"More mischief, Miss Wu?"

"Keep to your own business, Dr. Nødtvedt."

The man harrumphed and went back to his inventory.

Bosgraaf just shook her head as she led them to the left-hand door. "That man."

"Don't mind 'Dr. No,'" Morgan said. "He's all about his seeds."

The quarters that Mariel was given, windowless of course, were clean and livable. Like the cold outside, everything was relative; she had slept in far worse places.

Even before the proffered meal was brought, a phlebotomist came in to extract a vial of Mariel's blood.

"We are needing to establish a baseline before the real work begins," he said, as if Mariel's veins were a mine they'd be excavating.

"Better be careful with that," Mariel said. "My resources are limited."

The phlebotomist did not get her sarcasm. "*Claro.* But the human body can generate two liters of plasma per day, *más o menos.* Even more when well hydrated." His accent sounded Latin American, which she found comforting. Familiar. Although it did remind her a bit of Blas Escobedo, which was far less comforting.

Left alone, and in the silence of a mountain stronghold, she couldn't stop her thoughts from spiraling back to Rón. She must have been half a world away from him now. Where was he? Was he ensconced in his own "place of greater safety"— or at least his father's version of it? As an alpha-spreader, he wouldn't be allowed near other people. He was probably in a proverbial plastic bubble so he couldn't infect anyone. And it occurred to Mariel that under Blas Escobedo's authority, Rón might never be allowed to have human contact again. Rón had spoken of his father as a good man and loving father who had let his fear of Crown Royale drive his actions. But how loving of a father could he be if he kept Rón in perpetual isolation?

Well, one thing was clear: whatever situation Rón was now in, it was Mariel's fault he was in it. There were moments when she could live with that and moments when she couldn't.

When the food arrived, it was Morgan who brought it herself. Two place settings on the tray, because "no one should have to dine alone."

It was a pottage of fish and potatoes, oversalted, and short on other spices, but in a place like this, what else would you eat?

"I suppose you want to know about my experiences with Tiburón Escobedo," Mariel said as she ate.

"No," Morgan said right out of hand. "I know all I need to know. You realized what he was about, and you chose to not be a part of it. All that matters now is your path forward."

Which was a sentiment Mariel's mother would have approved of. Morgan, however, was nothing like Gena Mudroch. If Morgan was dismissive of the past, it was by choice, rather than out of necessity. There was something to be admired here. An older sister who knew how to make her mark on the world. Mariel found herself wanting to like Morgan more and more. She had a take on Crown Royale that was like the jarring jolt of their landing. Like a blast of that polar air. It was bracing in all sorts of ways.

"Do you actually believe society will collapse just because people are getting off on being happy?" Mariel asked.

Morgan took a moment to savor a spoonful of her soup before answering. "Civilization is not designed for everyone to be happy. There'll always be the haves and have-nots. Joy will always be at the expense of someone else's suffering. It's the way it's always been, the way it's always worked. That's the tension that creates civilization."

"But what if it doesn't have to be that way?" Mariel wanted to say. But after everything Mariel had been through, she wasn't up for it.

Morgan misread Mariel's silence—or perhaps simply chose to tap into a different vein—because what she said next drew a bad vial of blood.

"I know you feel guilt for the things you did with Tiburón Escobedo. Don't. You were under the spell of an alpha-spreader—you were a hostage of his disease. Classic Stockholm syndrome. Recoverees have a deranged sort of passion that can be very persuasive." Then she added, with a smirk, "And it didn't hurt that he's kind of hot."

Mariel let out a sudden laugh. Not the kind of truth bomb she was expecting from Morgan.

"The point is," Morgan continued, "you finally see recoverees for what they are; lost souls. They're doomed to lives of perpetual mediocrity. Feel sorry for them, but don't romanticize their crippling affliction."

Mariel returned to her soup as refuge from having to respond. What Morgan said made sense, and was wholly reasonable . . . and yet . . . These were weighty questions, so much grander than anything she had faced before. Mariel knew she was part of something larger than herself now. She felt that way with Rón, and she felt that way now. Two sides of the same coin.

"What you're doing here is important," she told Morgan. "A vaccine will slow Crown Royale down. It will give the world time to figure out how to deal with it."

"We deal with it," said Morgan, "by eradicating it."

"Maybe."

"There's no 'maybe' about it. When has a contagion been for the better? Disease has wiped out entire civilizations."

But although Morgan saw visions of Armageddon, it didn't jive with what Mariel had seen. At the pier. In the streets. Even at Helm House. Chaos came from the outside, not from within.

"Not everyone will want your vaccine," Mariel pointed out. "There are people who want to catch Crown Royale—I know I wanted to catch it when I thought I could. But a vaccine does level the playing field. It will let people to choose—and that brings balance."

"Yes," said Morgan. "Yes, of course. Choice and balance. But you really should think about this instead: you and I—

we could be partners in bringing something important to the world!" Morgan's excitement brimmed at the prospect. "Imagine it! Crown Royale defeated by two women!"

"Well, three if you include Dr. Bosgraaf . . ." Which brought to mind something Mariel had once learned in school. Or in a Disney movie. "The three Fates."

That made Morgan grin with appreciation. "I like that! What were their names again? Oh yes—Clotho, Lachesis, and Atropos; the spinner, the allotter, and the inevitable!"

Which made Mariel wonder . . . "Which one are you?"

Morgan leaned back, more than a bit self-satisfied. "I've always considered myself inevitable."

Two thousand miles south, a fourth hand of fate was plaiting a fabric of its own. But the weave was entirely dependent on the type of generosity that was once rare in the world.

Dame Havilland knew that going back to Thornwick Nab was out of the question, as Morgan most certainly had eyes on it. But she and Galen Rooks did need to get to London. The problem was, she and Galen were penniless now—and as such, needed the kind of assistance she was loath to ask for.

Dame Havilland was not accustomed to relying on the kindness of strangers. Perhaps because she never believed actual kindness existed. To her, it always had the semblance of secret self-interest, which made it all the more insidious. "Kind" people were to be distrusted for their ulterior motives. Of course, now her perceptions had changed in that regard— although she did wonder if any previral altruism was as pure as the sort of selflessness that Crown Royale imbued.

She was quick to discover that recoverees helped one

another, oftentimes without even having to be asked. Not quite an underground, because it was completely out in the open and aboveboard. No one hid their recovery status, rather the opposite—which posed its own problems. Because there were disruptors everywhere, happy to buy into all the lies that claimed recoverees did everything short of drinking human blood. "Fight the Spider," and all that. Attacks on recoverees were becoming commonplace, and nearly normalized. Things were always the same among the unembraced; never happy until there's someone to hate.

They knew rail fare to London would be an issue—a trip through the Chunnel was outrageously expensive by their current financial standards. But they found a recovered clerk who was happy to pay for their tickets from Cologne to London herself.

"Pay it forward," she said. "When you find yourself with money again, buy a ticket for someone else in need."

Upon arrival at King's Cross Station, Galen took the lead amidst the bustling city crowds. "I did bring change enough for the Underground," he told her.

"And deprive a London cabbie the pleasure of our company? I wouldn't dream of it." Glynis hadn't taken the London Underground—or, for that matter, a taxi—for half a lifetime, and although her old aversions to such things were gone, there was something to be said for appreciating the city from the spaciousness of a hackney carriage. And although they had very particular business in London today, they were early, so they could afford the time it would take to find a recoveree to drive them at little to no cost.

Patience and perseverance paid off, and they found themselves a cheery-cheeked cabbie who promised not to turn on the meter. "Truth be told, I'd give everyone free rides now, yeah? But bills are bills."

Galen gave him the address, which the cabbie recognized right away. "The Gherkin! Hope you already have your tickets for the observation deck, yeah? They sell out early—although that might be less of a problem these days, what with the pandemic being what it is." Then he offered to give them a personal tour of London, thinking they must be country folk on holiday. They decided to let him think that, but politely declined the offer.

"You'll like the observation deck. Not as high as The Shard, but The Gherkin's glass dome is impressive. Especially on a day like today, yeah?"

Upon arrival, they took some time to coordinate and review the plan in a café across the street. Then they went forth to take on the Havilland Consortium.

The lobby of The Gherkin was a study in curves and unconventional angles. Nothing was perpendicular; nothing was square. Every bit of the egg-shaped building was designed to inspire a sense of grand and glorious uplift to the future.

"An architectural ejaculation," Glynis had once complained, even as she reveled in the idea of setting up shop in a building that was both iconic and universally despised, by the dusty aristocrats *she* had so despised.

The entrance to the elevator bay was regulated by electronic glass gates that required a fob or passcard, neither of which were currently in Glynis's possession. One of the guards on duty recognized her right away, and came over.

"Good to see you, ma'am," he said, sounding more apologetic

than enthusiastic. "I'm afraid you'll need to check in with me first, now that you're no longer . . . well, now that things have changed. And begging your pardon, but you and your companion are violating the building's mask mandate."

"My dear man, we've had Crown Royale and have long since recovered," Glynis pointed out. "We're not a threat to anyone's health."

"Nevertheless, it's policy. So sorry, ma'am."

She turned to Galen, who produced their masks from his satchel.

"Now, then, you know who I am, but let me introduce you to my dear friend, Galen Rooks. Now please allow us to pass."

"I'm afraid it's not that easy, Dame Havilland." He sighed at having to speak this next part. "We have strict orders from your successor to refuse you admittance, should you turn up unexpected."

"Outrageous!" railed Galen, but it was just a performance. This was precisely what Glynis had expected.

"It's not my business to know what went on between you and Ms. Wu, but it is my business to enforce our tenants' security protocols, whether we like it or not."

"Willmon-Wu," Glynis gently corrected. "I imagine she might have you fired for neglecting to hyphenate."

"Thank you, ma'am. I'll remember that."

"Now be so kind as to call up, and ask her to either allow us entrance, or come down to deny us to our faces." Which Glynis suspected wasn't happening, because the chances of Morgan actually being there were slim. According to her one remaining contact at the Havilland Consortium, Morgan was most likely in Svalbard, or galivanting around the globe in the Havilland jet, creating a carbon footprint the size of Godzilla's.

Glynis expected it would be Ellis Bradway, her vice president, who came down from his office. A friendly face—or at least one slightly more friendly than Morgan's would be. But instead it was his assistant. Dame Havilland's old self would have been profoundly insulted.

Preston Locke suspected this day might come. Dame Glynis Havilland, even as a recoveree, would not go down easy. She would not allow herself to be put out to pasture without some sort of struggle. He had almost looked forward to the fireworks that might fly between the old woman and Morgan. But Morgan was off jetting around the world, leaving Preston to mind the proverbial store. And as much as he disliked being a lackey to Bradway, he disliked being vice president just as much. Perhaps if he had earned the position, rather than been appointed to it for spite, things might have been easier—but he was yet to be respected by his coworkers, who were now all his subordinates. In truth, he did his job well—but getting others to do their jobs well was an entirely different matter.

And now this.

He had always seen Dame Havilland as a dark, soul-sucking presence. A Nazgûl. A Dementor. An entity that thrived on the suffering of others. He could not imagine her as a Crown Royale recoveree—but as he counted the dropping numbers of the elevator readout, he knew he would not have to imagine much longer. He pulled out his phone and thought to call Morgan, asking her for direction in this matter, but quickly slipped his phone back into his pocket. No. She would just berate him for troubling her with it.

When he emerged into the lobby, and Dame Havilland saw him, she seemed taken aback. But that passed quickly.

"Good to see you, Preston," she said. He was surprised that she remembered his name. But then, that was probably tactical. Even though she rarely came to the office when she was in charge, there was power in knowing everyone's name. No hiding from the boss when she knew precisely who you were.

"Could you please let Mr. Bradway know that I'd like to speak with him?"

Preston cleared his throat and did his best to fill his double-breasted suit. "I'm sorry, Dame Havilland, but Ellis Bradway is no longer employed by the Consortium."

She nodded, but didn't as much as raise an eyebrow. Perhaps it came as no surprise that Morgan would make quick work with the axe once she took charge.

"I'm sorry to hear that. Who is it that you work for now?"

"I report directly to Ms. Willmon-Wu."

Then the guard who had called him down interjected, thinking he was being helpful, but really all he did was steal Preston's thunder.

"Mr. Locke, here, is the new VP of your . . . uh . . . of the Havilland Consortium."

She didn't miss a beat. "My word, things *have* changed since I've been around! Well, a hearty congratulations on your promotion, young man! Your mother must be proud."

It was both genuine and insulting at the same time. Only Dame Havilland could manage to be acerbic as a recoveree. He had no doubt she'd find a way to manipulate him into doing or saying something he did not want to. The quicker this encounter was over, the better.

"I'm sorry you've come all this way, but rest assured, everything here is in the best of hands, really. Thank you for coming. Have a nice day." Then he signaled to the guard to escort them out.

But as the guard advanced, Dame Havilland's companion stepped between her and the guard. "I will not have you manhandle the poor woman!"

"I wasn't going to—I was just—"

"Galen! No need to fight my battles for me!"

"Yes, but he was going to—"

"No, sir, I wasn't—"

Preston watched with growing horror. This was turning into a scene. The last thing he wanted was a scene. It would be caught on the security cameras, and Morgan would see him standing there, impotent to resolve the situation. Clearly this would not end well for anyone. He stepped forward to intercede, if only to make himself seem less useless—and just then Dame Havilland's cane flew out from under her, and she fell. Preston lurched forward to catch her, nearly losing his balance as well—but a young woman standing nearby came to his aide, and they both managed to get Dame Havilland back to her feet, saving her from what would most certainly have been a broken hip.

"Well, then," Dame Havilland said, only slightly ruffled. "There's my excitement for the day. Galen, let's let these good people be. It's not their fault Ms. Willmon-Wu has made me *persona non grata*."

They turned to leave, and once they were through the door,

the guard returned to his station, and everyone else observing the little kerfuffle went back about their business. Preston took a relieved breath and headed to the elevators, never knowing that his phone, and all his passwords, had been cloned.

He did notice, however, that the young woman who had helped him with Dame Havilland wore the most delightful perfume. It almost smelled like chocolate.

37
Turds All the Way Down

Morgan should have known that things in Svalbard were going way too well. That the universe, vindictive as it was, would find a way to kick a leg out from under her.

It began with a text from Preston in the London office. A turd emoji. Was this an attempt at humor? Then a second one appeared, and a third, and then a whole string of them. Whatever this childish display represented, she resented having to deal with it.

She tried to reply with a quite appropriate WTF, but the message didn't go through. Then, a few minutes later, a call came in from an unknown number. It was Preston.

"Could you be a little more communicative than sending me a barrage of little shits?"

"Turn off your Wi-Fi!"

"What?"

"Turn off your Wi-Fi before it's too late!"

And although she resented taking orders from him, she did as he asked. "What the hell is going on?"

"We've been hacked! Someone's infiltrated our network. All our data is being systematically replaced by those bloody emojis!"

"You can't be serious!"

"Every text we send, every email we transmit, it's turds all the way down. The firewalls have all fallen, and we can't stop its progression. We've already lost half of our files."

"Shut it down! Shut the whole thing down!"

"I already did—but the damage is done."

Morgan struggled to even process what she was hearing. A string of scatological emojis? That was an understatement for what this was. "Who could have done this? Someone on the inside? Do we have a mole?"

Preston's silence spoke volumes.

"Tell me, Preston. The longer you wait, the worse it gets for you."

"Dame Havilland paid us a visit this morning."

It was the last thing Morgan wanted to hear, but she should have expected it after the stunt she tried to pull with Morgan's mother. Damn that woman!

"And you let her in the office?"

"No! Absolutely not! I went downstairs to send her on her way. But we think she found a way to clone my phone, and that's how she gained access." And then he added, "It's just a theory—we don't know for certain it's her doing."

"*Of course it was her!*" growled Morgan. "She's toying with me! She's been toying with me since the moment she recovered—and if we're not careful, she could take down this whole operation!"

And then Morgan realized. *"You're calling me from an infected phone?"*

"No—the second I realized I was sending emojis, I had everyone in the office shut their phones down, and went across the street to find a land line. This call is safe."

Even so, those emojis landed on Morgan's phone before

she disconnected from Svalbard's Wi-Fi. Could the malware have wormed its way from her phone to Svalbard's network that quickly? She could only hope that she disconnected in time.

"This is *your* mess!" she yelled. "You'd better have it under control by the time I get there!" Then she disconnected, and powered her own phone down.

She took a few moments to try to settle her breathing. Then a voice spoke behind her.

"Something wrong?"

It was Bosgraaf—and in Morgan's current state, she wanted to slap the woman just for existing.

"There's been a breach," she informed Bosgraaf. "We have to cut ourselves off. No signals going in or out. No phones, no wireless—and pray that our network hasn't already been infected. Right now, I need you to collect all phones and destroy them—every last one of them."

"Destroy? I don't think our staff will take kindly to—"

"Do I look like I care? Destroy all phones! That's an order!" And to make it clear she meant business, she took her own phone, dropped it on the ground, and crushed it beneath her heel.

"No exceptions!"

Then she stormed off to find her parka and the pilots to fly her back to London.

From the moment Mariel arrived, she served one purpose, and one purpose alone. A veritable pipeline of bodily fluid.

Blood draws. Five, six, seven times a day. Mariel was developing a strange and somewhat surreal relationship with the phlebotomist. His name tag said SALCEDO. He never offered his first name. He had installed a PICC line in her left arm so he had direct access, and didn't have to jab her and dig for a vein every time. Although the vials he used were relatively small, he filled so many of them a day that Mariel constantly felt lightheaded.

"You must have been a vampire in a previous life, Mr. Salcedo," she commented on the third day of relentless blood-letting.

His eyebrows furrowed. "This is an insult?"

"Just an observation."

"Vampires live forever, ¿*verdad*? They cannot have a previous life."

Mariel shrugged. "Maybe you got staked through the heart, or caught by the rising sun."

"In this case, I would go straight to hell. Reincarnation is not an option."

The rest of Mariel's days were filled with bland diversions. Old DVDs, a limited library of books in a dozen different languages, and generic board games in the common area. When she did go out to the common area, where the medical staff hung out when they weren't working in the labs, there was an uneasy awkwardness around her. She tried to make conversation, but was always met with polite, but perfunctory responses. Only Dr. Bosgraaf would actively engage her, like a kindergarten teacher trying to draw in that one child no one would talk to.

"You don't have to coddle me, Dr. Bosgraaf, I'm a big girl."

"You must understand, these researchers and physicians have a certain reverence for you, because of what you represent to them. The holy grail of all their efforts, breathed into life." Then she leaned closer and whispered, "And perhaps they see you as an extension of Ms. Willmon-Wu—of whom they're terrified."

And while the rarified air in which Morgan existed must have been a lonely place, it tickled Mariel that the others saw her atop the same ivory pillar.

"When will Morgan be back?" Mariel asked.

Bosgraaf sighed and shrugged, clearly not keen on her return. "As of this morning, we've gone completely dark—no communication in or out, so I don't know."

"Gone dark?"

"Something to do with a virus." Then she laughed. "Well, of course—it's *all* to do with a virus—but in this case I mean a computer virus. I'm sure it will all sort itself out."

On the fourth day, the phlebotomist didn't come at the usual time. He didn't come at all. No explanation.

When Mariel went out for lunch, there weren't many people present—most were in the labs. The few that were there were even more standoffish than usual, and Bosgraaf was nowhere to be found. It was clear that something had changed.

She lingered awhile, and caught Salcedo leaving the labs for a short break. He looked exhausted.

"What's going on?" Mariel asked. "My blood's not good enough for you anymore?"

From a man who tended to take everything literally, his answer was uncharacteristically cryptic.

"The sun has risen," he said. "The vampires have all burned away."

. . .

"We're sorry, but the number you have called is not in service. Please check the number and try again."

Dame Havilland disconnected and handed Rooks back his phone.

"Verdict?" asked Galen.

"I venture to say we've been, at the very least, partially successful. I tried three of the Consortium's land lines, and all have been disconnected."

"Well, partial success is better than total failure."

"Yes, well, glass half-full doesn't help us much. We need it completely dry." She caught Galen looking at his phone with concern. "Something wrong?"

"Are you sure they can't trace us here through the phone?"

"Absolutely."

They were in a small hotel in Newham—not the glitziest of London neighborhoods, but crime rates had dropped with a steady rise of recoverees, and the hotel manager—a recoveree himself—offered them a free room as long as they left the place as they found it.

"How sure *are* you about the phone?"

She sighed. "Galen, do you remember when I was hell-bent on tracking Lord Gallick and his wife on their country holiday?"

"Yes . . . as I recall you were attempting to have condoms and erotic magazines delivered to them at every place they dined."

"Precisely! Which could only be accomplished by tracking his phone. But I failed miserably, because tracking a cellular phone requires the cooperation of multiple agencies that don't like to cooperate, and can't even begin without a warrant from Scotland Yard—and I guarantee you, with the shady dealings in which Morgan is involved, she won't go anywhere near law enforcement. So unless someone personally installed Find My iPhone on yours, we're perfectly safe."

"Well," said Galen, still unconvinced. "If you're certain. But she must realize that this latest bit of handiwork is yours."

"I'm sure she does. But I wish there was a way to know how deep the hack went. We have no idea if we actually infiltrated the computers in Svalbard."

"What does the girl think?"

Glynis sighed. "Freida says it all depends on how quickly they found it, and how seriously they took the threat. But without a contact in Svalbard, I'm afraid we have no way of finding out."

Then Galen looked dubiously at his phone once again. "And you're sure they can't find us?"

"Galen! Why are you so concerned? This isn't like you. Especially not since Crown Royale."

He put his phone down as if it might bite. "It's just that I've been getting these strange messages popping up on my Facebook account."

That made Glynis smirk. "YOU have a Facebook account?"

"Certainly. I'm not a complete technological Luddite."

That just made her smirk all the more. "Galen, these days having a Facebook account is the very definition of technological Luddite."

"Well, I have to have it," he said, a bit defensive. "It's the only way that my sister communicates. But these suspicious messages keep popping up." Then he handed her his phone. "Here, tell me what you think."

Glynis tapped on the message and began to scroll. Words, words, and more words.

"This makes no sense. . . ."

"Exactly! Gibberish. Why is gibberish showing up on my phone? I feel as if I've been hacked."

"'. . . first part of the third part, primary party notwithstanding . . .' What does it even mean?"

"I don't know, but it reeks of subterfuge."

"It reads like legal language, but this is the most incomprehensible, convoluted gobbledygook I've ever seen."

"I delete it, but it keeps showing up. Three times now."

Dame Havilland had seen enough contracts to parse out legalese. In fact, her solicitor, Linna McLeester—who now worked for Morgan—was a magician at slipping in entire continents of advantage in the small print of contracts. Which got her thinking . . .

"I do have a bit of déjà vu," she said. "As if maybe I've seen this before."

She read it again and again, trying to pull meaning out of the confusion. What a strange thing language was. It could enlighten you, or it could ensnare you. And then she let out the tiniest gasp. But not so tiny that Galen didn't catch it.

"Have you found something?"

To that, Dame Glynis Havilland only smiled, keeping what she found to herself. At least until she could confirm her suspicion.

"My dear Mr. Rooks, I do believe we owe ourselves a holiday away from all this toil and trouble."

He smiled right back at her. "And where, madame, do you propose we go?"

"I'm thinking Norway," she said. "A place we can see the northern lights."

38

Once More unto the Breach . . .

Had the raid on Svalbard been planned by the unembraced, it would have taken weeks, maybe months, to prepare. But Jarrick Javins's network of recoverees had neither egos, nor baggage to slow things down. No committees, no bureaucracy, no managers justifying their existence by marking the plan with their own particular urine, be it paperwork, or bad ideas, or a job for their unmotivated offspring. And while recoverees might not all be of one mind, they were most certainly of one heart. So with barely even lifting a finger, Javins had everything in place for the raid on Svalbard within seventy-two hours.

"My second recovery has given me intuitions and insights. There are things I sense now. Tender trip wires of pitfalls and possibilities. I can't see the results, but I know what will trigger them. I know what must be done to set the stage, but what the players do on that stage is out of my control."

At Javins's request, Rón visited the man each morning, so Javins could share his visions, his hopes, his apprehensions with him. By the third day, Rón could find his way through the woods to the *Triton* by recognizing the trees on the way.

"You're the only one he'll eat for," Javins's caregiver told him. So Rón always came with food.

"I have powerful visions of a day when the world as it is now is so strange to us, so primitive, as to be incomprehensible. All thanks

to the virus that evolves us. What will it be like when the human race has moved beyond selfishness, and aggression, and all the petty, destructive squabbles that plague us? We think we can imagine it, but we can't—not until it has been achieved."

His little missives reminded Rón of the things his father said in the book he was writing, but wiser. Javins never seemed at all wise before Crown Royale. In any interview Rón had ever seen with the man, he came off as the quintessential asshole. The unembraced would claim that Jarrick Javins had been "replaced." But recoverees knew better. He had been transformed.

"We've identified other alpha-spreaders like you out there. All blue-cone deficient, which you probably suspected. All barely survived Crown Royale. In free nations, they are being captured. In oppressive nations, they are being killed. Even so, I thought you might like to know that you are not alone. But you are the only one in a position to make a difference. I imagine there could be other double-recoverees like me out there in the world as well—all of us sensing the tide of great events, all of us seeking the best outcome. Perhaps there's one in every culture. Or perhaps it's only me. But however many there are, it will be precisely the amount needed to begin the task of saving humanity from itself."

In the warehouse, people were beginning to show Rón a sort of deference that bordered on awe, because everyone knew he was the one Javins called upon. Even Javins's emissaries in their silly rhinestone robes showed Rón a respect he didn't feel he had earned.

"If you matter to Him, then you matter to us," they told Rón. And although jealousy had no place in a recovered heart, Rón wondered if remnants of it remained.

"In this war, we need mythic figures, Tiburón. The emissaries believe they are those figures—which is precisely why they are not. But you—you are an alpha-spreader. The government sees you as an outlaw. You are the son of a man who was once my greatest adversary. That is the stuff of legend. And you are also the only one who can get a starving prophet to eat."

He said that last part with a wink, making it clear that it was part of a larger ploy. Establish Rón as mythic. Imbue him with some of Javins's own gravity. All in order to prime him to lead the attack on Svalbard. Although Javins didn't call it an attack. It was a liberation.

Rón had no desire to be a legend—but Javins pointed out that his trek across the country spreading Crown Royale had already set the foundations.

"Notoriety is the wake of great deeds. If you cut a powerful path, it can't be avoided—so you must learn to harness it. You are an alpha-spreader with a reputation. Add to that my personal blessing, and people will follow you into Svalbard like Henry V into war."

Which, if Rón recalled his Shakespeare correctly, involved sealing the breach with the dead.

An emissary came to wake Rón at dawn. "He wishes to see you now."

"This early?"

"He says it is a matter of some importance."

"You watch," said Rubian, half-awake across the room. "He's gonna finally teach you to levitate."

Rón left the warehouse, hurrying out into the chilly half light cutting through ground mist that swirled beneath his footfalls like a bog. When he arrived at the *Triton*, Jessa was waiting at the bottom of the steps, impatient and agitated.

"He hasn't slept all night," she told him. "Bouncing between screens like the old days."

Rón found him where he always found him—on the *Triton*'s bridge—but today all those dark computer screens were on, and at full intensity, data and communications filling each one, in competition for Javins's attention.

"What's going on?" Rón asked.

"Fortuitous news! There's been a system breach, and the facility at Svalbard has had to cut themselves off from the outside world. Which gives us a moment of advantage, because they won't see us coming!"

"A system breach? So you hacked them?"

Javins shook his head. "I had nothing to do with it. But I sense there are forces converging. Independent, unrelated, and yet working toward a common goal."

Rón had known that the raid on Svalbard was imminent, but making the leap from "soon" to "now" was too great a chasm for Rón to cross in a single bound.

"But . . . how do we get there? What do we do once we're there? How do we even get in if the place is a vault?"

Javins put up a hand to calm him. "Rest easy; everything is in place. The team is gathering, and is already familiar with the blueprints, the terrain, and the obstacles. They can bring you up to speed en route. Your task is simple. Lead the team to Svalbard, destroy the lab and all traces of the bioweapon, and infect everyone there with Crown Royale, so they won't attempt to create a weapon again."

What, Rón wondered, was simple about any of that?

Javins brought up the image of a jet on one of the screens. "It will arrive at Kokomo airport by nightfall. Half the team is already on board; the rest are in the warehouse being briefed. You have the day to prepare, and leave first thing tomorrow morning."

"Will you be there?" Rón asked. "Will you come to the airport to see us off? Let everyone see you—your presence will have meaning for them. As it has for me."

Javins stood still, staring forward. Rón followed his gaze. He was staring at the hatch, which led to the lower deck of the *Triton*. He didn't move a step toward it.

"I cannot leave the *Triton*," he told Rón. "As I am now, I find I need a buffer between myself and the world. Out there, the joy drives me to distraction. It addles my thoughts. It expands my heart to bursting." Then he glanced up at a light flickering above, threatening to go out. "Consider the lightbulb. Its incandescent filament must exist in a vacuum, or it will burn to ash. It is no different for me. It is a paradox; only in isolation can I stay connected to everything outside this hull." Then he looked to Rón with admiration, and perhaps the memory of envy. "Little did I know when I pridefully set this vessel here as a monument to my ego all those years ago, that it would become both my sanctuary and my sarcophagus."

Rón nodded, and respectfully said his goodbye, but just before Rón reached the hatch, Javins stopped him.

"There is one more thing I must ask you," he said. Rón could tell it was a subject the man did not want to broach. "The girl you traveled with. Was she . . . immune to Crown Royale?"

"Yes," Rón confirmed, "Mariel has natural immunity."

He took a deep breath and nodded. For a moment Rón thought he might have something to say. News to share. Perhaps knowledge of Mariel's whereabouts. But if he did, he kept it to himself.

"Godspeed, Tiburón," he said. "Destroy this bioweapon. And let nothing and no one stand in your way."

PART EIGHT
LA LLORONA

Subject Forty-Eight

Subject forty-eight is not happy. Other subjects are disappearing every day.

"They completed their service," the White Coats would tell her. "So they've been released, as per the contract they signed."

But that doesn't explain the body bag she saw being spirited out of the lab during the night. See, the problem with a lab with so many glass walls is that it's hard to hide bad shit going down.

"You can't treat us like we're stupid and don't know what's going on," she tells them. "We got rights!"

"No," says one of the White Coats, on the other side of the glass, calm as can be, "you don't. You signed those rights away when you signed up for this research project."

"Experiments, you mean! We're just lab rats to you!"

And he doesn't deny the claim.

There was this one convict—subject eleven. He had arrived with Crown Royale. After he recovered and became one of those nutjob recoverees, he actually tried to infect that skinny rail of a girl who controlled the purse strings. Yeah, he disappeared real fast after that. He was "released." More likely, he's now occupying a shallow grave in the ice, which is probably the White Coats' definition of "release."

No, subject forty-eight is not happy at all.

"You will not be infected with Crown Royale," Dr. Bosgraaf tells her. "I can assure you of that, Ms. Kintanar."

*She snorts at that. No one is ever so polite as to add a "Ms."
She's been just "Kintanar" for as long as she can remember. "Kint"
for short. Although people who wanted to lose teeth would switch
out the vowel.*

*"So what the hell do you need me for?" Not that she wants to
be infected, but she also doesn't like waiting around for something to
happen. She's done enough of that on death row.*

*Bosgraaf raises her penciled eyebrows at the question. "I'm
pleased to inform you that you have been chosen to change the world.
In the morning, you're going to be inoculated."*

"So you got a vaccine for me?"

"Something like that."

*They come to her cell at dawn. A medic and three security guards, all in
hazmat gear. She thinks they'll administer her a shot—which is ironic
since they've been threatening her with lethal injection for years—but
it turns out not to be a shot at all. The medic sets up a meticulous work-
station; a silver tray with perfectly placed tools, like at the dentist's office.
Then he opens a single test tube, dips a long swab in, and when he pulls
it out, there's a yellow mucus-like glob of slime on the tip.*

"Tilt your head back," he says.

"You'd better not be putting that shit up my nose."

"I'm not. Tilt your head back, please."

*Reluctantly she does, and the medic touches the swab to both
sides of her neck, leaving little dabs. Then he puts the swab and the
test tube in a biohazard bag, seals it, scrubs his gloves clean, and puts
the first biohazard bag in a second one.*

"That's it?" Kint asks. "Just some sort of fucked up perfume?"

*The medic eyes her for a moment. "Do you smell it?" he asks, like
he actually wants to know.*

Kint sniffs the air. "No, I don't smell a damn thing."

"Well, then, I guess it's not like perfume."

Then they all leave, locking her in with their high-tech cards and hermetic seals that are so much more refined than the heavy clang of prison. Really, she doesn't know what she has to complain about. Nice digs and the possibility of freedom, all for just a little swab on the neck. This is what her grandmother would have called "the catbird seat." A good place to be, at the right time to be there. Better than waiting to die in a place that can't seem to get around to killing you.

About an hour later, she starts to feel the itching.

It's almost subconscious at first; just little irritations on her neck that she's scratching without even noticing it. Then she realizes those were the spots where she had been touched by the loogie swab. Now her fingertips itch too, and every part of her face and body she's touched. And it's spreading. Not just across her skin but deep down, to places you can't scratch. It's maddening, the need to get at an itch that can't be gotten to. She thinks about those big plastic cones they put on dogs, because dogs don't got self-control enough not to rip themselves open. Maybe she needs that now—not just around her head, but over her whole body, because she just can't stop scratching. The need is as overpowering as an addiction.

She buzzes for help, and three White Coats come, standing outside her cell, looking in through the glass like aliens might observe an abducted earthling. She screams at them long enough that one of them finally goes and gets some itch cream, and those stupid pink allergy pills—but none of it does a thing. Eventually they leave her with, "Try and get some sleep."

When the fever comes, it's almost welcome because the aches and pains and shivers distract her from the deep, spirit-crushing itch.

Finally, exhaustion overtakes her and she slips into fever dreams. Vivid, hellish nightmares. The faces of her victims staring in accusation. Her father looking the way he did when he beat her. Her mother berating her and squealing about how she'll never amount to anything. And the pain. You're not supposed to feel physical pain in dreams, but she does. She relives every hit she ever took, every bone she ever broke. Every moment from the car accident that once landed her in traction. The worst moments of her life—not just flashing before her eyes, but imprinting on her soul.

And when she awakes, those dreams don't entirely go away. They linger like dreams sometimes do, leaving you stuck with that god-awful feeling that follows you. But this is worse. Way worse. It feels like every nightmare she's ever had is now coating her like a second skin, making it hard to breathe. Like there are fingers about to close around her throat but just haven't done it yet.

The itching is gone now—but the need *that came with it remains. Not a need to scratch, but for something else she can't put a finger on. All she knows is there's something she* needs.

And that sense she always had on death row, waiting for the other shoe to drop—it's tenfold now. It's like that story—the guy with a sword over his head, held by a single hair. Now she knows his unbearable anxiety. Not terror of the moment, but terror of the moment ahead, and the moment after that, and after that, and after that. It makes her want to crawl into a ball and disappear into a bottomless pit. A black hole that could swallow the universe and never be full. It feels eternal. Like this feeling will never go away— and it dawns on her that maybe it won't.

Subject forty-eight is not happy. And she suspects she'll never be happy again.

39

The Ninth Iteration

Morgan's flight back to Svalbard was more punishing than ever before. Bumps and drops, sudden rises and roller-coaster plunges. Morgan had never been so terrified. She could handle heavy turbulence on commercial flights—there was comfort in being surrounded by a planeload of random people. Because some primal part of her believed that, whether or not she was worthy of life, no God, real or fictional, would kill all these people just to get at her. But death by private jet would be more like a surgical strike.

"Sorry back there," the copilot said jovially. "The jet stream's taking a tight bend, and these wee jets don't like it." His casual Scottish brogue was not appreciated in this tense moment.

Preston Locke was with her. Perhaps he or the pilots were redeemable to the real/fictional God. But with turbulence so severe, she wasn't so sure. More than once Morgan found herself clutching Preston's hand, and it infuriated her that she felt compelled to do so. It also infuriated her that he himself wasn't in mortal terror.

"Mr. Bradway once had me accompany him to a conference in Milan," Preston told her. "We hit terrible turbulence over the Alps—just like this. All the while he sat there reading—and do you know what he said to me? He said, 'We won't die unless we hit a mountain—and we're way too high for that.'"

It made Morgan release a single nervous chuckle. As they continued to bounce, she found those words became a mantra.

When she had first arrived back in London, she had expected there to be chaos in the office. Preston running around like a headless chicken, hapless in his efforts to resolve the network breach. Instead, she arrived to find the situation, if not quite resolved, then acceptably managed.

"Most of our data has been lost, including backups," Preston had informed her. "But the bulk of it was rubbish; all of Dame Havilland's old spite projects, which we don't need anyway. So I'm treating it as a purge. Once we reenter our contact lists, the Havilland Consortium will emerge lean and ready for whatever we wish to take on next." Then he added, "But all considered, I think you should change the name."

Which Morgan was most certainly planning to do.

In the end, for all his inability to socially maneuver within a miasma of envious underlings, Preston was brilliant in a crisis. Morgan could now pat herself on the back for choosing him for the position—even if it was on a whim. With nothing left to do in London but watch people manually reenter data in the new computer system, Morgan decided to take Preston with her, figuring he might be useful in Svalbard—the only aspect of the Consortium that mattered right now. And if not, he could always be a test subject.

The hellish turbulence waned and smoothed once they began their descent to the lonely, snowcapped archipelago. Morgan didn't warn Preston of the hard landing, though. Because he deserved a little dose of panic too.

• • •

"Do you have good news for me, Dr. Bosgraaf? Because I only want good news today."

She and Preston had just entered the complex, and while Preston was taken to his quarters, Morgan got straight to business. To Morgan's surprise, the sour woman smiled at her. She hoped that was a good sign, and not just indigestion.

"We've had a breakthrough!" Bosgraaf could barely contain herself.

"Tell me."

"Better than that, I'll show you."

She led Morgan down to the vault, and through decontamination as quickly as the process would allow. The red light in the prep room indicated activity—and that they'd require hazmat suits.

In the primary lab, there were four medics in hazmat suits of an even higher grade than the ones Morgan and Bosgraaf wore. Thick enough material that it might have resisted the shiv of that deranged recoveree who had tried to infect her. It made her think of the space suit Dame Havilland had made her wear.

The medics loomed over a woman who was secured to a table with straps as thick as fire hoses. Her chest heaved. She writhed, trying to pull out of the bonds, but they were too tight to allow her much motion at all.

"This is our subject for the ninth iteration of the counter-virus. The first eight were failures—but, thanks to your friend's blood, this time we struck gold! Or more accurately, oil, because it just keeps coming!"

"This subject has the counter-virus?"

"She contracted it two days ago. The fever came on quickly and passed within a day. Right now, we're trying to determine how much of a viral load she's still shedding." From what Morgan could see of Bosgraaf's smile through her hazmat face mask, it seemed wide enough that her face might tear. "It's exactly as we had hoped! We've repeatedly exposed her to high concentrations of Crown Royale, and she hasn't contracted it. It's denatured within minutes of it being in her body. The countervirus makes it impossible to be infected by Crown Royale!"

No wonder Bosgraaf had that fun-house smile! This was more than a "breakthrough"—this was the whole wall coming down! Still, there was something about it that troubled Morgan.

"Why is she crying?" Morgan asked. "Are they hurting her?"

Bosgraaf shook her head dismissively. "No, not at all. Emotionality appears to be a side effect. I'm sure it will pass—the important thing is that we've done it! We've created a coronaform virus that can completely crowd out Crown Royale!"

Even so, the woman's sobs were unsettling. "Can't they sedate her?"

"We don't want anything in her system that might skew the results."

"Well, at least gag her! That wailing is awful."

Bosgraaf didn't respond. Instead she led Morgan away. "Come to my office, I'll give you the hard data. I think you'll be very pleased."

But a commotion in the lab made them turn back. One of the medics was trying to draw blood, but even tied down, the woman was able to knock the syringe from his hand, and it went flying.

"*¡Cuidado con La Llorona!*" he yelled.

It struck Morgan in a way that gave her a shiver. She wasn't sure yet whether it was a good or a bad shiver. "They're calling her La Llorona?"

"Yes—Dr. Salcedo's idea," said Bosgraaf, nodding toward the Spanish-speaking medic. "It's a Latin American legend; a spirit who cries for her drowned children."

"I know what La Llorona is," said Morgan, irked to be mansplained by a woman. "This counter-virus needs a name. I think that's what we should call it. But we'll flip the legend around! From corona, to Llorona—but *our* Llorona is crying out of happiness—because her children have all been saved." Morgan grinned at the prospect. "Everyone loves a good redemption story."

Dr. Nødtvedt, director of the Svalbard Global Seed Vault, was indifferent about the whole Crown Royale situation. He would avoid catching it if he could. And if not? So be it. He didn't buy into the whole "body-snatcher" theory. Whoever you were after the disease, you were still you, just a gentler version of you. As he had already devoted his life to the preservation of the planet through saving the world's heirloom seeds, he imagined nothing would change if he caught Crown Royale. Well, maybe he'd suffer fools with a little more patience and grace than he currently did.

"That couple is at the gate again, asking for a tour of the lab," his assistant director informed him.

People were idiots. Plain and simple. Which was why he much preferred the silence and the unbounded potential of seeds. They never made demands. They never showed up on the worst of all days. They just waited to be planted, and could wait for years.

"Have you told them we are *not* a tourist attraction?"

"Several times, but they keep coming back."

"And has the gate guard threatened them with arrest?"

"Well, they're still on the other side of the gate, so they're technically not doing anything illegal."

Nødtvedt sighed. He didn't have time to entertain an elderly couple's bucket list—especially today. Besides, the only people who received tours were dignitaries, donors, and the occasional reporter. No cash, no clout, no consideration. That was Nødtvedt's policy.

"What if I tell them to come back tomorrow?" suggested the assistant director.

Under normal circumstances, that would just kick the problem down the road. But these weren't normal circumstances.

"Excellent idea! Yes, tell them they'll be welcome with open arms tomorrow!"

Because things were changing at the Svalbard Global Seed Vault. Not by choice, but by necessity. And all because of that detestable young woman who had taken over the Havilland Consortium, invading his vault complex, and inserting herself and her white-coated mob into the gearworks like a flock of birds into a jet engine.

Nødtvedt knew early on that there would be no peace for his seed bank in the current environment. If that girl had her way, all of Nødtvedt's precious, priceless seeds would be cast to the wind so the girl could expand her lab even farther.

And so, weeks earlier, when he was contacted by someone who claimed they represented the newly diversified and restructured interests of Jarrick Javins, his ears perked up. They wanted intel on the Havilland Consortium's questionable activities on the island. Nødtvedt was more than happy to tell them every little thing—and while he personally didn't fraternize with the lab team, some of the Seed Vault staff would loiter just outside the main entrance with the lab workers for some fresh air—and the lab team talked more than they probably should.

However, once you were under the influence of someone like Jarrick Javins, it was a slippery slope. One thing led to another, and soon you were offering him use of your plane, and your vehicles, and you were sharing blueprints. . . . The gravity of the man, even at a distance, tended to pull you further and further in.

But that was fine, because your enemy's enemy is your friend—and it seemed Javins had it out for Morgan Willmon-Wu even more than Nødtvedt did.

The latest, and final, request from Javins was a simple one, and it came with a sizeable donation—enough for the Seed Vault to comfortably relocate—so Nødtvedt was more than happy to comply. According to his contact, all Javins's people wanted was for Nødtvedt to leave the outer gate, and the complex's singular entrance, unlocked and unguarded on a precise day, at a precise time. And then just walk away.

He had no idea what was planned, but he didn't care. Because once he walked away, it wouldn't be his problem anymore. And neither would that annoying geriatric couple requesting a tour.

The jet that Jarrick Javins had procured for the assault on Svalbard was smaller than most commercial craft, but larger than most private jets. It was white with no markings, logo, or brand to identify it. Humble—if a jet could ever be called humble. It seated twenty, although the team consisted of nearly twice that. They found spots for themselves around the cabin, sitting on floors, leaning against bulkheads. Sharpshooters, Navy SEALs, explosives experts. There were multiple languages being spoken among them, making it clear that they had been gathered from all over the globe. There was fuel to get to Svalbard, but not back. The unembraced might call that a suicide mission, but no one had any intent of dying—even though they knew it was a distinct possibility.

The plane, Rón learned, was owned by the Svalbard Global Seed Vault, which shared the vault complex with the laboratory. The vehicles, which were supposedly waiting for them at the tiny Svalbard airport, were owned by the Seed Vault as well. It would make it easy to land and approach the vault complex without arousing suspicion. As far as anyone knew, they were scientists who accepted an invitation to look at seeds.

There was only one pilot.

"Aren't there supposed to be two?" Rón asked, peering into the cockpit as he boarded.

"Why?" said the pilot with a distinct Eastern European accent. The man had deserted his nation's air force, having refused to blow up a target. Now he was here. "You think this is JetBlue flight? Drinks and nuts and crying babies?" Then he gave a hearty laugh. "What is it you say in America? 'God is my copilot.'" Then he gestured to the seat. "Come, you can sit. Company for the long flight."

Rón gave him a faint grin. "Wouldn't that make me God?"

"Only if you choose to be."

And since Rón had never sat in a copilot's seat before, he decided he might as well, and free up a seat in the back for someone else.

As the plane crossed the tarmac and cruised onto the runway, Rón turned to the pilot. "Shouldn't we tell everyone to put on their seat belts?"

Again, the pilot laughed. "More JetBlue?" Then he gunned the engines. "When you go to save the world, seat belts are optional."

40
What Blood Hath Wrought

When Mariel was little, she hit a tetherball so hard, it came swinging around the pole, smacked her in the back of the head, and knocked her down against a concrete planter, giving her a concussion. Her mother's response on the way back from the hospital was, "Well, now you know—what goes around comes around. In your case, literally."

Hard lesson learned.

That being the case, Mariel couldn't help but wonder if Morgan had betrayed her, the way Mariel had betrayed Rón. Not in so many words, but in so *few* words.

Mariel knew that Morgan was back from London—she had heard her voice out in the common area, but when Mariel came out to greet her, she was already gone, down into the labs. She assumed that Morgan would eventually pay her a visit. Update her on how things were going. But she didn't. No one did. Mariel was now the invisible girl. By the end of the day, she had to wonder if all of Morgan's talk about them changing the world together was just that: Talk. Weightless words to gain her confidence and cooperation.

Mariel had let her guard down—allowed herself to be taken in. And, as always seemed to be the case when she began to question herself, her thoughts came around to Rón. She had been drawn in by him as well. He and Morgan were alike, in a way. Both had powerful, all-consuming agendas. But that was where the similarity ended—because, while Rón was motivated to fix a broken world, Morgan was motivated to take *credit* for fixing a broken world. A subtle difference, with miles between.

So, who was the more misguided? Whose vision was the right one? Mariel still didn't know. The one thing she *did* know was that she was no longer needed, and that worried her.

Morgan's exuberance couldn't be contained by the confines of the vault. She felt positively claustrophobic down there, so she went out into the ridiculously long dusk. The clouds had cleared, and the winds had stilled. The cold was ever present, but bearable. She found a catwalk that led her to a nearby promontory, and there she stood to watch the northern lights waving across the sky, like celebratory fireworks just for her!

Preston found her there a few minutes later—which was fine. Because although she often preferred to be alone, she was positively bursting to talk about today's great achievement. Victory was something to be shared. And better with him than with Bosgraaf.

"I couldn't find a single bottle of champagne down there," Preston said. "All they have is vodka. And not even the good kind."

She took his hand. It was a little bit easier to do now, after having grabbed it on the plane.

"We've done it, Preston. It's official! Whosoever catches our proprietary virus will never catch Crown Royale!"

"What about people who've already had Crown Royale? Did Bosgraaf say?"

"Sadly, there's nothing we can do for them, it's either/or.

Either you have Crown Royale, or you're protected from it by La Llorona. A person can only contract one."

"So then it's airborne?"

"No—it's spread by fomites—by touch—but it has an amazingly high contagion rate, because it passes straight through the skin. You come in contact with anyone who's had it, or anything they've touched, and you've got it too. Which means it will spread just as efficiently—maybe even more so— than Crown Royale."

"I suppose we should inform Mr. Escobedo," Preston suggested—which felt like a wet rag on the moment.

"No—why should we tell him?" Morgan said. "He's out of this now—still in FBI custody for having helped his son escape, and not even his army of lawyers can get him out. Which means La Llorona is all ours!"

Preston sighed and shook his head. "Not for much longer, I'm afraid. You can monetize a vaccine, but you can't monetize something that spreads on its own. I hate to say it, but it's going to affect your bottom line."

"Oh, you are *so* wrong!" Morgan took a deep breath of the frosty air. This next part—she had been thinking about it for weeks, afraid to say it out loud before it was real. But there had been method in the madness all along.

"When Pfizer came up with the first COVID vaccine, they sold a hundred million doses to the United States for nearly two billion dollars," she told him. "But it took months for them to produce, store, and ship that many doses. Same thing with Moderna, AstraZeneca, and all the others." Then she beamed so brightly, it could put the aurora borealis to shame. "But here's the beauty of La Llorona: *We don't have to mass produce it!* We create just twenty doses! Then we sell them to the twenty nations who'll pay the highest price—and believe me, they will! No one will want to wait—not while Crown Royale is ravaging their population. They'll pay billions, and *thank* us. As for everyone else"—Morgan gave a royal flick of her hand—"they'll have to wait until it trickles down in a month or two. All the while hoping that Crown Royale doesn't topple their government, or crash their economy, in the meantime."

Preston stared at her, breathless. Perhaps in awe. Perhaps in terror. Either was fine.

"Morgan . . . ," he finally said. "That's . . . that's mad brilliant!"

"Isn't it, though?"

"I mean . . . no factory, no infrastructure. Just twenty doses . . ."

". . . and we walk away as rich as Blas Escobedo."

Mariel brought her dinner into her room, because she couldn't bear the palpable sense of isolation among the few people eating in the common room. It wasn't so much a cold shoulder as a *no* shoulder. She wondered which was worse—to be shunned, or to simply be ignored.

She had trouble sleeping that night. Too many thoughts to mull, too many bad choices to chide herself for. She went out to the common room to get a drink, and noticed, for the first time in days, the red light over the door that led down to the labs wasn't lit. No active work going on. No need for hazmat suits— but even so, she wouldn't need one anyway. A perk of immunity.

With no one around, and no one who deserved her good

behavior, she decided it was time to see what her blood had wrought.

She slipped into the air lock, not realizing that she had been seen.

The prep room that served as an air lock to the secure area of the vault was an intimidating space. Hazmat suits hung on the walls like biohazard scarecrows. Sinister sentinels to keep the squeamish away. Unlike most of the rest of the facility, the accessway to the lower vault, where the labs were, was part of an older system that predated its current use. Morgan had mentioned something about seeds. In any case, Mariel had to physically crank the door to the vault open, revealing a set of stairs. Mariel didn't know what she expected to find down there. Lab rats? High-tech equipment? None of that particularly interested her, but in her days at the facility, her curiosity was triggered by the simple fact that she was not allowed.

While the labs must have been brightly lit during the day, the night lighting was dim. There were the research labs, as she expected, filled with high-tech equipment, but beyond that, there was a hallway with glass compartments on either side, all fitted with doors sealed by multiple gaskets. Fail-safes within fail-safes. There was a cot in each cubicle, making it clear that these were designed for human test subjects. The thought of it gave Mariel a chill. She knew it had to be the case, but had avoided thinking about it, the way one avoids the thought of slaughterhouses. No one really wants to know how a cow becomes a burger.

The little glass rooms all seemed vacant, but showed evidence of having recently been occupied. Then she heard a noise toward the far end of the phalanx of cells. One cell that still held its guest. It sounded like a woman faintly whimpering, but as she got closer, she realized she wasn't whimpering at all. The multiple panes of glass had muted the sound. She was sobbing. Her arms were wrapped tightly around her, and she rocked slowly back and forth. She looked up as Mariel approached, her eyes freezing Mariel in place.

"Please . . . Please give me . . . Please give it to me. . . ."

Mariel wanted to help the woman, but wasn't sure how. "What is it you want?"

"Water. I need water. Please, please get me water."

Which didn't make any sense, because there was a cup and pitcher of water beside her.

"On the table," Mariel said, pointing. "There's plenty."

The woman glanced at the water, but even as she saw it, she made no move to fill the cup. It was as if she was disappointed that it was even there.

"No . . . No . . . It's food that I want. I'm hungry. Bring me food. . . ."

Mariel pointed to her other side. "But there's a plate there on the tray. A full meal . . ."

The woman glanced at the tray, and again gave that disappointed look.

"No, no, not food. Please give me . . . I need . . . I *need* . . ."

Mariel had no idea what she wanted, but she seemed to think that Mariel did. And when Mariel didn't present her with a solution, she put her head in her hands and went back to sobbing and rocking.

"Don't engage. It just makes it worse."

Mariel jumped at the voice behind her. She turned to see

a man, slim, early twenties. She thought she'd seen everyone in the complex, but this was someone new.

"Best if you just go back to your quarters," he said. "You're not supposed to be here anyway."

"Neither are you."

"I came to fetch you. I saw you go into the restricted area, and I didn't want you to get in trouble."

"And you are?"

"Preston Locke. Ms. Willmon-Wu's second-in-command, from the London office."

"I'm Mariel."

"I know," Preston said. "Everyone knows who you are, Mariel Mudroch."

Mariel wasn't sure she liked the prospect of that. Neither fame nor infamy appealed to her. She turned, sparing one more look at the troubled woman. Her sobs had eased, but her rocking continued.

"What's wrong with her?" Mariel asked.

"It's a reaction to the counter-virus, that's all. It should ease as she recovers."

Something about that snagged in Mariel's mind.

"Counter-virus? What do you mean, 'counter-virus'?"

"The competing viral agent we made from your blood."

"You made a vaccine," Mariel corrected.

"No, we made a . . ." And then he cut himself short, his eyes beginning to brew panic. "Wait . . . you mean Morgan didn't tell you?" He gauged her astonished silence, then took a physical step backward. "You know what? Forget I said anything."

Mariel could have laughed at that if any of this were even remotely funny. "Forget you told me that Morgan created another virus? Sorry, that's not a bell you can unring!"

Now Preston was in full damage-control mode. "Okay . . . okay . . . Well, it's *your* blood, so you have a right to know—but you have to promise not to tell Morgan you heard it from me."

And then from behind them, an all too familiar voice . . .

"Heard what from you, Preston?"

Like Mariel, Morgan had trouble sleeping. The sheer excitement of what lay before her was a powerful stimulant. She imagined it would be a long time until she needed caffeine again.

At Morgan's request, Bosgraaf's team had been able to cleanly divide the existing viral sample into five test tubes—and with swabs from subject forty-eight, they estimated they could culture fifteen more in less than a day.

The challenge would be arranging the auction. With the lab still running dark, with no Wi-Fi or outside communication, they couldn't begin the process until they were off the island.

Here's where Blas Escobedo could have been helpful, because a man like that had his pulse on the wrists of world leaders. But even without him, it wouldn't be hard to initiate. How could anyone ignore a celebrated Nobel laureate like Dr. Annika Bosgraaf making a high-profile public announcement about a medical breakthrough? *"Hear ye, hear ye! There's a way to take the crown from Crown Royale!"* What nation wouldn't come running? Once the word was out, all Morgan had to do was sit tight and wait for the world to come to her.

Just the way Preston did that night. And it turned out he wasn't the underachiever she took him for.

When he got up during the night, she thought he was

just going to the bathroom, because he wouldn't dare leave her the way guys often do. No—he wasn't going anywhere until *she* kicked him out, which she was in too good a mood to do. But then she heard the unmistakable sound of the prep room cranking open, and so she followed.

Things would have been different if she had gotten down to the glass hallway in time to keep Preston from opening his damned mouth. . . .

But . . . the hazmat suits.

Yes, the caution light was out, but Morgan wouldn't dare go down to the labs without wearing one. Because she already knew all too well, even when you thought you were safe, you were never truly safe. So she wasted a full minute putting the damn suit on. And by the time she got down to the labs, it was too late.

"You lied to me. All this time you've been lying to me!" Mariel could not remember the last time she'd been this furious. "So you're going to 'save' people from one disease by replacing it with another?"

"We are not talking about this," Morgan said with such imperious dismissal, Mariel wanted to pound her.

"You'd better talk about it—because you used my blood to create it!"

"It's the only way to truly defeat Crown Royale!" Morgan snapped, which made Mariel point to the poor woman in the glass cell.

"Look at her! She's miserable!"

"She'll get over it!" insisted Morgan. "She'll adapt. People adapt—that's what we do! And the world will be better for it!"

"So if this virus is the salvation you say it is, why are you in that hazmat suit? Why not infect yourself?" Morgan's reticence told Mariel all she needed to know. "You won't because you see what it's done to her! You said people will have a choice— but they won't! Because if one virus doesn't get them, then the other one will!" Mariel shook her head so hard it hurt. "Rón was right! This is a war, and I've just armed the enemy!"

Nothing Mariel had said fazed Morgan. Not until that. Morgan had certainly made enemies in her life. But being THE enemy was something wholly different. Mariel had driven a hot poker into a rare, unguarded place, and it surprised Morgan how much it hurt.

"I am not the enemy!"

"You are, Morgan. You are everything that's wrong with this world!"

"So you want Crown Royale to take down civilization? The ruin of everything we know?"

"You know what? Maybe that's exactly what we need; ruins we can rise from. All I know is I'd rather be happy during that kind of crisis than filled with despair!"

"Despair builds character!" countered Morgan. "It's what motivates us—but Crown Royale denies people that! You're just too naïve to see it!"

"I agreed to be a part of all this because I wanted balance— but you've taken away any possibility of that! You've created two extremes with absolutely nothing in the middle. You haven't saved the world, Morgan . . . you've split the world in two!"

And then something occurred to Morgan. Something bitterly simple, and entirely true. "You know what?" said Morgan.

"None of this matters. *You* don't matter. So you'd better get back to your quarters before I have security drag you there!"

Morgan could tell she delivered that red-hot poker right back to her, because Mariel's face got hard enough to crack, and she stormed away, too angry to fight for the last word.

Through all this, Preston stood impotently aside, not wanting to get caught in the cross fire. Only after Mariel was gone did he dare to speak.

"Morgan, I—"

"Not a single word!"

Because he didn't matter either. Hard lesson learned.

There were important things to be done. Earth-shattering affairs to manage. There was no room in Morgan's life to deal with trifling matters, such as paltry interpersonal drama. She had opened a door to intimacy with Preston. Mistake. Vulnerability is weakness, and people can only disappoint. She had taken a liking to Mariel. Mistake. Mariel was nothing but a means to an end. In Morgan's book, people fell into two categories: useful, or in the way. Mariel Mudroch and Preston Locke were now nothing more than obstructions. She vowed to jettison them from her mind. But it was easier said than done.

"What shall we do about the girl?" Bosgraaf asked first thing in the morning. The woman always said precisely the wrong thing at precisely the wrong time.

Morgan swallowed her frustration and feigned indifference. "Do we need any more of her blood?"

"We've made good use of what we had. We won't be needing any more."

"Well, then, why should I care what you do with her? Give

her a Svalbard key chain, and a thank-you-for-playing, then send her and Mr. Locke off on the next supply ship."

"Mr. Locke?"

"He no longer works for me. He just doesn't know it yet."

"I see," said Bosgraaf, and wisely did not ask for details.

The common room was empty now. The caution light above the lab prep chamber was on. Preston was confined to quarters and told if he left, his new room would be a cell in the lab. And Morgan made sure that Mariel was locked in her room, so she couldn't do any more exploring. The two were managed for now.

"I need some air," Morgan told Bosgraaf. "Walk with me."

"I need to get down to the lab and oversee the preparation of the new cultures."

"Your team isn't competent to do it without you?"

"Yes, of course they are, but—"

"Then get your coat and walk with me."

Bosgraaf breathed out her exasperation, but complied without further word.

There was a reason Morgan wanted Bosgraaf with her on her walk to the promontory today. Certainly not for the woman's company—the woman was a wet rag on a cold day—but Morgan had yet to inform Bosgraaf of the part she was about to play; the high-profile announcement the woman would make to the world about La Llorona. Better that she be informed personally and privately by Morgan, so she had time to get used to the idea—and, if necessary, Morgan would tie her performance to the sizeable payment Bosgraaf would receive for her work here.

But they never made it up to the main entrance. They were

barely out of the vault when something caught Morgan's attention. They had reached the vestibule between the two vault systems. To the right was the rising concrete tunnel to the main entrance of the complex. But just ahead was the east vault, where Dr. No tended to his seeds.

The Seed Vault door was open. It wasn't just ajar, but completely open, with trash strewn about on the ground in front of it.

"What on earth . . . ," mumbled Bosgraaf.

Morgan ventured forward and stepped inside. She had only once been inside the Seed Vault. It had been beyond neat, beyond orderly, with half a dozen permanent workers cataloguing, filing, and studying the viability of seeds that came in each week. The vault had been full of high-tech sealed crates, in a temperature- and humidity-controlled environment.

That's not what they found today. Today they found the detritus of abandonment. The crates, the seeds, they were all gone, leaving nothing but refuse and empty shelves.

"Well, good riddance," said Bosgraaf. "They weren't the most friendly of neighbors."

But Morgan's intuition was twitching in a dark direction. Nødtvedt was a meticulous man, and yet he left the vault as if it had been vacated in a panic.

"When did this happen?" Morgan asked. "When did they leave?"

"I don't know. I did hear activity yesterday. But the Seed Vault often has shipments coming and going."

This was off. Terribly, unmistakably off. "We need eyes on the gate. Eyes on the access road! Now!"

"Our security cameras are all wireless," Bosgraaf informed her. "They've all been offline since we went dark."

"Damn it! Then I need guards—all of them!"

Bosgraaf just shook her head, which infuriated Morgan.

"Do it!"

"But . . . security was provided by the Seed Vault. The guards were all theirs—I thought you knew that."

"You mean we have no protection?"

"We're inside a mountain on an island in the middle of nowhere," Bosgraaf told her, as if she needed reminding. "These vaults could survive a nuclear war. What on earth do we need protection from?"

Then the lights went out in the entire vault complex, giving them the answer.

41
Acolytes of the Dark Extreme

Morgan had no time to think, no time to consider the alternatives, or even to determine what nature of attack this was. She could hear feet—many feet charging down the entry tunnel toward them. This was clearly planned and well orchestrated. The only thing Morgan could do was get out of its way.

"Help me, Morgan!"

She turned to see Bosgraaf at the lab vault door, trying to close it in order to close the intruders out, and lock everyone inside—but the door was too big, too heavy, too slow.

"Morgan, help me!"

No. When in a crisis, one needs to take care of oneself because you can't fight another day if you don't live to fight another day. So she abandoned Bosgraaf and hid behind the Seed Vault door at the other end of the short corridor. Then she watched as the armed militia grabbed Bosgraaf.

"Intruders!" Bosgraaf yelled to anyone who could hear. "Don't let them reach the lab!"

Then someone else came down the tunnel. Someone who wasn't in combat gear. It was a blond kid. Late teens. A face she'd seen on security cam footage.

No, no, it couldn't be. That's not possible.

Morgan had to bite her lip to keep from gasping and giving herself away.

This was Tiburón Escobedo.

"Hello, ma'am," he said to Bosgraaf. "Don't be afraid." Then he leaned into the woman's airspace, releasing a long puff of air right into her face with a gentle whoosh.

Morgan had to stifle a scream from the mortal terror she felt. Tiburón Escobedo must not see her! He must not know she was there. She'd take a bullet, a blade, *anything* but a breath.

Bosgraaf screamed in rage. She fought back against the arms detaining her, and it was her commotion that provided enough cover for Morgan to quietly slip into the abandoned Seed Vault, where she covered herself with the trash they had left behind. And there she hid, hoping beyond hope that no one bothered to check the defunct Seed Vault. That the breath of this angel of death, this demon that was Tiburón Escobedo, would pass her by.

Salcedo couldn't wait to get home. With their mission accomplished, this miserable sequestering in this wretched mountainhold was no longer about counting the days—now he could count the hours!

Then he heard Bosgraaf's panicked scream. "Intruders! Don't let them reach the lab!" When he heard gunshots, the lab ceased to be his priority. He grabbed a flashlight in the common area, but before he could even turn it on, someone bumped into him in a panic, grabbed it from him, and ran off.

He thought to hide under a table, but before he could, the intruders swarmed the common room. Some of them had military gear, others not. And even in the dim light he could see there was something odd about their weapons. Who would paint such lethal hardware like children's toys?

Two of the geared-up intruders grabbed him and pushed him up against a wall, holding him there.

"Please," Salcedo said. "Take whatever you want. I just want to go home."

Then a third intruder approached. This one was young. He couldn't be any older than sixteen or seventeen, and wearing a smile completely out of phase with the moment.

"Of course you can go home," the boy said. "But first you'll have to stay with us for a few days. Don't worry—we'll take care of you, I promise." Then he leaned closer and breathed gently into the researcher's face. He could feel the boy's breath on his cheeks, on his eyeballs.

Now he knew what this was about. And he knew his fate was already sealed. The spider was on him. The spider was in him. The spider was weaving its web.

Dr. Annika Bosgraaf was an acolyte of the dark extreme. In other words, she had spent a lifetime assuming the worst. Worst-case scenarios, worst rumors, worst theories, and worst outcomes. She believed, with a terrifying certainty, that to contract Crown Royale was to die and to be replaced by a different, inhuman entity. And although you still might look the same, something monstrous was now living inside your body. Whatever that thing was, it would lie about being "happy," while secretly conspiring with the other false entities to usurp the entire human race.

Of course, as a scientist, she had to keep her inner wild conspiracist hidden—but her conviction lived in her heart like its own unholy entity.

When the alpha-spreader breathed his profane contagion upon her, she knew what she had to do.

The alpha-spreader had moved on to find other members of her team. Now she was in the hands of one of the militants—a camo-clad woman who zip-tied Annika to a railing in the entrance tunnel.

"This is just to keep you safe until we come back to fetch you," she said. "We'll be back, lickety-split, just as soon as we're done here." Then she offered a smile that Bosgraaf didn't believe for an instant, and would never believe while her mind was still her own. "Don't worry," her captor said, "soon you'll be one of us!"

Now it was Bosgraaf's turn to smile—and hers was as genuine as can be. "I will never be one of you!" she bellowed. Then she bit down on the cyanide pill she had slipped in her cheek just moments before.

She was dead before her words stopped echoing in the tunnel.

The bullets were rubber, but the explosives were real.

Rón knew timing here was everything. They received less resistance than they expected, but the blueprints Javins had given them only showed the vault as it was before the laboratory was built within it, and people were hiding everywhere.

The laboratory staff were their own worst enemies. All they needed to do was come out into the open, have a brief and painless encounter with Rón, and then they would be spirited out of the lab to safety before the place detonated. But if they hid, they would die when the lab blew. Were they so afraid of Crown Royale that they'd rather risk being buried under tons of mountain rubble than contract it?

"We're here to save you!" Rón yelled in the living area,

trying his best to convince those who were still hiding. "We're here to free you from this place, free you from your pain. I know some of you are still hiding, but your time is running out! Please, come out and let us see you."

And then one of his fighting team members shouted from another room, "We found it! We found the lab. It's down this way!"

Rón, and his armed escort, followed the voice through a room lined with hazmat suits and down a set of stairs to a glass hallway of medical stations. There was one door open—the lab where the biological weapon had been forged. And from that room burst one worker. He screamed and tried to get past them. He hit Rón with a flashlight, knocking him to the ground. The team was caught off guard. They turned to fire—not aiming at the man but just intending to fire warning shots. But he dodged as he went up the stairs and one of the rubber bullets hit him. He wailed in pain as if it had been a steel bullet—but it didn't slow him down.

"Let him go," Rón said, getting up and collecting himself. "If he's running, then he's leaving. He's getting out, and that's what we want."

"But you didn't get the chance to embrace him," one soldier lamented.

"Maybe it just wasn't his time."

In the lab, they found what they were looking for. Four clear cylinders, each holding a test tube with a puss-yellow substance coagulated on the bottom.

"There it is," Rón said. So much fuss over a smattering of biomatter. But it was biomatter that had no business existing.

"Torch it," he ordered.

Then a soldier with a flamethrower took aim and incinerated the counter-virus specimens, reducing them to molten glass and charred carbon in seconds.

With the samples incinerated, they could have just walked out and not set the explosives, but there was no telling if this was the only batch, or if more of it was lurking. And besides, the mission was also about sending a message: that recoverees might be beyond anger and aggression, but they *would* defend themselves, and defend their dreams of a better world.

The demolition team began to place the explosives at even intervals on every level. And although the others left the lab area, Rón remained.

He thought he'd only stay for a moment, just to take in the fullness of what they had done, and to prepare for what they still had to do. He looked at all the equipment—machines used to create a monstrosity—and he marveled at how healing and hurting so often went hand in hand.

And then he heard something. A voice. Faint . . . weak . . . It came from the far end of the hall. Rón went to investigate.

Hidden in the dark recesses of the abandoned Seed Vault, Morgan found it nearly impossible to stay quiet. The slightest twitch of a muscle, the rise and fall of her shallow breath, it all threatened to dislodge the trash that covered her. All it would take was the tumble of a single crumpled paper, and she was done for.

Because she wasn't alone in there. The explosives team had chosen the abandoned Seed Vault as its staging area for unpacking and arming brick after brick of C-4—enough to take down half the mountain.

A bug crawled up her nose and she had to allow it. She had no choice but to wait in silence, feeling it there, praying that it didn't make her sneeze, until it finally crawled out and went on its merry way.

The explosive team all spoke some Slavic language, and Morgan cursed herself for not knowing it, because she knew all too well that the right language at the right time with the right accent could turn any situation—even one as dire as this—to her advantage. It could mean the difference between life and death.

Finally, they left with their deadly assemblages, and the moment she was sure they were gone, she made her move, climbing out from the rubbish, making her way to the vault door. She had heard gunshots—more than one volley—but the sounds were all coming from the other vault. She wasn't going anywhere near it. Instead, she turned to head up the tunnel to the exit.

Far up ahead, the door to the icy mountainside was wide open, the twilight-blue sky inviting. Just a hundred yards. Nothing between her and freedom but a hundred yards of empty tunnel.

Whoever was behind this attack, they would rue this day. Yes, they might destroy the counter-virus, but Morgan had something almost as valuable: proof of concept. She did it once, so she could do it again—and more quickly next time. She would show them. She would show all of them.

Halfway to the exit, she was sobered by the sorry sight of Bosgraaf's body, zip-tied by her hands to a railing, eyes open, mouth dripping rancid foam—and although Morgan had no love for the woman, it pained her to see what these monsters had done to her.

Fifty yards to the exit now. Forty. She could feel the icy

flow of the mountain air now. Never had such a cold wind felt so good.

So focused was she on her escape, and that growing rectangle of twilight blue, that she never saw the figure lurking in the shadows just inside the door until it leaped out in front of her, grabbing her and pressing a cloth to her face. She gasped, breathing in something caustic and foul that was soaked into the rag . . .

. . . and then the sky before her changed. It all began to swim. Her legs seemed to vanish from under her, and she went away to a place no one remembers when they wake up.

"Help me . . . Please . . . please, help me. I need . . ."

Rón found a woman in a glass cell at the end of the hallway, in the far reaches of the laboratory level. She was rocking back and forth, rubbing her hands, her eyes red from tears.

"Don't be afraid," said Rón. "I'm here with you."

"Can you get me out?" she begged.

"I . . . I don't know how."

"The doctors, they have the keys."

"They're all gone."

Then she wiped a bit of mucus from her nose, the same color as the stuff in the test tubes . . . and suddenly Rón knew.

The sign on the door said SUBJECT 48. But this was patient zero.

"Don't leave me here," she said. "Please, I'm so scared. I'm so scared. I'm so *angry*. I'm so scared. I *need*, I need . . ."

"You're infected with the counter-virus. . . ."

"They did this to me. They made me sick. They made me *need*."

Rón knew he couldn't save her. This poor, poor woman. She couldn't be allowed to leave here.

In that moment, Rón made a decision. It wasn't a hard decision to make.

"I can't save you," Rón said. "But I won't let you die alone."

Then he put his hand to the glass, which was as close to her as he could get, and waited.

While around him, the lights on the explosive packs clicked from red to green. The bombs were armed, synced, and ready to blow.

Four containers of counter-virus were destroyed. But there had been five.

When the attack began, Preston Locke had seen the opportunity, and he had taken it. A chance to redeem himself—a way to get back in Morgan's good graces. The right move here, and all would be forgiven, and then some. But he had to act quickly.

The emergency lighting was a bare minimum. Small corners of illumination surrounded by large patches of darkness. Barely enough to find one's way. He had already heard gunshots, and someone shouting about intruders.

He stumbled his way out of his room into the quarters corridor, picking up speed as his eyes adjusted to the half light, and came into the common area, where one of the medics stood with an unlit flashlight, trying to find the switch to turn it on. Preston bumped him hard, grabbed the flashlight, and, while the man was reeling from the affront, Preston pulled the ID badge clipped to the man's shirt pocket without him even noticing. Then practically threw himself into the lab prep chamber, closing the door behind him.

He found the flashlight's on switch easily—and involuntarily flinched at the human forms it illuminated all around him, but quickly realized that they were just hazmat suits. No time for that. The shouts were louder. Gunfire closer.

He raced down the steep stairs into the glass corridor of the labs. He had only been here twice before; first when he arrived with Morgan, when Bosgraaf gave him a perfunctory tour, and then again, during the night—when he so completely screwed himself by talking to Mariel Mudroch.

Preston went to the main lab, swiped the stolen ID—which worked—but it took a long moment for the lock and gasket seals to disengage.

C'mon, c'mon . . .

The door opened, and he stepped into the dimly lit lab, shining his flashlight around. He wasn't exactly sure what he was looking for. A flask? Petri dishes? A little metallic suitcase like they had for such things in movies?

Finally, his light landed on five wax-sealed test tubes, each within their own clear cylinder. Bingo! He unscrewed the lid from one of the cylinders, and carefully removed the test tube, slipping it into his coat pocket—just as he heard voices, and footsteps, coming down to the labs. No time to get the other tubes. He had to get out.

He tried, but again, that damn door mechanism slowed him down. By the time he was out of the room, the intruders were already in the glass hallway. He shone his light into their eyes to disorient them, then he charged, barreling toward them, and smashing the heavy flashlight as hard as he could on one of their heads. The intruder went down, but the others were quick to react. As he bolted forward, they fired on him. Bullets hit the glass around him—but the glass didn't shatter. The bullets bounced off. These were rubber bullets.

"Stop! We don't want to hurt you!"

But just as he reached the stairs, he was hit by a single bullet in the hip—and even though it didn't penetrate, he couldn't believe how much a rubber bullet hurt. But he swallowed his pain, bounded up the stairs, and hid in a locker, waiting until he was sure the coast was clear.

Mariel missed most of the battle, because Morgan had locked her in her room before the lights went out. She heard the commotion, Bosgraaf warning of intruders, gunshots. Could be the safest place was to be locked in her room, but she couldn't abide being a sitting duck, waiting for something to happen, probably bad.

Mariel kicked and kicked and kicked at her door to no avail. In the end, she managed to break off a chair leg and use it as a crowbar to pry the bottom part of the door wide enough for her to crawl out. She made it into the dim hallway, and stumbled on a brick of gray clay with wires and a blinking light. It didn't take a rocket scientist to figure out what that was.

Jesus, these people mean business.

Then she was spotted.

"We found another one!"

Suddenly, hands were on her, and she was pulled out into the common room. A military woman in a flak jacket, who looked hard but probably not as hard as she used to look, smiled at Mariel.

"Don't be scared. You're safe now. Better than safe! You're going to be embraced."

"I can't be embraced, you idiot! Let me go!"

"Oh, don't be like that," she said. "You deserve to be happy too. You'll see."

Then one of the others called, "Go get Tiburón," which made Mariel's head spin halfway around.

"Wait, Rón's here?"

"I'm sure Tiburón would love to meet you. I'll bet you'll like him!" Then she turned to one of her compatriots. "Where is he?"

"I don't know," said one of the others. "Last time I saw him, he was down in the lab."

"No, we're done there," said one of the demolition guys. "Explosives are set."

"Then he must have gone out already."

Then someone else bolted out of a hiding place, and Mariel used the distraction to break away. They didn't chase after her.

Mariel went down to the labs, and found Rón just where they said they last saw him. A line of green detonator lights blinked on the ground like runway lights leading to him at the far end of the hallway.

She knew he'd be there. And she knew why. Because she knew him too well.

Rón had already accepted his fate before Mariel arrived. He was going to die today. It was not an act of desperation, not an act of self-destruction, but an act of pure compassion and sacrifice to spare this poor infected woman the misery of dying alone and unloved.

"I'm here for you," he told her. "Even if no one else cares, I do."

It just made her wail even harder. And then Rón heard a voice he thought he'd never hear again.

"Rón?"

When he turned and saw Mariel standing there, he thought it was a vision. It was his mind, or maybe it was Crown Royale itself giving him the perfect final moment. He would die with Mariel in his eyes, in his mind, and in his heart. What a perfect way to leave this world. He believed that right until the moment she came over to him, grabbed him, and tried to pull him away.

"Rón, we have to go! We have to go now."

It snapped him out of his daze. "Mariel? Wh-what are you doing here? You have to get out! This whole place is about to blow!"

"I'm not leaving you, Rón."

"But I can't leave *her*."

"You have to. There's nothing you can do for her."

"That's not true. I can be here!"

"There's still time," the woman begged. "Find the key, open the door."

But Mariel shook her head. "You're sick because of me, and you're carrying something unthinkable. There's only one way to fix this. I'm sorry."

"No! Don't leave me! I need to get out. I need, I *need* . . ."

Rón couldn't will himself to move. He kept looking from Mariel to the woman, and back again. And then Mariel got in his face in a way she never had before.

"*Rón, if you don't come, I don't leave! If you stay here, three die instead of one—and that will be entirely your doing! You will have sacrificed three people, three lives, when only one needs to die!*"

Rón found himself wavering, the answer not so easy, the conclusion not so clear. And Mariel was relentless.

"Where is your empathy, Rón? Where is your compassion? How can a recoveree let this happen? Save two lives, Rón. If you're embraced, then embrace *me* and let's get the fuck out of here!"

Rón's desperation resolved into acceptance. His life could be forfeited. But Mariel's could not.

"What's your name?" he asked subject forty-eight.

"Kay. Kay Kintanar."

"I'm sorry, Kay," he said, with all the remorse in the world. "I will honor your name until the day I die."

Then he turned with Mariel and they ran.

The local police were already alerted to the attack. All four squad cars from the nearby village of Longyearbyen were on their way, speeding up the mountain. More excitement than they'd seen in years.

Most of the liberation force had already ridden off, trying to get to the fork in the road that led to the airport before the police cars cut them off. But the explosives team remained because their job was not yet done.

"Musimy to zrobić teraz!" one of them said. "We have to do this now! Everyone's out, yes?"

"I think so. Have you seen the boy?"

"He was, I think, in the last Jeep to leave."

"Are you sure of this?"

"We do this now, or it doesn't happen!"

The first police car crashed through the gate. Time had run out. The explosive team leader hit the button. If Rón was still in there, the man would never forgive himself. And yet, as a recoveree, he couldn't help but forgive himself. And he couldn't forgive himself for *that*.

Mariel and Rón almost made it. They had gotten out of the vault and were racing up the tunnel past Bosgraaf's body, past the chloroform cloth that had been dropped on the ground. They were ten yards from the exit when the blasts came, synchronized and rhythmic like a requiem bell: boom, boom, boom, boom, *boom*. And the mountain came crashing down.

Preston Locke had never known cold like this. He was barely two hundred yards from the entrance, having escaped the vault complex and evading the last of the intruders. But with no parka, no jacket, nothing but his meager button-down shirt to protect him, he might as well have been naked on the surface of a Jupiter moon.

I'm going to die out here, his inner voice kept telling him. *This was a mistake. You thought last night was a bloody mess; now you've really done it.*

His hands ached, and every blast of wind felt like it would rip his soul from his flesh, leaving him frozen in the ice. The airport, which had only been a five-minute ride by warm, cozy, covered Jeep when he had arrived, might as well have been on another continent.

That was when the vault complex blew, and a shock wave rolled down the mountain. Preston was actually happy for it—because there was a blast of sudden heat at his back. He turned to look up the winding mountain road to see flaming chunks of concrete launched into the air, landing, sizzling, in the snow.

The monolithic entrance caved in on itself. Black smoke poured out of the hole that remained.

Part of him wanted to run back there just for the heat of the fire, but he didn't let himself. He was more than halfway to the airport now.

I'll either get to the airfield or I'll die, he thought. In some strange way, that was comforting. There were only two outcomes. There were no decisions to make, no options to ponder. There was only this or that—the beautiful simplicity of a simple computational binary. So he forced his feet to move faster. Determined that his own personal binary code would leave him at "one" instead of "zero."

Mariel lay beneath the smoldering debris. She was broken. Mariel felt crushed by the tonnage around her—but she wasn't dead yet. Grimacing, she sat up to find Rón wasn't moving. A heavy piece of concrete had come down on his side, and another one was on his leg. But she put her ear to his lips and could hear he was still breathing. Unconscious, but alive.

They had made it this far, and she was determined not to die this way. This mountain would not have her. It would not have him. She drew on her anger. She summoned greater and greater fury, building it into a storm. They would not die like this!

Her rage brought her a surge of adrenaline, and with it she found strength enough to topple a stone from herself and then heave even heavier ones from Rón. She found strength enough to lift him, even though one of her arms was broken, even though her ribs were cracked.

She carried him on her one good shoulder out of the debris, fighting the pain with everything she had, until the wind swooped around her and the snow and ice were beneath her, and she fell into it, dropping Rón to the ground like a rag doll, and letting herself crumble into a wailing pile of agony. She cast her eyes back to the mouth of the beast that had tried to consume them; the smoking hole in the mountain that used to be the entrance to the safest place on Earth. She was in more pain than she ever thought she could withstand, but she was alive. They were *both* alive. And that was something.

42

The Faucet, the Sink, the Doorknob, the Wall, the Counter, the Passport, the Armrests, the Tray, the Cup, the Doorknob, the Sink, and the Faucet

There was a tiny terminal next to the Svalbard airfield. Preston hadn't realized this was an actual working airport, since no one had been there when he and Morgan had landed. But now there was a small Scandinavian Airlines jet sitting on the tarmac, preparing to board people who were leaving the nearby town of Longyearbyen. He had to get on that plane. But first things first. He threw himself into the terminal bathroom, trying to lock the door, but his hands were too stiff from the cold—they just scratched like paws on the doorknob. He tried to stop himself from shivering. It wasn't just his teeth chattering; he was in a full-body shiver. He knew that was good, though—when you were so cold that you stopped shivering, that was when you had to worry. Going to the sink, he flipped on the hot water—thank God the faucet fixture wasn't knobs he had to turn. Then he thrust his hands beneath the flow of hot water.

He heard a flush behind him, and a scruffy man dressed much more warmly than Preston stepped out of a stall and looked at him, chattering teeth, shaking hands, and all.

"*Er du ok?*" he asked. Preston didn't need to understand Norwegian to get that one.

"Yes, yes, I'm fine. Cold out there."

"*Kaldt?*" the man said. "*Ha!*" And he walked out, shaking

his head at the lightweight Brit, who clearly didn't know the meaning of the word "cold." *Well, screw you, too, Olaf!*

When Preston felt warm enough to steady his jaw without having to clench it, he left the bathroom—but his legs were weak from the run, and he stumbled against the wall, onto his knees. He looked around, but no one saw him. It turned out the travelers there had something else to grab their attention.

Sitting against a wall were several people in camo, hand-cuffed, watched over by three police officers, while a fourth one waved people away with the Norwegian equivalent of "move along, nothing to see here." These few attackers had been caught before they got to whatever plane they arrived on—he didn't imagine they flew in on SAS. The thing was, they didn't seem at all bothered. They sat as if they were just sitting in a pub, laughing and tossing one back. *The fools think they accomplished their mission, so they'll go to jail happy as clams. Bloody recoverees.* Preston patted the tube in his pocket, just to make sure it was still there.

"*Munnbind, takk,*" said the ticket agent as he approached the counter—"mask, please"—pointing to a little box of cheap paper masks on the counter. Preston grabbed one and slipped it on, almost laughing because, after all he'd been through, it seemed like a joke. He asked for a ticket on the SAS flight, Oslo connecting to London. He didn't look at the price. What did it matter? He was just thankful he had had the presence of mind to cram his wallet and passport into his back pocket. The agent took his passport to check it, but gave him a suspicious glance, so he tried to play clueless.

"What's that all about, then?" he asked, gesturing to the handcuffed group.

"Is trouble at seed place," the agent said, her Norwegian accent strong. "I think is fire on purpose. What is word for that?"

"Arson."

"Yes. That."

She gave him his ticket and passport. He took a deep breath, joined the end of the boarding line, and ten minutes later, he said goodbye to Svalbard forever, gripping the armrests of a middle seat in the last row, which he was thankful for. Never had wheels-up been such a cause for celebration.

Half an hour later, after putting up his tray, and handing his empty coffee cup to the flight attendant, he got up to go to the lavatory.

Only now did he reach into his pocket to pull out the test tube to take a good look at it. Amazing! The yellow puslike glop in the tube was more valuable than the rarest of diamonds. All he had to do was take care of it until he got to London. It was as he turned it in his hand that he caught a glint of reflected light from the edge of the tube.

The top lip had the tiniest crack.

It was barely visible, but it still gave Preston pause. Had that been there before? Perhaps it happened when he was hit by the rubber bullet.

Not a problem, he told himself. The glop was still clinging to the bottom. The seal didn't appear broken. Not a problem.

But just to be sure, he grabbed paper towels and wrapped the tube, and wrapped it again, before putting it back into his pocket. Then out of an abundance of caution, he washed his hands, not once, not twice, but three times. He knew he was being silly, but better safe than sorry. Satisfied, he returned to his seat, letting the next passenger into the lavatory.

Seated again, he took a deep breath and smiled, finally allowing himself to enjoy his victory. If Morgan survived the attack, she would herald Preston as a hero. If she didn't survive it, then he was now fully in charge of the Havilland Consortium. Either way, it was a win/win for him.

As for his hands, he knew it must have been the frostbite that made them so terribly, terribly itchy.

Morgan thought she was in a hospital. That she had been caught in the blast, and all these wrappings were bandages. But the only pain she felt was a persistent ache in the middle of her head. She tried to move her arms in these bandages, but it was difficult. Heavy.

And somehow familiar.

This was a sensation she had experienced before, but couldn't quite place. When her eyes focused, the view before her wasn't entirely clear. It was distorted, as if through a fishbowl. There was a face looking down on her, silhouetted against a dead gray sky. This was not a hospital. And the woman before her was definitely not a nurse.

"Hello, dear."

"You!" Morgan swore if she ever saw Dame Glynis Havilland again, she would throttle her with her own hands. Morgan tried to move but found she was restrained. And what she took for bandages were not bandages at all. It was a space suit.

"Not the face you hoped to see?" Dame Havilland taunted, in the disgustingly cheerful tone that only a recoveree could muster. "Not even a smile for your beloved benefactor?"

"I'll have you arrested! No, I'll have you taken out and shot!"

"Ah! A firing squad at dawn. I'm afraid those days are long

gone, dear. Oh, I'm sure you could hire some goons to do the job. For all I know, you've already sent a few hired assassins to the cottage to put us down. I must admit, even in my worst days before Crown Royale, I could never bring myself to sink that low. But I'll admit that, once or twice, I amused myself with the idea. You, on the other hand—I do believe you might go through with a hit."

The ground heaved beneath them, and Morgan realized it wasn't ground at all. She was able to shift just enough to see that they were on a boat. A weathered fishing boat. Havilland's butler/man-toy was piloting. He tossed a glance back, caught her eye, and gave Morgan an expressionless stare before returning his attention to the helm. This was between Morgan and the old woman.

"It's good to see you, Morgan," said Dame Havilland. "I hope you'll forgive me for the space suit! It was an effort to get you into it, but worth it—because I do love the theatrical—especially when it brings things full circle."

"Forgive you? Do you think I can forgive any of this?"

"It's a figure of speech, dear. Don't take it literally."

Morgan shifted and strained against her bonds. "Let me go!"

"I can't do that, Morgan. You know why. Even if your viral agent has been destroyed, you'll be at it again. I know you will, because your tenacity and your ingenuity are why I chose you. And so, the only way to stop you is to stop you myself."

"Where are we?" Morgan demanded. "Where are you taking me?"

"So many questions! If it pleases you to know—although I can't see how any of this would please you—we are in the Norwegian Sea, just west of Svalbard."

"The Greenland Sea," interjected the butler from his post at the helm. "The Norwegian Sea is much farther south."

"Yes, well, Rooks is navigating, so he would know."

"Headed where?"

"Here," said the old woman. "Or there," she added. "Elsewhere. Most definitely elsewhere."

Morgan growled in frustration. It echoed within her helmet, and fogged up the glass.

"I had the space suit fetched by Mr. Bradway, by the way—the man who you so unceremoniously dismissed. He hasn't even had Crown Royale and yet was more than happy to help me retrieve it for you, as he still has a capacity for revenge."

"Is that what this is all about, then? Revenge?"

"Heavens no, I couldn't feel that if I wanted to. All I can feel is pity. Some viruses steal your sense of smell or taste; this one steals your sense of vengeance. I do miss it, though. It would be quite the tasty treat today, served hot or cold."

"Someone will come up with a way to fight Crown Royale, whether I'm here or not."

"Yes, yes, the elusive vaccine against happiness," said Dame Havilland with a wave of her hand. "I'm sure it will arise in time. But by then, it won't matter. Crown Royale will have transformed and elevated the larger part of humanity. . . ."

Dame Havilland labored against her cane to sit on a low bench across from Morgan. Close, but not close enough for Morgan to strangle the woman with her thickly padded fingers. "You'll be interested to know that there was a clause in the paperwork you signed, Morgan. Hidden in all the indemnifications, guarantees, contingencies, and considerations. A little convoluted clause that is the absolute epitome of fine print."

As Dame Havilland spoke, Morgan focused on her situation. She was secured to a pipe with duct tape—and not all that much of it. If she could wriggle, she could loosen it. And once she was free, she would give this geriatric couple exactly what they deserved!

"I didn't even know about the clause until it was brought to my attention," Dame Havilland continued. "My attorney—excuse me, I mean *your* attorney—slipped it in as some sort of secret fail-safe. She indirectly informed us of it through a Facebook message, of all things, once she recovered from Crown Royale—I suppose she kept that bit of news from you, but then, how would you know? You've been jetting around the world! In any case, the clause, when unraveled, states that if you were to die prior to creating a will of your own, the entire kit and caboodle reverts back to me."

Yet as awful as that sounded, Morgan saw a ray of light in it. This was just another bluff! "That means you'd have to kill me, and we both know you won't do that; you're a recoveree."

"Yes, I am, which poses quite a dilemma, doesn't it? Overcoming this irrepressible good nature, this restrictive kindness, could be quite a challenge. I admit it; I don't know if I'm capable of ending your life. But I do believe we'll soon find out."

"And even if you do manage it—do you think you'll get away with it? It won't take long until they figure out exactly who it was!"

"Yes, and I'll likely go to prison—but not before I shut down the many questionable undertakings of the Consortium. Particularly the ones involving biotech."

Something was striking Morgan about this whole interchange. Why was the old witch talking to her at all? If she meant to kill her, she would have done so already. Something more was going on here. Could this all be a ruse? The opening volley of a negotiation? If so, maybe Morgan could still play this to her advantage.

"All right. You've got me," Morgan said. "I'm all ears. What do you want? What's your angle? Because even as a recoveree, there's got to be something in it for you."

"I already told you the angle, dear, haven't you been listening? You die, and I get back my money—which I will then use to serve the greater good. There's nothing hidden to that agenda."

From the very beginning, Glynis knew this was a test that she might heartily fail. Rooks, the dear man, had faith in her, but cold-blooded murder had not been in her wheelhouse even in her old days. She knew if this was going to work, she would have to contrive a work-around. Which meant Morgan was correct in thinking that something more was going on here. But it wasn't a negotiation.

Glynis rose to her feet, and moved toward Morgan, who had been futilely trying to loosen the tape that held her in place. "That suit is rather heavy, so it will sink quickly," she told Morgan. "I don't know if the pressure will crush you, but if it does, it will be quick, painless, like those people who were lost in that little submarine some years back. A blink and they were gone."

Morgan's fury was building with Dame Havilland's every word. Good. Let it build.

"If you send me to the bottom of the sea, I'll probably never be found. Without a body, there's no proof of my death, which means the entire estate will rest in limbo until I'm pronounced dead in, what, seven years? Isn't that how long it takes for the missing to be deemed dead? I'm sure you'll be rotting in your grave yourself before that knot unravels!"

"Oh, they'll find you; that suit has a very powerful homing beacon—and we're not exactly dropping you into an abyss. We've mapped the depth. You'll simply be another piece of debris strewn across the sea floor, easily retrieved."

Then Dame Havilland pulled out a knife. Not sharp enough to puncture the suit, but that wasn't her aim. Instead, she cut the tape, freeing Morgan from the pole—

And the moment Morgan was free, she rose to her feet, a menacing presence, bulky and lumbering, and knocked Glynis down.

Glynis wailed in surprise, but she wasn't surprised at all. This was exactly what Glynis had hoped for. Morgan fighting back. Morgan angry enough to kill. The threat to Glynis's own life had to be real . . . because now anything she did would be purely in self-defense.

Morgan gloated—practically preened—at the sudden reversal of fortune. "You should have killed me when you had the chance! But who were you kidding? You pathetic recoverees couldn't hurt a fly!"

Then she charged toward Glynis, hands grasping, fully intending to throw Glynis into the churning sea.

"You're right, Morgan. But you, my dear, are not a fly." Then Glynis lifted her cane to defend herself against Morgan's charge. The cane's rubber tip connected with the chest of the clumsy, top-heavy suit, and—in order to protect herself—Glynis gave the cane a hefty, hearty, jab—

Which sent Morgan stumbling backward, over the boat's low railing.

She disappeared, space suit and all, in a single splash, gone beneath the waves as if she had never been there at all. And yes, Glynis felt the urge to jump in and try to save her—an instinct that all recoverees shared. But she found, as with all instincts, the power of one's will counted for something, and she was able to resist the urge.

Now Glynis felt Rooks right behind her. Had he watched? Had he seen what had happened? Did he understand why she had to risk herself as she did?

"You were right, Galen. When push came to shove, I did what had to be done."

"Yes, and that was a right good shove."

"I know. I feel positively awful about it."

"Crocodile tears, madame?"

Glynis sighed. "Even a crocodile can grieve for its prey, my love."

As Morgan sank to the depths, there was nothing in her universe but rage. She screamed at the top of her lungs, even though she knew her fury could not be heard. At last, she forced herself to stop screaming, and the silence immediately became overwhelming. She was still plummeting through the murky void, but she must have reached terminal velocity, because she didn't feel any acceleration to her fall. She felt suspended in place. Floating. Like Alice's long journey down the rabbit hole. The only clue that she was sinking was the slow diminishing of daylight.

When she hit bottom, it wasn't hard, but it was jarring.

Like the jolt of a plane landing. Expected, yet unexpected. Her left leg made contact first, and the rest of her body followed. She wound up on her back looking up at the distant surface. It wasn't entirely black—there was still a dim shimmering of sky far above. However deep she was, she had not been crushed. The space suit had not sprung any leaks. It was designed for a vacuum, not for the pressure of an ocean floor, but still it held its integrity.

There was a small red light blinking on her wrist. The homing beacon Dame Havilland had spoken off. It was the only electronics on the suit that seemed to function—if there was a visual display to tell her how much oxygen she had left, it wasn't working. For all she knew, the tank on her back that had made it so easy for Dame Havilland to push her off balance was empty. Morgan had no way of knowing if she was to die in seconds, or minutes, or hours.

And still rage filled her. It was all so unfair! To lose her life, for no reason other than an old woman's whim. To die slowly, all the while having to chew on the fact that Dame Havilland had won.

Morgan contemplated unsealing her helmet and letting the water rush in to drown her and get it over with. But when it came down to it, she couldn't do it. She wanted to squeeze every last second out of this life that she could—if for no other reason than to spite Havilland.

A creature undulated close to her in the half light. An eel, just about the size of her arm. Beady black eyes surveying her with profound, soulless stupidity. She swatted at it, and it wriggled away.

With great effort she pushed herself up into a sitting position. Her eyes had adjusted enough to the dimness of the deep to see the terrain around her for a few yards in every direction. The sea floor here was mostly flat and speckled with rocks. It looked like the surface of the moon.

In a moment, the eel was back; a gloomy companion at best. But she didn't swat it away this time. It kept her from being entirely alone in her final moments.

What will you do, you pathetic creature? Will you try to eat me when I'm dead? You won't be able to.

She supposed nothing short of a shark could bite through the suit—and maybe not even that. Which meant it wasn't really a suit; it was a formfitting coffin.

Then, following the eel's gaze, she realized what had attracted it. It was the little red blinking light of the homing beacon. And slowly it dawned on Morgan that there was still one small victory she could claim. She could deny Dame Havilland hers!

Morgan found a rock that fit into her thickly padded hand and brought it down on the blinking light on her wrist again and again until the light was smashed, and the homing beacon destroyed.

With the light out, the eel lost interest and left, creating a faint serpentine pattern where its fins brushed the ocean floor.

It was possible that Dame Havilland, thorough as she was, might have had the forethought to drop a buoy at the spot where Morgan was dumped, to mark the resting place of her fortune. And so Morgan resolved not to be there. When divers came to exhume her from the deep, they would find nothing but ever-shifting sands where she had been, her footprints wiped clean by ocean currents. She would get as far away from here as she could before her oxygen ran out, dying alone and undiscovered, a mystery of the deep. It would ensure that every penny of the Havilland fortune would spend years tied up court.

She had no idea in what direction she faced, but what did it matter? She rose to her feet and turned to follow the path of the eel—as good a direction as any. Then, placing one foot in front of the other, Morgan walked on the surface of the moon.

While You Were Out

Rón awoke to a deep blue sky beyond a hospital window. The window's edges were frosted like a Christmas display. Every part of him hurt, but he was partially numbed by what he suspected was morphine or something along those lines. He was okay when he didn't try to move.

A doctor was leaning over him. He wore no mask. He must have been a recoveree.

"Good. You're awake!"

"Mostly," he croaked.

And then Mariel moved into his field of view. It was a relief to see her. More than a relief. But she was injured as well. Bruised. She had a casted arm in a sling. He tried to come up with something clever to say, but his brain was in power-saver mode.

"You've been out for a long while," Mariel said. "They've stabilized you, but they're going to need to airlift you to a city with a bigger hospital. Longyearbyen doesn't have what you need."

"Longyearbyen," he said. "Yeah, it has been a long year."

Not even a courtesy laugh. It's okay. He blamed the morphine.

"Mostly just the past couple of months," said Mariel.

Was that all it had been? It seemed like forever ago he had met her up in the penthouse.

There was someone else at the edge of his field of vision. His eyes focused enough to see an armed guard just outside the door. He knew what that meant.

"I suppose I'll be facing charges somewhere. Everywhere."

Mariel looked to the doctor, and the doctor looked back at her, then said, "You're not under arrest. The Norwegian government is offering you asylum. As are several other countries sympathetic to your cause. But you may not need it. . . ." He let Mariel deliver the rest.

"They found evidence of a mass grave on the mountain," Mariel told him. "Test subjects."

Which didn't surprise him. It must have shed their ragtag incursion in a different light.

"There's more," Mariel said, and took a deep breath. "The president—*our* president—has just died from Crown Royale. The vice president is being sworn in as we speak." Then she leaned a bit closer. "No one's certain . . . but they think the VP's a recoveree. . . ."

"So," said the doctor. "All may be forgiven."

"Not by everyone," Rón noted. He had only been unconscious for a few hours, and in that time the world had gotten twisted into an even tighter knot than it was already in. He turned to Mariel. "Tipping point?"

"Maybe," she said. "We'll see."

"So much, so quickly," the doctor commented, waving in a nurse to check Rón's beeping IV. "Every five minutes something new out there. And now there's word of a new sickness. Oslo, but maybe now London, too. Could be nothing. Who knows?"

Rón looked to Mariel, but neither wanted to say what they were thinking. As if saying it would make it so.

"Don't think about it now," Mariel said. "You need to heal. We both do. The world will do what it does without us for a while."

The nurse reset his IV and stepped away, revealing the window once more. "I thought it was dawn," Rón said, "but it's already getting darker."

"The days get shorter now," the doctor said. "Until December, when there's no daylight at all."

"That's okay," said Rón. "You can't see the aurora in the light of day."

Mariel reached out with her good hand and gently clasped his. "You recoverees. Always seeing the bright side."

Then they both turned to look out the window, waiting for the coming darkness and the glorious glow of the northern lights.

Elsewhere:
Barentsburg, Norway

The shore on the outskirts of Barentsburg is windswept and rocky, stretching to a lighthouse point in the distance. The lonely strand marks the spot where Svalbard's largest fjord opens to the sea.

Every day when the weather allows, the little girl goes down to the beach from her family's cottage—a beach made not of sand, but of rocks, all worn and weathered, as smooth as eggs. They are a natural mosaic of every earthen color. Red, yellow, and brown; white, gray, and black—and in certain light some even appear blue! The girl keeps a collection of the best ones, which she lines up on her windowsill. Her favorites are those that are perfectly round, with lines of different shades encircling them, so that they look like tiny little planets that fit in the palm of her hand. Proof that the world is a wondrous place!

Today she picks up a few, surveys them, and puts them back. The sea needs to tumble them a bit more for the rocks to be up to her standards.

Far out to sea, she spots a container ship on its way west. Probably to Iceland, or maybe farther, to the Americas. She has never been out of Norway—only rarely does she leave the little town of Barentsburg. Her main contact with outsiders is the occasional visitor to the Isfjord Radio Adventure Hotel farther down the beach. Sometimes she would sell her rocks to the visitors, who come from all over the world—and maybe even farther, because her father, on his more whimsical days, would tell her the Isfjord Radio dish reaches into outer space.

Someday she might see other places in the world where her rocks have gone, but not now. Neither she, nor her parents, will be setting foot out of Barentsburg for a good while.

"Better to stay home in a storm," her father always says—and what is a pandemic if not a kind of storm?

Right at the edge of the water, where the cold sea gently laps at her shoes, she finally finds a superb round stone, deep red and glistening, with little pockmarks like tiny craters. A perfect planet for sure!

But as she leans over to grab it, something farther out in the surf catches her eye. There are many things that wash up on the beach. Seaweed. Driftwood. Junk that has fallen from passing ships. But this is different. She blinks and refocuses to make sure her eyes aren't playing tricks on her. Then she runs off to fetch her parents. They won't believe her, of course. Not until they see it for themselves. Then they'll know she's telling them the truth.

It is, indeed, a wondrous world. She never thought she'd see something so marvelous and strange as a spaceman walking out of the sea!

ACKNOWLEDGMENTS

All Better Now has been a joy to write, but none of it could have happened without an epidemic of talented people.

My publisher and editor, Justin Chanda, as well as assistant editor Daniela Villegas Valle were the first responders, there on the front line to guide me while the rest of the publishing house worked the mysterious magic that makes books happen: Jon Anderson, Anne Zafian, Lisa Moraleda, Michelle Leo, Amy Beaudoin, Nicole Benevento, Caleigh Flegg, Chrissy Noh, Amanda Brenner, Chava Wolin, Ashley Mitchell, Brendon MacDonald, Alex Kelleher-Nagorski, Emily Varga, and Amanda Adams, to name just a few.

Love the cover? So do I! Thank you, Matt Roeser, for your shining cover art, and Chloë Foglia for another great cover design.

My endless gratitude goes to my literary agent, Andrea Brown; my entertainment agents, Steve Fisher and Debbie Deuble Hill; contract attorneys Shep Rosenman and Jennifer Justman; and managers Trevor Engelson and Josh Turner McGuire—all of whom are already at work getting *All Better Now* to the screen.

Thanks to social media magicians Bianca Peries and Mara DeGuzman for keeping me visible in the world, even when I'm under a rock; Symone Powell for her research and newsletter puzzles; and the family TikTok team of Jarrod Shusterman and Sofía Lapuente for creating fantastic videos that get me millions of views!

A very special shout-out to the incomparable Claire Salmon,

my creative director / tour coordinator / assistant, who orga-
nizes my chaotic life. Thanks, Claire! It would all fall apart
without you!

I'm thrilled with the global contagion of my books, which
wouldn't happen without literary super-spreaders like Deane
Norton, Stephanie Voros, and Amy Habayeb in Simon &
Schuster foreign sales, as well as Taryn Fagerness, my foreign
agent—and of course all my foreign publishers, editors, and
publicists, including Doreen Tringali and Antje Keil in Ger-
many; Frances Taffinder, Non Pratt, and Kirsten Cozens in the
UK; Irina Salabert, Lorenzo Garrido, and Paula González in
Spain; Liesbeth Elseviers in the Netherlands; Maciej Marcisz
and Emilia Mazur in Poland; Ana Pinto, João Gonçalves, and
António Fonseca Tavares in Portugal; Nathália Dimambro and
Julia Schwarcz in Brazil; Eunkyung Kwon and Eunmi Choi in
South Korea; and in Norway, my friend and translator Olga
Nødtvedt—no relation to this book's Dr. No! (Okay, maybe.)

Thank you all. My gratitude is viral!

ABOUT THE AUTHOR

Neal Shusterman is the winner of the 2024 Margaret A. Edwards Award and the *New York Times* bestselling author of more than thirty award-winning books for children, teens, and adults, including the Unwind Dystology, the Skinjacker Trilogy, *Downsiders*, and *Challenger Deep*, which won the National Book Award. *Scythe*, the first book in his Arc of a Scythe series, was a Michael L. Printz Award Honor Book. He also writes screenplays for motion pictures and television shows. Neal is the father of four, all of whom are talented writers and artists themselves. Visit Neal at storyman.com; @Nealshusterman on Instagram, TikTok, and X/Twitter; and at Facebook.com /NealShusterman. Join Neal's Substack for exclusive content and a look behind the scenes at Substack.com/@Nealshusterman.